PRAISE FOR BEYOND WOUNDED HEARTS

Cynthia Roemer once again dazzles with a tale of sacrifice and pain in *Beyond Wounded Hearts*. Luke and Adelaide's story is the perfect example of what it means to love someone to Christ, and weaves a glorious message of acceptance for those with even the deepest scars.

— TARA JOHNSON, AUTHOR OF *ENGRAVED ON THE HEART, WHERE DANDELIONS BLOOM,* AND *ALL THROUGH THE NIGHT*

Set in the aftermath of America's Civil War, *Beyond Wounded Hearts* is a touching saga of love and reconciliation that will touch the heart of every reader.

— KELLY GOSHORN, AWARD-WINNING AUTHOR OF *A LOVE RESTORED*

Beyond Wounded Hearts is a journey of confronting one's greatest fears and heartaches, and finding grace and healing--even restoration--on the other side. Tender, heartfelt, and genuine characters build a story world of Reconstruction easy to enfold. A story for such a time as this from a gifted writer makes this book a must-read for every fan of hope-filled historical fiction.

— KATHLEEN L. MAHER, ACFW GENESIS AWARD-WINNING AUTHOR OF THE SONS OF THE SHENANDOAH SERIES

D1590169

Beyond Wounded Hearts is another fantastic novel from Cynthia Roemer. This beautiful story will captivate you from the first page with its message of grace, hope, and the power of redemption in the midst of tragedy. The characters grab your heart and their tale may draw you to tears, yet leave you with hope in the joy of a life lived serving Christ. I highly recommend it!

— MISTY M. BELLER, *USA TODAY* BESTSELLING AUTHOR OF THE SISTERS OF THE ROCKIES SERIES

To 'love our enemies' has no truer test than during wartime, and author Cynthia Roemer portrays beautifully this captivating tale of one woman's struggle to move beyond the pain and loss of war and embrace truth, trust, and acceptance. Only in the kindness and caring of those considered enemies does she see a reflection of God's love, and the chance of forgiveness, healing, and hope. Roemer's talent for creating well-drawn characters and her heartfelt message of faith make *Beyond Wounded Hearts* an inspiring, romantic journey that Christian historical fiction fans are sure to enjoy.

— KATE BRESLIN, AWARD-WINNING AUTHOR, *IN LOVE'S TIME*

BEYOND *Wounded* HEARTS

Wounded Hearts • Book Two

Award-winning Author

CYNTHIA ROEMER

Scrivenings
PRESS
Quench your thirst for story.
www.ScriveningsPress.com

To those who have sacrificed something of themselves to bring another person to Christ.

©2023 Cynthia Roemer

Published by Scrivenings Press LLC
15 Lucky Lane
Morrilton, Arkansas 72110
https://ScriveningsPress.com

Printed in the United States of America

Paperback ISBN 978-1-64917-276-1

eBook ISBN 978-1-64917-277-8

Editors: Amy R. Anguish and Linda Fulkerson

Cover by Linda Fulkerson, www.bookmarketinggraphics.com

Beyond Wounded Hearts is a work of fiction. Where real people, events,
establishments, organizations, or locales appear, they are used fictitiously. All
other elements of the novel are drawn from the author's imagination.

All other scriptures are taken from the KING JAMES VERSION (KJV):
KING JAMES VERSION, public domain.

ACKNOWLEDGMENTS

When I consider all that the Lord has done and the beautiful people He's placed in my path these past several years, I am overwhelmed with gratitude. My dream of becoming a published author stems back to my high school days, and I am indebted to so many for helping make this novel-writing dream a reality. First and foremost to the Lord. Without His abundant love and guiding hand, none of this would have been possible. May His name be praised, and may each word I write bring glory to Him.

I'm so grateful to the staff of Scrivenings Press for believing in my stories. Thanks to Publisher, Linda Fulkerson, for her tireless efforts to aid, encourage, guide, and promote my work as well as the numerous other authors she's taken under her wing. Thanks to Content Editor, Amy Anguish, and Virtual Assistant, Elena Hill, who is ever the encourager and diligent to keep things running smoothly behind the scenes. Your spunk and sense of humor keep us smiling! Thanks to the support staff for all their help and assistance. The staff and writers of Scrivenings Press are truly like family. God bless you all for your commitment to excellence in writing and caring for us as individuals.

My heart is full of appreciation for my dear friends and beta-readers Savanna Kaiser and Cara Grandle. Since we met in 2014, you have been there for me every step of the way. You are both such an encouragement to me as friends and writing pals. The Lord truly blessed me when He allowed our paths to cross at ACFW all those years ago.

What a huge blessing it was to partner with my dear friend and fellow historical romance author, Kelly Goshorn. I feel I gained a sister when we joined forces to spur each other on in our writing endeavors. You have been such an incredible critique partner for my Wounded Heart Series, and I look forward to sharing more ventures together in years to come.

I am so grateful to gifted authors and friends Misty Beller, Kate Breslin, Kelly Goshorn, Tara Johnson, and Kathleen Maher for their willingness to read advance copies of *Beyond Wounded Hearts* and lend such sweet words of endorsement. What a blessing you are.

I'm ever grateful to my husband, Marvin, for enduring my endless hours of research and writing. Thanks for your understanding and for sticking by me even though writing is so "not your thing." Thanks for your patience and enduring love through every project and deadline. I love you!

Lastly, thanks to my parents for buying my first computer, believing in my writing from the start, and backing me each step of the way. Though my dad is no longer with us, what a joy is was to have his love and support while he was here. Thanks to my mom for your continued support and for encouraging this girl of yours to follow her dream!

"When a man's ways are pleasing to the Lord,
He makes even his enemies live at peace with him."
(Proverbs 16:8)

1

An explosion pierced the night, shattering the windows of the upstairs apartment bedroom and jarring Adelaide Hanover from fitful slumber. She held back a scream, trembling as she pulled her bed sheet tighter to her chest. Shrill cries and the hasty rattle of wagon wheels echoed from the street below.

This was madness.

She squeezed her eyes closed to block out the amber glow filtering through the inside shutters. Why had Aunt Polly been so stubborn? They should have fled Richmond the moment President Davis declared the Yankees would soon be upon them.

Numbness threaded through her. There was nothing left for her here now anyway.

A second blast sounded, closer this time. Her pulse quickened. With a groan, she buried her head beneath the cotton sheet. "Do you s'pose it's the Yankees?"

When the comment garnered no reply, Addie peeled back the cover and placed a hand on the vacant spot where her aunt should have been. She sat up and glanced around the darkened room, heart racing. "Aunt Polly?"

Dryness tore at her throat as she caught a whiff of smoke. Harried voices drifted from the street below, along with the crackle of fire. The entire city sounded in a din. Tossing her cover aside, she looped her legs over the side of the bed and sprang to her feet.

With careful steps, she ventured toward the shuttered window. Shards of broken glass peppered the floor, slicing her exposed feet in more than one place. As she opened the shutters, more glass sprayed down in a bone-rattling clatter. Ignoring the pain of the cuts, she peered into the fiery haze blanketing the night sky. It appeared the stiff south breeze had morphed Richmond into a raging inferno.

Turning, she took another quick sweep of the apartment and rested her hands on her hips. Had Aunt Polly just up and left her with the whole city crashing down around them?

By morning, all of Richmond would likely be in shambles.

And in the hands of thievin' Yankees.

The blood drained from her cheeks. What would become of her if the Yankees overtook the city? Seventeen was a vulnerable age to fall prey to enemy soldiers. A shiver ran through her. She must find Aunt Polly.

Picking her way through the shattered glass on tiptoe, Addie went to retrieve her black taffeta dress. She let out a huff. If she knew Aunt Polly, she'd gone to look after her precious millenary shop—likely the reason she'd refused to leave in the first place. The thought pricked Addie. Did Aunt Polly care so little for her that she'd leave her to fend for herself at such a time? The least her aunt could have done was take her along.

Hurriedly donning her dress, Addie paced the room. With quivering hands, she struggled to fasten the string of buttons lining her front. No wonder Aunt Polly had never wed. All her attentions were thrown into her business. It seemed effort after foolishness now. Whether the store be overtaken by fire or Yanks, her aunt's attempts to spare it would likely be for naught.

Another "boom" sent Addie scrambling for her boots. Though she hadn't agreed with her aunt's decision to stay, Aunt Polly was all the family she had left.

Thanks to the cursed Yankees.

She plucked a shard of glass from the ball of her foot and slid her boots on with a frustrated sigh. One way or another, she must convince her aunt it was foolhardy to stay. She jerked at her bootstrings, determined not to sleep another night in this crazed city which, if not already, would soon be overrun with Yankees.

Stomach knotted, she scurried into the hall, down the stairs, and into the chaos of the street. Pillars of fiery smoke clouds billowed overhead, shielding the stars from view. Driven by the stout wind, hot embers seared her neck and face. Even in dead of night, it was obvious the city had become a mass of ruins.

She choked back a cough and maneuvered her way through the flurry of people—more coloreds than whites. Some rejoiced, while others were in panic, racing—arms laden with belongings —from the incessant flames threatening to engulf the city. Addie pushed through the onslaught of people, her pulse thumping in her ears. Part of her wished to turn and flee with them.

But she couldn't.

Not without Aunt Polly.

Addie's breath caught as she rounded the corner leading to the business district. She stood with mouth agape, spellbound by the chaotic scene playing out before her. Looters bashed through doors and windows, darting in and out of stores, arms loaded with goods. Shouts and merriment intermingled along the congested street. The foul stench of liquor oozed from broken bottles littering the gutter, competing with the smell of smoke.

Addie puckered her face in disgust. "How dare they?"

No sooner had she spoken the words than a selfish thought darkened her spirit. Better to have Richmond vandalized and destroyed than for the murderous Yankees to get their hands on its goods. She set her jaw. After what the Federals had done, she'd sooner see them blown to smithereens by cannon fire than have them seize a single shred of gain from the once grand city.

She glanced farther down the street to her aunt's shop and gasped. Flames spewed from the broken-out windows and holes in the roof. A nervous twinge shot through her. Surely Aunt Polly wasn't inside.

Hiking her skirt, Addie sprinted toward the blazing structure, moisture stinging her eyes. She suppressed the urge to pray. God hadn't answered her prayers in the past. Why should He now?

A wave of heat enveloped her as she neared the burning building. She shielded her face with her hand and panned the street, struggling to catch her breath. Desperate people rushed to and fro. No Aunt Polly.

The clang of fire engines echoed in the distance, and Addie's hopes rose, but fell just as quickly. With so many fires to extinguish, the firefighters would never reach the millinery in time. With the frantic way people were dashing about, she'd be hard-pressed to find anyone willing to help. Determined, Addie balled her hands into fists. If Aunt Polly needed rescued, Addie must go in herself.

With a resolute huff, she ripped a section from her shift and dipped it in an ash-tainted water trough. Tying it over her nose and mouth, she held her breath and bolted through the burned-out doorway. Thick smoke obscured her vision, threatening to choke off her air. She squinted and took a shallow breath, eyes darting from one corner of the sweltering building to the next. Greedy flames licked the walls and ceiling, transforming her aunt's shop into a consuming beast.

She cried out, cowering against the oppressive heat. "Aunt Polly!"

Amid the roar of fire, a weak cough sounded to her left. Turning, she peered through the smoke-filled millinery and glimpsed the faint image of someone lying on the floor. Heart pounding, she rushed over and dropped to her knees. "Aunt Polly?"

Polly's eyes flickered open, and she uttered a slight moan. "Add-ie. You shouldn't ... have come."

Ignoring the tempered scolding, Addie tugged at her aunt's arm. "Can you stand?"

Aunt Polly shook her head. "My legs are ... trapped."

Through the haze, Addie eyed the heavy timber stretched across her aunt's legs. Her heart sank. Aflame at both ends, the menacing plank seemed insurmountable. She edged toward it, heat singeing her forehead and brows. Mustering her strength, she gripped the smoldering beam and gave it a shove, barely budging it. She pushed harder, muscles quivering under the strain. The timber finally gave way and slid from her aunt's legs, sending a barrage of sparks flying.

Fire sprayed down from the ceiling, setting Addie's sleeves ablaze. With a loud scream, she slapped at the flames scorching her arms. She ground her teeth against the agonizing sting, finally laying atop them to smother the flames. Tears welled in her eyes as she slinked back to her aunt.

Aunt Polly tried to rise, but fell back, releasing a string of coughs. "It's too late ... for me. Save ... yourself."

"No! I'll not leave you." Despite the throbbing burns on her forearms and hands, Addie looped her arms under her aunt's and pulled with all her remaining strength. Numerous attempts left her only inches from where she'd started.

Addie fell back with a grunt, struggling for air. Aunt Polly's weight being twice Addie's, she would never accomplish this alone. Leaning close to her aunt's face, she hollered through the soaked rag, "I'll find help."

Aunt Polly raised a hand to Addie's cheek. "I'm sorry." Something in her eyes hinted of a deeper meaning, as if she'd made a costly mistake for both of them. She swallowed, fighting for breath. "Find ... Clarissa. Don't let him ... have her."

Addie shook her head. "I don't understand. Who's Clarissa?"

Her aunt's eyes flickered and closed. With a final intake of breath, her head slumped to the side.

"Aunt Polly?" Addie choked back a sob, the flames closing in around her. She stood and weaved her way through the fallen planks, the burning in her hands and arms as excruciating as the sting of another loss. Tears welled in her eyes as she rushed into the noise and bedlam of the street. Ripping the cloth from her face, she yelled, "Help! Someone please help!"

The throng of people scurried by, ignoring her pleas.

With effort, she caught a passerby by the sleeve. "Help me, please. My aunt's trapped inside."

The older gentleman tugged his arm from her grasp, sending a surge of pain through her fingers. "See to her yourself. I've troubles of my own."

He rushed past, and Addie let out a heart-wrenching groan. With a frustrated glance around, she cried, "Won't anyone help me?"

A loud "crack" sounded above her, and she flinched. Sharp pain sliced through the top of her head, blurring her vision and driving her to her knees. Heaviness engulfed her, stealing her breath as the clamor of the street faded to dark silence.

Richmond, April 3, 1865, 11:30 am

CORPORAL LUKE GALLAGHER doused the small fire with his bucket of water. A plume of smoke billowed in the breeze as the flames flickered and died. He paused, wiping his sweat-drenched brow with his sleeve, and peered at the fiery remnants of the prized city. For months, years even, Richmond had eluded them. Now, it had fallen into their hands without resistance. And yet, its crippled remains stood as a reminder of the viciousness of war.

Sergeant Delmar stepped beside him, his bushy, wheat-blond hair nearly concealing his eyes. "Hard to believe, ain't it?"

"Sure is. Never thought I'd see the day Richmond would fall."

The sergeant folded his arms over his chest. "You surprise me, Gallagher. Aren't you the one always telling me to have a little faith?"

A corner of Luke's mouth lifted. "I never knew you listened."

Chuckling, Delmar clapped him on the back. Several years Luke's elder, the sergeant had taken him under his wing like a brother. "You make it a challenge not to."

Though Luke grinned, his insides churned. He couldn't afford to be quiet about his faith. Not after Jacob. Luke would bear the guilt of his friend until his dying day. Never again would he keep silent and allow someone he cared about to spend eternity apart from God.

Widening his stance, Sergeant Delmar puffed out his chest. "And to think, after all the fuss the Rebs gave holding us off all this time, they lit out of here without so much as a shot fired again' us."

Luke passed the empty bucket to the man next to him and propped his boot on a stone slab. "They sure ravaged the place. Not much left to claim."

Delmar wiggled his eyebrows. "Except victory."

With a snicker, Luke nodded. "It's only a matter of time now, don't you think? The end of the war, I mean."

"Oh, you bet. We've got 'em on the run now. Grant won't let up until he finishes the job."

Luke inhaled a long breath. What a blessing to finally have the end of war in sight. A chance encounter with his big brother, Drew, earlier in the day made it a double blessing, leaving him all the more eager to return home to his mother and sister.

Joining the army at sixteen had seemed the thing to do following his father's untimely death in battle. But the year and a half away from home had done little to lessen the sting of loss.

"I, for one, can't wait to shed this uniform and don my work clothes. After this, the rigors of farming sound pret-ty good."

"To you and me both, Gallagher."

"Sergeant Delmar!"

The sergeant straightened and turned to face Lieutenant Fowler. "Yes, sir."

"Assemble your men," The stout lieutenant barked out his order. "We need to create a firewall to contain the blazes destroying Main Street."

"Right away, sir." As the lieutenant tromped away, Sergeant Delmar called to his men.

Passing off their water buckets, the squad of soldiers fell into formation. Luke strode at their rear, conscious of the sorrowful array of townspeople looking on.

Upon first glance, he'd cheered the ruined capital city, knowing its occupancy by Union forces meant the war's end was imminent. But now, as he gazed into the eyes of its defeated, half-starved citizens, something within him grieved. His brother was right. These were the innocent ones caught in a web of war they had no control over.

Sweat dripped from Luke's temples as he marched into the thick of the fires. The blistering heat and stifling scent of smoke left him wishing they'd been allowed to remain part of the bucket brigade. But no matter how challenging the circumstances, nothing could shake him.

Now that going home was within reach.

———

April 3, 1865, 4:30 pm

"HAVE A HEART, Corporal. The bucket brigade was child's play compared to this."

Luke brushed soiled hands together and peered at the

disgruntled private. "Look at it this way, Cummings. Would you rather be fightin' Rebs or cleanin' up after 'em?"

The burly private scratched his stubbled chin. "I reckon you've a point there."

Luke smothered a grin as the private returned to work without further complaint. Long months traipsing after Johnny Rebs and sparring with them in the Petersburg trenches had them all ready to chuck this war and head home.

A soot-covered Private Fenton tossed aside a charred beam and let out a weary huff. "The Rebs sure left this place in a sorry state. It'll take months t' clean up this mess, not to mention track down Jeff Davis and his cronies."

"One thing at a time, Fenton. For now, our job is getting these fires under control." Luke pushed his kepi higher on his forehead and skimmed the string of gutted buildings along the cluttered street. Block upon block of what appeared to have been the town's business district lay wasted. Many buildings still ablaze.

With the fall of Richmond, thousands of lives had been uprooted, their homes and livelihoods destroyed. By joining the fight, Luke had hoped to hasten the war's end, as well as avenge his father's death. In reality, the violence and bloodshed had only left him empty, depleted. He glanced at the charred remains of the once-grand city. God forgive them for all the senseless killing and devastation.

"Hey, Corporal. Looka here."

Luke shook off his ponderings and turned to see Private Fenton squatted beside something in the rubble. As he made his way over, others gathered around, concealing his view. Whatever it was had gained the troop's full attention. Shouldering his way through, he strained to see what had the soldiers so entranced.

The pair of tattered boots and frayed black material protruding from the spot where Private Fenton had been clearing debris brought Luke to a standstill. The tiny, leather boots were hardly bigger than ones his younger sister, Lydia, wore.

Private Fenton peered up at him like a startled deer. "It's a ... girl."

Luke grimaced and reached for one of the charred timbers. "Don't just stand there. Help free her. Gently, though."

With slow, careful movements, they worked to uncover her. Dreading the almost certain outcome, Luke knelt beside the lifeless form lying face-down on the ground. One of her arms rested outstretched, much of her sleeve melted away, revealing extensive burns to her hand and arm. Her singed black tresses lay strewn about her, tangled and matted in clumps.

With a hard swallow, he brushed aside her hair and pressed a hand to her temple. Warmth surged through his fingertips, and he released the breath he'd been holding, thanking the Lord above. "She's alive!"

Stunned murmurs circulated through the group of soldiers.

Luke moved his fingers to the artery in the girl's neck and cringed.

Barely.

2

"Where's the nearest hospital?" Luke blurted to a group of soldiers in passing.

Their gaze trailed to the limp girl tucked in his arms. One of them pointed farther down the street. "The two-story frame house a few blocks ahead, corner of Third and Main."

With a brisk nod, he hurried on. Though the woman's breaths were steady, they were extremely shallow. Every moment counted.

A soft moan emanated from the young woman, and Luke glanced down. She looked to be about his age or possibly a bit younger. Beautiful, despite the coat of ashes and soot soiling her features and the mass of burns lining her arms. It was a wonder she'd survived. And yet, the Lord had allowed them to find her. Surely, she was meant to live.

Or so he hoped.

There was something endearing about her long, dark lashes and the slight pout of her crimson lips. Who was she? Were other members of her family trapped beneath the rubble? Clothed in a drab mourning dress, she obviously had lost someone close to her—a father or brother? Surely not a husband.

His throat clamped. Could one so young be a widow? It

saddened him to even consider. Whoever she grieved had likely been taken from her by Union forces. And yet, her own Confederates had inflicted *this* travesty upon her.

He gently shifted the nameless girl in his arms, returning his gaze to the path ahead. When he'd arrived in the Confederate Capital, he'd been overjoyed at the long-awaited victory, never giving thought to the lives the conquest might affect. Seeing this lovely young woman clinging to life put the situation in a different light. When the Rebs set Richmond ablaze, chances are their intentions were to keep anything of value out of Union hands.

Not devastate the entire city or kill their own.

The scent of smoke grew fainter as he left behind the burnt-out business district and entered the part of town which had sustained less damage. A yellow flag with a green *H* designating the hospital came into view. Increasing his pace, he set his sights on the two-story frame house, its front and back lawns astir with activity. With heavy breaths, Luke upped the porch steps and pounded on the door with his foot.

A dark-haired lady opened, and with one glance at the listless girl, ushered him inside. "Take her in there," she directed, pointing to the room on the left.

With quick strides, Luke made his way into what must have once been an elegant parlor. Now, a dozen or more civilian patients lay clustered about the spacious room. Ever so gently, he lowered the girl to one of the few empty cots. Her eyes flickered open a brief instant and her brow creased as if in pain. Then, just as quickly, she retreated back into quiet slumber.

Troubled by the extent of her wounds and the limpness of her body, Luke sought out the closest nurse. "Where's the doctor? That girl over there needs help."

The woman raised a brow. "We have no doctors. They vacated the city before you Yanks arrived. There's only a few of us volunteers to tend the wounded."

"But she needs assistance. Now."

The nurse glanced to where the girl lay then returned to tending the badly burned man before her. "Like countless others. Her turn will come."

"But she's ..."

The woman's intense gaze fixated on Luke. "We'll get to her as soon as we're able, Corporal. We can only do so much."

Panic rose in Luke's chest. "Who's in charge here?"

She nodded to the lady who'd met him at the door. "Captain Sally Tompkins over there."

Luke tromped toward the woman who continued to direct patients to rooms. "Miss Tompkins?"

Turning, her dark eyes perused him. "*Captain* Tompkins." Even in her short response, her Southern drawl rang thick.

"I brought a young woman in just now who needs immediate attention, or I fear she won't make it." He gestured toward her, and the woman craned her neck for a look.

"Where is she injured?"

"Her arms and hands are badly burned, and she appeared to have taken a hit on the head." He fell into step behind her as she wove her way through the roomful of patients.

Bending down, she lifted first one of the girl's eyelids, then the other.

"Can you help her?"

She glared up at him. "We have the lowest mortality rate of any hospital here in Richmond. Supplies are low and we're short-staffed, but we'll do what we can."

"Is there anything I can do?"

Her expression softened. "Your concern for the girl is commendable, Corporal. But I assure you, she'll be well taken care of. Now, I'd appreciate if you'd leave me to my work."

With a tentative nod, Luke ventured a final glance at the young woman. It pained him to see someone so young caught in the hazards of war. Somehow, he felt responsible for her. And yet, all he could do was entrust her to the Lord's hands and pray this nurse knew what she was doing.

He turned to leave, then hesitated. "Could I check back tomorrow to see how she's doing?"

Captain Tompkins paused from examining the burns on the girl's arms. "Suit yourself. So long as you don't get in the way."

Luke fingered his kepi. "Thank you, Captain."

As he turned to go, an overpowering sense of dread encompassed him. There was every chance the young woman would not survive. He whispered a silent prayer on her behalf, uncertain if he would have the heart to return and find out.

Robertson Hospital, Richmond
April 3, 1865, 10 p.m.

SEARING pain and heat pulsed through Addie's arms. She moaned and opened her eyes, her vision fading in and out as the dim glow of lantern light invaded her senses. Her eyes perused the plastered ceiling and the flickering shadows along the walls. Where was she?

She tried to move and cringed, an unbearable ache in her head forcing her to still. Thick bandages adorned both of her arms. What had happened to her?

Fragmented images pricked at her fogged memory. The last thing she recalled was struggling to pull Aunt Polly from the burning millinery shop.

The fire.

Her arms had been burned in the fire. But, why this throbbing pain in her head?

Wait. She squeezed her eyes shut, envisioning the burning building. Now she remembered. She'd lacked the strength to free her aunt and had gone for help. Something had struck her.

Tears welled in her eyes. Her poor aunt. She let out a string of coughs. "Why... would no one ... help us?"

"Shhh. Keep still. You're safe now."

A cool hand stroked her damp forehead. Addie slowly shifted her face toward the soft voice, wincing at the intense pain. Her brow pinched at sight of the woman standing over her, the *MS* on her sleeve designating her as Medical Staff. "Where am I?"

"Robertson Hospital."

Addie cringed, her breaths heavy. "I-It hurts."

"Here. Drink this." The woman tipped Addie's head forward and held a cup to her lips.

Addie took a tiny swallow and grimaced. "What is it?"

"Laudanum. It will help reduce the pain and allow you to rest."

Reluctantly, she finished drinking the bitter medicine and laid her head back with a cough. Within moments, she could feel the medicine's effects. A bit woozy, she closed her eyes and succumbed to the fatigue. When next she opened them, daylight streamed through the windows. She inhaled shallow breaths, the oppressive odor in the room making her thankful the windows were slightly ajar.

The woman she'd encountered in the night stood with her back to her, tending a patient on the cot next to Addie's, her chestnut hair drawn in a tight chignon. Across the room, another nurse swabbed the forehead of an injured man. His eyes held a dazed expression as he stared unblinking at the ceiling. Several others in the room showed no sign of alertness whatsoever.

"Well, you've finally awakened. How are you feeling?"

Slowly turning her head toward the voice, Addie gazed into the face of the dark-haired nurse. "Tired."

"Are you in a great deal of pain?"

Addie licked dry, chapped lips, managing a weak nod.

"Your arms or your head?"

"Both." The gravelly voice barely seemed her own. "My head is throbbing and my arms feel as though they're on fire."

The nurse's brunet eyes filled with compassion as she leaned in closer. "You've suffered extensive burns to your hands and arms, along with a blow to the head. We'll do what we can to make you comfortable, but I'm afraid we may not be able to completely alleviate your pain."

Addie glanced at her bandaged limbs. "At least my hands don't hurt."

The woman's eyes crimped, her mouth growing taut. "You feel no pain in your hands?"

"Only a little. They're more stiff than sore." She tried unsuccessfully to wriggle her fingers beneath the bandages. "I can't seem to move them, or hardly even feel them."

Something akin to alarm flickered in the caretaker's eyes.

Addie swallowed, the dryness in her throat hampering her speech. "Is that bad?"

The nurse's drawn-out breath and creased brow sent a tremor through Addie, but the woman merely passed off the question with a weak grin. "It's nothing to concern yourself with just now. Let's have a look at that bump of yours."

Gently, the nurse tilted Addie's head to the side. "Hmm. Still rather swollen. I think another cold compress is in order."

"Might I have a drink?"

"Certainly." Retrieving a pitcher, the nurse poured a half-filled glass of water and the remainder into a large bowl.

Addie stared up at her, mind bogged with questions. "How did I get here?"

Glass in hand, the nurse sat on the edge of the thin cot and tipped Addie's head up for a drink. "You were carried in by a soldier."

Greedily gulping the water, Addie choked slightly.

The nurse pulled the glass away. "Easy now. Not too fast."

After another sip, the nurse eased Addie down and dabbed her wet lips with a cloth. She followed the nurse's every move, her mind still seeking answers. "Do you recall the soldier's name? I'd like to thank him."

"I'm sorry. I don't." The woman dipped the cloth in the bowl of water and wrung it out. "But you may have your chance to express your gratitude. He seemed quite concerned over you and promised to return. In fact, I could hardly prompt him to leave."

A flash of heat spilled onto Addie's cheeks, and she wished it away. "But I thought all our able-bodied men had fled the city?"

"They have." Pressing the rag to Addie's head wound, the woman raised a brow, an odd sort of expression spilling onto her face.

Addie flinched at the touch of the cold compress, her mind struggling to process the nurse's unspoken implication. At last, her eyes flared wide. "You don't mean. Not a Yankee?"

"Yes indeed. And a handsome one at that."

Suddenly antsy, Adelaide shifted on the cot. "Then I've no wish to thank him at all. He can fall in a hole for all I care." She gnawed at her lip. "What about my aunt? She was trapped inside the burning building. Did he find her as well?"

The woman gave a disheartening shake of her head. "I'm sorry. He brought only you and made no mention of anyone else."

Tears stung Addie's eyes as the weight of reality coursed through her. Then she truly had no one.

Seeming to sense her dismay, the nurse gave Addie's shoulder a soft pat. "I wouldn't give up entirely. It's possible someone else found her and took her to a different hospital."

A glimmer of hope rose within Addie, though recalling the severity of the fire, it seemed unlikely. "Perhaps."

"Captain Sally?" The distraught voice pulled the caregiver's attention to the approaching nurse.

"Yes?"

"The man's fever is continuing to rise."

She hung her head. "I was afraid of that. We need to get his temperature down. Fetch some chunks of ice, and I'll be right over."

With a nod, the nurse went on her way.

Addie searched her attendant's dark eyes. "Captain?"

The woman nodded. "Yes. I'm Captain Sally Tompkins. Known to most as Captain Sally. I supervise this hospital."

Addie blinked. "A lady captain?"

"Unusual, I know, but in order to receive the necessary medical supplies, Richmond hospitals require military personnel to be in charge. Therefore, I was given the rank of captain." Her brow creased. "Though, I'm not sure it will matter much longer, what with the Yankee takeover."

Addie's eyes glossed over. "Then, it's true. The Federals have overtaken our glorious city. 'Tis a sorry day indeed."

Captain Sally sighed. "Richmond is not so glorious at the moment. From what I hear, most of the businesses, the ironworks, and warehouses are destroyed. Not to mention the bridges and ship fleet."

"Those wretched Yanks!" Addie shifted her head and moaned at the twinge of pain kneading through her.

"Easy, now. You must lie still." Bending low, the nurse placed a steadying hand on Addie's forehead. "And it wasn't the Federals who set the fires. It was our own soldiers."

Addie's brow creased. "You can't mean it."

"Indeed. From what I understand, our men were ordered to set the blazes to keep anything of importance from falling into enemy hands."

Addie clenched her teeth. "Then I don't blame them. I'd just as soon die as be subjected to Yankee rule. Perhaps it would be just as well if I did die."

Captain Sally shook her head. "Come now, one so young shouldn't speak of dying. You've your whole life ahead of you. And think of all those who'd mourn your loss."

The comment wielded a heavy blow, stirring further emptiness inside Addie. Moisture pooled in her eyes. "I've no one left to grieve me. Those horrid Yankees killed my father and brothers. My aunt is all that remains. *If* she survived."

Genuine remorse swept over the woman's face. "I'm truly

sorry. I hope she's found." She squeezed Addie's shoulder. "Rest now. I'll have Miss Jane bring you some nourishment."

Addie nodded, concerns for Aunt Polly's fate superseding any thought of food. She stared at a crack in the plastered ceiling. What would she do if her aunt wasn't found? In years past, she would have taken her worries to the Lord.

But not now. Not when He'd forsaken her and her family.

She had only herself to rely on.

That, and the hope her aunt still lived.

3

Richmond, April 4, 1865
Early Afternoon

L uke fingered the charred locket in his hand—the only identifiable remains of what he assumed had been a woman inside the burned-out building. Uncovering her remains so near where they'd found the girl had him wondering if the two were related. The heirloom necklace would provide the answer.

If the girl still lived.

He stuffed the keepsake in his pocket and swiped a sleeve over his brow. The horrendous heat made rummaging through the ruined buildings all the more intolerable. So much destruction. So many homeless, destitute people lining the cluttered streets. The gutted city seemed more like an eyesore than a coveted prize. No telling how long it would take to rebuild the place.

Was it even possible?

Excited shouts sounded in the direction of the James River. Luke and the other soldiers paused from their work and peered toward the commotion. Though the dilapidated buildings obscured their view, the uproar made it plain something unusual was amiss. Yet, it was hard to tell if the ruckus was initiated by friend or foe.

Private Fenton stepped toward Luke. "What goes on, Corporal?"

"I'm not sure, but keep your firearms handy." Luke locked eyes with Sergeant Delmar as he strode toward him from across the street.

The sergeant jerked his head toward the uproar. "Go have a look, Corporal."

"Yes, Sergeant." Luke headed out at a spry walk, tension pulling at his shoulders. Had the Rebs tricked them and doubled back? He wouldn't put it past them. Yet, the closer he strode to the riverfront, the more the raised voices sounded like shouts of jubilation.

Rounding the corner of a building, he could see a cluster of liberated slaves rushing down the street. Curious, he followed them, keeping his eyes trained ahead of him and his rifle half-cocked. A larger mob of people had gathered along the riverfront, leaping and shouting, even lifting their voices in song.

Luke strained for a closer look. What could cause such a stir? Obviously not the Rebs.

He caught a glimpse of a tall, silk hat and a bearded man at the center of the pack, his head towering above the rest. Wide-eyed, Luke stopped short. It couldn't be. Stretching his five-foot ten-inch frame taller, he shielded his eyes against the midday sun until certain they hadn't deceived him.

With a chuckle, he clapped a hand atop his kepi. "Sufferin' polecats. Lincoln? Here in Richmond? If that don't beat all."

He watched the procession move as one along the riverfront and into the street. Several naval officers encircled the president, their attempt to keep the crowds at bay fruitless. Ignoring protocol, Lincoln clasped hands with ecstatic former slaves as he passed, while what remained of Richmond's downtrodden citizens gazed on from a distance. A reverent hush fell over the group as they pressed deeper into the city.

Luke edged back, taking in the scene as if a piece of history was unfolding before his eyes. His shoulder bumped against someone, and he turned to see a teary-eyed woman looking on. Donned in a modest brown dress rather than the mourning garb like the majority of Richmond women, she wore her brunette hair pulled back, a cluster of ringlets gathered at the nape of her neck. The smile on her face asserted the tears were ones of joy not sorrow. "Is it truly him? The president?"

Caught off guard by her elated tone, Luke gave a slight nod. "Yes, ma'am. I believe so."

She pressed her hands prayer-like to her lips, her prominent chin dipping lower. "How I've longed for this day."

Luke stared at her, baffled that a Southerner would applaud the president's entry into the Confederate Capital. Her accent, though milder than most, lent to that of someone reared in the South. "Are you from Richmond, ma'am?"

"Indeed, I am. Born and raised here. Though I left for a time to attend school in Philadelphia."

Confused, Luke scrunched his brows. "And you're ... happy Lincoln has come?"

She blinked moisture from her pale blue eyes. "I assure you there are none happier." Sniffling, she tipped her chin higher. "You might say, I helped bring him here."

By the humored look on the woman's face, Luke's eyes must have swelled to the size of silver dollars. "How's that?"

Her thin lips spread in a wide grin. "Are you, by chance, familiar with the Richmond Underground?"

"No, ma'am." He lowered his voice a notch. "Is that in connection with the Underground Railroad?"

"Not exactly. Their purpose is to usher slaves to freedom. My network's intent is to bring an end to this war so that the loathsome practice of slavery will be abolished. And that day, my dear corporal, is near at hand. The president's visit here is testimony to that."

Intrigued, Luke rubbed a hand over his chin. "That's a tall

order. How do you manage such an undertaking here in the heart of the Confederacy?"

She cast a quick glance in both directions and leaned in closer. "Let's just say my associates and I are adept at sharing undisclosed, vital information with the right sources to tip the war in favor of the Union."

"You're a ... spy?" The words rolled off his tongue in a whispered squeak.

She angled her head side to side in a triumphal sort of way. "I prefer the term 'liberator.' I may not be well thought of by the residents here, but I'm in rather good standing with your sort."

Uncertain what to make of the odd woman's claim, Luke cast a glance over his shoulder, eager to report Lincoln's presence to Sergeant Delmar. "The best to you in your efforts, ma'am. I'd ... uh ... better return to my squad. Nice meeting you."

She gave a slow nod. "If you're ever in need of assistance, don't hesitate to call on me. The name's Van Lew. Miss Elizabeth Van Lew."

Luke tipped his kepi, not quite convinced such a commonplace lady could help topple the Confederacy from within its capital city. "Thank you, ma'am."

He turned and sprinted back to his squad, dodging the bedlam of debris in his path. With heavy breaths, he hustled over to the sergeant. As if sensing the importance of what he had to say, the soldiers stopped what they were doing and gathered around.

"What is it, Corporal? The Rebs?"

Swallowing, Luke fought to catch his breath. "Furthest thing from."

Sergeant Delmar's brows pinched. "What then?"

Luke's lips spread in a lopsided grin. "President Lincoln just arrived."

A rumble of laughter circulated through the group, and the sergeant crossed his arms over his chest. "Nice try, Gallagher."

Luke shifted his gaze from one disbelieving face to another.

"No. Honest. Lincoln's right here walkin' the streets of Richmond, a whole crowd of freed slaves swarmin' around him, shaking his hand."

Another round of boisterous chuckles sounded. Sergeant Delmar's eyebrow raised higher. "You expect us to believe that? Jeff Davis and his cronies ain't been gone much more than a day. Now, why would the president risk comin' here?"

Bristling at the challenge to his integrity, Luke met the sergeant's gaze, mouth taut. "Ever known me to lie?"

The group stilled, and the sergeant's rounded eyes searched Luke's. Finally, he shook his head. "Can't say I have. A good-natured tease, yes, but you're about as strait-laced as they come where your word's concerned."

Just then a soldier hollered from across the street. "Hey fellas, did ya hear? Lincoln's arrived, and General Weitzel ordered all work to cease so everyone can congregate."

With a satisfied nod, the tension in Luke's muscles eased. "Like I said. Lincoln."

Sergeant Delmar grinned and slapped the closest gawking private on the arm. "Well, don't just stand there. Let's go."

With joyful hoots, the men brushed off their uniforms and clamored in the direction from which Luke had returned, their task forgotten. The singed locket jingled in Luke's trouser pocket as he followed along. With duties suspended, maybe later he'd have time to check in on the girl he'd transported to the hospital.

Alive or dead, the trinket most likely belonged with her.

Robertson Hospital, Richmond
April 4, 3:30 p.m.

ADELAIDE'S EYELIDS fluttered open at the sound of murmured activity around her. A tremor of pain surged through her murkiness, making her wish she'd remained asleep. She sensed a presence to her right and turned her head, startled at sight of a wavy-haired corporal seated beside the bed. She eyed his blue uniform, then scowled up at him. "Who are you?"

His striking blue eyes stared back at her, a hint of a grin lining his lips. "Corporal Gallagher. The fella who brought you here."

She blinked, attempting to make sense of his words, her mind still foggy from the laudanum. "So, you're the one." Her gaze trailed to her bandaged arms, her clouded mind beginning to clear. "I suppose you want me to thank you." She stared up at him, eyes narrowed. "Well, I'm not so sure you've done me a favor. I'd likely have been better off if you'd left me where you found me."

His brows pinched and his grip on the cap he held tightened. "I suppose that depends on how acquainted you are with the Lord. Since I had no way of knowing that, I figured it best to make the effort to spare your life."

Taken aback by the unexpected response, Addie chewed on her lip. Little did he know, he'd just given her another reason not to like him. "So, you think highly of God, do you?"

"I do."

She tried not to notice his winsome smile, but there was something appealing about the young man's candid nature. Shifting her gaze to the ceiling above, she clenched her teeth. "Well, I don't share your convictions. If there truly is a God, He's brought me nothing but heartache. Same as you vicious Yankees."

His lack of response pulled her eyes back to him. The corporal's head had dipped downward, his long blond lashes pressed to his cheeks. Was he praying?

For her? The very thought made her insides squirm.

At last, he opened his eyes and released a long breath. "I s'pose that's why the Lord allowed us to find you in time. Your soul isn't ready."

Stricken by the sincerity in his tone, she moistened her lips. "You a preacher?"

With a shake of his head, his lips formed a weak grin. "No, miss. Just someone who loves the Lord."

Before Addie had time to frame a response, the young soldier reached in his pocket and brought out a blackened piece of jewelry. "I was wonderin' if you recognize this."

As he stretched out his palm, she sucked in a breath. "My aunt's locket. Where did you find it?"

The moment the words left her mouth, she guessed the answer. When he hesitated to respond, her spirit plummeted. "She's dead, isn't she?"

His mouth twitched, and he gave a slow nod.

Fighting tears, she turned her face to the wall, panic surging through her. "I told her we should flee with the rest. But she wouldn't listen. Now all is lost."

"I'm truly sorry, miss." After a moment's pause, he cleared his throat. "Have you anyone else we should try to locate? Your parents? Brothers? Sisters?"

She shook her head, anger flaring in her tone. "No one. I have no mother, and you blasted Yankees killed my father and brothers!" She glared up at him. "Now, do you see why I don't hold to your God?"

His cheek flinched, and a pained look stole the luster from his eyes. The jab seemed to pierce his very soul. She'd wanted to hurt him, the way his kind had wounded her. Yet, part of her regretted being so spiteful. Though she hated to admit it, he'd been nothing but kind to her.

The clatter of those around seemed to intensify as she awaited his response. At last, he wet his lips and looked her in the eyes. "I see why you're hurtin', miss. I just don't see how you can blame God when it's us who chose to do the fighting."

Addie opened her mouth to speak, then clamped it shut. How could she argue that?

A tear slid down her temple, and she sniffled. "I suppose we're all to blame."

Without a word, Corporal Gallagher slipped a kerchief from his pocket.

Addie tensed as he reached to dry her eyes and nose—a simple act she could no longer accomplish herself. Not since she was a young child had anyone offered her such a thoughtful gesture.

She eyed him. He didn't seem a bad sort. For a Yank. He was almost charming with his blond waves, vibrant blue eyes, and ruddy complexion.

Her gaze dropped to the locket still cradled in his palm. "Could you open it? I've often wondered what was inside. It never left my aunt's neck."

Corporal Gallagher rubbed off some of the charred fragments and then wedged his fingernail in the tight crevasse. With a bit of prying, the locket clicked open. After venturing a peek, he turned it toward her. "Is this you?"

Craning her neck for a better look, Addie focused on the two, small daguerreotypes—one of Aunt Polly holding a young child, the other an older version of the fair-haired girl. She shook her head. "No. The woman is definitely my aunt, but I have no idea who the child is."

Corporal Gallagher pulled the locket back for a second look. "If not you, it appears to be someone she thought a great deal of. A daughter maybe?"

"My aunt had no children. She never married." Addie dropped her head back on the makeshift cot, a wave of disgruntled curiosity trickling through her. "Who could she be?"

Her mind raced back to the moment just before she'd left her aunt and the desperate words that had poured from her lips. *Find Clarissa. Don't let him have her.* Was the child in the photograph Clarissa? But who was she? A shiver worked through Addie.

Better yet, who was the *him* Aunt Polly wished the child spared from?

LUKE TOSSED another log on the fire outside his tent, casting a glance at Sergeant Delmar. "You ever hear tell of Miss Elizabeth Van Lew?"

The sergeant brushed his hands together, then scratched his unshaven jaw. "Van Lew? Ain't she the gal who's suspected of feedin' information to some of the higher-ups in the Union ranks?"

Stunned, Luke murmured under his breath. "Then she was telling the truth."

"What's that?"

Picking up a mallet, Luke ran his palm along the smooth handle. "I ran into her today. She told me she and some others were passing on vital information to help end the war. I wasn't sure whether to believe her. Guess she was on the up and up after all."

"Could be. From what I hear, soon as the Union cavalry crossed into Richmond, Van Lew plunked an American flag outside her home. Created quite a stir among her neighbors. The angry mob threatened to burn down her house."

Private Fenton edged closer, obviously eavesdropping. "I heard somethin' about that. They claim she stopped 'em short by sayin' her friend, General Grant and his army would be there within the hour to set their houses ablaze if they so much as touched hers."

"I hear tell General Grant even joined her for tea," Private Cummings chimed in.

Gazing past the rubble to the vibrant sky in the west, Luke shook his head. "After seeing her determination, I wouldn't put it past her to invite the president himself."

"Sure was somethin', wasn't it? President Lincoln waltzin' up the rebel Capitol steps and inside like he owned the place?"

At Private Fenton's loud guffaw, Luke nodded and finished

pounding in the pup tent peg. "Like nothing I ever thought to see."

Luke stood and stared into the dying embers of the fire he and the men had routed earlier. In truth, he wasn't sure which was more astonishing—witnessing the president stroll the streets of Richmond or seeing the near-lifeless girl he'd carried alert and coherent.

Even a bit feisty.

Something about her stirred his senses. Maybe it was the fact she'd been rendered helpless, or that she had no one.

Or maybe her violet eyes, coal-black hair, and rosy lips had something to do with it.

Whatever the reason, he couldn't get her out of his head.

With her hands and arms badly burned, how would she manage? By her own admission, she had no one to care for her. She couldn't so much as wipe her nose or scratch her cheek, all bandaged up and in too much pain to move. Would the hospital staff tend to her needs? They seemed hard-pressed to keep up with the growing number of patients.

"I cain't see how the South can hold out much longer, now that we've got Lee's army on the run." The gangly private's nasally voice broke through Luke's concentration.

He leaned on his mallet. "One can hope."

He'd never forget the haggard look on Lincoln's face as he passed. Years of tension and worry told in the creases of his eyes and mouth. If anyone wished the war to end more than the soldiers, it was their commander-in-chief.

When the freed slaves made him out to be some sort of messiah, he'd redirected their praise toward God. But what amazed Luke most was the rumor that Lincoln had advised General Weitzel to go easy on the Confederates. An attitude that went against the majority of Union thinking. How Luke longed to become such a humble, forgiving man—a man after God's own heart.

His mind returned to the girl with the burned arms. He'd not even asked her name, and yet somehow, he felt liable for her welfare—both physical and spiritual. Maybe, amid the flickering embers of this irksome war, the Lord could use him to spark renewed hope into this lonesome, young woman's heart. Though he couldn't shirk his duties as corporal, his off-duty time was his to do as he pleased. Spending time and speaking a few godly truths to the young woman couldn't hurt.

The question was, would she pay any attention to a "blue-belly"?

4

Robertson Hospital, Richmond
April 5, 1865, Evening

A delaide glanced up just as the curly-headed corporal approached. "*You* again." Though she did her best to sound agitated, deep down her heart thrilled to have a visitor outside of the poking and prodding attendants.

Even if he was a Yank.

He edged down beside her, his warm smile melting her resolve to remain unsociable. "You're sitting up. That's progress."

She gave a soft shrug. "Sitting or lying, makes no difference. I'm still helpless. The only advantage is I don't choke on my food."

The corporal's smile deepened. "Well, that's something anyway."

She arched a brow. "Are you always so chipper?"

He shrugged and twisted the cap in his hands. "Never hurts to be positive."

Her bandaged arms glared up at her, the throbbing pain as relentless as the putrid hospital air. "I've not much to be positive about."

"You will, in time. The Lord has a plan for you, else you wouldn't have survived."

Her eyes narrowed as she met his gaze. "A lump on my head, a bruised body, and burns on my arms and hands that will likely leave me crippled for life. Just what sort of plan does this God of yours have for me?"

Corporal Gallagher wet his lips. "I can't rightly say, but you might find your answer in Scripture. I'd be pleased to read to you from my Bible sometime."

Addie sank her head back against the plastered wall. "Save yourself the trouble, soldier. I've no use for fanciful tales and empty promises."

That pained expression returned to his eyes as he lowered his gaze. He obviously had a strong faith which, twice now, she'd offended. And yet, he showed no sign of resentment, only remorse.

"Time for your supper, Adelaide."

The female voice pulled her attention to the opposite side of the cot. A weary-eyed Miss Jane stood with tray in hand, her haggard appearance conveying overburden.

"Here, let me help with that. I'm sure you've a dozen other patients to tend to."

As the corporal clasped the tray, Addie wasn't sure who seemed more stunned—her or the nurse. Miss Jane's long face brightened. "Why, thank you, Corporal. I wouldn't have expected such thoughtfulness from a Federal soldier."

Before Addie could protest, the nurse turned on her heels and padded away.

"Adelaide. Is that your name?"

Addie pursed her lips. "Don't you have anything better to do than play nursemaid to a helpless invalid?"

With a decisive shake of the head, the soldier pulled up a chair and placed the tray on his lap. "Not really."

Uncertain how to respond, Addie merely breathed a bewildered sigh.

Instead of offering her a forkful of food, he bowed his head and closed his eyes. No doubt he wished to speak a blessing over the meal. Unwilling to comply, she tipped her chin higher. She had nothing left but contempt for God. Not once since the war began had He answered her prayers. He'd forsaken her, her family, and her Southern kinsmen. Faith was but a farce to her now.

And yet, this man's sincerity intrigued her. She'd never known anyone so grounded in his beliefs. He was either the most genuine man she'd ever met, or the most naïve.

Refusing to close her eyes, she studied him, noting his smooth jaw and bronzed complexion as he prayed.

"Heavenly Father, I thank you for watching over Miss Adelaide, for sparing her life and giving her the ability to sit and eat. May her pain be minimal and may this food provide the nourishment she needs to face another day. In Jesus' name we pray. Amen."

As his head lifted, she glanced away, embarrassed to be found staring. Her stomach rumbled, and her eyes darted to the plate of smoked ham, string beans, and potatoes. "How I despise being dependent on someone else to feed me."

Slicing the meat into bite-sized pieces, he glanced over at her. "It's only for a while. Besides, when people are in need, it gives others a chance to serve."

She shook her head. "You're an odd one, Corporal. Not at all how I pictured a Yankee."

He jabbed the fork prongs into one of the pieces of ham and grinned. "And how did you picture us? With horns, a pitchfork, and a tail?"

Taking the bite he offered, she weighed her response. In truth, she'd thought all Yankees devils. But everything about this man defied that thinking. She shifted the meat to her cheek. "I had that general impression. Though I suppose there's good and bad in the lot of us. Yankees as well as Southerners."

"True." He fed her a bite of potatoes, his azure eyes concentrating on guiding the fork to her mouth.

Addie lowered her gaze, humbled by his unexpected kindness. She swallowed the bland mouthful, wishing this all a nightmarish dream. From the moment she'd received word of her father's death just over a year ago to the hellish night her aunt had perished and her own arms had been burned in the fire, Addie's life had been one solid mass of hurt and disappointment. An act of kindness from a Yankee stranger seemed as uncanny as sharing an evening at the White House with Mr. and Mrs. Lincoln.

"It suits you."

The corporal's soft tone pulled her eyes back to him. She knit her brows. "*What* does?"

"Your name. Adelaide. I've not heard it before. It's real pretty."

She gave a slight nod, hoping the warmth in her cheeks didn't tell on her face. "Mostly I go by Addie."

He lifted a glass of water to her lips. "I like Adelaide."

The heat in her cheeks intensified as she sipped a drink. Something about this man tied her in knots. She swallowed as he pulled the glass away. "Papa always insisted on calling me Adelaide, but he was the only one."

"Then, he was a wise man."

They fell silent as she finished eating, the only sounds the scraping of the fork against the tin plate and an occasional groan from one of the other patients. Addie eyed the young corporal, wanting to dislike him. He was a dreaded Yankee, after all. Her sworn enemy. His sort had killed her father and brothers. But he was making it very difficult to harbor a grudge against him personally.

Why did he have to be so kind and so pleasant to look at?

She bit her tongue to keep from asking his given name. More than likely, with his Christian upbringing, it was a biblical one. David or Daniel perhaps? She remembered reading of valiant men of God who had strong faith such as his. It only seemed fitting that he share one of their names. She chided herself for even considering the curiosity. Why should she care what his name might be?

Setting the empty plate aside, he brushed crumbs from his uniform. "It's good to see you have an appetite."

A twitch of lightheadedness coursed through her, and she closed her eyes. "I fear I may have indulged a bit too much."

"Do you need to lie down?"

"I think I'd better."

Corporal Gallagher placed a warm hand on Addie's back and another on her shoulder. With his help, she eased herself down. She stared up at him, a bit winded. "Thank you." Though the words sounded forced, her gratitude was genuine.

"My pleasure."

For a brief moment, Addie's eyes locked with his, and she longed to know more about this intriguing soldier. Who was he? Where was he from? And why had he taken it upon himself to cater to her needs?

A shadow fell over the room, and he glanced out the window at the darkening sky. "I'd best head back."

Addie hesitated, then gave a slight nod. Why he'd come, she couldn't say. But, as much as she hated to admit it, his visit had brightened an otherwise humdrum day.

Donning his cap, he tipped its brim. "Good evening, Miss Adelaide."

As he turned to leave, she fumbled for a reply. "Will I see you again, Corporal Gallagher?" As soon as the words left her mouth, she wished them back. Had she truly welcomed a Yankee to visit her?

He paused and pivoted toward her, a hint of a grin lining his lips. "You can count on it. And the name's Luke."

The corners of her mouth lifted. *Luke.* A biblical name, just as she'd supposed.

Though his name was the only thing predictable about this surprisingly kind-hearted soldier.

"W HERE YOU BEEN HIDING?"

Luke sat on his rolled-out blanket and tugged at his brogans. He cast Sergeant Delmar a sideways glance, hoping his response wouldn't draw further questions. "I was ... checking on a patient."

The sergeant stretched out on his blanket. "Anyone I know?"

Certain if the sergeant learned the truth, he'd dish out a lot of unnecessary and unwanted ribbing, Luke shook his head. "I don't think so." He pulled a piece of hardtack from his haversack, though the thought of eating it was almost worse than hunger pangs.

He sensed Sergeant Delmar's scrutinizing stare. "Must be someone special to cause you to miss grub."

Heat welled in Luke's neck and face as he eased down on his bedroll. There'd be no getting around the sergeant's pointed questions. "Just the girl I carried to the hospital the other day. I wanted to see how she was faring."

Sergeant Delmar smirked, his bushy brows lifting. "Uh-huh. And?"

Luke held back a groan. Obviously, the sergeant wouldn't be satisfied until he'd pried out every detail. "Her hands and arms are burnt to the extent she can't use them. Her father and brothers were killed in the war, and her aunt died in the fire. She has no one. The least I can do is help her out."

With a nod, Delmar reached to dim the lantern. "Oh, of course. I'd expect nothing less from you, Gallagher." He paused briefly before adding, "But it doesn't hurt that she's pretty."

Luke clenched his jaw at the muffled snicker from the opposite side of the tent, letting his eyes adjust to the darkness. He bit his tongue to keep from saying something he'd regret.

Though he couldn't deny Miss Adelaide's features were pleasant to the eye, he disliked the sergeant's insinuation. His was an act of mercy, a way of expressing Christlike love to someone who was hurting—a lost soul.

Like Jacob.

Looping his hands behind his head, Luke stared at the canvas covering that seemed to glow with the brightness of the moon. He couldn't deny being drawn to Adelaide. Not only was she pretty, but she had a kind of spunk he'd not witnessed in girls back home.

He'd have to guard his heart. To become too attached would not fare well for either of them. He had no business pursuing any sort of relationship with someone who didn't share his convictions. In time, he hoped and prayed that would change.

As well as her distaste for Yankees.

5

Richmond
Sunday, April 9, 1865

"Hey, Gallagher! Your turn for sentry duty with the old lady."

Sergeant Delmar's rather rude remark broke through Luke's Sunday afternoon quiet. Regardless that Mrs. Lee's husband fought against them, as a general's wife, she deserved the respect and protection due her. He stood and brushed debris from the back of his trousers. "Where do I find her?"

The sergeant thumbed over his shoulder. "Two blocks that way. Brick house on East Leigh Street."

With a nod, Luke started in the direction of the house. His duty would last well into the evening. Too late for his usual trip to the hospital. The assignment had been sprung on him only this morning, allowing no opportunity to let Adelaide know he wouldn't be stopping by. Would she miss the nightly visit? Or be relieved he hadn't come? Though she seemed to enjoy the company, her adamant refusal to hear any reference to his faith made Luke wonder if she viewed him a pest.

As he neared the three-story, brick house, a look of relief

spilled over the face of the sentry he'd been sent to replace. Jogging up the steps, Luke offered a salute.

The tall, lank soldier returned the greeting and, without hesitation, started down the steps. "She's all yours."

Rifle in hand, Luke widened his stance and braced himself for a long, uneventful evening. He stood for what must have been a couple of hours, listening to the clamor of soldiers' voices in the distance and watching some of Richmond's remaining citizens wander aimlessly along the street, their hollow expressions tugging at his heart. So much about this war wasn't right. Countless lives had been shattered ... on both sides. When the conflict ended, would the country have any hope of reconciliation?

The sound of shuffling feet drew his attention behind him. The door to the house opened, and a trim, dark-haired woman pushed an older lady in a wheelchair out onto the sparse veranda. Luke tipped his kepi to them and moved aside to make room. "Evenin'."

The white-haired woman gazed up at him from her wheelchair, myriad emotions streaming from her dark, deep-set eyes. "Good evening, Corporal."

Her voice was surprisingly pleasant, her thick, Southern accent almost cheery. "This is my daughter Mary, and I suppose you know who I am."

Luke returned a friendly nod. "Yes, ma'am."

As the younger woman retreated inside, Mrs. Lee picked up the meager tray of food on her lap and handed it to him. "Provisions are a mite scarce these days, but you're welcome to what we can spare."

Taken aback by the kind gesture, Luke stared at the plate of potatoes, peas, and biscuits, his mouth watering. After a week of hardtack and missed meals, the food looked grander than he'd seen in months. "Much obliged, Mrs. Lee." He bowed his head in a moment of silent prayer, then heartily scooped up a forkful of potatoes.

Turning her gaze on the gutted street, Mrs. Lee drew a long breath. "By your pause to give thanks, I take it you're a man of faith."

Luke lowered his fork. "Yes, ma'am. I am."

With a slight nod, she laced her fingers together in her lap. "Have you noticed anything extraordinary about the view here, Corporal?"

He scanned both sides of the street, for the first time noticing the stark contrast to the damage—one direction gutted with fire, the other virtually unscathed. "Now that you mention it, I do. It appears the fire stopped very near this house."

"Indeed. Your General Weitzel and his men tried to convince my daughter and me to leave, but I refused. And in just the nick of time, the Lord answered our prayers and the wind shifted the fire away from us."

Dumbfounded, Luke ventured another glance at the charred section of the street. "Remarkable."

"Have you never experienced the hand of God at work in such a way, Corporal?"

Luke rifled through his thoughts, then turned to Mrs. Lee. "I've been spared countless times over the past year and a half from bullets and cannon fire. Once a Reb—er—Confederate soldier, not five feet from me, had his barrel pointed at my chest, but just before he pulled the trigger, another gun sounded, and he fell to the ground dead. I never knew who spared me, so I figure it must have been the Lord's angel of mercy watchin' over me."

The corners of her lips tipped upward. "Then, it appears the Lord doesn't take sides where this war is concerned, but rather He considers those who put their trust in Him."

The refreshing thought revitalized Luke. "I like to think so."

Mrs. Lee eyed the untouched plate of food in his hand. "Don't let my carryings on keep you from your supper. Eat up before it's cold."

"Yes, ma'am."

As he raised the forkful of potatoes to his lips, several rounds of cannon fire blared to the north. Mrs. Lee pressed a hand to her blouse. "Merciful heavens. What do you suppose?"

"I'm not sure." Luke stared in the direction of the disturbance, his meal once again on hold.

More shots sounded to the west followed by men's raucous shouts. Luke set his plate aside and took up his rifle, intent on rushing to see what the trouble was. But, remembering his duty, he held his position.

The house door flew open and a frantic Miss Lee stepped toward her mother. "What's happened?"

"We were discussing just that," the general's wife answered matter-of-factly.

Miss Lee's eyes probed the street then darted to Luke. "I think you'd best come inside, Mother. These Yankees are full of mischief."

With a spirited tip of his cap, Luke held back a grin. Obviously, Miss Lee wasn't as big-hearted as her mother. He couldn't blame her. He'd feel the same if his home were in danger. Whatever the ruckus, he had his orders and would do whatever it took to protect the Lees.

Mrs. Lee nodded. "Perhaps you're right, dear. Though I'm certain we're in good hands."

Luke caught her quick wink and smiled. "Yes, ma'am. We all are."

As her daughter backed her wheelchair toward the door, Mrs. Lee pointed to the plate of food. "With all this caterwauling, you can't seem to get a bite in, can you, Corporal?"

He shook his head and chuckled. "No, ma'am."

Turning to face the now-deserted street, Luke listened intently to the continuing bombardment of gun shots and yells. What was happening?

Moments later, a lone Union cavalryman cantered along the street, bringing Luke to full alert. Luke called to him. "What's the trouble, Sergeant?"

The soldier reined his horse to an abrupt halt in front of the house, a huge smile wedged across his face. "Ain't no trouble. Just the opposite. Lee surrendered at Appomattox Courthouse this mornin'. Inform Mrs. Lee the war is over."

As the sergeant rode away, Luke let out a loud "whoopie" and tossed his kepi high in the air. Leaning his rifle against the rail, he plopped down on the top step, stunned and a bit giddy. The war was finally over.

A hundred thoughts pummeled him. After so many hard-fought battles, news of Lee's surrender came as a shock. Time and again, he'd outsmarted them with his cunning and tenacity. Now, it seemed, the general had come to the end of his road. Luke glanced over his shoulder at the quiet house, and a tinge of regret washed through him. How would Mrs. Lee take the news?

How would Adelaide?

Luke's stomach rumbled and the plate of food called to him. No sense spoiling Mrs. Lee's supper with the news. He licked his lips. Might as well not waste what he'd been given. He shoveled in a forkful of the lukewarm potatoes. The lack of flavor bore witness to the shortage of luxuries such as salt and butter. But it would fill his belly. And right now, he could almost eat dirt and not complain.

As he scooped another bite into his mouth, he breathed a soft sigh. The task before him wasn't a pleasant one, but if Mrs. Lee had the resilience and faith she professed, she'd manage the news well.

But he couldn't venture to say the same for Adelaide.

Robertson Hospital, Richmond
April 9, 1865, Evening

ADDIE GRITTED her teeth as Miss Jane wound a fresh layer of bandages around her arm, the sting of the burns unrelenting.

Even small movements caused excruciating pain. Not to mention the cloth pressing against the raw, blistered wounds. "I can't say which is harsher—the scraping off of skin or the wrapping."

The thin-lipped nurse shook her head, continuing to bind the arm. "I'm sorry, miss, but it must be done."

With a groan, Addie sank her head back against the wall. While the agony of the burns was horrid enough, her forced dependence on others was almost worse. "It's been nearly a week and my arms still feel as though they're on fire. I thought by now they'd show signs of improvement."

The wrapping complete, Miss Jane sat back, her white frock stained with smudges of dried blood. "Wounds this severe take time to heal. Be thankful only your hands and arms were damaged. Many here have suffered worse."

A glance around verified the stark reality of the nurse's words. Some in the room had been injured to the point they could neither talk nor move. Others had not survived. "I realize that, but I tire of relying on others to feed and tend me. If I could only regain use of my hands."

The nurse patted her on the shoulder, eyes brimming with compassion. "Patience, child. You've a long road ahead, but you're young and strong. In time, your wounds will heal."

As the nurse moved on, Addie glanced toward the doorway for the dozenth time, disheartened by its vacantness. Corporal Gallagher hadn't missed a day coming to see her since she'd arrived. Though difficult to admit, his visits had broken the monotony of the long days and given her something to look forward to. Had she offended him one too many times? It being Sunday, perhaps he'd chosen to spend his day in rest and worship rather than endure further rejection.

She sighed. Why should she care if he came anyway? He was a blue-belly. He meant nothing to her.

And yet, she couldn't deny the void his absence created.

She lowered her gaze to her soiled black taffeta dress, the

scent of smoke still lingering in the frayed material. Perhaps she should have obliged his repeated offers to read Scripture. Words that had once brought her solace.

But not now. Not after all that had transpired. Now, she couldn't bring herself to listen to words of God's faithfulness and love. Her life had become accursed, and no words of comfort could remedy such hurt.

Her gaze flicked to the open locket beside her. The more she pondered the photos the more perplexed she grew. Had her aunt harbored a secret all these years? Who was Clarissa and how could Addie hope to find her with nothing more than a photo to go on ... and without the capability to even manage on her own?

Though Aunt Polly had, for the most part, kept to herself, she'd been the closest thing to a mother Addie had known. Especially over the past year, since Papa and Addie's oldest brother, Thomas, were killed. When her other brother, Eli, was killed a few months later, what could she do but sell their property and accept Aunt Polly's offer to move in with her?

Not once had her aunt mentioned a Clarissa. But, now that Addie thought of it, Aunt Polly had had the peculiar habit of closing her millinery shop and taking leaves now and then without explanation. Her excursions usually lasted more than a week at a time. Though Addie never probed to learn where her aunt went, upon her return, Aunt Polly always seemed a bit downhearted.

Addie arched a brow. Perhaps she hadn't known her aunt as well as she thought.

Movement in the hall pulled her attention back to the doorway. Her breath caught when, rather than the lean, blue-clad corporal, a burly fellow stared back at her from just outside the entryway, his silvery eyes boring into her. She turned away, hoping to deter him, and yet, she could sense his eyes still fastened on her. At last, she ventured another glance in his direction, relieved to see he'd gone.

A commotion outside the building set her heart pounding.

The roar of cannons, gunfire, and shouting filled the street. Addie craned her neck to see out the nearest window, listening for some clue as to what the trouble was. All at once, an excited voice filtered through the open windows. "Lee surrendered! The war's over!"

The words ripped through her like the prick of a thorn. "It can't be. General Lee would never surrender."

But even as she mouthed the words, her heart told her it must be true.

6

Robertson Hospital, Richmond
Monday, April 10, 1865

"Y ou're Polly's niece, ain't ya?"

Adelaide woke from her nap with a start. The man from yesterday stood over her, studying her with narrowed, slate gray eyes. There was something familiar about the man. Her eyes crimped. Where had she seen him? "You know my aunt?"

He sneered, his gruff voice as unsettling as his vulgar stare. "Polly and I are sort of ... business partners."

Addie's brows pinched as she recalled seeing him in her aunt's shop on occasion and how jittery Aunt Polly had become when he happened in. "I remember you. You've been to the millinery shop a few times while I was there. Collecting payment on a loan if I recall."

"That's right." He glanced around the room. "Where is she? I need to talk to her."

The muscles in Addie's shoulders tensed. Something told her the less this man knew about her and Aunt Polly the better. "I-I'm not sure. We became separated during the fire." The lie slipped out almost too easily.

He stroked a hand down his whiskered face. "Well, she'll find you, and when she does, tell her Simon's lookin' for her."

With a hesitant nod, Addie shifted to conceal the locket under her skirt. "Have you considered she might be injured? You'd do well to search for her in some other hospital."

"Already have. She's not to be found." He pointed an index finger at Addie. "I saw the sorry state her shop's in. There's nothing left. But don't let her think she won't have to pay what she owes."

Addie grimaced. "Surely you don't expect ..."

"Oh, but I do." His brow creased. "And you can tell her so for me. She can't hide forever."

A tremor rippled through Addie as he pivoted and stormed toward the door. Was money so important to this Simon fellow that he'd scour the hospitals in search of Aunt Polly, knowing she could be injured and her business ruined?

Her mouth went dry. Worse yet, what would he do when he discovered she'd perished in the fire?

LUKE STARED at the back of the bulky man leaning over Adelaide. He wore no uniform to distinguish him as Confederate or Union and, by the looks of his salt and peppered hair, was old enough to be Miss Adelaide's father.

But she'd said she had no family.

Luke bristled. Surely, he wasn't a beau.

From the doorway, he couldn't make out the muffled exchange of words, but Adelaide's paled expression hinted they weren't ones she wanted to hear. While he wavered as to whether or not to interrupt, the disgruntled man pivoted and stomped toward the door, brushing past Luke without so much as a glance.

He strolled toward Adelaide, the distressed look on her face fading as her eyes met his. Pulling a chair up beside her, he gestured over his shoulder. "Who was that?"

She pursed her lips as though hesitant to answer. Finally, she gave a soft sigh. "His name is Simon. He was looking for my aunt. I fear she owes him a good sum of money ... a debt he intends to collect."

Luke's cheek flinched as he eased into the chair. "Did you tell him what happened?"

With a shake of her head, Adelaide's eyelids fluttered downward. "Just that my aunt and I were separated in the fire."

Protectiveness steeled over Luke, and he balled his fists. The man looked like someone who'd make good on a threat. "Was he unkind to you?"

"No, but he seemed annoyed I couldn't help locate my aunt."

The stammer in her voice tore at Luke. Obviously, the man had upset her, and Luke didn't wish to add to her worries by causing her further alarm. Relaxing his jaw, he forced a grin. "Well, hopefully he'll not bother you again."

She stared up at him, a strange sort of quandary in her violet eyes. Her mouth opened as if to speak, but no words came.

"What is it?"

"You didn't come last night," she said at last, her voice barely above a whisper. "I thought perhaps you'd tired of seeing me in my predicament."

His spirit lifted at the hint of disappointment in her tone. Had she missed him? He cleared his throat. "I had sentry duty at the Lee house and couldn't get away in time."

The luster in her eyes returned, and her face brightened. "General Lee's house? Did you see Mrs. Lee?"

His lips tipped in a sideways smile. "Both her and her daughter."

"What were they like?"

With a shrug, he scratched at his cheek. "Mrs. Lee was friendly enough. Even fed me supper. Her daughter seemed a bit more standoffish, especially when the ruckus started, and I had to tell them General Lee surrendered."

His words seemed to suck the life right out of Adelaide. She glowered. "Then it's true. All our efforts have been for naught, and my family died in vain."

Luke leaned forward, resting his elbows on his knees. How should he respond? To have one's entire family snuffed out for a lost cause seemed too great of sacrifice for anyone. The entire war had been nothing short of a conflict-ridden bloodbath.

Give me the words, Lord.

He sighed. "I know it seems that way, but fighting for something you believe in, even dying for it, isn't without merit. They died attempting to protect you and their home."

Her eyes lifted, and her tone turned raspy. "That's little solace when you've been stripped of everyone and everything you hold dear."

Tension welled in Luke's chest. "I understand your hurt. My own father also fell victim to the war."

"But you surely have other family and a home to return to and two good arms." Tears trailed down her cheeks, and her voice hitched. "I have nothing."

Luke couldn't deny her losses dwarfed his own. But he wanted her to know God was bigger than her pain. "You've had a rough go, that's certain. But the Lord promises to be near the brokenhearted."

She glared at him, her lips thinning in a taut line. "If God is near, why are so many people suffering? Look around, Corporal. Do you see God at work here?"

Luke glanced around the room filled with burn victims, many in worse shape than Adelaide. His mouth twisted. "No, miss, I don't. I see the repercussions of war. A war of our own choosing. God doesn't want to see us suffer any more than we do. He'd help you through this, if you'd only give Him the chance."

Her eyes narrowed into slits. "I want no part in a God who allows such pain and devastation. And ... and I want no part in a

Yankee who cottons to such nonsense, so I must ask you to please leave." With a sniffle, she looked away, a hardened expression settling over her face.

Shaken by the harsh words, Luke slowly rose to his feet. He was getting nowhere with this distraught young lady. Though convinced Adelaide spoke out of hurt and not hatred, now was not the time to point that out.

LUKE STARED out over the James River, listening to the sounds of celebration drifting from deep within the city. He tuned out the lively melody of a harmonica and the hoots and hollers of the soldiers in the distance. Any other time, he'd be in the midst of it. He'd been as eager as anyone for the war to end. Yet tonight, his heart refused to find joy. Not while Adelaide was hurting so in both body and spirit. How many other lives had been devastated as well?

He tossed a pebble into the murky water and watched the ribbon of moonlight threaded across its surface fan out into dozens of glistening ripples only to calm and be restored to one solid beam moments later. He raked a hand through his hair and stared into the starry sky. If only wounded hearts could mend so easily.

Adelaide's a closed door where You're concerned, Lord. I don't know how to reach her. She's right. My losses are minuscule compared with hers. How can I speak words of life and wisdom to someone whose heart is so battered and bruised? My words seem as empty as those of Job's friends.

"That you, Gallagher?"

Startled by the unexpected intrusion on his prayer, Luke peered over his shoulder as Sergeant Delmar approached. "Yep."

The sergeant cast Luke a dubious glance as he stepped up beside him. "What are you doin' standin' out here in the dark? I thought you'd be back at camp, kickin' up your heels with the rest of 'em."

Returning his gaze to the river, Luke folded his arms across his chest. "Just needed time to sort through things."

Sergeant Delmar gave a low grunt. "You're a hard one to figure, Gallagher. Either you're cuttin' up with the fellers or off alone in some forlorn place. Why is that?"

Though the sergeant didn't share Luke's faith, his superior never maligned his beliefs and, deep down, seemed to respect him for them. He cleared his throat. "Getting off by myself helps me put things in perspective. Do some praying."

Delmar chuckled and gave Luke a friendly nudge on the arm. "The time for prayer is passed. Haven't you heard? The war's over, and we won!"

Luke was still coming to grips with that reality. Yet, Adelaide's words hung heavy on his heart. "There are other things to pray about besides the war. Lee may have surrendered, but there's a lot of heartbroken people caught in the crossfire."

The sergeant clamped a hand down on Luke's shoulder. "Ah, now Gallagher. Surely the Good Lord would give you some leeway to celebrate before praying away the rest of our troubles."

A grin edged out the solemness in Luke's expression. Turning, he nodded to Sergeant Delmar, his face half shadowed by the night. "I s'pose so."

"Well, come on then. Let's go."

Guided by starlight and flickering campfires in the distance, they meandered their way from the river's edge back to the outskirts of the city. The sounds of merriment overtook the steady chant of frogs and nightlife as they neared their campsite.

Doing his best to push aside the burden he carried, Luke's step and mindset grew lighter. "How soon do you figure they'll send us home?"

"Can't say. Not till Richmond is better secured, I'd venture. We for sure can't leave things as is. These poor souls don't know their left hand from their right."

The comment funneled Luke's thoughts back to Adelaide. Her life had truly been turned upside down. What would become of her now that the fighting had ended? "What do you s'pose will happen to the people here at Richmond with their homes in such shambles?"

Sergeant Delmar sighed. "They'll rebuild, start their lives over as best they can, I reckon. But we can't worry about that now. Come on. We've some celebratin' to do."

As Luke followed the sergeant into the throng of carousing soldiers, his heart sank. One army's victory was another army's defeat. Somehow meeting Adelaide and getting a firsthand view of her plight had crushed his spirit of celebration. He couldn't blame her for holding a grudge against him. Not after all the hardship she'd suffered.

Though it wasn't his choice, he'd abide by her wishes to keep his distance. But that didn't mean he couldn't pray for her. And right now, prayers were what she—and the entire country—needed most.

7

Saturday, April 15, 1865

With Miss Jane's help, Addie eased into the wicker chair on the hospital veranda. Gazing into the desolate street, she gave a soft sigh. "Useless. That's what I am. Utterly useless."

The willowy nurse bent low, lines creasing the outer edges of her eyes. "Oh, you shouldn't say such, miss. Of course, you're not useless."

"But I feel so helpless. I still can't accomplish even the simplest of tasks."

"Give yourself time, child. Your arms will soon mend. Be grateful you have use of your legs to move about."

"I suppose." Addie drew a long breath. "It is rather refreshing to breathe in something besides stale air and body odor. Thank you for helping me outdoors."

"My pleasure, child. Perhaps tomorrow being Resurrection Sunday, we can get you out sooner, in time to watch the sunrise."

Addie pivoted toward the kind nurse. "I'd forgotten tomorrow is Easter."

"It is indeed. And what a blessing we have the end of the war to celebrate as well."

Addie's eyes glossed over as she recalled happier times. Before the war. When she'd dressed in her finest and accompanied Papa and her older brothers to Easter church service. She'd been but a girl of twelve or thirteen then and full of life and vigor. Her brothers' pride and joy. How they'd doted on her, taking turns escorting her to and from the church pew. Practicing, she supposed, for when they'd marry.

A pleasure neither of them would ever know.

She gnawed her lip. God had seemed so real to her then. But the war changed that. Now, He was nothing more to her than a distant memory, a fanciful notion. He'd answered her prayers with silence. So, rather than think of Him as an ogre who'd allow her family to be slaughtered like cockroaches, she preferred to disown Him.

Such a cruel God she couldn't fathom or champion.

The touch of Miss Jane's hand on her shoulders pulled Addie back to the present. "What's happened to that young soldier friend of yours? Corporal Gallagher, was it?"

At mention of the handsome corporal, Addie's throat tightened. She squirmed under the added warmth of the shawl. Five long days had passed since she'd hastened him away. She wet her lips, a tinge of regret trickling through her. "I asked him not to come."

The nurse drew a hand to her chest. "Whatever for? He was such a help to us both."

Addie dropped her gaze and mumbled under her breath, "He's a Yankee—a reminder of everything I loathe and abominate."

Chuckling, Miss Jane cupped a hand under Addie's chin. "Does that make him the devil that you should shoo him away?"

Her brows knit. "Men like him killed my father, my brothers, and now my aunt."

With a shake of her head, the nurse propped her hands on

her hips. "Now miss, don't go placing blame where it isn't due. That young man is no more responsible for the death of your loved ones than I am. The war's to blame, along with us all. We chose to let our differences divide us, and we're all paying the price."

Heaviness tugged at Addie. Perhaps she had been a bit hasty. After all, the corporal had shown her nothing but kindness. And he, himself, had done her family no harm. His visits had actually given her something to look forward to each evening.

It was his talk of God that niggled her.

She shrugged her shoulder. "I suppose that's true. I just don't cotton to some of his spiritual notions."

Miss Jane wagged a finger at Addie, her loose chignon bobbing back and forth with each movement of her head. "Even so, if you ask me, that young man showed a lot of gumption giving up his free time to play nursemaid to you. And, whether you realize it or not, you're indebted to him for saving your life."

Adelaide sat back with a huff. She couldn't argue that. Though, knowing Corporal Gallagher, he would likely give God the credit.

Miss Jane tugged the shawl tighter around Addie's shoulders, tempering her tone. "I need to return inside. Will you be all right here a while?"

"I'll be fine."

With a brisk nod, the nurse retreated indoors.

Addie glanced haphazardly down the street, eyes searching. She had to admit, Corporal Gallagher had been a help to her, along with relieving some of her loneliness. Given the opportunity, she might even welcome him back.

Eyeing each soldier who passed, Addie's heart plummeted when none favored the wavy-haired corporal with striking blue eyes. A sigh escaped her as she leaned back and molded herself to the chair. More than likely, she'd frightened him off for good.

And somehow, she'd never felt more alone.

The clop of horse hooves echoed down the near vacant

street, pulling her attention to the right. A distinguished looking soldier astride a white horse with dark mane and tail moved steadily toward her. Her heart hammered. There could be no mistaking the white beard, the stately manor, and the tidy uniform of what, in her mind, was the greatest military leader of all time—General Robert E Lee.

Eyes wide, she edged forward and rose to her feet. Others on the street gathered round to pay homage to the defeated, yet renowned, general. Dressed in gray and head held high, General Lee stared straight ahead, not venturing a glance at those standing by. Addie gave a slight curtsy, bowing her head as he passed, sadness squeezing out the wonder of the moment.

The celebrated general had come home, not to cheers or fanfare, but to a quiet, unassuming trickle of onlookers. Many of them Yankees. And yet, all seemed to hold an element of respect for the man who had outwitted the Northern army time and again.

A quiet hush seemed to fall over the city as his dazzling horse, Traveller, pranced down the street, proudly carrying his master. Addie watched until the pair slipped from view, her heart drumming in her chest. With his return came a finality of the war. The life she'd known no longer existed.

And nothing would ever be the same.

Dear Ma and Lydia,

How I wish I could be with you to celebrate Resurrection Day. And yet, I'm confident this will be our last holiday apart. With the war ended, I hope to return home very soon. I happened across Drew here in Richmond a few days back. He is well, but said to tell you he will be delayed in his return home.

LUKE PAUSED to dip his quill in the inkwell, a grin tugging at the corner of his mouth as he continued writing.

Though he didn't say so directly, I'm certain a lady friend is the reason. He never was good at concealing his emotions. Richmond is in shambles, and the people here are at a loss. It will require much work to restore the city and their lives.

His thoughts returned to Adelaide, his heart aching at the image of her sitting alone and unattended. Surely his company had been better than none. Resting his freshly inked quill tip on the paper, he continued.

I've witnessed firsthand the hardships of some of the people here and it saddens me. One girl in particular, who was found injured beneath the rubble ...

A commotion outside the pup tent brought a halt to his writing. Murmured voices fell silent as he laid aside his quill and moved to the tent opening. Drawing back the flap, he peered outside to see a cluster of soldiers gathered nearby, heads hung low. Sergeant Delmar's face was ghostly pale as he glanced up from the paper in his hand.

Luke stepped toward him with a sudden sense of dread. "What is it? What's happened?"

The sergeant's Adam's apple bobbed, a stunned look in his dark eyes. "It's President Lincoln. He's been shot."

"What?" A numb sort of panic coursed through Luke. "Is he alive?"

Sergeant Delmar lowered his gaze, shaking his head ever so slightly. "He died early this morning. They're still searching for the killer."

Luke braced himself against the trunk of a tree, the news hitting him like a cannonball in the gut. President Lincoln dead? Shot by an assassin? It seemed too incredible to be true. Just a few days ago, he'd strolled the streets of Richmond. Luke could still hear the celebrative cheers of the freed blacks and envision the president reaching out his hands to them, his lank frame and tall hat standing out amid the crowd.

With a heavy sigh, Luke raked a hand over his face. Less than a week had passed since Lee's surrender. The short-lived victory now seemed hollow.

Without a word, he retreated inside his tent, wondering how such news would affect the nation. Would peace prevail? Or would the President's untimely death stir up a whole new initiative where the South was concerned?

He shoved his paper and ink aside, unable to finish the letter he'd written with such fervor moments earlier. Lying on his blanket, he latched his hands together behind his head and stared up at the dingy tent canvas. *I'm not a vengeful person, Lord, but what this assassin did is pure evil. May they find him and may he reap his just rewards. And may this incident not cause further tensions between North and South.*

He blew out a breath. Moments ago, home seemed all but within reach. Now, he wasn't certain of anything.

8

April 16, 1865
Easter Sunday Morning

Addie's heart stammered as the blue-clad soldier approached the hospital veranda. She sat taller in her chair, grateful for the opportunity to redeem herself. "Corporal Gallagher. Whatever brings you here?"

Removing his cap, he cleared his throat. "I was passing by on my way to Easter Sunday service. I ... uh ... noticed you out here and thought I'd check how you're doing. I hope you don't mind."

"No, no. I'm pleased you came." She cringed, reeling in her eagerness. Had she truly said she was pleased? "I mean, it's quite all right you stopped. The days have been rather monotonous."

"Well, at least you're up and about. That's good." He turned his head, allowing her a glimpse of his handsome profile.

She chastened herself for noticing. "The nurse thought I would benefit from some fresh air. But I find the morning a bit chilly."

"Would you like me to take you inside or ask for a blanket?"

She shook her head, touched by the sincerity in his voice. "I'll be fine. It's warmer now that the sun has risen higher."

Her breath caught as he moved to pull her shawl tighter around her shoulders. The scent of lye soap enveloped her, an indication he'd cleaned up for Sunday service. His blue eyes found hers. "I don't suppose you'd want to go to the service with me?"

Her mouth twisted. He didn't give up easily. "No, thank you."

He gave a slow nod, displaying no visible sign of disappointment. "Well then, I'll be on my way. Good to see you're doing well."

As he turned to leave, she fumbled for something to say. "I-I heard about Mr. Lincoln. I had no love for the man, but he didn't deserve what happened."

The corporal's grip on his cap tightened. "He longed for peace. I'm glad he saw it come before he died."

She could only nod. That "peace" had come at a high price for her and many others. But she didn't wish to argue the point.

Donning his cap, Corporal Gallagher eased down the veranda steps, the tips of his wavy hair turning golden in the sunlight. He glanced up at her, eyes sparkling. "Take care of yourself."

Addie nodded, edging forward in her chair. Feelings of loneliness seeped back in as she watched him go. She called after him. "Do stop again, Corporal. *If* you're of the notion."

He pivoted toward her, confusion lining his brow. "But I thought ..."

"I was rude to you the other day." She hesitated, softening her tone. "I-I'm sorry."

A smile edged out the seriousness on his face as he backed down the street, his step a bit lighter. "I may just do that."

Addie grinned as she crumpled back in her chair. If there was one thing she needed right now, it was a friend. Yankee or not, she was grateful she'd found one in Corporal Luke Gallagher.

"HEY GALLAGHER! WAIT UP!"

Luke turned to see Sergeant Delmar jogging toward him. "Who was that you were talking to?"

Luke kept up his pace, a bit reluctant to answer. "The girl we found in the rubble."

"You don't say?" The sergeant tossed a glance back over his shoulder. "Purty little thing, ain't she? A bit young though, don't ya think?" He let out a chuckle. "'Course, you're barely out from beneath your Ma's apron strings yourself."

He bristled at the sergeant's crass comments, but out of respect for his superior rank, held his tongue. Instead, he kept his gaze fixed on the church building ahead.

Sergeant Delmar's laughter quieted. "Say, what's gotten into you, Gallagher? All the fun's gone out of you lately."

He shrugged, tempering his response. "I s'pose I've seen a side to things I hadn't seen before."

"Like what?" The sergeant's words held a hint of challenge tinged with curiosity.

"Like how this war has devastated lives on both sides. And, that there are more important things at stake than who wins or loses. If we can't help each other and foster peace, we all lose."

Sergeant Delmar snorted. "Here we're helpin' these Southern rebels clean up their burned-out city and tending their wounded, and one of 'em goes and puts a bullet in our president. I don't call that very peace-loving."

The reminder of the heinous act of Lincoln's assassination renewed Luke's sense of loss. "No, and I hope they find the fellow who did it. But the hatred and killing has to stop somewhere. As far as I'm concerned, there is no more North and South. We're Americans, neighbor helping neighbor."

The sergeant clapped him on the arm. "Gallagher, if you think all the bitterness and turmoil are gonna die away so easy, you're more naïve than I thought."

Luke tossed him a sideways glance, slowing his pace as they neared the church. "Not naïve. Hopeful. Healing takes time, and this land is in need of a heap of it. I have faith, in time, the Lord will do just that. But we all have to do our part."

Sergeant Delmar arched a brow. "Don't know if I can handle two sermons in one day, Gallagher."

Luke grinned. "Can't hurt."

Delmar scratched his chin. "I don't know. One at Christmas and Easter is my usual limit for the year. But, since you've joined our ranks, seems I hear some tidbit of faith most every day. You sure you ain't missed your calling to be a pastor?"

The thought humored Luke. He could never imagine himself a fist-thumping pulpit preacher. He was a farmer, a simple outdoorsman who happened to love the Lord. He shook his head. "No, Sergeant. I believe I'm right where the Lord wants me."

Sergeant Delmar knit his brows. "How can you be so sure?"

"'Cause you have yet to give your heart to Christ."

With a shake of his head, Delmar stared at him. "I do believe if anyone can get me to repent, it'll be you, Gallagher."

Luke's lips spread in a sideways grin. "Whatever it takes."

The sergeant gave a soft snicker and slapped Luke on the back as they started up the church steps.

Luke's thoughts returned to Adelaide. He and the men had happened upon her in the nick of time. And though she'd needed saved in both body and spirit, her heart was more closed to God than the sergeant's. The Lord had placed the two of them in his path for a reason.

His chest tightened. He'd missed his chance with Jacob. Maybe now was his chance to redeem himself.

A SHADOW FELL across Addie's face and her eyelids bobbed open. When had she drifted to sleep? She startled awake and squinted up from the wicker chair at the shaded figure standing over her. Though the silhouette was that of a man, the sun at his back made the face difficult to distinguish.

"Well, now. If it ain't Polly's niece."

The man's voice was gruff, abrasive. So unlike Luke's soothing one. Addie bristled but gave no response.

He widened his stance. "Ya know, I've looked high and low for that aunt of yours, and I can't find her anywhere. I don't guess you've seen her either?"

Addie wet her lips, attempting to hide the unsteadiness in her voice. "No. I'm afraid I haven't."

"That's what I figured." He edged closer, until Addie could glimpse his close-set eyes and square, unshaven jaw. He pointed to the charred necklace dangling from the darkened chain around her neck. "That's an interesting piece of jewelry you're wearing."

Heat rose in her cheeks. Did he recognize it? When she'd asked Miss Jane to clean and place the locket around her neck, she'd not bargained on the return of her unwelcome visitor.

His brow creased. "She's dead, ain't she?"

Ignoring the pointed question, Addie let out a huff. "What is it you want, Mister ...?"

"It's just, Simon." His thick lips curled slightly upward. "And, what I *want* is to know how you intend to pay off your aunt's debt?"

Addie's breaths shallowed, her mind awhirl. "I-I have some money from the sale of my family's property. I just need time to retrieve it."

He raised a brow. "Graybacks?"

"Yes, of course."

With a shake of his head, he crossed his arms over his chest. "Won't do. Now that the war's ended, they ain't worth the paper they're printed on."

Her shoulders sagged, along with her spirits. Then she truly was destitute, the money she had to live on now worthless. "Then, I'll need time."

"How much time?"

"A few months perhaps."

He jutted out his lower lip and scrunched his brow as if deliberating. "I'll give you six weeks."

Sitting forward in her chair, she stretched out her arms. "But that's impossible. Surely you can see I'm in no condition to seek employment."

She caught a whiff of his foul breath as he leaned closer. "Oh, I don't know. Your hands and arms might be damaged, but you have other assets that would work in your favor."

Addie eased back, eyeing him apprehensively. "And just what do you mean by that?"

He bared a mouthful of yellowed teeth. "You can work for me."

Her eyes narrowed. "And do what?"

"There'll be a lot of lonely soldiers returning home from the war. And you're a very pretty lady." Reaching out a hand, he brushed the back of his fingers against her cheek. "You could ... entertain them."

It took a moment for Addie to grasp his meaning. As the words sank in, she spit in his face, repulsed, wishing her hand was healed enough to slap him.

Jerking back, he wiped his face with his sleeve. "Why you little ..."

Addie met his gaze, jaw set. "Get away from me, you filthy scoundrel."

He snickered as he backed away. "You may change your mind when you hear the full story. With Polly dead, the debt falls to her nearest kin." A devious look flashed in his eyes. "How is Clarissa anyway?"

Addie's breath caught. "Clarissa? What do you know of her?"

He smirked. "More than you, I imagine. What is she now, twelve? Thirteen?"

Addie swallowed, attempting to appear as though she knew what she was saying. "She's thirteen."

His scoff affirmed his knowledge on the matter was greater than her own. "Just what I thought. You know nothing about her. She turned twelve last November. Polly must have known her time was up else she would never have mentioned her."

Speechless, Addie could only stare at him. Who was this man who seemed to know more about her aunt's personal life than she did?

He lowered his voice. "She did a good job keeping her hidden, but a promise is a promise. Polly's death changes nothing. I expect payments every month same as always."

Addie squinted up at him. "And just how long do you expect to receive money on a millinery shop that no longer exists?"

He paused. "It's not the shop she owes me for."

Thrown off guard by the unexpected reply, she knit her brow. "What then?"

With a glance around, he leaned in closer and softened his voice. "She paid me twelve dollars a month to keep quiet about the girl."

Addie shook her head. "I don't understand. Keep quiet about what?"

"Apparently, your aunt didn't like the notion of anyone, least of all her family, knowing she was a sullied woman who'd mothered a child out of wedlock."

Lightheadedness tore at Addie, the disturbing words almost causing her to swoon. Inwardly shaken by the news, she did her best not to let it show. Instead, she tipped her chin higher. "Well, I have no family or friends left to disclose such a secret to, so I don't see why I should feel obligated to pay what you ask."

His face gnarled. "Is that so?" Reaching out, he slid his fingers under the locket and cradled it in his palm. "This never left Polly's neck. I wonder what's inside that made it so ... special?"

Addie tried to lift her arm to snatch it from him, but stopped midway, cringing in pain. "Put it down."

Ignoring her plea, he smoothed his thumb over its marred

surface. "Polly hid the girl from me all these years. I agreed not to seek her out so long as I got my payments. But, if you decide not to follow through, that could change."

He tugged the chain tighter until it cut into the back of her neck.

Fearing the charred links would snap, she leaned forward to slacken the chain. "Please. It's all I have left."

He tightened his grip on the locket as if to yank it from around her neck.

"Is this man bothering you, miss?"

The man's voice from the street stilled Simon in mid tug. The keepsake thudded against Addie's chest as Simon straightened and pulled his hand away. He stared at her, his eyes demanding she make light of the situation. She craned her neck to see around him. A Federal soldier watched them from the bottom step. Mustering her voice, she feigned calmness. "Uh ... no. But I believe he's in need of assistance. He seems to be lost."

The stout private tipped his cap higher on his forehead. "Where is it you're going, mister?"

Simon glared at Addie, then pivoted toward the soldier. "I'm, uh, looking for my injured friend. He must be at a different hospital."

"There's one farther down. I'm heading that way if you wanna come along."

"Sure thing." Simon's expression sobered as he again turned to face Addie. He bent closer, his eyes boring into her. "I'll be back," he whispered. "And don't get any notions of leaving. Like I said. I know how to find people."

His lingering stare sent a shudder through Addie. As he turned to go, she wilted down in the wicker chair. How thankful she was the soldier had happened by when he did. Though Simon's promise to return assured her the reprieve would be short-lived.

She had only one hope left and needed Corporal Gallagher's help to attain it.

9

Addie perused the solemn procession of soldiers and freed slaves making their way along the street from Easter Sunday service. Obviously sullen from news of their president's untimely death, they trudged along like whipped puppies. To the point she nearly felt sorry for them.

When more than one fellow cast her a brazen stare, she retreated back into the shadows of the hospital veranda. How could she ever hope to capture Corporal Gallagher's attention amid the throng of soldiers? Or even spot him, for that matter?

Still shaken by the mid-morning visit from Simon, she nervously jiggled her foot, continuing to scan the sea of blue uniforms. Oh, why hadn't she thought to ask Luke before he'd left? Flagging him down amongst the other soldiers was so ... unladylike.

And would likely embarrass them both.

But she needed the use of his arms and the security his presence would provide.

She pulled in a breath. There he was! She craned her neck to be certain. Yes. Who could mistake those blond curls protruding from beneath his cap or the spring in his step?

Venturing into full view, she gathered her courage and called to him. "Corporal Gallagher! Corporal Luke Gallagher!"

Every eye veered her direction. Warmth leached up her neck and into her cheeks. A string of whistles and shouts rang out among the soldiers, making her wish she'd let them pass without uttering a word. She was about to slink away and forget the entire thing when she saw the corporal break rank and head her way. Those nearby whooped and prodded the poor fellow along, his face as flushed as hers felt.

Ignoring their jests, he made his way over, his winsome face revitalizing her. "I didn't expect you'd want me to stop by quite so soon."

She swallowed. "I-I need to ask a favor."

He propped his foot on the veranda step and shrugged. "Name it."

With a hesitant glance over his shoulder, she waited for the soldiers to pass. When only a few stragglers remained, she leaned toward him, lowering her voice. "I'd like you to escort me home."

His brows pinched. "I thought you didn't have a home?"

"That's what I need to find out. I know my aunt's shop was destroyed, but it's possible her apartment was spared."

The hospital door creaked open, and Addie turned to see Miss Jane peering at them. Her eyes widened when she saw Corporal Gallagher. "Well now, this is a pleasant surprise. I thought Miss Hanover ousted you for good."

"So did I."

Addie glanced from one to the other. "It was ... a mistake."

Miss Jane gave a firm nod, her thin, oval face seeming in agreement. "I'm glad you've come to your senses, but you'll have to continue the conversation later. Your dinner is ready, then you must rest."

Addie tensed and took a step back. "Oh, but the corporal was about to escort me to my aunt's apartment to see if it was spared the flames." She glanced at Corporal Gallagher, a quiver in her voice. "A-At least that was my hope."

Luke opened his mouth to speak, but before he could respond, Miss Jane intervened. "Well, it will have to wait. You've been out here far too long as is. It's time you take your nourishment and rest a while."

"But I ..."

The nurse's upper lip flattened in a thin line. "I'll hear no arguments, young lady. Captain Sally has given her orders. Perhaps you can persuade her to let you go later in the day."

Addie flashed Luke a pleading look.

The softness in his eyes robbed her defenses. He nodded toward the nurse. "Go on. I'll get some grub and check back later."

With a defeated sigh, she nodded and turned toward the door then paused, glancing back at him. "Promise?"

"You have my word." With a tip of his cap, he downed the steps.

As he started down the street, Addie stared after him. Never did she imagine she'd take the word of a Yankee. But something told her she could trust this one.

Though she refused to admit it to him or anyone else.

He was a means to an end. That was all.

MISS ADELAIDE'S black dress swished side to side as she paced back and forth on the hospital's small veranda. Guessing the reason for her impatience, Luke quickened his pace.

She glanced his way and paused, her expression brightening. With careful movements, she downed the steps. "I thought you'd never get here."

He paused as she strolled right past him. Doing an about-face, he jogged after her. "I was fortunate to get away as soon as

I did. I don't know if you realize it but, even on Sunday, I'm at the mercy of my commanding officer."

Without responding, she hurried on. "My aunt's apartment is quite a ways from here. On Eleventh Street. So, we'd best get going. We'll not find anything once the sun sets."

Luke fell into step beside her. "You sure you're up to this?"

"Quite sure. It's my arms that are injured, not my legs."

He shook his head. Her determination astounded him.

They fell silent, her taking the lead. As they neared the burnt-out segment of the city, her gait slowed, the hopefulness in her eyes waning. Charred timbers and shattered bricks still lined the devastated Main Street. Destruction that had become commonplace to him over recent weeks, she was viewing for the first time, and her paled cheeks and tormented expression gave clue to her anguished spirit.

The scent of ash and soot enveloped them as they ventured into the rubble. Adelaide paused and glanced around, a dazed look in her eyes. "I hardly recognize the place."

"It was much worse right after the fire. We've spent the past two weeks just making the streets passable."

She glanced side to side, her raven black hair contrasting with the milkiness of her ivory skin. "I had no idea the flames had devoured so much." She stilled and gaped at him, as if his words had only now sunk in. "You mean to say Union soldiers are clearing away the debris?"

Luke grinned. "We're not all as bad as you think. Not only have we worked to rid the streets of rubble, but we've ensured your fellow Richmonders have roofs over their heads and food in their bellies." Arching a brow, he motioned to her bandaged arms. "Not to mention medical care."

Her violet eyes widened and then turned stormy. "Well ... it's the least you can do after pilfering our livelihood." With that, she tramped forward.

Humored by her spirited disposition, Luke chuckled to

70

himself as he started after her. "Isn't there anything that will change your mind about us Yankees?"

She shook her head. "Nothing."

Enjoying his bit of fun, he pressed her further. "And yet, you allow me to visit and accompany you of your own accord. So, you must not hate me entirely."

She cast him a sideways glance, a sudden flush in her cheeks. "I don't hate *you,* in particular. Merely what you and your Yankee cohorts have done."

"And what is that?"

Her face scrunched. "Kill and destroy!"

The hem of her skirt snagged on the corner of a charred timber, pinning her in place. Stooping down, Luke freed her from its grasp. He stood, the tip of her head barely level with his chin as he met her gaze. "We're not killing and destroying now. We're aiding and restoring."

She seemed to flounder for words. "W-Well, of course. Now that you've run us off and taken over the place."

Luke raked a hand over his face. "Do you think your Confederate soldiers would have done any different if they'd seized our Capital?"

Her pursed lips and averted eyes hinted he was on the brink of being exiled a second time. Perhaps for good. Deciding it best to change the topic, he cleared his throat. "Do you recognize where you're at in all this ruin?"

With a quiet huff, she glanced around, seeming to shake off the incident. "I'm not sure. It's a huge, jumbled mess. Even the street signs aren't legible."

Luke scanned the area. "There's a sentinel up ahead. Maybe he can help."

"Wait! Over there." Adelaide fixed her gaze on some unknown object in the distance. "There's Capitol Square. At least it's standing proud as ever."

Peering around the gutted buildings up ahead, Luke caught a glimpse of the Capitol building and grounds, untouched by the fire that had devastated entire blocks of houses and businesses just to its west.

As they ventured closer, Adelaide jutted her chin. "What are those Federals doing milling about our Capitol? Have they no respect?"

"They're doing no harm, merely keeping watch." Luke hadn't the heart to tell her that, days earlier, President Lincoln himself had entered the Capitol building and spoken to a hoard of excited freed slaves and Union soldiers from the front lawn.

"Why, hello again, Corporal."

Luke shifted toward the voice, surprised to see the tiny woman he'd encountered days earlier no more than a few strides away. He tipped the brim of his kepi. "Miss Van Lew. How are you?"

"Very well, thank you." Her gaze swung toward Adelaide. "And who's this with you?"

He sensed his companion ease back into his shadow like a frightened kitten. "This is Miss Adelaide ..."

"Hanover." Adelaide called from behind him.

"Ah! A Union soldier and a Richmonder strolling side by side. There's a sight I'd enjoy seeing more of." Miss Van Lew dipped her head to one side, her smile fading as she fixed her gaze on Adelaide's bandaged arms. "Were you injured in the fire, my dear?"

Her gumption returning, Adelaide stepped forward. "I was, and we really must be going."

Taken aback by the rudeness of her tone, Luke sought to explain. "We're seeking her aunt's apartment to see how badly it's damaged."

The woman's pale blue eyes sparked. "Oh, I see. Would you like me to accompany you? In all this mess, it's a struggle to find your way."

Adelaide bristled and nodded to the cluttered street ahead. "No, thank you. I know exactly where we are. The apartment is just beyond the Capitol grounds. Come, Corporal." With that, she started on.

Luke shrugged and grinned in attempt to smooth over Adelaide's impoliteness. "Forgive her. She's been through a great deal."

Understanding lined the woman's eyes, and she smiled. "Believe me, her response to me is not one I'm unaccustomed to. In fact, it's rather mild compared to most."

Recalling what Miss Van Lew had disclosed earlier, he could only guess Adelaide, as well as others, had an inkling of the woman's Unionist loyalties. He brushed the brim of his hat with his fingertips. "Nice to see you again."

"And you, Corporal," she called as he started after Adelaide. "If I can assist you or Miss Hanover in any way, don't hesitate to ask."

With a backward wave, he fell into step with Adelaide. She flashed him a disgruntled scowl. "Did you have to be so friendly?"

"Did I have reason not to be?"

She blew out a breath. "Do you know who that was?"

"Elizabeth Van Lew is what I was told."

"Crazy Bet, you mean."

"She didn't seem crazy to me."

Adelaide shook her head, glossing over the comment. "Of all people, she is most despicable. The entire town suspects her of underhanded dealings with those ornery Federals."

Luke held back a grin. Had she forgotten he was one of them? "Is that so?"

She scoffed, refusing to slow her pace as she skirted around a pile of rubble. "I suppose you hold her in high esteem, you being a Yankee?"

Not wishing to escalate the dispute, Luke tempered his response. "War makes people do strange things sometimes ... like cause a Yankee soldier and a Confederate civilian to join ranks for a common cause."

Though she gave no reply, the pink in her cheeks was enough to convince him his words found their mark.

The farther they ventured, the narrower the passageway along the dirt-laden street. As they neared the end of the burnt-out district, Adelaide slowed her pace and released a soft moan. He followed her gaze to the remnants of a building in shambles. The despairing look in her eyes confirmed his suspicions. "Was that it?"

With a slight nod, she gnawed her lip. "All is lost. What will I do?"

The desperation in her voice tugged at Luke. "I'm sorry."

She turned moist eyes on him. "We'll never find it in all this mess."

"Find what?"

She hesitated before responding. "My aunt kept a metal box in a hidden compartment of the corner cabinet in the kitchen. It held ... our valuables. Though the money no longer has worth, I'd hoped there might be something of value in it. It's all I have to live on."

Luke pushed his kepi higher on his head and glanced at the pile of debris. The last thing he wanted was to spend Easter Sunday digging through more charred ruins. He got his fill of that through the week. But Adelaide needed help, and it appeared he was the one to lend it. Rolling up his sleeves, he cast her a sideways glance. "Well then, I s'pose we'd better find it. Where abouts was the kitchen?"

Something akin to gratitude flashed in her eyes. "The left front corner of the building. The cabinet rested against the outer wall."

He gave a brisk nod. "We'll start there then." As he reached for a singed board, he called over his shoulder. "Hope you don't mind me saying a prayer."

Her soft sigh voiced her lack of faith. "Do as you must. Though I doubt very much it will help."

Tossing the board aside, he straightened. "Now, that's where you and I differ. You can't expect God to answer if you doubt Him. Scripture says we're to ask in faith and not doubt."

Rather than the scoffing he expected, the remark met with silence. Though he longed to turn and view her expression, he returned to his work, praying something he said would penetrate her heart and that, little by little, the Lord would prove His faithfulness to her.

"THAT'S IT!" Addie could barely contain her eagerness. "I never would have believed it."

"A little prayer does wonders." Corporal Gallagher flashed that winsome smile of his, melting her resolve.

"It appears in this instance you may be right."

Hands black with soot, he set the locked box on the ground in front of her. Squatting down, he tugged at the burnt padlock. "Looks like we'll have to bust it open."

He sought out a jagged rock and gripped it tightly in his fist. Using his full strength, he smacked it hard against the charred lock, snapping it in two. With a questioning glance, he gazed up at her. "Open it?"

Addie nodded, though it didn't seem fitting for a Yankee to rummage through her aunt's personal belongings. She hadn't even been allowed in the box herself. And yet, Corporal Gallagher was so different from what she'd envisioned a Yankee to be. She'd expected Northerners to be rude and uncouth.

More like Simon.

Instead, the young corporal had made every effort to help her. Nothing had stunned her more than to learn Federal soldiers were working to repair the burnt-out city rather than plunder it.

Still, they'd killed her dear father and brothers. She could never forgive them that.

Addie's heart pounded as the corporal pried open the lid.

The jingle of coins offered renewed hope. But would there be any of value?

Or would all this be for naught?

Her spirit fell at sight of the wad of Confederate graybacks on top. The decision to sell her family's estate had been a heart-wrenching one. In doing so, she'd hoped to secure her well-being for many years to come. To learn the funds she'd received no longer held value was devastating.

With an apologetic glance, Corporal Gallagher set the worthless funds aside and dug deeper in the metal box. He pulled out three hand-written letters and several daguerreotype photos. Standing, he fanned the photos out in his hands. "Are these people familiar to you?"

Addie craned her neck for a look, and the corporal obliged by turning the photos toward her. The first two were larger versions of the ones in her aunt's locket. Another depicted a couple she'd never seen with a girl that resembled the child in the picture with her aunt, only older. Perhaps five or six years of age.

But it was the final photo that took her breath away. Endearment shone in her father's eyes as he stood alongside a young woman resembling Addie, her raven-black hair accenting her ivory wedding gown. A long veil framed her oval face. A tender smile played on the woman's lips, her face full of youthful vigor. Who could guess that a mere five years later, her life would end?

Addie's throat squeezed, threatening to choke off her words. "That's ... my parents."

Corporal Gallagher flipped the photo toward him and glanced at the couple, then at Addie. "You look very much like your mother."

She stepped beside him, mesmerized by the image. Moisture pooled in her eyes. It was true. She had her mother's coal-black hair, petite frame, and large eyes. Though she couldn't imagine she was half as beautiful. "I've never seen my mother."

"Why's that?"

Addie peered down at the photo, her voice soft, wispy. "She died when I was a baby. My brother Thomas said Papa was heartbroken and couldn't bear to look at her picture. So, there were none to be found."

"I'm sorry." His comforting tone sparked of sincerity.

"I would sometimes sense him staring at me, as though I reminded him of her. Now I see why." Pricked by the loss, she hung her head.

Corporal Gallagher was silent a moment, then gathered the photos and notes together. "Maybe I oughta take you back, give you the chance to view these on your own."

His thoughtfulness surprised her. And though she yearned for the ability to explore the contents in private, she had no wish to wait. She nodded toward a flat stone from a fallen building. "If you'll just spread the letters on that boulder, I'd like to read them now."

With a shrug, he unfolded the letters and laid them on the flat surface, handling them lightly so as not to coat them with soot. He edged back, as if to allow her privacy.

Trembling, Addie eased down onto the thick stone slab. Whether the coins inside the box were worth much or little, right now, she didn't care. If her suspicions were correct, she had found missing pieces of her heritage that were of greater worth to her than money.

She only hoped the letters would tell her what she longed to know.

10

Addie quivered with anticipation at the three letters stretched out before her. It felt intrusive reading letters not her own. Letters that had long been kept for her aunt's eyes alone.

Surveying their dates, she began with the one dated December 10, 1852.

Dear Miss Hanover,

> *Our pastor informed us of your dire circumstances and your reasons for surrendering your infant daughter. Do not fret over your arduous decision. The Lord has answered our prayers for a child through you. I assure you she will be raised in the Christian faith and, in honor of your wishes, will retain the name you chose for her. We pray this knowledge brings you comfort.*
>
> *Regards,*
> *Mr. and Mrs. Stuart Banks*

A wave of disbelief coursed through Addie. What dire circumstances had forced Aunt Polly to make such a decision?

Though the note explained how the girl came to live with the couple in the photo, it did little to clarify the circumstances that led her aunt to give the child up or how she came to be.

Addie glanced again at the date. December 10, 1852. If the baby was born before that date, she would be twelve years old—the very age Simon had declared Clarissa. Her gaze flicked to the second letter dated April 2, 1854. Perhaps it would provide more details.

Dear Miss Hanover,

>*We have prayed long and hard over your request and have come to conclude there could be no harm in you visiting, so long as you hold to your word not to reveal your true identity. Clarissa Jane is thriving under our care and is in every respect our daughter. To interfere with our rearing of her would only bring heartache to us all. We hope you understand.*

>*Regards,*
>*Stuart and Emma Banks*

Clarissa Jane. Addie bit back tears. Jane was her aunt's middle name. There was no mistaking the connection now. Clarissa was indeed Aunt Polly's daughter.

And *her* cousin, regardless of where she was or the circumstances surrounding her birth.

She turned to the third letter dated July 12, 1856, and, with eager eyes, devoured each word.

LUKE WATCHED Adelaide as she pored over the letters. Her expression was difficult to read, seeming to fluctuate between confusion and disbelief. Feeling intrusive, he turned away. Fingers stiff from soot, he trudged to a nearby water trough and dipped his hands in the murky water. He rubbed his palms together, though the layer of sludge made him doubtful his hands would emerge much cleaner.

"Then it's true."

The soft-spoken words pulled Luke's attention back to Adelaide, her small frame and bewildered expression lending her a look of innocence. Beneath her guarded exterior lay a fragile girl, frightened and alone.

Drawing his hands from the water, he dried them on his uniform pants. He stepped toward her. "What is it?"

Her large eyes brimmed with tears as she glanced up at him. "It seems I'm not the last of my family after all. Aunt Polly has a daughter."

The knowledge obviously meant a great deal to her. Luke refrained from probing for details—how her aunt had kept such a secret or how she'd come to have a child without a husband. Instead, he merely nodded. "Is she here in Richmond?"

Adelaide's voice hitched. "That's just it. I have no way of knowing. The postmarks and return address have been marked out. Aunt Polly clearly didn't wish anyone to know where her daughter is."

Luke bent to pick up the box. "Maybe we just need to dig deeper."

His words seemed to spark something within Adelaide for she left the display of letters and moved to join him. But, other than a couple of worthless bank notes, a few personal items, and the pouch of coins, there was nothing.

"What's that wedged along the side?"

At Adelaide's prompting, Luke tugged the thin slip of paper lodged in a crevasse at the back of the box. Flipping the paper over, he gave a confused "humph."

"What is it?"

"A bunch of crossed out dollar signs and the initials S. B. at the bottom." He turned the page toward her. "Can you make sense of it?"

Her delicate face pinched, then her eyes grew wide. She shook her head, not quite meeting his gaze. "N-no. I'm afraid it means nothing to me."

But the flicker in her eyes and the edginess in her voice hinted she knew more than she was telling.

ADDIE LAY on her cot and stared at the darkened ceiling. She yawned, exhausted from her eventful afternoon. Around her, the groans of burn patients only fueled her despair, as did the throbbing in her arms.

Unable to sleep, her mind played over the contents of her aunt's box. Unlike Corporal Gallagher, she'd known exactly what the *X*'s over the dollar signs and the initials on the slip of paper represented. Of the eighteen emblems, twelve had been marked through. Aunt Polly was counting down years until she was free of Simon's harassment. The initials surely stood for Simon, his unknown last name beginning with *B*.

There was no disputing that Clarissa was her aunt's child. A relative Addie never knew existed. And she had names now for the couple who appeared to be the girl's adoptive parents— Stuart and Emma Banks. But how could she ever hope to find them without a notion of where they lived? And without funds to even try?

Confident Aunt Polly's undisclosed trips must have included visits to Clarissa, Addie racked her mind to recall if she'd ever given clue to where she'd been. The third letter from Mr. and Mrs. Banks mentioned them living a good distance away.

But, where?

Obviously, Aunt Polly had taken extreme precautions to keep her daughter's location a secret.

Addie tensed. Knowing Simon, she could understand why.

The bundle of silver half-dollars would be enough to sustain her a short while but would in no way satisfy Simon's demands.

Here, surrounded by medical staff and patients, she felt safe from his threats. But when she recovered, what then?

Her bruised head had all but healed. Other than the uselessness of her hands and arms, she was strong and healthy. She was more liability than anything now, taking up far too much of the nurses' valuable time. How much longer would they allow her to stay? And, truly, how much longer did she wish to?

The more time spent in the fresh air, the less bearable the stale confines of the hospital became. But, with nowhere to go and limited money to live on, she was at Simon's mercy. Though she was fairly certain he would *show* no mercy.

What she hadn't learned was how the brute knew her aunt's secret, and how he'd had the audacity to hold it over her. Mysteries she intended to find the answers to should he pay her another unwelcome visit.

11

April 18, 1865
Tuesday Evening

Addie cringed as Captain Sally examined first one of her arms, then the other, her expression vague. "You're still in quite a bit of discomfort, I take it?"

Unable to stand the sight of the blotchy, raw-looking arms, she nodded and turned her head. "They sting worse with the binding off."

"Yes. Exposure to air will do that. Are you able to bend your fingers?"

An attempt to flex her raw, stiff fingers left Addie shaking her head. "I can't."

Captain Sally gave a soft sigh. "Well, the burns are healing, but it will be several weeks, possibly months, before you'll regain use of your hands and arms."

Standing, she motioned for Miss Jane to apply the fresh layer of bandages soaked in a blend of white, lead paint and linseed oil. "We'll give it a couple more days, but it's safe to say you'll soon be able to return home and have someone tend to you there."

The very mention of home and loved ones to care for her nearly brought Addie to tears. She moistened her lips in attempt to still their trembling. "But I have no family and no home to return to."

Captain Sally's eyes softened. "That's right. I'd forgotten." With a sigh, she crossed her arms. "Well, you'll definitely need someone to tend you for a number of weeks yet. Surely there must be someone who could put you up. A neighbor or friend?"

Addie dropped her gaze to her lap. "No one. Everyone I knew evacuated before the Yankees arrived."

The nurse brushed a wisp of dark hair from her cheek. "That *is* a problem."

Addie's eyes lifted. "Couldn't I just stay here until I'm well?"

Captain Sally's face pinched. "I'm afraid our staff is in short supply and must concentrate on those in dire need of medical attention. And, I just received word our little hospital will be closed down soon."

Addie sucked in a breath, the startling announcement crushing any hope she had left. "But why?"

The captain shrugged. "It seems the Yankees have no interest in the upkeep of a small, Confederate hospital. I had to appeal to the Union medical director just to remain open long enough for my patients to recuperate or transfer to a larger Federal-run hospital."

Numb, Addie slumped against the wall. "I can't stomach the thought of rotting away in some infested, Yankee hospital."

Captain Sally placed a hand on Addie's shoulder, her expression sullen. "Don't worry. I wouldn't think of sending you to one of those miserable places full of diseased and mutilated soldiers. Now that you're faring well and mobile, we'll have to make other arrangements."

"But where can I go?"

The question seemed one the caretaker had no answer to, for she sighed and dropped her hands to her sides. "There must be some place. I would put you up myself, but as soon as this place closes, I'm leaving town."

Addie turned in hope to Miss Jane who wagged her head as she fastened a fresh bandage on Addie's arm. "I'm afraid I can't be of help to you either. I'm away from home much of the time and live in a tiny apartment with strict rules against extra boarders."

Despair coiled around her heart like a noose, squeezing the life from her. Her head dipped lower. "Then I've nowhere."

"She can stay at my home."

The astonishing words reverberated through the room like a blast of cannon fire. All eyes pivoted to the doorway. Flabbergasted at the sight of Corporal Gallagher peering back at her, Addie nearly melted dead away. Was he jesting? The sincerity streaming from his eyes and the straight-forward set of his jaw suggested otherwise.

Miss Jane paused her wrapping, eyes wide. "Just what are you proposing, young man?"

"Nothing improper, I assure you." A crimson-faced Corporal Gallagher stepped closer, gripping his cap in both hands. "I have a mother and sister back home in New York. I'm certain they would be willing to look after Miss Adelaide, if she's willing."

Addie's mouth dropped. "Are you mad? *Me* live under a Yankee's roof? I'd sooner wander the streets of Richmond as a beggar."

A tinge of hurt flashed in her friend's eyes. He moved to the foot of the cot. "From the sounds of it, you may do just that, if you remain so stubborn."

She pursed her lips. *What gall.* She'd known this young man only a matter of weeks. Did he expect her to jump at the chance to accompany him to a place she had no knowledge of or desire to be? "Do you truly think I would agree to such an arrangement? Turn my back on my heritage and take up your Northern way of life?"

Widening his stance, he crossed his arms over his chest. "I'm not suggesting you give up your Southern roots. I'm merely offering you a place to recuperate."

She rolled her eyes. "Well, the notion is absurd. New York, indeed!"

"Do you have a better idea?"

"Enough." Captain Sally raised a hand to intervene, then turned to Addie. "This soldier has been helping tend to you, has he not?"

Unable to deny it, Addie offered a reluctant nod.

"Is he someone you trust?"

Her mouth twisted as she studied him more carefully. "I suppose he's given me no reason not to. Other than he's a Yankee."

Lacing her fingers together behind her back, Captain Sally gave a brisk nod. "Well, Yankee or not, it wouldn't hurt for you to at least consider the option." She shot Luke a pointed glance. "Provided you have a chaperone. With the railroads disabled, that would entail quite a long trip."

The corporal shifted his feet. "I-I'd need a couple of days to work out the details."

Addie tipped her chin higher. "There's no need, because I have no intention of going."

Captain Sally turned to her, softening her voice. "It would only be a temporary arrangement, until you're able to function on your own."

Miss Jane gave Addie's shoulder a gentle squeeze. "Yes, dear. You can always return and start anew once your arms and hands heal."

Addie wavered, realizing Luke's proposition was truly a selfless one. But, as the faces of her fallen brothers and father flashed through her mind, her resolve deepened. "I'm afraid it's out of the question."

She and Luke locked eyes but an instant before his gaze fell away. Heaviness pulled at her chest. Had she disappointed him? She released a long breath. "I appreciate your gesture, Corporal, but my roots are here, and I don't intend to leave."

His jaw flinched. "Your mind's made up, then?"

The despondency in his voice pricked her, and she mellowed her tone. "I'm afraid it is."

Her words seemed to wield a crushing effect, for he hung his head.

The poor fellow. It seemed all she did was cause him grief. Compelled to offer a kind word, she forced herself to sound pleasant. "I do thank you for your generosity. It was very considerate of you."

His eyes lifted, and a strange sort of understanding seemed to pass between them. At last, he donned his cap. "If you change your mind, let me know."

With that, he turned on his heels and left.

As he did, a hint of remorse rippled through Addie. She flicked a brief glance at both Captain Sally and Miss Jane. Neither spoke a word, but instead returned to work, their ruffled expressions alluding that she was a fool.

Perhaps she was. Corporal Gallagher had proven himself a trustworthy friend in her time of need. But, fool or no fool, she couldn't bear to turn her back on her family's legacy, all they'd died to preserve. Even for a short while.

It was asking too much.

Miss Jane finished wrapping Addie's arms, then swept a stray wisp of hair from her forehead. "What will you do then?"

Addie gave a soft sigh. "I haven't the slightest."

LUKE JOGGED down the hospital steps and trekked out into the street, Adelaide's firm rebuff still ringing in his ears. Heat singed his cheeks. What had he been thinking? The impulsive words had spewed from his mouth before he'd given thought to what he was saying. Her adamant response both relieved and crushed him. He had no way of knowing if he could even follow through with such a promise anyway.

He blew out a breath. It was just as well she'd declined. What would Ma and Lydia think of him offering to bring a Southern-bred girl under their roof to tend? Most likely, they'd say he'd lost his senses.

A twinge of regret ripped through Luke, and he kicked at a rock in his path. He'd only wished to help. Despite her infuriating stubborn streak, something about Adelaide beckoned to him. Like it or not, she needed help. Regardless of her attempt to conceal it, he'd seen the desperation in her eyes and heard it in her voice.

He just wasn't sure he was the one to aid her.

Elongated shadows fell over the street as the evening sun dipped lower in the west. Luke locked eyes with the man passing to his left. Vague recollection pulled at him. He'd seen him somewhere. But where? He glanced over his shoulder for a second look and caught the man peering back at him. Obviously, he'd recognized Luke as well.

His stomach clenched as he turned back around. Now he knew. He was the man he'd seen leaving Adelaide's room a couple weeks back. The one who'd upset her.

Though his mind yearned to know where the fellow was headed, he kept walking. Was he paying Adelaide another unwanted visit? Luke slowed his pace, then forced himself to press on. It was none of his concern. Adelaide made that quite clear.

Yet, he couldn't shake the urge to turn and follow the man. There was just something about him Luke didn't trust.

What should I do, Lord?

Another backward glance assured him the burly fellow was indeed heading toward the hospital. Luke worked his jaw, warring within. If he returned, Adelaide would likely tell him it was none of his business and send him on his way.

But, if he didn't ...

"WHAT ARE *YOU* DOING HERE?" Though Addie spoke in hushed tones, her voice was anything but pleasant. Nor did she intend it to be.

Simon sneered as he pulled a chair up beside her. With a glance around, he kept his voice low. "Protecting my interests."

She glanced around the room of sleeping patients, wishing Miss Jane hadn't already left for the night. Refusing to be intimidated, Addie glared at him. "You said I had six weeks. I'd appreciate you honoring that and not pestering me every other day."

His pitted brow furrowed. "Just wanna be sure you know I'm not goin' anywhere."

"Don't worry. You'll get your precious money. Though I've half a mind not to bother. I don't think you have the slightest idea where Clarissa is."

He leaned closer, his foul breath nearly gagging her. "Maybe not, but I assure you I'll find her if need be."

"Why? What possible interest could you have in a twelve-year-old girl?"

With a sideways glance at the patient nearest them, Simon bent lower, steely gray eyes boring into her. "There's more to it than you know."

"You needn't bother holding my aunt's indiscretions over me. What's done is done. And there's no one left to care." The words raked a hollowness through the pit of her stomach. Had she become so calloused?

He gripped her chin, his rough fingers pressing into her skin. "That may be so, but ..."

"You, there. What are you up to?" Though the words came out forceful, Captain Sally's voice held a tremor.

Simon pivoted toward her, jerking Addie's head to the side as he pulled his hand away. "We was jus' havin' a friendly discussion."

The captain stepped closer. "Well, it's time you leave."

"Is this man bothering you ladies?" The man's voice though familiar, sounded strained. Addie leaned to see around Simon and melted with relief at sight of Luke.

"Yes!" The emphatic reply, spoken in unison, brought him a few steps closer.

His eyes crimped as they focused on Simon. "You heard the ladies. You've overstayed your welcome. Now get going."

Addie warmed at the protective tone in her friend's voice. She'd seen that firm set of the jaw on her brothers' faces numerous times when they sensed someone bothering her. But she'd not expected such concern from a Union soldier she'd known only a short time. Though bulkier and broader in the shoulders than Luke, Simon's muscles didn't appear as firm beneath his shirt.

She had a feeling the young corporal could hold his own in a confrontation with the larger man if necessary. Though the thought of championing a Union soldier over a Southerner was a bit alarming. Yet, there was something to be said for a person's character.

And the corporal outshined this Simon fellow by a long shot in that respect.

Simon slowly stood, his stare lingering on Luke. Addie's breath caught. Would he challenge her friend? At last, he strode toward the door, bumping Luke's shoulder as he passed. A bit shaken, Addie released the breath she'd been holding.

Leaning down, Captain Sally swept hair from Addie's forehead. "I'm so sorry. Are you all right, dear?"

"I'm fine." Addie worked to still her trembling limbs. She

wasn't fine. With her hands disabled, she had no means to defend herself. Her jaw still ached from Simon's firm grip.

Creases formed above the bridge of her caregiver's nose. "Is that man an acquaintance of yours?"

Exhaling a harried breath, Addie pondered how to answer. "He was an associate of some sort of my aunt who perished in the fire."

"This is at least the second time he's troubled Miss Hanover."

Detecting an element of concern in Luke's voice, Addie sought to downplay the incident. "I'm certain it won't happen again."

Captain Sally shook her head. "I do apologize. Apparently, I need to lock the doors earlier than I'm accustomed. I'll bolt them as soon as the corporal leaves."

Straightening, she turned to Luke. "Thank you for your assistance, Corporal. Your appearance here was timely. How did you happen back so soon?"

Equally curious, especially after her recent refusal, Addie eagerly awaited his response.

He twisted his cap in his hands like a school boy who'd neglected to do his homework. "I ... uh ... met him on the street. I had an inkling he might turn up here, so I doubled back."

"Well, we're grateful you did."

Captain Sally's appreciative words compelled Addie to offer her own. "Yes. Thank you, Corporal."

"My pleasure." He met her gaze, his shy grin nearly reducing her to a puddle.

Under Captain Sally's scrutinizing stare, he donned his cap. "Well, I'd best be getting back to camp."

"I'll see you out."

With a nod and a tip of his brim to Addie, he followed Captain Sally from the room. A feeling of void spilled over Addie as he left, her sense of security vanishing with him. His offer to welcome her into his family's home had been a valiant one indeed. But not one she could imagine agreeing to. And yet, she yearned for a safe haven, away from the pangs of loss. Away from memories that had dissipated into sorrows.

Away from Simon's menacing presence.

But even these yearnings could not erase the swath of bitterness churning inside her for those who'd killed her loved ones. She couldn't stomach living in the same house as cruel Yankees.

Like it or not, she must bear the burden her aunt left behind.

12

April 19, 1865

Luke chucked a stray rock onto the pile, then brushed his hands together, squinting against the noontime sun. All morning he'd struggled to wrap his mind around last night's incident with Adelaide and the man he'd chased off. What did the fellow want from her anyway?

He had the feeling there was a lot Adelaide wasn't telling. She obviously didn't trust him. No matter how hard he sought to prove himself a friend, she'd forever view him as a Yankee—an enemy to her and her family.

"You look about as far away as home."

Luke turned to see Sergeant Delmar coming up beside him. Unwilling to divulge his true thoughts, he merely agreed. "Home sounds pretty good about now."

"Well, between this wreck of a city and that fugitive assassin, I wouldn't get any ideas about leaving too soon."

With a nod, Luke propped his boot on a stone slab. "Any news on Booth's whereabouts?"

Delmar shook his head. "Nothin'. Even with every available

man hunting for him, no one's laid eyes on that Rebel since the night he shot Lincoln. At least no one who's talking."

"They should get my big brother, Drew, on his trail. He can track anything that moves."

"Maybe they will. They need someone with a bit of foxhound in him to sniff Booth out." The sergeant scanned the squad of privates piling debris. "By the long faces, it looks like the whole lot of you are itchin' to be done with your duties and back home."

Private Cummings straightened and rubbed a hand over his lower back. "Any notion of when that'll be, Sergeant?"

"You just keep working and let the higher-ups worry about that."

Private Fenton swiped a hand over his brow. "It can't come soon enough as far as I'm concerned. I've a sweetheart back home who's likely plumb forgotten what I look like."

Cummings snickered. "With your mug, that may work in your favor."

Luke held back a grin as mirthful laughter erupted from the squad of soldiers. It was good to see the fellows having a bit of fun. Even Private Fenton smiled and shook his head, seeming to get a chuckle out of the good-natured poke. The long, grueling war, followed by the president's shocking assassination, had sapped the men's spirits. They deserved a bit of blithe humor to rejuvenate them.

"All right, you hooligans, back to work." Sergeant Delmar strode through their midst, pointing to the rubble. "The sooner we get this place on its feet, the sooner we can head home."

Mild grumbles ensued as the men returned to their duties.

Luke reached for a charred timber.

Home.

Since news of Lee's surrender, he'd dreamed of nothing but home. Yet, incidents like the one last night made Luke a bit leery to leave. What would happen to Adelaide? Once he left and the hospital ousted her, she had nowhere to go and no one to look after her.

Except God.

And she'd turned her back on Him.

He straightened and thumbed his kepi higher on his forehead with a sigh. Her stubbornness would be her undoing. Maybe he'd do well to stay away this evening and give her time to think things through. It wouldn't do any good to try to convince her to change her mind. God alone could pierce a heart that had grown cold.

Turning his eyes heavenward, he lifted a silent prayer. *Look after her, Lord. Whether she knows it or not, she needs You. Penetrate her heart. Help her realize You're not to blame for her troubles. She needs someone in her corner, someone who'll look after and protect her. May she open her heart and allow that One to be You.*

ADDIE GLANCED over the letters spread on her lap in hopes of gleaning more information about her undisclosed cousin. And yet, nothing new stood out. So many unanswered questions.

Questions only Aunt Polly could have answered.

With effort, Addie flipped the letters over on their backs with her bandaged hands and peered at the smudged postmarks. Bending lower, she examined the markings on the third letter more closely. Though the postmark had been blotted out, part of it was still visible. The last two letters were definitely *IA*. Virginia? And yet, the first letter didn't look like a *V*. It was too rounded. More like a ...

Addie's breath caught. Surely she was mistaken.

Miss Jane stood with her back to Addie at the opposite side of the room, peeling back the bed sheets from a recently vacated cot. "Miss Jane?"

The woman pivoted toward her, arms laden with bedding. "Yes?"

"Would you have a look at this? I can't quite make it out."

With a nod, the volunteer nurse dropped the sheets in a heap and started across the room. Coming up beside Addie, she placed her hands on her hips and peered down at the letters. "What is it you're trying to decipher?"

"The postmark there. Can you make out where that one originated?"

Miss Jane lifted the letter closer to her face, turning it in all directions. "I can't distinguish the town name, but I believe the state must be Pennsylvania."

Addie's eyelids fluttered. "Pennsylvania? Are you sure?"

Miss Jane squinted for another look. "Well, I can't be positive, but it looks to be."

Addie pursed her lips. How shrewd of Aunt Polly to hide Clarissa on Yankee soil—where Simon would never think to look. Pennsylvania was a vast state. Without a town to go by, this bit of knowledge did her little good. And yet, she felt one step closer to finding her cousin.

"Is that all you needed?"

Shaking off her musings, Addie nodded toward the letters in her lap. "Could you put these away for me please?"

"Certainly." Offering a faint smile, Miss Jane folded the letters and placed them back in the metal box before returning to her task.

Addie leaned her head back and riffled through her muddled thoughts. Clarissa being in Pennsylvania shed new light on Luke's offer to accompany her north. Traveling to New York meant passing through Pennsylvania. She wavered, for the first time finding Luke's proposition almost tempting. Could such an arrangement work to her favor?

The thought niggled her. Would using Luke to gain free access north be abusing his kindness? She had a feeling his offer would stand regardless of her motives. He'd been nothing but generous. A friend when she'd had no one else.

Lowering herself onto the cot, she attempted to flex her stiff fingers beneath the confines of the bandages. Given time, she'd hopefully regain some use of her hands and arms. But would she forever remain crippled? The nagging fear twisted her insides into a knot.

She blew out a prolonged breath. Perhaps a short time convalescing with Luke's family would prove tolerable—if doing so meant bringing her one step closer to locating Clarissa.

Yet, no matter how strong her desire to find her only living relative, the question remained. Could she do what she'd sworn never to do—set foot inside the home of a Yankee?

April 19, 1865, 11:30 pm

THE CREAK of a floorboard at the foot of Addie's cot startled her from light sleep. She opened her eyes to the dim room. A solitary lantern, its wick turned low, shed a faint glow from the corner of the room. Dark shadows danced along the walls and ceiling. Assuming the sound had come from Captain Sally checking patients, Addie nestled back down and closed her eyes.

And then, as if the flame had been snuffed by a gust of wind, the room blackened. Her eyes popped open at the sound of scuffing boots. Raising her head for a look, she pulled in a breath as calloused fingers gripped her mouth, pressing hard against her cheeks. The hand squeezed tighter, muffling her attempt to scream. Hot breath blew against her ear, and something cold and sharp pricked her side. "Quiet."

Addie stilled, her heart pounding. She struggled to breathe, the stench of whiskey and thick fingers pressed just under her nose threatening to block her air. Though unable to see him, there was little doubt who the assailant was.

Who but Simon would single her out?

She longed to cry out to God for mercy, but her heart refused to believe He would hear. Asleep or too incapacitated to aid her, the other patients were as helpless to her as her own bandaged arms. How she yearned for Captain Sally to come, or by some miracle, Luke, or even Miss Jane.

But hope died within her as he pressed closer. She fought to wriggle free of his hold, determined it better to die than be molested. But, the sharp blade in her side eased as he slid his arm around her waist, stealing any thought of escape. He snickered softly in her ear, his foul breath repulsing her. "Not to worry, little missy. I've only come to prove I'm calling the shots. Not you or your Yankee suitor. I can do whatever whenever I please. Got it?"

Nodding, she blinked back the moisture blurring her vision.

"Just get me my money, and you'll have no trouble. But cross me, and you and the girl will ..."

The sound of footsteps in the hall stilled his words and his grip tightened. As lantern light seeped into the room, he jerked his arm from around her and dashed toward the open window. Gasping for air, Addie sank down on the cot with a groan, a stab of pain surging through her bandaged arms.

Hurried footsteps approached and the room brightened. Gentle hands pulled her to a sitting position. "Addie! Are you all right?"

Numb and sore from Simon's rough grip, Addie gave a weak nod.

Sitting beside her, Captain Sally brushed stray hair from Addie's cheek. "What happened? I thought I saw someone."

Addie cast a glance at the window, open much wider than when she'd gone to bed. Its thin curtains flapped in the gentle breeze, the darkness of night concealing any signs of the intruder. Her voice quivered as she choked back sobs. "That awful man came."

"Who?"

"Simon. The one here earlier. He fled out the window."

Sally's face pinched. "Did he ... hurt you?"

With a shake of her head, Addie shifted her throbbing jaw back and forth. "Aside from a few bruises and aggravating my burns, no."

"You poor dear." The nurse placed a hand under Addie's chin, examining her by lantern light. "It appears locking the doors isn't enough. The windows need secured as well. Though it may get a mite stuffy in here."

She stood and made her way around the room, pulling the windows closed before returning to Addie. Leaning over, she offered a weak smile. "I'll put in a request for a guard first thing in the morning. But for tonight, do your best to get some rest."

Addie settled back on her cot, too anxious to sleep.

Captain Sally patted her leg. "Rest assured. That man won't set foot in here again."

Though the caretaker's words were meant to comfort, they offered Addie little reassurance. She had a feeling posting a guard and securing the hospital wouldn't keep Simon out if he chose to return. A cold sweat trickled through her. Since the fire, this hospital had been her one safe haven. Now that, too, felt threatened.

ADDIE SHIFTED onto her side in attempt to get comfortable. Long hours had passed with little or no sleep, her mind sated with disturbing thoughts. Even if she could come up with the money Simon demanded—which was unlikely—would he truly let her be? Thinking back, she recalled how tense and jittery her aunt had become whenever he'd stopped by the millinery shop. Though Addie never saw funds pass between them, she understood now why Aunt Polly had conveniently sent Addie on an errand or to tend to a customer while he was in the store.

There was so much that made sense now about her aunt that hadn't before. And so much she had yet to grasp. Such as how

Clarissa had come to be, and why Aunt Polly found it necessary to mention her when death seemed inevitable? She might easily have let the secret die with her. And yet, she'd pleaded with Addie to find the girl.

Why?

Was she so certain Simon would cause her harm? What would it gain him?

With a huff, Addie shifted on the cot. Part of her longed to forget she'd ever learned of Clarissa, while something deep within yearned to find her one remaining relative. But, even if she did, would the girl be so content with her life that disrupting it would do more harm than good? Even knowing Mr. and Mrs. Banks were from Pennsylvania wasn't much help. She had no inkling how to go about tracking them down.

Surely Simon wouldn't either.

The first glimmer of daylight dawned outside the windows. Addie yawned, her eyelids growing heavier. She mustn't sleep. Not yet. Not until daybreak, when more people were around to ensure Simon would be less of a threat.

She rolled her shoulders, nerves raw. Clearly, she needed to leave this place, find somewhere to elude him. If she threw herself at the mercy of some benevolent group, perhaps they would take her in.

A sigh escaped. It was no use. She could never feel safe here in Richmond. If Simon's claims were true—and he'd given her no cause to doubt them—he would find her. Was she destined to live the rest of her days in fear?

Yea, though I walk through the valley of the shadow of death, I will fear no evil: for thou art with me.

The verse from the familiar Psalm droned through her cluttered thoughts. If only she could claim the comforting words as her own. Once, she'd believed God loved her. But no more. Despite her heartfelt pleas, He'd abandoned her when she'd needed Him most.

Fixing her gaze on the dim rafters above, she blew out a long breath. How could she not fear when there was no place to run and no one to protect her?

Her eyes flared, a thin ray of hope breaking through her cloud of angst.

Or was there?

13

April 20, 1865
Thursday Evening

Luke gulped down the boulder-sized lump in his throat. "You're sure?"

Adelaide's reluctant nod was anything but reassuring.

He propped his boot on the hospital porch step, his mind probing for answers. He would have a hard time explaining this one to Ma and Lydia. "What changed? Two days ago, you wouldn't have a thing to do with the idea."

The wicker chair creaked under Adelaide as she shifted, lips pulled taut. "I-I decided it's my best alternative ... for now."

He leaned against the rail and studied her, her words and demeanor unconvincing. "Did something happen?"

With a shake of her head, her eyes drifted to the floorboards. "No. I-I merely realized I could bear living on Yankee soil for a short while. Though I ask you not make mention of the arrangement to anyone."

The odd request only puzzled him further. Was it so demeaning to her for others to know? "And why is that?"

"It's just better that way." The tremor in her voice hinted of fear rather than regret or embarrassment.

What wasn't she telling him? He cleared his throat. "I'll need to secure a short leave and contact my mother and sister. As yet, they know nothing about this."

Her eyes lifted, a glimmer of unease rippling through them. "Then there's a chance they may not wish me to come?"

"Oh, you've no worries there. They're the giving type. They may even meet us part way."

The tension on her face eased. "How soon would we be able to leave?"

Luke arched a brow. "That all depends on what sort of mood my superiors are in and how soon I can arrange to get you there. I'd say sometime next week at best."

"Next week? But I need to le ..." She pursed her lips, unwilling to finish.

"You need to what?"

Lowering her gaze, she shrugged. "Nothing. I was just hoping to leave a bit sooner."

Luke crossed his arms over his chest. Something didn't set right. Why the sudden change of heart? Not only was she willing to do what days earlier she'd adamantly opposed, but she seemed eager to do so. Who would hold such persuasion over her?

The Lord?

Not likely. Not by the troubled look in her eyes.

Captain Sally or the nurse, perhaps?

Doubtful. Their comments had garnered little effect.

As his mind riffled through their recent encounters, his muscles tensed. *Simon.* It had to be. Somehow, he'd frightened her into leaving Richmond. That would explain why she wanted to keep the arrangement a secret.

With a tip of his kepi, he gave a reassuring nod. "I'll see what I can do."

ADDIE'S HEART drummed in her ears as Luke paused to speak to the guard posted outside the hospital's picket fence. She craned her neck in attempt to hear the conversation, but all she gleaned was the troubled look on her friend's face. He cast a quick glance her way, then headed down the street, the darkening hues of twilight shadowing his features. Had he learned the reason for the guard? If so, he knew of Simon's nighttime visit.

Just what she'd hoped to keep from him.

No sooner had he disappeared from view than Addie grew restless, leery of every shadow and noise. After last night, even a guard couldn't ward off her fears. Luke's presence calmed her. Made her feel safe, protected.

Would she feel that way under the care of his family?

A chill coursed through Addie as the setting sun sank below the horizon. Her eyelids heavy, she yawned, her sleepless night catching up with her. Though she'd dozed much of the morning, it had been a restless slumber, her mind cluttered with uncertainties. Had she done the right thing in accepting Luke's offer? At times, she felt at peace with the decision. Other times, she revolted at the thought.

What would Papa and her brothers have thought of such an agreement?

She'd not wished to leave Richmond, let alone Virginia. It nearly turned her stomach to think about subjecting herself to Yankee ways, even for a short while. New York was so far from all that was familiar. Would she be spurned by the Northerners? Or would they treat her with the same benevolence Luke had?

A nervous tremor kneaded through her. Like it or not, Simon had pretty well made her mind up for her. Her only comfort came in knowing the arrangement would be a temporary one. As soon as able, she would seek out Clarissa.

Addie gnawed at her lower lip. Reared in Pennsylvania, would her cousin even have any desire to forge a relationship with her? Or shun her as the stranger she was? Was she even aware Aunt Polly was her mother? Or that she'd been adopted?

So many unknowns.

If need be, she would return south alone to make a fresh start.

Tears pricked her eyes as she peered at her bandaged limbs. Her hands and arms would indeed heal.

But, like the wounds in her heart, she would never rid herself of the scars.

SO *THAT* WAS IT.

Luke's steps grew more clipped with every stride. His instinct had proven right. According to the private stationed outside the hospital, there'd been a break-in and a threat to one of the patients. No doubt Adelaide had been the victim and Simon the intruder.

No wonder she was eager to leave. He'd known something wasn't right. The snap decision made sense now. The fellow must have frightened her awfully bad to convince her to make such a desperate choice. What exactly did he hold over her?

Whatever it was, he knew better than to ask. If she wanted him to know, she would have said as much, instead of trying to conceal it.

He kicked at a stone in his path, sending it skidding to the side of the street. Maybe someday she'd come to trust him.

The important thing was, she'd decided to take him up on his offer. Was this the Lord's way of answering his prayers for her?

He eyed the street ahead. The telegraph office was just two blocks away. If he hurried, he could get word to his mother tonight. Tomorrow morning he'd tackle asking for leave. With the war ended, surely a week's pass wouldn't be too difficult to finagle.

A twinge of uncertainty washed through him. Hopefully Ma and Lydia wouldn't get the wrong impression about Adelaide. A brief telegram could hardly explain the situation. Yet, he was confident they'd not turn her away ... regardless of their assumptions. He'd made the offer, and he had every intention of seeing it through.

The sooner the better for Adelaide's sake.

He rubbed a hand over the back of his neck. He'd completely forgotten about the need for an escort. Every railroad out of town had been ransacked, the tracks laid waste. How far north they were out of commission, he wasn't certain. But it wouldn't be proper to accompany a young lady unchaperoned any length of travel. The trouble was finding a suitable escort. He wasn't acquainted with anyone in Richmond outside of soldiers.

He jolted to a stop outside the telegraph office, his hand gripping the door latch. He did know one person who might be willing to help. *If* he could locate her.

He just wasn't sure the choice would settle well with Adelaide.

14

Van Lew Home
April 21, 1865

L uke whistled at sight of the vast mansion and grounds stretched out before him. Flanked on both sides by overgrown shrubs and shade trees, the grand house perched atop Church Hill looked more like a congressman's estate than one owned by a pint-sized lady doubling as a spy for the Union. Surely this couldn't be the place.

He glanced at the street address the telegraph attendant had given him—2311 Grace Street. Sure enough. This was it. The armed guards stationed in front of the house and the American flag displayed boldly at the top were further testament to the fact.

Luke shook his head. How could such a tiny woman manage such a lavish estate? But then she must be a gutsy lady to head up a whole spy network. He'd learned more about Miss Van Lew from Sergeant Delmar, how her web of underground spies had accomplished everything from smuggling Richmond newspapers and relaying secret, coded information to General Grant, to freeing slaves and helping Union prisoners escape from Libby Prison. Even harboring them in this very house.

Still in a bit of awe, Luke nodded to the sentry several yards to his left then upped the stone steps. The click of his boot soles echoed in the stillness as he started down the long pathway to the house. Six white pillars towered over him at the front of the three-and-a-half story mansion. Passing between them, Luke paused outside the door to brush off his dusty uniform jacket. He hoped Miss Van Lew's offer to help was a sincere one, else he'd feel plumb foolish. If she declined the offer, perhaps she could suggest a fitting replacement.

He hiked a brow. In an all-fired hurry to leave, Adelaide best not be too picky about his choice of escorts.

With a steadying breath, he lifted the doorknocker and tapped it down twice.

He waited, listening, the chortle of birds his only reprieve from the quiet. Was no one home? Surely more than Miss Van Lew occupied the king-sized house. After a generous span of time lapsed, he again raised his hand to the knocker, then drew it away at the sound of leisurely footsteps within. Taking a step back, he removed his kepi and raked a hand through his hair, trying to gather his thoughts. How would he explain his plight in a convincing manner?

The door eased open, and he straightened, peering inside the dim interior. An older lady stared out at him, eyes full of quandary. Though a mite taller and more stooped in the shoulders than Miss Van Lew, the woman shared her prominent chin and pale blue eyes. Ribbons of silver lined her chestnut hair. "Yes? May I help you?"

Caught off guard, Luke hesitated. "Is ... uh ... Miss Van Lew at home?"

"I believe she's out back." The woman's eyes swept over him, bewilderment spilling across her craggy features. "You're far too young and handsome to be a suitor and too straightforward to be one of her *associates*. So, I'm at a loss as to why you'd be calling on my daughter."

"Why, good evening, Corporal. This is an unexpected pleasure."

Luke pivoted toward the voice, Miss Van Lew's timely approach sparing him an awkward response to her inquisitive mother. With a polite nod to Mrs. Van Lew, he stepped away from the door.

Looping her basket of greens over her arm, Miss Van Lew waved to her mother, and the older woman dutifully retreated inside the house. Her over-sized bonnet flopped forward as she glanced up at him. "Don't mind Mother. She'd question her own sister before letting her in."

Luke held back a grin. "I suppose every mother wants to know what company her daughter keeps."

"Indeed. No matter how old one gets." She motioned to a stone bench at the corner of the house and started toward it. "As you can well imagine, we've been inundated with visitors on both sides of the conflict since the war's end."

"No doubt." Luke fell into pace beside her, adjusting his gait to allow for her shorter stride.

Setting her basket aside, she sat on the bench and slapped her hands lightly on her thighs. "Now. Tell me, Corporal, what's brought you here to see me?"

Luke eased down beside her. Obviously one to get to the crux of the matter, the tiny woman offered him her full attention.

He sat forward, elbows on his knees, struggling how to broach his awkward request. There seemed no other way around it but to be equally as straight-forward. "Do you recall the young lady I was with the other day?"

A hint of a smile crossed Miss Van Lew's thin lips. "You mean the one who would sooner throw me to the wolves than join me for tea?"

Luke chuckled, the amusing comment putting him more at

ease. "I wouldn't go so far as to say that, but I think you've got the right gal in mind."

"Yes. Her arms had been injured I believe."

With a nod, Luke blew out a breath. "That's why I've come. You see, she doesn't have anyone to care for her until she's well enough to manage. She has no family, and the hospital she's in is closing soon. So, I offered for her to stay with my mother and sister in New York until she's recovered."

Miss Van Lew's eyes crimped. "New York? Such a long way."

"Not far into New York. Our farm is just across the Pennsylvania border, near Elmira." He dipped his head, staring down at his dusty brogans. "I never truly thought she'd accept the offer. Especially knowing how she feels about Northerners."

"Well, I've plenty of space here. Why not simply have her come stay with me?"

His head lifted. It made sense, but when he recalled the tremor in Adelaide's voice and her urgency to leave Richmond—not to mention her contempt for Miss Van Lew—his glimmer of hope was snuffed out like a candle in the breeze. "That's real generous of you, Miss Van Lew. But ... as things are, I think Miss Adelaide has her heart set on leaving."

The curious glint in her eyes pleaded for more. He clenched his jaw, uncertain how much Adelaide would wish him to divulge. "It's complicated."

"I see." Miss Van Lew wet her lips. "And how do you propose to travel all that way with the trains out of commission?"

"Horse and buggy, most likely. To Washington, anyway. I've telegraphed my mother in hopes she and my sister, Lydia, will meet us there and accompany Miss Adelaide the rest of the way. I've been granted a week's leave. It'll take every bit of that to make it to Washington and back by buggy."

He paused, not quite meeting her gaze. "Only trouble is, it wouldn't be proper for the two of us to travel all that way alone."

"Ah. And you wish me to accompany you?"

Luke rubbed sweaty palms over his knees, looking her in the eye. "Yes, ma'am. If you're willing."

"Does your friend know your plans include me?"

He tugged at his shirt collar. Though hesitant to admit the truth, hiding it would solve nothing. "Not yet."

One corner of her mouth lifted. "If you intend her to go through with it, I suggest you don't."

Stifling a grin, Luke returned a brisk nod. "You'll consider it then?"

"I might." The woman's small fingers strummed her hollow cheek, her voice low and eyes glazed over as though speaking more to herself than him. "I've always longed to visit the capital city. Mary Jane could keep Mother out of trouble a while."

At last, she glanced up at him, a twinkle in her eyes. "How soon do you intend to leave?"

15

April 24, 1865
Monday, 5:30 a.m.

L uke hopped from the carriage and gave one of the horses a quick pat on the shoulder. The bay mare arched her neck toward him and gave a soft nicker. Miss Van Lew's generosity in offering her own carriage and team allowed for a nicer rig than he could have afforded from a livery stable. Maybe Adelaide wouldn't find Miss Van Lew's presence so imposing with her riding in the back seat.

Shades of rose and turquoise streaked the eastern sky as the tip of the early-morning sun crested the horizon. The street was quiet, but for a few Richmonders and soldiers milling about. At Adelaide's request, he'd come at dawn to get an early start. Though, he suspected the plea had more to do with the desire to slip away unnoticed.

He cut a quick glance at Miss Van Lew. Though more than a couple decades his elder, her oversized bonnet and slight frame made her appear almost childlike. Her reassuring grin helped bolster his courage to face Adelaide. The woman had truly proven a godsend. Why she'd agreed to accompany them, he couldn't say. But knowing how Adelaide felt, it would be a wonder if the three of them survived the trip.

He chuckled to himself. What a picture they would make—a Federal soldier, a Southern girl, and a Union spy—traveling Richmond's streets. Only God could arrange such unlikely travel companions.

A nervous twinge worked through him as he turned toward the hospital. Shadowed movement on the small veranda assured him Adelaide was eager to get the trip underway. She cast a cautious glance in both directions as he strode toward her. A simple bonnet now framed her oval face, and she carried a small bundle of what smelled like fresh baked goods in the nook of her bandaged arm. Most likely a kind gesture on the part of Captain Sally or one of the volunteer nurses.

Uncertainty flashed in her eyes as they settled on him.

Topping the steps, he offered a heartening grin. "Ready?"

With a hesitant nod, her gaze drifted to the carriage. "Who's that?"

"Her? That's our escort." Heat singed Luke's cheeks as he diverted his eyes to the metal box at her feet, still not ready to face the coming maelstrom.

She made no comment, her view obviously obscured by the dim light of morning and Miss Van Lew's ample bonnet.

He scanned the veranda. "Is this everything?"

"Yes."

At her sorrowful expression, Luke scolded himself. Why had he even asked? When he'd pulled her from the rubble and rushed her to the hospital, she'd had only the tattered dress she wore to call her own. She'd been so pale and lifeless, on the very cusp of death. And though her life had been spared, one small box held all she possessed.

No wonder she was so willing to leave.

The front door creaked open, and Captain Sally eased onto

the veranda, a meager bundle of supplies in her arms. "These are all the bandages I can spare. Hopefully they'll get you through until you reach your destination."

Adelaide mustered a weak grin. "Thank you for everything."

With an affirming nod, the woman turned dark, pleading eyes on Luke. "Do see that she's well looked after and her wounds kept clean."

Taking the wrappings and tin of paint and linseed oil from her, he met her gaze. "I assure you she'll be in good hands."

The woman studied him as though not quite certain she could take him at his word. At last, she returned her attention to Adelaide. "Be sure to exercise your fingers. In time you'll regain use of your hands, but you must work at it consistently lest the stiffness worsen and become disabling."

"I will. Thank you." The response, though soft-spoken, brimmed with determination. With a sudden intake of breath, Adelaide dipped her chin and started down the steps. "Shall we go, Corporal?"

Shifting the supplies to one arm, Luke tipped the brim of his kepi to Captain Sally. "Bye, ma'am." Without awaiting a response, he retrieved the metal box and hurried after Adelaide, catching up to her almost halfway to the buggy. Breathless, he fell into pace beside her. "For someone opposed to living in the North, you seem in an all-fired hurry to get there."

She shot him a sideways glance. "We've a long way to travel. I'm merely eager to get started."

The tremor in her voice belied her reasoning. Was she more concerned about getting a head-start on the trip or changing her mind if she lingered?

Or was it her troubles she was eager to leave behind?

Her pace slowed to a near stand-still, the pallor in her cheeks deepening. Luke followed her gaze to the woman seated in the carriage, his muscles tensing in anticipation of what was to come.

"That's Crazy Bet! What is she ...?" Adelaide's head whipped toward him, her glare as sharp as her pointed question. "How could you?"

Conscious Miss Van Lew could decipher every word, Luke wedged himself in front of Adelaide to block her view and lowered his voice. "I'm sorry. She was our only option, and she was gracious enough to help fund the trip."

A blend of hurt and anger collided in Adelaide's violet eyes. "Are you intent on making this trip miserable for me?"

"He's done nothing of the sort."

Luke cringed at Miss Van Lew's defensive tone, fighting the urge to march Adelaide back to the hospital and forget the whole thing.

"Step aside, Corporal. I want to speak with Miss Hanover."

Hesitant to obey the woman's plea, Luke locked eyes with Adelaide hoping the look he gave would temper her response. Instead, her chin tipped higher, the set in her jaw intensifying as she peered up at him. "Do as she says."

Reluctantly, Luke eased from his spot. This was gearing up to be a battle of the wills. He could only pray it would end peaceably and not prove the onset of another war.

Miss Van Lew's expression leveled as her gaze fell to Adelaide. "No matter what you've heard, my dear, I'm not the devil."

Adelaide's jaw worked back and forth, but she gave no response.

Undaunted by her silence, Miss Van Lew laced her fingers together in her lap and continued. "Corporal Gallagher has told me of your hardships. You've suffered a great deal, and it's my desire to help in whatever way I can."

A tremor seemed to vibrate through Adelaide's very core until it burst from her lips like a cyclone. "*Help* me?" All caution aside, she strode to the carriage and glared up at Miss Van Lew. "The only help you've succeeded in giving is to murder my family, along with a vast number of others."

Compassion streamed from the older woman's eyes. "I've not

murdered them, child. The war's done that. My efforts were intended to bring a swifter end to the hostilities and killing, never to cause pain or grief."

Though Adelaide's lips clamped tighter, a soft whimper sounded in her throat.

Stepping to her side, Luke placed a hand on her shoulder. Though he ached to intercede, he held his tongue, confident if the two didn't hash out their differences here and now, the trip would not fare well.

Miss Van Lew's voice softened. "I'm truly sorry for your losses, my dear. No one should endure what you've had to, especially at such a tender age." She gestured toward Luke. "But this young man and I are willing to help you. And so, you have a choice to either accept our help or refuse it. Don't let your disparaging feelings toward me keep you from seeking what's best for you."

For a long moment, Adelaide stood motionless, her features stoic. With bated breath, Luke watched her, conscious of the conflict warring within. There was something heartbreaking in her stooped posture and downcast head. He lifted a silent prayer, certain if left to fend for herself, Adelaide's life would take a turn for the worse.

At last, her head lifted, and her boots scuffed the ground beneath her skirt. With a soft sigh, she edged toward the carriage.

Though Luke thrilled inwardly, he made every effort not to let his enthusiasm show. Placing her meager possessions on the floorboards, he touched a hand to her bandaged elbow to help her onto the carriage. As he took a seat beside her, she lowered her head once again, no doubt devastated at the thought of leaving behind the only life she'd known.

How he yearned to slide an arm around her shoulders and allow her to lean into the comfort of his embrace. She had nothing, save the clothes on her back, a box of old photos and worthless monies, and a charred, keepsake locket. And yet, for the first time, Luke had hope that, like Naomi in the story of Ruth, the Lord would one day turn Adelaide's bitterness to contentment and her mourning into joy.

16

Ashland, Virginia
April 24, 1865, 11:30 a.m.

The turn of the buggy wheels slowed, and Adelaide lifted her head. For much of the morning, she and her companions had ridden in silence, with only an occasional comment posed by either Luke or Miss Van Lew. Now, as they approached the small, depleted town of Ashland, curiosity nipped at Addie. "Why are we stopping?"

Luke reined the team to a halt outside what looked to be a telegraph office, though the lettering on the sign out front was too weathered to read. "I need to send a telegram to let Ma and Lydia know we're on our way. Then afterward, maybe we can get a bite to eat and let the horses rest."

He hopped from the buggy and tied the reins to the hitching post, then glanced up at her. "Wait here."

As he entered the building, Addie ventured a look around. Compared to Richmond, the damage to the town appeared minimal, and yet, many buildings were rundown and its streets cluttered and nearly deserted. Her heart ached for her beloved

South. The war had devastated its vast splendor and turned it into a wasteland.

In that moment, her heart revolted at the thought of leaving. The Yankees had ravaged her homeland and stolen those she held dear. How could she entrust herself to their care? Doing so went against every fiber of her being. And yet, what choice did she have with her hands and arms crippled?

A man lumbered by on the opposite side of the street, his burly physique and coarse, unkempt hair reminiscent of Simon's. A nervous twinge ripped through her. Even here, miles from Richmond, she didn't feel safe from his clutches. Not until she set foot on Yankee sod would she feel free of his grasp.

I know how to find people. Addie shuddered at the memory of his words. Would he seek her out? Worse yet, would he make good on his threat to find Clarissa?

A stab of guilt sliced through her. Aunt Polly had entrusted her to safeguard her daughter. But how could she? Even if she were physically able, there was no way to locate the girl. She had only the couple's names to go on. Without that knowledge, surely Simon would be unable to track her down.

At least that was the hope she clung to.

"Have you been to Ashland before, Miss Hanover?"

Having momentarily forgotten Miss Van Lew sat behind her, Addie tensed, the unwelcome query grating at her like fingernails on a slate. She only half turned her head, a bit embarrassed to answer. "I've never been outside of Richmond."

A slight gasp sounded from the back seat. "Oh, my dear, then you have an adventure ahead of you. There is much to see between here and where you're headed. I've not been so far north as New York, but Pennsylvania is quite pleasant."

Addie pivoted toward her. "You've been to Pennsylvania?"

As though surprised by her interest, a curious grin spilled across Miss Van Lew's lips. "Oh my, yes. My Grandfather was mayor of Philadelphia for several years, until his death. And I attended classes there as a girl."

"But I thought you and your family were from Richmond?"

"Indeed, we are. I was born in Richmond and have lived there most of my days."

A blend of disbelief and resentment burned inside Addie. "Then how could you do it?"

"Do what, Miss Hanover?"

"Turn your back on Richmond and betray the South."

Miss Van Lew leaned forward on the carriage bench, the intensity of her stare making Addie almost regret asking. "Betraying Richmond was never my intent. I simply loath and abominate slavery and chose to concentrate my efforts on seeing it ended."

Though Addie had never relished slavery, she'd known nothing else, nor had she given much thought to it. "The war wasn't so much about slavery as it was protecting our freedom to live as we please."

Miss Van Lew pursed her lips, edging back on her seat. "May I ask you something, Miss Hanover?"

Addie hesitated, then nodded.

Lacing her fingers together in her lap, Miss Van Lew hiked a brow. "If the situation had been turned, and you and your family were the ones enslaved and forced to endure unthinkable brutalities, would you want someone to fight for your freedom, whether openly or in secret?"

Addie nibbled at her lower lip, the thought of being enslaved one she couldn't fathom. Though her family had owned only a handful of house servants and field hands, she'd never considered their personal feelings in the matter, never taken time to get to know them as individuals. They'd worked without complaint, never questioning what they were told to do.

Though their servants had been treated fairly, more than once, she'd witnessed her father and brothers callously shove or poke slaves who tired and grew slack in their work. The thought of giving up one's freedom and being forced to labor to the point of exhaustion with barely enough food to fill one's belly was unimaginable. "I ... I don't know. I suppose."

The woman's tone softened, the expression in her eyes deepening. "The Lord never intended one person to own another, Adelaide. I know you view me as a traitor to the South, but I would do it all again if it meant gaining countless men and women freedom from thrashings and being severed from their families to be sold like cattle."

Addie's stomach gripped. When she'd sold her father's property, she'd marketed the slaves as well, never once giving thought to what life would hold for them or if they'd be separated from loved ones.

Unnerved by the thought, she peered toward the telegraph office, suddenly antsy for Luke's return. Miss Van Lew's words were ones she couldn't quite wrap her mind around.

Yet ones she found impossible to ignore.

North of Ashland, Virginia
1:00 p.m.

"I BELIEVE I'll stretch my legs a bit and take a stroll along the creek. Would you care to join me, Miss Hanover?"

Luke shifted his gaze to Adelaide, expecting a stark refusal to the invitation. Instead, she merely shook her head and offered a polite, "No, thank you."

Seeming satisfied with the response, Miss Van Lew stood and brushed off her skirt. "I'll see you in a bit then."

With an affirming nod, Luke brushed crumbs from his hands. Having found no suitable place to eat in Ashland, they'd traveled north until they'd come to a cluster of hickory and oak trees along the roadside and made do with the bundle of goods Captain Sally had packed for them. Spreading a blanket beneath the budding branches of an oak tree, they'd shared their meal while allowing the horses to graze.

Certain Adelaide would spurn Miss Van Lew's offer to help her eat, he'd been stunned when she'd not put up a fuss. In fact, Adelaide seemed to be tolerating Miss Van Lew much better than expected, as if something notable had transpired between them while alone in the carriage.

Had they somehow made their peace?

"I can't believe how open everything is. There's nothing but grass and trees for miles."

Luke startled at the sound of Adelaide's wispy voice. Propping one of his knees against his chest, he glanced around and attempted to envision the landscape through her eyes. Unwilling to let her first attempt at conversation since leaving Richmond pass without comment, he scrambled for a response. "I imagine it's quite different from what you're used to."

She shifted her face toward him, allowing a better view of her striking features. One of her dark brows lifted. "Indeed, it is. Richmond is all I've ever known. Whenever I tired of looking at buildings, I'd stroll to the riverbank and stare out over the James, wondering what was beyond. I never imagined such vast landscape."

A grin pulled at the edges of Luke's lips as he leaned against the rough bark of the oak. "This is nothing. Wait'll you see the area where my family lives. I'm homesick for its tree-topped hills and valleys, its wide rivers and rich fields and meadows."

A trace of sadness flashed in her eyes. "It's been so long since I've seen anything but destruction and decay, it's difficult to imagine such beauty." Her gaze drifted to the damaged railroad tracks several yards to the west. "Even here, the effects of the war are evident."

Never straying far from the wrecked rails, the road allowed a clear view of the damage that had forced them to seek a slower means of transportation. While short sections of track remained intact, the majority of the iron rails lay twisted and broken in useless heaps. "From what I hear, they're like this much of the way to Washington."

Adelaide blinked, two faint creases lining the bridge of her nose. "Washington? Must we go there to get to your home?" Her disheartened tone hinted the notion of venturing to the Union Capital wasn't one she relished.

Luke cleared his throat. "That's where my mother and sister plan to meet us. They'll accompany you by train from there."

"They? You mean you're not coming?"

Catching the slight tremor in her voice, he sat forward and tossed a blade of grass into the breeze. "Believe me, I'd like nothing better, but with the railroad out of commission, a week's leave is barely enough time to make it to Washington and back."

Though she gave no reply, a strange sort of panic hardened over her face.

Luke shot her a lopsided grin. "Don't worry. Ma and Lydia will take good care of you."

She offered a weak nod, her thick lashes brushing her cheeks as she lowered her gaze.

Though warmed at the thought she might miss him, he couldn't blame her for being uncomfortable with the arrangement. Ma and Lydia were strangers to her, as well as Northerners. Living under their care would take some getting used to for this daughter of the South.

Part of him ached to accompany her the full way, protect her from all the fears and anxieties that plagued her. That she'd trusted him enough to come this far seemed amazing in itself—considering her opinion of Yankees. In a world where she felt alone and abandoned, she'd looked to him for friendship. And he'd freely given it.

But Adelaide needed hope. The kind only God could provide. Maybe He'd allowed their paths to cross for that very reason—so Luke and his family could help ease her burden of hardship and point her toward God.

He just hoped she'd stay around long enough for him to see that day come.

Taylorsville Inn, Evening

ADDIE SAT on the edge of the bed a bit unnerved at the thought of sharing a room with Crazy Bet ... Miss Van Lew. Yesterday, she'd not have even considered the possibility. But after long hours of travel, she was too exhausted to argue. Besides, what choice did she have? She couldn't very well expect Luke to help with her private care matters.

If you and your family were the ones enslaved, would you want someone to fight for your freedom? Miss Van Lew's poignant words from that morning still rang in Addie's ears. They'd penetrated deeper than she cared to admit. And though she didn't entirely approve of the woman's methods, Addie found she could no longer despise her for her convictions regarding slavery.

Miss Van Lew set her luggage in the corner of the room, then arched her back and mumbled, "My aging bones are not accustomed to such lengthy travel." Propping her hands on her hips, she turned toward Addie. "Well, young lady. Let's see about changing those bandages and getting you set for bed. It's been a long day."

Addie yawned. It had indeed. Even at her young age, the endless hours of sitting and the constant jostle of the buggy seat had proven tiresome. How she yearned to stretch out on the bed and rest undisturbed until morning. She only hoped Miss Van Lew didn't snore. "How long will it take to reach Washington?"

Miss Van Lew's face scrunched in thought as she crossed the room. "A good two more days' travel, I would say." She reached for Addie's arm and set to work loosening the cloth. "It's a shame the train isn't running. We could have been there in a matter of hours instead of days."

Addie nodded. "Yes. It would have been less troublesome for you and especially Corporal Gallagher."

A hint of a grin spilled onto the older woman's lips. "Oh ... I have a feeling the young corporal isn't minding. He's obviously quite fond of you."

Heat rushed to Addie's cheeks, and she struggled to meet the older woman's gaze. "What makes you say that?"

"Why, any man who'd go to such lengths to bring you all this way must think something of you." Miss Van Lew tossed her a wink and continued to unwind the strips of cloth.

Even as Addie tamped down the notion, her pulse raced faster. She'd given little thought to the reason behind Luke's generosity, assuming it stemmed from his charitable nature. She hung her head. "More likely, he pities me."

Pausing, Miss Van Lew gave a soft chuckle. "Come now. I've just spent an entire day observing you two from the back seat of a carriage. It's not pity glistening in his eyes when he looks at you."

Uncomfortable with the rather personal exchange, Addie remained silent, the warmth in her cheeks intensifying. Though she couldn't deny being drawn to Luke, she thought of him as merely a friend and assumed he considered her the same.

Miss Van Lew leaned to Addie's eye level, creases forming in the corners of her eyes. "Ah, I've embarrassed you. Forgive me. I'll speak of other things."

Relieved, Addie peered at her partially exposed right arm, the sleeves of her dress having been cut away to allow for ease in changing the bandages. Raw, blistered skin glared back at her, reminding her how much healing remained. She flexed her misshapen hand, disheartened by the lack of movement. Would she regain full use of her fingers, or would they forever prove a malady?

She felt the pull as Miss Van Lew gave the final strip of cloth a gentle tug. Free of the bandage, she winced at the sting of the open air against her bare skin.

Miss Van Lew's head shook side to side. "My, but you did suffer some extensive burns."

"They looked much worse right after the fire."

Her companion let out a string of tongue clicking. "You poor dear."

Releasing a soft sigh, Addie averted her gaze to a crack in the plastered wall. She'd tired of looking at her distorted limbs. Even after healing took place, she would likely bear nasty scars. How would anyone ever find her attractive?

Until Miss Van Lew's comment about Luke, she'd given no thought to how a man might react to her blemishes. Someday she hoped to marry. Would her husband view her as damaged, repulsive to look at? The war had taken her home, her family, her heritage. Had it stolen her hope of a future as well?

Her breathing shallowed, the tightness in her throat threatening to choke off her air. Maybe Simon was right. Maybe all she was good for now was the life he'd proposed.

She hung her head. Perhaps this journey was doomed before it even started.

17

Road to Fredericksburg, Virginia
April 25, 1865, Tuesday

Luke shifted on the carriage seat, the hours of travel leaving his backside a bit numb. He reined the horses around a washed-out place in the road, feeling a slight jolt when the back wheel caught the edge of the rut. Beside him, Adelaide sat with head bowed and shoulders drooped, seeming too preoccupied with her thoughts to notice. Her lips angled downward in a sad sort of frown, the afternoon sun adding a bit of color to her sallow cheeks. She'd hardly said two words all morning. Even stopping for lunch hadn't pried her from her shell.

Had bringing Miss Van Lew along been a mistake?

Though he realized their sharing a room would be touchy at best, Miss Van Lew seemed perfectly content and in good spirits, her faint hum sounding above the clop of hooves and jingle of harness. But something wasn't right. Yesterday Adelaide had begun to open up. Today, she'd retreated deeper inside herself.

When he'd endured all the lack of conversation he could stand, he turned toward her and spoke loud enough for both women to hear. "I've never known two ladies with so little to say. I figured I'd have to fight to get a word in."

Though Adelaide offered little response, Miss Van Lew's steady humming ceased. "I'm merely taking everything in, Corporal. It's been quite some time since I've experienced a long ride through the countryside."

Luke gave an affirming nod, then peered over at Adelaide. "How about you, Miss Adelaide? Are you enjoying the ride?"

As if shaken from a trance, Adelaide's head lifted. "What? Oh, yes. I suppose so."

Unconvinced, Luke leaned toward her. "I have a feeling, given the right circumstances, you'd have a lot to say."

Her head shifted toward him, allowing him a fuller glimpse of her ivory complexion and taut mouth. "I might. When I was a girl of six or seven, I would prattle on so that my older brothers tired of me."

His chest warmed at the morsel of personal knowledge his comment garnered. There was so much he wished to know about this elusive young lady, so much she'd kept tucked inside that he longed to unlock. Risking rejection, he pressed her further. "And how did they put an end to your chatter?"

Her full lips tipped slightly upward. "They gave into my request."

"And what was that?"

As though hesitant to answer, she gnawed at her lip. At last, she met his gaze, her grin deepening. "A pony."

Joy of the memory shimmered in her eyes an instant and then fell away, like a shooting star flaring across the sky before it faded to darkness. Each glimpse into her hidden past left Luke hungry for more. She was a puzzle, a mystery to unravel. A lost soul that needed found.

And he hoped to be there when and if she was.

"What town is that up ahead, Corporal?"

Miss Van Lew's query snapped his attention back to the road

ahead and to the wide cluster of buildings in the distance. "I believe it's Fredericksburg."

Leaning forward, Miss Van Lew placed a gloved hand on the back of the buckboard seat between him and Adelaide. "Fredericksburg. Praise be. Then we're more than halfway to Washington."

"Yes, ma'am, and if it's all right with you ladies, I thought we might end our travels a bit early and stay here the night. It'll take another day and a half to reach Washington. No sense pushing the horses."

"I, for one, think that's a splendid idea." Miss Van Lew rapped her fingers on the wood, her voice animated. "Yes. An evening in town would be most agreeable. And I know just how Miss Hanover and I shall occupy our time."

The comment gained an immediate reaction from Adelaide, her eyes flashing wider and lines forming at the bridge of her nose. Whatever Miss Van Lew had planned, Luke had a feeling she might have a struggle on her hands.

ADDIE SAT on the edge of the hotel lobby chair, jiggling her knee up and down. "I don't see why Miss Van Lew insists on being so secretive," she complained to Luke under her breath.

He leaned toward her with that alluring sideways grin. "Maybe that's the way *spies* like to do things."

"Well, it unnerves me." She glanced toward the door for the dozenth time. "Where did she go, anyway?"

"Didn't say. Only that she'd be back within an hour."

A pair of women strode past, whispering to each other as their eyes perused Addie's bandaged arms and unkempt appearance. Slumping back in the upholstered chair, she tamped down the awkwardness plaguing her. "Well, I wish she'd hurry. I feel I'm on display."

Evidently sensing her angst, Luke touched a hand to her elbow. "Would you like me to escort you to your room?"

With a relieved sigh, she nodded. "Would you please?"

As he stood, Miss Van Lew entered the lobby, brown-paper packages tucked in her arms. She approached, all smiles. "Come, Miss Hanover. There's work to be done."

Addie blinked, slowly rising to her feet. "What sort of work?"

A mischievous grin edged across Miss Van Lew's lips. "You'll find out soon enough." Turning to Luke, she offered a quick nod. "Good evening, Corporal. Miss Hanover and I will take our evening meal in our quarters. We'll see you first thing tomorrow morning." With that she started down the hall.

Addie peered at Luke who simply shrugged, seeming as bewildered as her. Barely evening, it seemed far too early to say goodnight. But confident the petite lady wasn't one to accept arguments, she followed her to their room.

Stepping inside, Addie tried not to show her disappointment. Other than the metal frame bed, the rather sparsely furnished room contained only a modest oak dresser and mirror, a worn, cushioned chair in the corner, and a wash tub and basin.

Miss Van Lew pushed the door shut behind them and took a glance around. "Hmm. Not exactly up to Richmond's standards, but it will do." Dropping the packages onto the bed, she brushed her hands together. "Now, my dear, we can get down to business."

Addie eased onto the lumpy mattress, her patience wearing thin. "And just what do you intend for us to do here all evening?"

The tiny woman propped her hands on her hips. "I thought it high-time you enjoy a bit of primping. I imagine you're quite a fetching young lady when your hair is styled and you're suitably dressed."

Addie glanced at herself in the mirror, heat rising in her cheeks. She truly was a sight, with hair in disarray, arms bandaged, and black taffeta dress tattered and smudged. Since the fire, she'd received little grooming to make her presentable.

A gentle hand touched her shoulder and Miss Van Lew smiled down at her. "Don't fret, child. When I'm finished, you'll look and feel yourself again."

The very thought of yielding to Miss Van Lew's control left Addie a bit nauseous. This entire venture had her longing for the life she'd once had. When, as a girl of twelve, war was but a vague notion, something mentioned but never acted upon.

Her life had forever changed when the conflict turned to reality—one that invigorated her high-spirited brothers and left her father on edge. One by one they'd left home to fight—never to return. And in a short span of time, she'd gone from contented youth to orphaned and alone.

"Miss Hanover? Are you well?"

Miss Van Lew's anxious tone cut short the unpleasant memories. Seeing the genuine alarm in her companion's eyes, Addie nodded. "Yes. I'm fine."

The tension in Miss Van Lew's forehead eased, and she released a short huff. "Well, all right then. For starters, I'll ask the hotel attendant to draw a warm bath and give you and your hair a much-needed scrubbing."

"But my arms. The water will burn ..."

Miss Van Lew motioned her to silence. "Not to worry, my dear, I'll be most careful. Just leave everything to me." She leaned to untie one of the packages. "I took it upon myself to purchase a few items on your behalf." Lifting out a cotton nightgown, she held it in front of her. "What do you think?"

Addie shifted her gaze between the gown and Miss Van Lew. "For me?"

The older woman gave a humored chuckle. "Why, yes dear." She laid the nightdress on the bed and reached for the larger bundle. "I wasn't certain when your time of mourning would end, so I purchased two dresses." With a wink, she unwrapped the parcel.

As Miss Van Lew unfolded first a black, taffeta dress then a blue and white checkered day dress with navy trim, Addie sucked in a breath. "You shouldn't have."

"And why not? You'll certainly need something to wear besides a mourning dress in time. The one you have is well overdue for replacement, wouldn't you say?"

"Yes, but ..."

The older woman's brow creased. "No arguments, now. It's my wish to give them, and the truth is, you need them."

Unable to argue the point, Addie stared at the handsome dresses. "They're beautiful, but with these bandages, my arms won't fit inside the sleeves. It would be a shame to cut them."

"Then we'll thin the bandages until they fit." She stared at Addie, as though assessing the situation. At last, she clapped her hands together and grinned. "And we'll use the spare cloths to tie up your hair. In the morning you'll have perfect curls."

Taken aback by the woman's generosity, Addie's eyes moistened. "Why are you doing this?"

"Because it pleasures me. The Lord gifted me with the means to help others, and as long as I'm able, I intend to do so." She softened her voice, her expression sobering. "Though I admit my funds are somewhat depleted since the war."

Addie gnawed her lower lip. It made no sense. Why would this woman risk her life and savings to aid the Northern cause only to turn around and help a Southerner she barely knew? And yet, hadn't Luke done the same—first saving her life and now going out of his way to ensure her well-being?

An unsettled feeling churned inside her. If a Yankee had come to her door in need of aid or shelter, would she have offered assistance? In truth, most likely not. Rather, she'd have done her best to alert her fellow Confederates to his presence. Anyone responsible for killing her loved ones didn't deserve grace or pity. And yet, both Luke and Miss Van Lew had undoubtedly suffered loss at the hands of the Confederates. Why did they willingly show mercy to someone who opposed them?

She shook her head. Both travel companions were difficult to figure. Perhaps someday she would understand what compelled them to offer such kindnesses. With Luke, she felt certain it had to do with his faith. Perhaps that was Miss Van Lew's motivation as well.

Addie pressed down the thought that faith in God could warrant such actions. Given her situation, she had no choice but to accept their generosity. And yet, she longed for the day she'd be able to manage on her own ... and return to her beloved South.

18

Fredericksburg Hotel
April 26, 1865

Luke tied the reins to the hitching post outside the hotel. Having risen early to retrieve the horses and buggy from the livery stable, he'd hoped to return before Adelaide and Miss Van Lew missed him. He gave the horses each a pat on the neck, breathing in the musty scent of hay and horseflesh. The team appeared rested and well-fed, which was more than he could say for himself.

A thin layer of mist hung in the still air. Even here in town, there was a tranquility to the early morning hour, when only a handful of soldiers, businessmen, and early risers roamed the quiet street.

Fredericksburg had endured much during the war. Two fierce battles had raged within its streets. Both Confederate victories. Several of its stores looked abandoned, and others were in ill-repair as though the town had struggled to recover its losses. Now that he considered it, they'd been fortunate to find a suitable hotel to stay the night.

Wiping his hands on his trousers, Luke stepped onto the

boardwalk, the weathered planks creaking beneath his brogans. After the long, uneventful evening, he was eager to be on their way. Tired as he'd been last night, he'd expected to fall right to sleep. But rest hadn't come easy. Though the lumpy mattress and noise from the adjoining room were partly to blame, his unsettled thoughts were the real culprit.

Particularly those surrounding Adelaide.

She seemed so troubled and discouraged. Did she regret coming? Whatever Miss Van Lew's plans for last evening, he couldn't understand why she'd felt it necessary to exclude him. He only hoped she hadn't made matters worse by trying to sway Adelaide to her way of thinking.

Opening the hotel door, he stepped inside the lobby that had stirred to life since he'd left. Miss Van Lew waved a gloved hand at him from the dining area to the right. He started toward her and noticed a young woman in a satiny, black dress seated beside her with her back to him. Ringlets of ebony hair dangled along the nape of the young lady's neck from beneath a fashionable bonnet. He looked past the girl for Adelaide, but saw only Miss Van Lew.

The muscles in his shoulders tensed. Had she refused to join them for breakfast? Whatever the reason for her absence, he would insist Miss Van Lew fetch her and incite her to eat.

As he approached the table, the woman in black turned her head, allowing him a view of her profile. Jolting to a stop, his jaw slackened. He edged up beside her, eyes wide. "Adelaide?"

Shifting toward him, she flashed a shy smile. Though he'd thought her beautiful before, with her unkempt hair and tattered dress, now, she was absolutely captivating. Unable to tear his eyes from her, he took in every detail of her soft cheeks, dove-like eyes, and silky hair.

A chuckle sounded. "I see you approve of how Miss Hanover and I spent our evening, Corporal. She's stunning, is she not?"

Still enthralled by Adelaide's transformation, it took a moment for Miss Van Lew's words to filter through his fogged mind. At last, he nodded, his gaze still fixed on Adelaide. "Yes, ma'am. She surely is."

A tinge of pink flared in Adelaide's cheeks, and her gaze flittered to the ivory tablecloth.

Luke slipped into the empty chair beside her. "But your arms. How ... ?"

"It wasn't easy," Miss Van Lew intervened. "We wrapped them in a thinner layer of cloth and slowly inserted them into the sleeves."

Adelaide's eyes lifted. "It's not the most comfortable, but perhaps now at least I won't be gawked at. Except for my hands and having to be fed like an infant."

Luke's chest squeezed. He should have realized what a hardship her dependencies were. To be tended to in a hospital full of ailing patients was one thing, but quite another to be looked upon as an invalid by passersby in settings such as this. If his sister, Lydia, were strapped thus, she would refuse to show herself in public.

As the dining hall began to further fill with guests, Luke sensed Adelaide's newfound joy diminishing. On a whim, he stood and took hold of the back of her chair. She glanced over her shoulder at him. "What are you doing?"

"We're leaving."

Miss Van Lew flashed a curious scowl. "What? But we haven't yet eaten."

Pulling the chair back for Adelaide, Luke peered across the table at Miss Van Lew. "Take Miss Adelaide and gather your things. I'll see if I can sweet-talk the cook out of some victuals, and meet you at the carriage. We'll eat on our own from now on."

Adelaide pivoted toward him, gratitude streaming from her violet eyes. Though she spoke not a word, he knew at once he'd made the right decision. A grin threatened to spill onto his lips as the two women started across the dining hall. Adelaide's shoulders no longer slouched nor did her head droop. Instead, she walked with shoulders tipped back and head held high, as though her sense of dignity had been restored.

A mixture of emotions washed over him as he watched her go. He'd been drawn to Adelaide from the start, and the more time spent with her seemed only to enhance those feelings. But, as thrilled as he was by her outer transformation, it was the condition of her heart that he ached to see reborn.

Something inside him longed to ease the burden she carried, help her find contentment. Peace. If only she had faith to cling to. The Lord could do for her what Luke or no one else ever could. Someday he prayed she'd discover that for herself.

ADDIE SQUINTED against the morning sun, its welcome warmth soaking into the dark fabric of her dress, warding off the April morning chill. Seated beside Luke in the buggy, she took in the town of Fredericksburg as they traveled its streets. Even here, reminders of the recent conflict were everywhere—in the debris along the roadside, the abandoned buildings, the strong presence of Federal soldiers, and the abundance of hospitals and medics. Once a Confederate stronghold, like Richmond, the town had now fallen to Yankee dominance.

As they reached the outskirts, Luke urged the horses faster. Addie caught him stealing a glance her way and smiled. Never would she forget the expression in his azure eyes when he'd taken his first glimpse of her. She'd turned boys' heads in the past, but Luke's response seemed to run much deeper than youthful infatuation.

She swallowed, her heart pumping faster. Could there be some truth to Miss Van Lew's assumption? Did Luke hold some semblance of affection for her?

Though at first leery of Miss Van Lew's intentions, Addie had to admit the evening of pampering provided her a much-needed renovation. Subconsciously, she flexed her fingers under the thin bandages and tried to tuck them out of sight. Though the ugliness of her scars remained, at least having her arms concealed saved her some scrutiny.

As well as the constant reminder of her infirmity.

A cluster of buildings stood at the edge of town, wounded Confederate soldiers convalescing at their front. Some with bandaged heads or arms in slings; others with missing limbs. They stared across the landscape with ashen faces, their stony expressions carrying the look of downtrodden defeat. Repulsed, she turned away, tempering the hostilities threatening to consume her.

Her stomach reeled. Had her father and brothers suffered long from their injuries or passed from this life into the next in a matter of breaths? The only news she'd received was that her father and oldest brother, Thomas, had both been cut down in the Wilderness Battle, and young Eli five months later at Cedar Creek. Their few possessions had been returned, news of where they were laid to rest unknown. After the fire, even their keepsake belongings were lost to her.

The muscles in her jaw tightened. Perhaps it was best she didn't know the details surrounding their deaths. It was enough to know they'd fought valiantly for their beloved South. She would rather not have that image tainted by considering the circumstances of their mortal wounds.

Forcing her mind onto more pleasant ponderings, she peered at the landscape stretched out ahead of her like some unknown adventure. Whatever the future held, she was convinced she'd made the right decision in coming. If she'd stayed in Richmond, no telling what would have become of her. Luke and Miss Van Lew had been good to her. At least she didn't feel quite so alone and helpless.

A flutter of unease coursed through her. But would Luke's family be as accepting? The thought of being taken into a Yankee home still turned her stomach. Would they look down upon her as some sort of lesser being? Worse yet, would they pity her or attempt to fit her into the mold of their way of life?

Her chin tipped a notch higher, Southern pride burning in her chest. They'd best not even try. She might willingly subject herself to their Northerner ways for a time, but she would never be a part of them.

19

Washington D.C.
April 27, 1865

Addie's stomach gripped at the sight of the Capitol dome looming in the distance. The past three and a half days of travel, she'd been able to fool herself into believing this moment would never come. And yet, here they were about to enter the city whose officials and army had bested the South and would impose changes many had given their lives to oppose.

Luke and Miss Van Lew were a part of that. Both had fought to bring an end to her cherished South. No matter how gracious they'd been, a part of her could never forgive that.

"Are you certain your mother and sister don't mind my coming? I mean, to travel all that way for someone they've never met is quite an inconvenience." She glanced down at her bandaged hands. "Especially someone who'll be a burden."

Luke's eyes beckoned to her as she met his gaze. "Believe me, you're no burden. With my brother, Drew, and me away, they'll welcome the company. If I know Lydia, she'll think of the train ride as a sort of grand adventure ... and be happy to have someone besides older brothers around to pester her."

Addie mustered a weak grin. "I suppose we'll have that in common, both growing up the only girl in the household."

He tapped the reins across the team's back, spurring them to a faster walk. "I've no doubt you'll take to each other like a couple of flickering fireflies."

Addie swallowed, wondering what her father and brothers would think of the arrangement. The entire venture sparked of betrayal. "I have no means to repay them."

Casting a brisk glance in her direction, he sat taller on the seat. "There's no need. Helping others is a blessing—a way of showing love for Jesus."

She studied him through narrowed eyes. "Are you always so blatant about your religion?"

For a brief instant, his expression turned stony as if the question dredged up an unwanted memory. "I wasn't always." He turned to her, the shadow over him lifting. "But it's not *religion* I champion, it's *faith*."

"There's not much difference between the two in my estimation," she mumbled.

"Oh, but there is. Religion is holding to rituals and routines." He glanced out ahead of them, working his fingers through the reins. "Faith is, well ... trusting God and living life to please Him."

Addie blinked, pondering his words. She'd never met anyone so passionate about their faith. If he wasn't so genuine, his comments might grate on her. But there was something so unpretentious about the young man, she could only stare in wonder. Part of her wished she could share his strong convictions. Since the day they'd met, he'd done nothing but offer assistance, with no thought to himself.

She turned to the path ahead, recalling a time when she'd been nearly as heartfelt in her faith as Luke. When, at the tender age of nine, she'd received Jesus into her heart and been cleansed of her sins in the wide creek outside of Richmond.

Those had been happier, simpler times, when God seemed

real and dear to her. When He'd heard and answered her prayers. But she'd been younger then, and more naïve, she supposed. Things were more complex now. The war had sapped any semblance of faith from her. With each tragic event and unanswered prayer, her confidence in the Lord had waned. Until it was eaten away entirely.

She cut a glance at Luke, who seemed oblivious to the tumultuous battle warring within her. True, the war had taken his father. But he'd never know what it was to lose everything, as she had. God had ignored her fervent pleas and, one by one, her loved ones had been stripped from her.

Her faith had died with them, and no amount of flowery talk could revive it.

LUKE TUGGED AT HIS KEPI. He never would understand women. Adelaide's mood seemed to shift from pleasant to sullen at the drop of a hat. Were all women so touchy? Lydia and Ma didn't seem so. His gut gripped. But then they hadn't endured all that Adelaide had either. Losing one's family and being uprooted from your home, not to mention being disabled and in the company of those you deemed enemies, was enough to cause anyone to be out of sorts.

He'd not soon forget the tender look of gratitude in her eyes when he'd spared her the indignity of being fed in public. How he wished for more snatches of joy from her. He had a feeling her silence had something to do with his mention of God. She'd simply have to accept that. His faith was one thing he wouldn't apologize for.

But then, maybe a bit more subtlety was in order.

"What a grand sight the Capitol is," Miss Van Lew called from the back seat. "It's well worth the long trip just to see it."

Luke's gaze pulled to the newly completed Capitol dome. It

truly was a sight to behold, its alabaster exterior shining in the sunlight. "She is a beauty."

The scene seemed to have the opposite effect on Adelaide, her face turning ghostly pale. Perhaps their destination had something to do with her melancholy mood. Or was it meeting Ma and Lydia that had her on edge? If so, he was confident they'd soon put her at ease.

"Where are we to meet your mother and sister?" Adelaide's soft voice sliced through his thoughts.

"The Willard Hotel."

"Oh, how grand." Miss Van Lew piped. "I've heard it's the very hub of the city. The preferred place for all the top officials to stay. It must be quite expensive. Of course, I'll help defray the cost."

Luke nodded his thanks. Ma must have saved every penny to pay for such a venture. Though his family had done well for themselves, they were by no means wealthy. And with no one at home to provide an income, she would be hard-pressed to manage. Did Adelaide realize what a sacrifice his family was making on her account?

A faint whistle sounded in the distance, drawing Luke's gaze to the iron tracks leading into the city. His eyes fastened on the train as it glided along the rails, a plume of smoke pouring from the engine's stack. Were Ma and Lydia aboard? Or had they already arrived?

Suddenly more eager to reach their destination, he slapped the reins down on the horses' rumps and spurred them into a lively trot. Adelaide braced her boot on the sideboard as though caught off guard by the burst of speed. Luke shifted the reins to one hand and reached an arm around her waist to steady her.

Her muscles tensed under his touch, though her eyes remained fixed on the string of passenger cars worming their way steadily closer.

The flush in her cheeks was enough to persuade him to

withdraw his arm. "Sorry. I guess I'm a bit too eager to see my mother and sister."

The tension in her shoulders seemed to ease as she offered a weak grin.

Fighting distraction, he forced his attention back to the train until it became swallowed by the buildings. "Have you ever ridden a train?"

Adelaide shook her head. "No. Though I've often watched them come and go through Richmond wishing I could."

"Well, then. You're in for something." Slackening the reins, he leaned forward and rested his elbows on his thighs. "I'd not ridden one myself until I joined the army. 'Course that wasn't much of a pleasure—being stuffed in a box car with a bunch of fellers like cattle. This ride should be more enjoyable. And you'll have Ma and Lydia for company."

She gave a slight nod. "What are they like, your mother and sister?"

"A lot like me, I suppose, though a mite prettier." He smiled, pleased to see her sharing the grin. "Ma's never known a stranger. She took it hard when my father died, and when my older brother, Drew, left to fight early on." He fixed his gaze on the path ahead, the memories rushing back like birds at springtime. "She used to sit on our porch of an evening with her mending or garden goods and stare out over the landscape for hours, no doubt praying the Lord would bring Drew home safely."

"And for you as well, I'm certain, after you left."

"I 'spect so. She thinks the sun rises and sets on our account." He expelled a long breath. "I should have written home more often."

She allowed a gentle pause before adding, "And your sister?"

He sat back, loosening his hold on the reins, the clop of hooves drumming a steady beat. "Ah, Lydia. As sisters go, there are none finer." He gave a lighthearted chuckle. "She had her fill of me in her younger days. Drew was older and gave her no trouble, but I used to tease her unmercifully. She stomached it well and never held it against me. In a sense, I think she relished the attention."

"The poor girl. So, have you learned to curb such mischiefs?"

His smile faded, more recent memories wedging a knot in his shoulders. "The war did that. With news of our father's death, Lydia seemed to grow up overnight. Suddenly, she was no longer a child, but a young lady with a heart for the hurting."

Adelaide tipped her head to one side, eyes softening. "When did you last see them?"

"When I left home, a little over a year ago."

"No doubt they'll be glad you've come, even for a brief visit."

The hint of sadness in her voice tugged at Luke. Here he was prattling on about his family when she had none of her own. "And I've no doubt they'll welcome you as well. I'm glad you came."

Uncertainty brimmed in her oval eyes as she returned a shy smile.

Luke yearned to reach out and touch her ivory cheek, assure her all would be well. Instead, he prayed in time spent with his family, the Lord would soften her heart and give her reason to hope.

20

Addie's eyes swelled at sight of the huge, marble columns lining the Willard Hotel lobby and the elaborate chandeliers dangling from the lofty ceiling. In all of Richmond, she'd not seen anything half so grand. She followed Luke and Miss Van Lew past the cluster of patrons lounging in wingback chairs to a vacant area beyond.

Looking as lost and uncomfortable as her, Luke craned his neck to scan the onslaught of people for a familiar face. He set down their belongings and smoothed the kinks from his uniform jacket. "Stay here. I'll see if I can find out if they've arrived."

He'd barely ventured a step when a soprano voice hailed from deeper within the lobby. "Luke!"

A huge smile erupted onto his face as he pivoted toward the sound. Addie followed his gaze to the young girl and older woman scurrying toward them, their expressions radiant. With a hearty laugh, Luke broke into a trot and rushed to meet them.

Deep ache bubbled inside Addie as her friend offered his mother a warm embrace, then twirled his young sister around. Placing a hand atop her hat, the girl giggled and hugged tightly to his neck. Addie turned away, glad for Luke and his family, and yet dismayed she would never experience such a joyful reunion with her own.

"It appears they've been found," Miss Van Lew quipped in Addie's ear. "Shall we join them?"

With a hesitant nod, Addie waited for the older woman to gather their things, then fell into step behind her. A nervous twinge worked through her middle, and she drew a deep breath. Why was meeting Luke's family so difficult? Perhaps it was the thought of being taken in like a stray cat, an unfortunate soul in need of assistance.

The very thought niggled her.

Well, she would not burden the Gallaghers any longer than necessary. As soon as she could manage, she would make her way to Pennsylvania in search of Clarissa. Once found, if willing, the two of them could return to the South and start a life together.

She squared her shoulders, thankful she at least did not have to face Luke's mother and sister with unkempt hair and dress.

At her and Miss Van Lew's approach, the trio broke off their happy chatter and greeted them with welcoming smiles. Luke's face fairly glowed with pride. Stepping between his mother and sister, he placed an arm around their shoulders. "Ma. Lydia. This is Miss Elizabeth Van Lew and Miss Adelaide Hanover."

Mrs. Gallagher gave a polite nod, her blue eyes a shade paler than Luke's, tinges of gray woven through her wheat-blonde hair. "Pleased to meet you." Her voice was soothing, pleasant, like a gentle brook. Instead of haughtiness, genuine kindness streamed from her eyes as she turned her gaze on Addie. "We're looking forward to getting to know you, Miss Hanover. May I call you Adelaide?"

The unexpected appeal left Addie at a loss for words. She managed a slight nod. Would she ever get past the awkwardness?

Miss Van Lew, on the other hand, wasted no time responding. "How good to meet you, Mrs. Gallagher, Miss Gallagher." Her eyes swept over the threesome. "My, but it's easy to see the family resemblance. You favor each other quite strongly. Have you other children as well, Mrs. Gallagher?"

"Yes. My oldest son, Andrew."

"And does he share a resemblance to you as well?"

A sliver of sadness marred Mrs. Gallagher's expression. "No. He takes after his father."

Miss Van Lew reached to clasp the woman's arm, her voice softening. "Luke told me of your loss. I'm so sorry."

"Thank you." Though the soft-spoken words sounded heavy of heart, Mrs. Gallagher's expression never lost its pleasantness. "The war shattered many a family." Her eyes veered toward Addie. "On both sides."

Addie met her gaze, and in that moment, some of the uneasiness stoved up inside her loosened its grip. Mrs. Gallagher didn't seem the judgmental sort she'd feared, but instead someone who might offer her solace.

Luke's sister took a step forward, her vivid eyes and wavy, blond hair so like her brother's. "I'm Lydia. My, but you're pretty. No wonder Luke took a shine to you."

Heat flared in Addie's cheeks, and she stifled a giggle as Luke tugged his sister back into place, a tinge of pink in his own cheeks. With a sheepish grin, he tipped his head to the side and shrugged. Addie decided then and there, like her older brother, young Lydia would be impossible not to like. Though she was resolved not to allow herself to grow too fond of any of them.

There could be no place in her heart for Yankees. No matter how kind.

———

LUKE SET their belongings inside the spacious room, whistling under his breath. "This is some fancy place. I'm assuming my quarters are around here somewhere?"

His mother nodded and pointed to the door on her left.

"There's an adjoining, smaller room through that door where you'll stay."

"I must say, Mrs. Gallagher, your choice of accommodations has made the long trip well worthwhile." Miss Van Lew panned the plush beds and elaborate dresser. "This shall be an experience I'll long remember."

A gentle smile stretched across his mother's lips. "It is rather splendid. And only a few blocks from the train depot." She turned to Luke, her smile fading. "I'm afraid our train leaves early tomorrow morning. I do wish we had more time with you."

Luke planted a kiss atop her bonnet. "I wish so, too, but Miss Van Lew and I will need to head out early, too, if I'm to make it back to Richmond before my leave ends."

Miss Van Lew touched a finger to her cheek. "You know, Corporal, now that I'm here, I'd like to stay a while. You'll travel faster on your own."

"But how would you get back to Richmond?"

Pivoting toward him, she waved a hand in the air. "Not to worry. I'll lend you one of the horses to ride and sell the other, along with the carriage. I'll catch a train home once the railroad to Richmond is up and running again."

"But that could be weeks. Months, even."

She clasped her hands together and rested her chin atop them. "Ah, but there is so much to see here. I'm certain not a moment will be wasted. I'll telegram Mother first thing tomorrow morning and explain. She's used to my eccentric ways." She chuckled. "And I dare say, won't be a bit surprised."

Luke shrugged. "Well, all right. If you're sure."

Miss Van Lew strolled to the window and pulled back the sheer curtain. "I've never been more certain of anything."

Though Luke agreed Washington had a lot to offer, for him, the biggest draw would be leaving on tomorrow's train. He glanced at his mother and sister, already aching at the thought of parting ways.

A copy of the *Evening Star* rested atop the console table

beside him. The newspaper heading caught his eye, and he leaned for a better look.

EXTRA. Thrilling news!!
Capture of the assassin Booth!

"What is it, son?"

The stunning headline must have registered in his expression for urgency tinged his mother's voice. He skimmed farther, then held the paper out to her. "It says here John Wilkes Booth was shot and killed yesterday in a barn in Maryland."

Eyes widening, she snatched it from him.

Miss Van Lew pressed a hand to her chest and released a loud sigh. "Praise be."

Ma glanced up from the newspaper, the creases at the corners of her eyes deepening. "Will this have a bearing on your release from the army?"

Luke crossed his arms over his chest, feigning optimism he didn't feel. "It might."

Edging closer, Lydia propped her hands on her hips. "I'm glad they caught him. Maybe now you and Drew can come home."

A grin tugged at Luke's lips. "I imagine I'll beat Drew home, if he's being detained by a lady as I suspect."

With a giggle, Lydia clasped her hands together. "If Drew brings home a girl, it'll be like having two new sisters."

At the comment, Adelaide's complexion pinked and her gaze flicked from one face to another. "I'll not stay long. Just until my wounds heal, and I'm able to manage."

Luke stared at the rug. He'd hoped to see Adelaide again. But with her eager to leave, it seemed unlikely. He breathed a quiet sigh. Maybe, it was better that way. Maybe the Lord was sparing him heartache. He'd determined years ago not to become entangled with someone who didn't share his love for God. Though Adelaide had many appealing attributes—resilience, tenderness, beauty—she lacked the one thing that mattered most.

Faith.

If they spent more time together, he'd be tempted to fall for her.

And *that*, he was determined not to do.

21

B & O Train Depot, Washington D.C.
April 28, 1865, 7 a.m.

The train engine hissed and grounded to a halt in front of the depot, billows of steam rising from beneath it. Though a similar train ran through Richmond, never had Addie stood so near one. Awed by its impressive size, she stepped back to take it all in, a twinge of anticipation mingling with her nervous stomach. What would it be like to glide over the silvery rails and travel at such great speed, many miles in a single hour?

An array of passengers poured from within—soldiers, freed slaves, foreigners, ladies in fine dress—all seeming in a hurry to get where they were headed. Others clustered around awaiting their chance to board. She drew a steadying breath, realizing the time had come to say goodbye to her friend ... and everything familiar.

Turning, she watched Luke hug his mother and sister, heartbreak evident in his eyes. They'd had so little time together, the fleeting moments like sparse droplets of rain on drought-ridden land—a mere taste that seemed not to quench their thirst to be a family again. Lydia and Mrs. Gallagher released their hold, eyes moist.

Luke bent to kiss his mother's cheek. "I'll see you again soon."

Her lips pulled in a weak grin, and she reached to straighten his collar. "God go with you, son."

He winked. "Always."

Turning to his sister, he brushed a strand of hair from her cheek. "You take care of Ma and Adelaide for me till I get home."

"I will." The young girl's eyes brimmed with admiration for her older brother, much as Addie's had for Thomas and Eli.

Touched by the tender exchange, she averted her gaze to the stream of passengers boarding the train. It seemed, in respect to goodbyes, Northerners and Southerners shared similar emotions.

A whistle sounded, and Mrs. Gallagher patted her daughter's arm. "We'd best go. Goodbye, son."

With heads bowed, they took up their belongings and edged toward the train. Lydia peered over her shoulder at Addie until her mother tugged her forward.

Eager for her own chance to say farewell, Addie lagged behind, taking in Luke's ruddy complexion and wavy hair one last time. In a few short weeks, he'd become a trusted friend, someone she relied upon more than she cared to admit.

A nervous tremor coursed through her as he turned to face her. The unexpected reaction left her a bit breathless. The thought of leaving without him stirred a sense of loss within.

One she'd not anticipated.

He slid his hands in his trouser pockets and shuffled toward her like a timid schoolboy. Early morning sunlight shone through the tips of the blond curls above his ears, turning them frosty white. A small dimple dinted one cheek as he tossed her a half-hearted smile. "Well, I guess you're on your way."

His tone carried a hesitancy she couldn't quite read, almost as if he didn't relish the thought of parting any more than she did. Brushing the thought aside, she returned a brisk nod. "It appears so." She glanced at Mrs. Gallagher and Lydia waiting by the train. "It's good of your mother and sister to go out of their way for me like this."

He followed her gaze, then turned to look her square on, his eyes wistful. "They'll take good care of you."

The corners of her mouth lifted. She was beginning to believe that. As misplaced as she felt in this Northern capital city, she felt strangely at home with Luke and his family. She would miss his winsome smile and good-natured charm. "Thanks for everything. I don't know what I would've done if you hadn't come along."

His modest shrug assured her the compliment hadn't gone to his head. "You needed help. I was there. Simple as that."

"True." She arched a brow. "Though your visits to the hospital were more than mere happenstance."

A crooked smile framed his lips. "I'm not sure anyone could blame me, choosing your company over that of a bunch of foul-smelling soldiers."

She held back a grin, gazing deeper into his eyes. "Still, it was kind of you, and I'll not forget it, nor the sacrifice you made in bringing me so far."

A second whistle blasted, and Addie saw Lydia motioning. "I-I'd better go." Despite her words, her feet remained firmly in place. She hadn't realized how much she would miss him.

He edged closer, narrowing the gap between them. Raising a hand to her cheek, he brushed his knuckles along her jawline. "Goodbye, Adelaide."

The warmth of his touch sent a tingle through her. Her eyes searched his, the finality in his tone settling heavy in her chest. He didn't expect to see her again.

She took a step back, her eyes still fastened on his. How ironic that he would return to her home, and she to his. He'd come all this way for her sake. Whether out of friendship, Christian duty, or something more, she couldn't say. She only knew she was grateful. Swallowing down her emotions, she forced a gentle "Goodbye."

His Adam's apple bobbed. "I'll pray for you."

Though the sentiment meant little to her, she knew his words were heartfelt ones. With a quick nod, she turned away, willing herself not to look back as she strode toward his mother and sister. Would she ever see him again? Not likely.

The sting of that reality unsettled her. In all honesty, she *wanted* to see him again. *Needed* to see him again.

The very thought frightened her. And yet, she couldn't deny it.

Only time would tell what lay ahead. She only knew there was no going back.

———

LUKE PRESSED his heels deeper into the mare's flanks, emptiness clawing at his insides. Every stride took him closer to Richmond and farther from his home and loved ones. Being severed from them again so soon proved almost harder than when he'd left to join the army. *Then*, he'd been bursting with gumption to fight the Rebs, avenge his father's death, and end the war. Now that the conflict had ended, all he could think of was going home.

Slowing his pace, he peered over his shoulder at the trail of dust in his wake. How he longed to wheel his mount around, forget his obligations to his country, and settle back into normal life. But he had a stint to fulfill, one he prayed would soon end.

He'd expected to miss Ma and Lydia. Yet, he'd not anticipated this other ache inside him—the one leaving Adelaide had wedged. What started as an act of compassion to spare a girl's life had blossomed into friendship and unexpected attachment.

His chest clenched. He'd grown too fond of her. And something in her eyes when they'd parted gave him an inkling she returned the sentiment.

He threaded the reins through his fingers, thankful he was making the return trip alone. Not that Miss Van Lew was difficult to manage. *He* was the one unfit for company. True to her word, Miss Van Lew had gifted him the horse to borrow and gone her way. The days of solitude would give him time to sort through the unanswered questions hampering his thoughts.

One thing he did know. It was best he and Adelaide be apart. Given time, deeper fondness might have developed between them—something that couldn't be. She was too full of contempt for the North and even more so the Lord. When he surrendered his heart, he intended to choose a wife he could bond with completely—body, soul, and spirit.

As things were, he could never have that with Adelaide.

It would never work. She was a closed book where God was concerned.

Like David in the Bible, he'd made it his aim to become a man after God's own heart. Though he failed at times, he knew enough not to kindle a flame that was certain to scorch him. King David's downfall began with infatuation over a woman. And he was resolved not to make the same mistake.

––––––––

THE SWIFT MOVEMENT outside the passenger car was dizzying, though the sway of the train over the iron rails was a tad smoother than the jostle of the carriage. To travel at such great speed was a venture Addie had only dreamt of. It had taken but an hour to arrive in Baltimore after leaving Washington. Following a short delay, she and her companions had boarded the Northern Central for the longer journey north to Elmira, New York.

Mesmerized from the moment the train departed the station, Addie had barely taken her eyes from the fast-flowing scenery. As city streets and buildings transformed into rolling hills and forests of budding trees, Addie realized Luke had been right in saying this final stretch of the journey would be the most enjoyable.

But she had to admit, she missed his company.

Lydia proved an amiable enough companion, though there seemed no end to her curiosity. With Luke, Addie had done most of the inquiring. But Lydia's inquisitiveness knew no bounds.

"How old are you?"

Addie shifted her gaze from the misty, tree-lined hills and valleys to the girl seated on the narrow bench beside her. Taken aback by the bluntness of the question, she hesitated before responding. "Seventeen."

Lydia's eyes danced, and a generous smile blossomed on her lips. "Same as Luke!"

The unsolicited information gave Addie a sense of satisfaction. She'd often wondered her friend's age but had been too timid to ask. Struck once again by Lydia's overwhelming resemblance to her brother—same wavy texture to her flowing wheat-blond hair and crystal-blue eyes that shimmered with vitality—she could only stare. "And you are ...?"

Her mouth twisted. "Fourteen, but I'd give anything to be your age."

Addie's mind careened back to her own bittersweet fourteenth birthday just ahead of her father's departure to fight in the war. The nearly four years since had been a blur of raw memories too gnarled to untangle. She mustered a weak grin. "It will come soon enough."

Lydia glanced at her mother resting with eyes closed and head bowed in the seat across the aisle. She'd nodded off shortly after switching trains in Baltimore. Leaning closer to Addie, Lydia softened her tone to a whisper. "Mama still treats me like a child. Me being the only girl, as well as the youngest, she tends to coddle me as though I haven't the gumption to do anything of my own choosing. Was your mother so protective of you?"

Heaviness weighted Addie's chest, and her mind fled to the

photo tucked in her aunt's box. "I have no memory of my mother. She died when I was very young. Until recently, I'd not even seen a photo of her."

Lydia's face pinched. "How sad for you. Luke said you had no family, but didn't share the details. Forgive me."

Addie shrugged and managed a weak grin. "Not to worry. I suppose we all have our sufferings to bear."

As quickly as Lydia's smile faded, her face brightened. "I bet she was pretty. Like you."

Addie's shoulders dipped, the compliment difficult to accept. Though her mother was indeed beautiful, and Addie favored her in many ways, her blistered arms and hands left her feeling damaged, unattractive. "Much prettier, I would say."

"Do you have the picture of her with you?"

The noticeable uptick in Lydia's voice made the query impossible to ignore. "In the box under the seat."

Eyes sparkling with curiosity, Lydia scooted to the edge of the seat. "Could I see it?"

The earnest plea ignited a maelstrom within Addie. Forever etched in her mind, the image of her mother resurrected all Addie had missed without the comforts of motherly affection or a female confidante to guide and teach her the intricacies of being a woman.

The very attributes Lydia viewed as intrusive and overprotective in her mother, Addie had been denied. Her father's insecurities robbed her of precious memories she might have treasured. Instead, her mother's nature and character would forever remain a mystery.

She forced a slight nod. "If you like."

Without hesitation, Lydia leaned down and reached under the seat, probing with her fingers until they tapped against the metal box. Pulling it up, she examined the charred case. Her expression softened as she peered over at Addie. "Was it damaged in the fire that burned you?"

The drumming of Addie's heart in her ears drowned out the

rhythmic rattle of the train as she swallowed down the memory of that horrific night. She nodded, the tightness in her throat choking off words.

Lydia set the box on the seat between them and brushed bits of debris from her palms.

Addie's breaths shallowed as the girl lifted the rickety lid and peered inside. Not since Luke first found the box had anyone riffled through her aunt's personal effects. How she wished she herself could hold the few remaining fragments of her family's heritage. As agreeable as Luke's sister seemed, she had Yankee blood flowing through her veins, a detail Aunt Polly might have deemed offensive.

Lydia drew the thin stack of photos from the box, her gaze flicking between the wedding photo and Addie. "My, but you do look similar."

Despite her reluctance, Addie couldn't resist craning her neck for a look. Her heart squeezed as, once again, she was struck at how closely she resembled her mother. Did they share other similarities as well? Was her mother's voice soft and lilting, or giddy and full of mirth?

Haunted by the unknowns, Addie turned away. She understood now why Papa found it difficult to look upon her mother's image. The pain of his loss must have been great. Still, to never speak of her had deprived Addie and her brothers of treasured remembrances that would forever go unfulfilled. In sparing himself, he'd denied them all.

"Who's this?"

The forthright question jarred Addie from her thoughts. Her stomach lurched when she noticed Lydia peering at the photograph of Aunt Polly and Clarissa. Certain her answer would only lead to further questions, she hesitated. "My aunt ... and cousin."

"Are they gone too?"

Addie released a jagged breath, the stark reality all too painful. With all that had happened, she'd had little time to grieve. She dropped her gaze to her lap. "My aunt perished in the fire."

Lydia gave a soft moan. "I'm sorry. What about your cousin? Did she survive?"

Uncertain how to respond, Addie merely stared out the window.

The rumble of the train intensified as Lydia, too, fell silent.

After a moment, the lid to the metal box clicked shut. "I didn't mean to make you sad. I promise I won't ask any more questions."

Turning, Addie breathed easier when she saw Lydia no longer held the photographs. She slid the metal container back under the seat, then sat with arms in her lap, lips pursed. Grateful her companion had made no attempt to delve deeper into the box's contents, Addie offered a reassuring smile before returning her gaze to the sprawling countryside. In time, perhaps she'd be ready to confide the truth, but for now, she was content to shoulder her burdens alone.

Her eyes skimmed the vast scenery. Clarissa was out there somewhere, and Addie intended to find her.

22

Gallagher Residence
Friday, April 28, 1865, 5:30 p.m.

Tension knotted Addie's shoulders as she peered out the opening of the hackney coach, the slow-moving carriage a stark contrast to the fast-paced locomotive they'd departed in Elmira. Though the tree-lined hills and fields dotted with wildflowers held boundless beauty, every clop of a hoof and turn of the carriage wheel carried her deeper into the unknown. She turned to Mrs. Gallagher seated across from her. "How far out is your place?"

"About four miles." Mrs. Gallagher glanced at the landscape then smiled at Addie. "Not much farther. We should be home in plenty of time for you to rest before the evening meal."

Nodding, Addie eased closer to the opening in the side of the coach, the gentle breeze cooling the perspiration on her forehead and upper lip. She hadn't realized how raw her nerves had become. However pleasant-looking, this place was foreign to her, these people strangers. Her heart ached for the familiar, for what her life had once been.

Before everything went askew.

She missed Papa, Thomas, and Eli tramping in after a day's work, their teasing and lively banter leaching into the very fabric of their home, making the walls and floors spark with life. She even missed Aunt Polly and having someone to call family when she had no one else.

Her stomach dipped. Truth be told, she also missed Luke—his winsome smile and calming presence. His unexpected companionship had carried her through a time when she'd needed the comfort of a friend to cling to. His allegiance to God both irked and fascinated her. To believe so strongly in the Lord's sovereignty and goodness was admirable, but something she could no longer adhere to.

"There's our place. Over there," Lydia announced, gesturing to the two-story farmhouse in the distance.

Nestled between groves of trees, with rolling hills beyond, the place truly was picturesque. Even the abundance of barren fields surrounding it lent to its charm. "It's lovely."

A soft sigh pealed from Mrs. Gallagher. "I'm afraid the property is a shadow of what it was when my husband and sons were tending it. It didn't take long for the fields to fall into disarray in their absence."

Addie shook her head, scanning the vast acreage. "Still, I can't get over all the wide-open spaces. Growing up in the city, I've not seen anything quite like it. Have you no neighbors?"

"A few. Hal and Celia Perkins are our closest. They live three-quarters of a mile to the west through those trees."

Leaning closer to Addie, Lydia's face lit in a smile. "Mrs. Perkins is a wonderful cook, and Mr. Perkins is a bee fancier. He harvests their honey to sell and trade with all the neighbors and stores."

Mrs. Gallagher's response was less animated as her deep-set eyes sought out Addie's. "Mr. Perkins farmed a section of our land for us last year, but he's not in the best of health these days and getting on in age." A trace of regret seeped into her voice. "With the war ended, we were in hopes Luke or Andrew would be home in time to put a crop in this year. But the way it's looking, that doesn't appear likely."

With a slow nod, Addie clamped her jaw tighter. Though she understood the woman's disappointment, she had to bite her tongue not to mention she and Lydia were fortunate to have them coming home at all.

The coach maneuvered along the rocky trail, edging closer until it halted at the front of the house. No servants came to greet them. Instead, the driver helped retrieve their luggage and set the bags on the porch before collecting his payment and starting his return trip.

Addie surveyed the large farmhouse from the bottom step. The closer angle allowed a view of the chipped paint on the porch rails and loose boards in the flooring. The many months without a man to upkeep the place had indeed taken its toll.

Mrs. Gallagher adjusted her hat, peering at the cracked upstairs window. "I'm certain it's nothing as fancy as you're accustomed to, but I hope you'll feel at home here."

"It's fine. Thank you." Despite its flaws, the place held a certain charm.

The older woman's lips lifted in a weak grin as she glanced at Addie. "Come. Let's get you settled."

Addie started up the porch steps, feeling useless as she witnessed Lydia's struggle to lug Aunt Polly's metal box under one arm and the bulky satchel in her other. How she loathed being reliant on others. Especially Northerners who were all but strangers. What she wouldn't give to regain her ability to function on her own, and with it, her sense of dignity.

With bated breath, she waited for Mrs. Gallagher to open the door, her heart pounding. What did a Yankee home look like? Would it differ vastly from what she was accustomed to?

Her muscles tensed as the door swung open and Mrs. Gallagher stepped inside. Addie's feet froze in place. This just didn't feel right.

Her hostess pivoted toward her, compassion streaming from

her eyes. "Come, my dear. You must be exhausted after your long trip."

As though embracing a life not her own, Addie slowly striddled across the threshold. She was indeed fatigued. Since the night of the fire, her unsettled mind and scorched body had robbed her of much-needed rest. Would she find any sort of solace in these unfamiliar surroundings?

A narrow hallway awaited her with a wide doorway on either side, and, deeper in, a carpeted stairway leading to the upstairs. While the exterior of the building had fallen into ill-repair, from this vantage point, the interior appeared immaculate.

Depositing her satchel to the side of a small table in the hall, Mrs. Gallagher gestured to the room on Addie's right. "This is the sitting room and across the hall, our parlor."

Addie peered inside the sitting room, glimpsing a pair of upholstered chairs before a sizable fireplace and a rather commonplace settee at the room's center. A rounded, oak table bearing several framed pictures rested against the inner wall.

A glimpse across the hall revealed a more stylish settee atop a woven rug with an elegant console table at its front. A cherry, rolltop desk graced the far wall. Though not particularly ornate or fancy, the furnishings possessed a flare for quality, their arrangement impeccable.

Surprised at the ordinariness of the rooms, Addie breathed easier. Strange, one's misconceptions. She'd anticipated a place utterly foreign to her. There was nothing here that could not be found in any ordinary home in Richmond.

"Come, Adelaide. I'll show you the rest of the house." Lydia swished past, arms still burdened with luggage.

Like a compliant puppy, Addie fell in step behind her.

"Show her to Luke's room, then come help with supper." Mrs. Gallagher called after them. "And don't pester Adelaide with a lot of questions. She's due for a bit of quiet."

"Yes, Mama." Lydia's tone, though respectful, harbored a smidgen of annoyance. She waited for Addie at the bottom stair, nodding to the spacious room with a sturdy table and chairs on their left. "That's the dining room. The bed chambers are upstairs." With that, she lumbered up the stairway, dragging the overstuffed satchel.

Addie eyed the thick mahogany banister as she started after her. Similar to the one she used to slide down into her father's waiting arms. Heaviness pulled at her chest. Selling her home had proven nearly as difficult as uprooting herself to come here. And yet, Richmond held only bitter memories for her now. She had no wish to return. Even if she had, she couldn't—so long as Simon posed a threat.

Lydia plopped the satchel down at the top of the stairs with a weary huff. "I shall need a rest myself after toting this hefty baggage all this way."

Another irksome pang of regret trickled through Addie. "I'm sorry to trouble you."

Pivoting toward her, Lydia leaned against the banister, hands on her hips. "Don't be. It's worth it to have you here. I've had only brothers to chum with all these years, and we both know how taxing that can be."

"Yes." Addie held back a grin, memories of traipsing along after Thomas and Eli flooding back. At times, they'd been more than pleased to have her tag along. Other times, she'd proved nothing but a nuisance. Having a girl near her age to converse with would be a new experience. One she admitted, might have its enjoyments.

Hefting the bag once more, Lydia gestured toward the closed door on the left. "That's Drew's room. Luke's is this way."

The floorboards creaked under Addie as she topped the stairs and followed Lydia to a room farther down. Small cracks in the plaster walls—patched and painted over—hinted the farmhouse had stood for quite some time. "Has your family always lived here?"

"Yes. My grandparents built this house and deeded it to my parents when they married. I can't imagine living anywhere else."

A stale smell wafted out as Lydia unlatched the door and pushed it open. She dropped the satchel on the bed with an "*umph*." "The room's been closed up since Luke left. I'll open the window to air it out." Setting Addie's box on the dresser, she edged toward the window.

Addie stepped through the narrow doorway and ventured a look around. The small room contained only a bed with a trunk at its foot, a three-drawered dresser, and a stand table holding a wash basin and pitcher. She drew a satisfied breath. Much like her brothers' rooms. Simple, and yet, all that was necessary. And much more private than the hospital in Richmond.

Lydia brushed her hands together. "There. That should do it."

A gentle breeze filtered through the open window, relieving some of the musty smell. Addie eased down onto the bed, surprised at the softness of the mattress. She eyed the hand-stitched tan and rust quilt atop it, impressed by the evenness of the stitches.

"Mama's a fine seamstress, isn't she?"

Addie glanced up to see Lydia standing beside her. "She certainly is. What a lovely pattern."

"It's called Evening Star. Mama made each of us a keepsake quilt for when we marry."

"What a wonderful gift." Addie's throat hitched. What she wouldn't give to have such an heirloom from her mother. Even something as small as a favorite book with her inscription, or a locket, like the one she now wore of Aunt Polly's. Minus its charred casing.

Lydia opened the satchel and removed the night gown and day dress Miss Van Lew had given Addie. Standing on tiptoes, the young girl held the blue and white checkered dress up to her front and spun around. "It's so pretty. I'd love to see it on you. Forgive me for asking, but when will your time of mourning end?"

Addie's muscles tensed. In truth, her mourning time had

ended long ago for Papa and Thomas and more than a month ago for Eli. But she'd grown so accustomed to wearing the drab taffeta she'd forgotten what it was to wear anything else. She swallowed. "Just a bit longer."

With a weak grin, Lydia smoothed a crease from the skirt. "I'd best keep the dress in my room. I have a wardrobe where it can hang and work out some of its wrinkles."

Addie nodded. "I would appreciate that."

Draping the dress over one arm, Lydia gripped the bag handle with her free hand. "Well, I'd better go help Mama with supper. Is there anything you need? A drink of water? Another pillow?"

"No. I'm fine. Thank you."

Lydia backed toward the door. "I'll let you know when supper's ready. Oh, and my room is just across the hall, so if ever you need anything, just call out."

"Thank you. I will."

Pausing, Lydia hugged the dress tighter to her chest and peered over at Addie, head cocked to one side. "I know you don't intend to stay long, but I hope you do. It sure would be grand having you for a sister."

Something within Addie melted. At a time when she felt utterly alone and helpless, this family had extended hospitality and kindness, the likes of which she had never experienced. Choking down her emotions, she gave a slight cough to steady her voice. "That's very sweet of you."

With a satisfied smile, Lydia exited, leaving the door open a crack.

Easing down onto the bed, Addie stared at the plaster ceiling.

> *"If thine enemy be hungry, give him bread to eat;*
> *and if he be thirsty, give him water to drink."*

The verse of Scripture shot through her mind before she

could block it. Was that what this was about? Were the Gallaghers fulfilling some sort of Christian duty to aid the less fortunate?

Their enemy?

She gnawed her lower lip. If so, she had no intention of yielding to it.

23

Addie shook her head at Lydia's attempt to feed her another bite of honey-coated biscuit. "I'd better stop." Not wishing to offend, she cast a glance across the table at Mrs. Gallagher. "The meal was very good, but I'm afraid all this traveling has stolen my appetite."

"That's perfectly all right, dear. I'm glad it was to your liking."

Though reassuring, Mrs. Gallagher's soothing tone did little to curb Addie's turbulent spirit. More than mere travel had churned her stomach. This whole affair had her muddled.

Addie leaned against the back of the oak chair, hands dry and tight beneath the thin layer of bandages. She tried unsuccessfully to flex her fingers. Captain Sally assured her she would regain at least some use of her hands and arms. Though, likely, she would bear the dreadful scars the rest of her days. She held back a yawn, too exhausted to think about it.

"You look plumb worn out. A good night's rest is what you need."

Not quite able to look her hostess in the eyes, Addie nodded agreement. "I am a bit fatigued." Not to mention the dull ache in her head.

Mrs. Gallagher set her silverware on her plate and stood. "Come. I'll help you ready for bed."

Addie's chair skidded on the hardwood floor as she pushed back from the table too quickly. She'd expected Lydia to assist her. Somehow the young girl seemed less intimidating. It had taken the entire trip to Washington to feel the least bit at ease under Miss Van Lew's care. As kind as Luke's mother seemed, Addie felt a tad self-conscious having her witness the ugliness of her injuries and be burdened with her personal needs.

The truth was, she would never grow accustomed to the humbling act of being fed or clothed by someone. No matter who they be.

Hiking her skirt, Mrs. Gallagher started up the stairs ahead of Addie. "I'm glad you've come, Adelaide. I hope you'll feel at home with us."

"Thank you, Mrs. Gallagher." Unable to lift her dress from around her feet, Addie quickly fell behind, struggling not to trip on the floor-length taffeta. "You've been ... more than ... kind."

"Please. Call me Martha." Her hostess peered over her shoulder, noting Addie's difficulty. "Oh, my dear. Let me help you." Retracing her steps, she lifted Addie's dress from around her feet with one hand and her own with the other.

Heat rushed to Addie's cheeks as they climbed the stairs side by side. Would she ever again know the freedom of tending to her own needs?

Pausing outside Luke's room, Martha gestured across the hall. "My bedroom is downstairs opposite the dining room. Lydia will be more accessible if you need assistance using the chamber pot in the night. But, should anything out of the ordinary arise, please don't hesitate to wake me."

Addie gave a tentative nod, determined to do her utmost not to call upon either of them in the night.

The room had aired out considerably from when they first arrived.

Martha turned down the covers and jostled the mattress. "I hope the bed suits you."

"It's fine. Thank you." As tired as Addie was, she could sleep on a bed of leaves.

A robin's sweet, evening chortle sounded outside the window. How different this quiet haven was from the chaos of Richmond, with its patrolling soldiers and crowded streets. She could understand now why Luke longed for home.

The setting sun cast an amber glow over the clear, western sky stirring remembrances of the fateful night of the fire. Her moment of peacefulness shattered, Addie forced herself to look away, suppressing the unwelcome memory. In years past, the beauty of a sunset would have evoked joy, not fear. Too much anguish had stolen the splendor of such simple pleasures.

Lifting Addie's nightgown from the foot of the bed, Martha sat on the mattress. "Come, Adelaide. I'll help you into your nightgown."

Addie strolled over, dropping her gaze to the floorboards as she took a seat beside her. It felt odd being referred to by her given name instead of Addie. In time, perhaps she'd feel comfortable entrusting the nickname with them. But for now, Adelaide would suffice.

They might even prefer her full name, as Luke did.

Martha's hands moved to unfasten the string of buttons. "Luke tells me your arms and hands suffered significant burns."

A nod was all Addie could manage.

"Burns of that magnitude are slow to heal. Yet, I imagine each day brings a slight improvement, each week a bit less pain and rawness."

Not wishing to be rude, Addie forced a reply. "A little."

A warm hand cupped her chin, drawing her eyes upward until she met Martha's gentle gaze. "A little healing is still healing. Given time, our nation will mend as well. Restoration will take a great deal of effort on everyone's part. But, day by day and week by week, we must work toward reconciliation. And trust that, in due time, the Lord will heal our land."

It was clear where Luke inherited his tendency to believe the best of things. And while Addie had no doubt the atrocities of war would fade in people's minds over time, they would never be forgotten. To believe otherwise was naïve. Though Martha's words held some element of truth, Addie's heart was no more hopeful now than the day she'd received the news of her father and brothers' passing.

Addie's lips trembled, months of heartache bubbling up inside her. "I wish this awful war had never happened and things could be as they were." The words poured out before she could stop them.

Martha gave a soft sigh. "I suspect there's not a one of us who doesn't feel that way. I daresay the war brought greater hardship and more bloodshed than anyone anticipated."

It was true. When Papa and Thomas left home, they'd boasted the war would be over in a matter of months—with certain victory for the South. But months had soon stretched into years, and neither had come back alive.

When Addie remained silent, Martha paused and drew her hands back. "Did Luke share with you his reason for joining the army?"

Venturing a glance up, Addie shrugged. "I assumed out of desire to avenge his father's death."

The older woman's face pinched. "In part, yes. But before he left, he expressed his desire to bring a swifter end to the war."

Addie arched a brow. "That sounds like Luke."

Martha leaned back and released a long breath, her eyes glossing over. "He was young, barely sixteen when he left, with not a shred of fear in him. From the time he was old enough to grip a rifle, he hunted game and soon became quite a marksman." She smiled, the creases at the outer edges of her eyes deepening. "He's our adventurous one, eager to conquer any challenge."

Addie nodded, memories of his brave efforts to save her flooding back.

"He wrote home often at first, but soon, his letters came less frequently. I could sense by their tone his initial zeal was waning."

Moisture glistened in her eyes as she finished unbuttoning Addie's dress. "Luke is ever the optimist, strong and sure in his faith. Killing and maiming others doesn't come easy for him. I worried he would soon end up like his father."

Addie's throat thickened at the myriad emotions encompassing the woman's face. She knew full well what it was to fret over the welfare of a loved one. In her case, she'd had every cause for concern. Addie struggled to speak. "And yet, he survived."

"Yes, and for that I'm deeply grateful." Martha's hands stilled, her gaze snapping back to Addie. "He didn't often share details of the battles he fought but seemed to always find some bit of hope to cling to."

She shook her head, a look of wonderment in her eyes. "He once wrote that he purposely shot the rifles out of opposing soldiers' hands rather than take their lives. Even went so far as to stuff verses of Scripture written on scraps of paper in the pockets of the wounded."

"Why, that's foolhardy! It's a wonder he wasn't killed."

Reaching for Addie's sleeve, Martha gave it a gentle pull. "That's Luke. He'd rather forfeit his life than take another's if there's any way around it."

Addie shook her head. "I don't understand. Why would he willingly make such a sacrifice?"

With a tug on the other sleeve, Martha blew out a breath. "There was an incident years ago involving a friend of his that nearly shattered him. Since then, he's determined not to let anyone he cares about die without ensuring their heart is right with God."

Addie blinked, recalling him making a similar remark to her.

Though she couldn't fathom such heartfelt convictions, she couldn't help but admire her friend. "You must be proud of him."

Martha's lips spread in a wide grin. "Indeed, I am. When too much time passes without hearing from him, I take out his letters and soak in the encouragement they offer and reread the verse he ends each letter with."

Her uneasiness lifting, Addie stood and let the dress slip down around her feet, envisioning Luke's ready smile. Only this morning they'd said their goodbyes, and yet, it seemed so much longer. He was indeed a man of sincere faith—one she'd come to respect. Pricked by curiosity, Addie couldn't resist asking, "Which verse did he include?"

Lifting her face to the ceiling, Martha closed her eyes. "Joshua chapter one verse nine. *Be strong and courageous. Do not be afraid; do not be discouraged, for the* LORD *your God will be with you wherever you go.*"

The verse was not an unfamiliar one to Addie, and once would have offered her great contentment. But she no longer sensed God's presence or His comfort.

Nor, most likely, would she ever again.

A gentle hand touched her shoulder, and she met Martha's compassionate gaze. "If we look for it, I believe some good can come out of even the most trying of circumstances."

Addie edged back, her thoughts conflicted. She held out her bandaged arms. "And what good can come of disfigured, useless hands and arms? What benefit can there be in the deaths of my family or your husband, for that matter?"

The older woman's eyes crimped. "I can't answer that, Adelaide. I don't know the mind of God. But I do know there are blessings to be found even in the midst of sorrow, if we search for them. Just look at the ways the Lord has provided for you since your injury."

Addie clamped her lips tighter so as not to say more than she should and instead pondered the words. Though she didn't entirely agree with the woman's sentiments, one thing was certain—it was time to let go of her painful past and press forward.

Like it or not, these people were all that stood between her and a life of privation.

———————

April 29, 1865
Saturday, 5:45 a.m.

THE SNAP of a twig woke Luke from a light sleep. He sat up and gripped his Springfield rifle, panning his surroundings. Something weightier than a coyote or deer was out there.

Likely a two-footed something.

Having spent the night under the stars rather than in the stuffy confines of an inn, his senses were heightened. Though the war had ended, it would be naïve to think the animosity had died away.

A shuffling noise drew his gaze to a cluster of trees to the north. Rifle raised, he scrambled to his feet and squinted into the early morning shadows, the promise of dawn etched along the eastern horizon. "Who's there?"

A rifle cocked and a soldier stepped from behind a tree several yards away, his gun pointed at Luke's chest. "Me."

The booming voice ricocheted down to Luke's toes. Though the dim light rendered the color of the man's uniform indistinguishable, his massive frame brought to mind the name Goliath. Luke gulped as the soldier stepped out into the open, laying to rest any hope of Union blue. Though no giant, the Reb had several inches on him, not to mention a good number of pounds and shoulders broad as a cannon. Stringy hair, a smudged uniform, and a gaunt complexion hinted he'd been without the comforts of military life for some time.

On instinct, Luke glanced around to ensure the soldier didn't have company, quickly determining the fellow was alone. Most likely a deserter.

And desperate.

With a silent prayer on his lips, Luke lowered his rifle enough to show he meant the man no harm, but not so much he wouldn't shoot if he had to. He hadn't survived the war to be killed by some renegade. "What say we both set our rifles aside, so we can talk more friendly?"

The soldier grunted and took a step closer. "Not on your life, Yank."

Undaunted, Luke widened his stance. "Haven't you heard, Reb? The war's over."

Steadying his aim, the man gave a taunting smirk. "Not for me it ain't."

24

For a prolonged moment, Luke held the soldier's rigid gaze, trying to determine if he were a man of reason ... or just plain hungry for blood. Though he tended toward the latter, he decided to risk it. With a silent prayer, he raised his rifle and aimed. "All right then, shoot. I'm ready to meet my Maker. How 'bout you?"

The bulky private made no move, and yet no bullet came.

Luke held his ground, his palms growing clammy and his arms shaky beneath the weight of the rifle. Movement in the underbrush behind and to the left of the renegade soldier brought renewed hope and a smile to Luke's face. Just like the ram in the thicket when Abraham was about to sacrifice Isaac.

Thank you, Lord.

He raised his voice a notch, his confidence bolstered. "Or ... we can put our rifles to use the way they were meant to and shoot us that rabbit over there for breakfast."

The soldier's head bobbled slightly to the right. Seeming flustered, he lowered his gun a tad then quickly raised it. "Nice try, Yank, but I'm not that stupid."

Luke gave a slow shake of his head. "If you don't believe me just promise not to shoot when I do." Without waiting for a response, he shifted his aim a trifle to the left and pulled the trigger.

The private jerked back and lowered his rifle, frantically looking his uniform over. A relieved grin crept onto his lips, and he gave a loud guffaw. "You missed, Yank. Now it's my turn."

As the soldier raised his gun, Luke pointed toward the underbrush. "I hit just what I was aiming at. See for yourself." He strode toward the confused Reb, walking right past him to where the rabbit lay. Picking his limp quarry up by the ears, he flashed a lighthearted grin. "It's not eggs and bacon, but it'll fill our stomachs just the same."

The private's bloodshot eyes scrunched tighter, and he licked his lips. With a snort, he scratched his stubbled chin. "I reckon it will, Yank. And right now, fillin' my belly sounds a heap better than goin' belly up."

A half-hour later, the rabbit was skinned and roasting on a spit. Agreeing to put their differences aside, they unloaded their rifles and leaned them against a tree while they waited for breakfast. Luke glanced at his unlikely companion. "Do you have a name, Private?"

The scraggly soldier glanced up from peeling dried mud from his boot. "Cass. Cass Newberry." He leaned back, brushing dirt from his hands. "You?"

"Luke Gallagher."

Cass eyed him curiously. "Where you headed?"

Luke gave the spit a turn. "Richmond."

The soldier's brow furrowed. "*Richmond?* Ain't you travelin' the wrong direction for a Yank? From what I hear Richmond's nothin' but a heap of rubble."

"That's about the size of it and the reason we're there. To get things back in shape."

"Humph. What do you blue-bellies care what sort of shape the South's in? Was you who destroyed it."

Certain the topic would only escalate into an argument, Luke let the comment slide. He hugged his knee to his chest. "Where you headed?"

The private chucked a clump of dirt into the underbrush. "Home to Raleigh, North Carolina."

Luke arched a brow. "Long ways to travel on foot."

Cass shrugged. "Nothin' new from what I've been doin' all these months." His gaze swung toward Luke's horse, and his gray eyes narrowed. "'Course a mount would get me home to my wife and boy a lot quicker."

The gleam in his new acquaintance's eyes made Luke a bit leery that once the shared meal was over, their next tussle might involve Miss Van Lew's horse. Seeing as he likely wouldn't make out so good in a fist-to fist confrontation, a distraction seemed a good idea about now. "How long since you've seen them?"

Cass blew out a long breath. "Over a year now."

"Long while." Luke gave the rabbit another quarter turn, studying his companion. Knowing the man had a wife and son awaiting his return put a new slant on things. His gaze flicked to Miss Van Lew's sturdy bay mare, disliking the idea formulating in his head. And yet, he couldn't shake the impulse to pose the suggestion.

Sitting up straighter, he wiped sweaty palms over his trousers. "Say, uh. Why don't you ride along with me as far as Richmond? I figure the horse is stout enough to ride the both of us, if we switch off from time to time."

The private peered at him as if he had two heads. "Ride with a Yankee? You must be daft."

Almost in agreement, Luke shrugged. "Just a thought. I figure it would spare you some time and your feet some callouses."

Cass seemed to waver, his expression difficult to read. He cast a greedy glance at the horse.

Luke scolded himself, fearful he'd just given his companion an idea. Both knew Luke couldn't out-muscle the stocky soldier.

Still, he didn't regret the offer. Didn't the Good Book say to live in such a way to make your enemy be at peace with you?

Instead of scoffing laughter, Cass turned to Luke with questioning eyes. "If'n I was to ride along, what's to keep you from claimin' I'm your prisoner once we get there?"

Luke tipped his chin a smidge higher. "My word. That's the only guarantee you need."

Cass eyed him wearily, as if sizing up Luke's integrity. At last, he snickered. "You're an odd one, Yank."

A grin edged across Luke's lips. "You're not the first to make that claim."

The gray-clad soldier looped his hands behind his head and puckered his lips. "Well Yank, I reckon I'll take you up on that there offer just to quicken the pace and spare my feet."

Befuddled by the soldier's change of heart, Luke gave an affirming nod. Though his gut told him not to let his guard down.

Gallagher Estate
Outside Elmira, New York
April 29, 1865, 6 a.m.

A TAP on the bedroom door brought Addie to a sitting position. A wave of dizziness flooded over her, last night's headache still clinging to her like a burr. She pried her eyes wider, surprised at being summoned while it was still half-dark. "Come in."

The door creaked open, and a fully-dressed Lydia peeked her head in. "Are you awake?"

Barely, Addie wanted to say. "Yes. Is anything wrong?"

"No. I just thought you might like to come with me to milk Penny."

"Penny?"

"Our cow." Striding in, Lydia peered more closely at Addie. "You look still asleep."

Addie stifled a yawn. "I'm not used to being awake at such an early hour."

The mattress jiggled as Lydia plopped down beside her. "Oh, we rise early here on the farm. Penny starts bawlin' something awful if she's not milked out before the sun fully peaks the horizon." She tossed her thick, blond braid over her shoulder. "Ever milked a cow?"

Almost choking at the thought, Addie shook her head. "Can't say I have." She'd hardly seen a cow, let alone milked one.

"Well, we'd best get you dressed then. It's Saturday, and Mrs. Perkins is due to come by." Lydia hopped to her feet and gently tugged at Addie's nightgown sleeve, talking as she worked. "We had to sell off all our livestock 'cept Penny and our plow horses. Mr. and Mrs. Perkins sold their cow, but kept their chickens, so we trade milk and butter for their honey and eggs."

Standing, Addie struggled to raise stiff arms shoulder high. As she wriggled free of the nightgown, Lydia prattled on about anything and everything. Addie suppressed a grin. How different the girl was from her subdued, even-keeled brothers.

Was this what it was like to have a sister?

Lydia's eyes trailed to the charred locket around Addie's neck which, until now, had remained concealed. She slid a hand under the singed piece of jewelry. "Oh my. What happened to your locket? Was it damaged in the fire too?"

Nodding, Addie surveyed the marred necklace. "Yes. It belonged to my aunt."

"I bet it was pretty. Are there pictures inside?"

Addie jerked back, her tone a bit harsher than intended. "Only ones you've already seen."

The locket slipped from Lydia's palm, garnering a wide-eyed stare. "I'm sorry. I don't mean to pry."

Seeing the girl was in earnest, Addie immediately regretted her abruptness. "Forgive me." She sat on the edge of the mattress, staring at her bandaged arms. "It's hard being reminded of all I've lost."

Lydia eased down next to her. "I felt that way when Papa was killed. I was eleven at the time, and I remember chasing after him when he left, not wishing him to go. He lifted me in his arms and gave me the longest hug, almost as if he knew it was the last one."

The tender scene played out in Addie's head, stirring remembrances of her final farewells with her own family. She remembered well a similar longing to cling to every fleeting moment. And the emptiness once they'd departed.

Addie fidgeted, pricked by the compulsion to share her own story. She worked to steady her voice, the tightness in her throat nearly choking out her words. "My father and both of my brothers perished in the war."

Moisture glistened in Lydia's eyes. "That must be so hard. I couldn't have stood it if Drew or Luke had died as well as Papa."

Somehow the words of sympathy helped ease the burden Addie had harbored so long.

Lydia's small hand gripped Addie's shoulder. "I know it isn't the same, but I hope while you're here, you'll think of Mama and me as family." Her lips turned upward in a tearful smile. "And if Drew and Luke make it home before you leave, consider them brothers."

Addie tensed. Though touched by the offer, considering Yankees as family was unthinkable. Lodging with them was one thing. Endearing herself to them was quite another. Though Lydia and her mother were likeable enough, Addie could never fully open her heart to them.

And Luke?

A ripple of unease trickled through her. As highly as she regarded him, it was best they'd parted ways ...

Or "brother" might not accurately describe her feelings for him.

25

Lydia patted the honey-colored cow on the shoulder, gripping the metal milk pail in her other hand. "This is Penny. She's a Jersey cow."

The creature gave a low "moo" and twisted her head toward Addie as if distinguishing her as a stranger. Timid of the short, squat animal, she took a step back.

A giggle sounded from her companion. "Don't worry. She won't hurt you." The girl hugged the cow's neck. "Isn't she pretty?"

Pretty was not the word Addie would use to describe her. Though she had to admit her large, fawn-like eyes had a certain allure. "She's ... something all right."

Lydia scratched Penny behind the ear, and the cow leaned into her, bobbing her large head up and down. The pair seemed to truly enjoy each other. Moving to the cow's side, Lydia slipped the pail under her. She tossed Addie a grin as she pulled a three-legged stool up beside Penny. "Too bad you can't try milking. Maybe in a few weeks, once your hands have healed more."

Forcing a smile, Addie feigned agreement. For once, she was almost relieved her hands and arms were hindered. She only hoped by the time her fingers were agile enough, the offer would be forgotten.

An orange cat appeared from nowhere, tail in the air, its "meow" reverberating through the near-vacant barn. Reaching down, Lydia gave the cat a stroke on the back and it rubbed against her. "This is Basil. He never misses a meal."

As Lydia settled onto the stool, the cat sat beside her and watched her spray steady streams of milk into the pail like a sentry guarding his plunder. Each spurt struck the metal pail with a loud *ping*.

Addie craned her neck for a closer look. "You make it look easy."

Cutting a quick glance over her shoulder, Lydia never slackened her pace. "It's not hard once you get the hang of it."

Basil edged closer, meowing more intently as the bucket filled. A mischievous grin slid across Lydia's lips. "Watch this." Redirecting her aim, she gave the awaiting cat a squirt on the mouth. Instantly, his meows quieted and his pink tongue worked to clean the milk from his face.

Addie chuckled. "You're pretty good at that."

Lydia's grin widened. "Luke taught me. He's full of ideas."

Mention of Luke stirred Addie's attention. There was something invigorating about the thought of learning more about the man who'd sacrificed so much for her sake. Knowledge he'd likely never share himself. "What sort of ideas?"

"Like attaching a rope to the tree over by the pond and teaching me to swim by swinging me across and dropping me in."

Addie's mouth hinged open. "He didn't."

With a giggle, Lydia returned to milking. "There wasn't any real danger. He jumped in, too, and stayed within arm's reach."

Though the measure seemed drastic, knowing first-hand Luke's protective nature, Addie had no doubt he'd kept a careful eye on his young sister. She arched a brow. "What else has your daring brother taught you?"

"Well ... he taught me how to make a hen turkey call to flush a gobbler out of hiding."

"He takes you hunting?" Addie's raised voice caused the cat to scurry behind the pile of straw on the opposite side of the stall.

"A couple of times. I'd flush them out, and he'd shoot 'em."

The tension in Addie's muscles eased. "Oh, well. I'm glad to hear that. For a moment I thought he'd taught you to shoot."

The milking stopped, and Lydia slowly shifted her gaze toward Addie, her expression resembling a fox who'd just cornered someone's prize chicken.

"He *did*?"

With a reluctant nod, Lydia swiveled toward her. "Just before he left for war. With Mama and me here alone, he thought it best one of us know how to load and shoot a rifle. Since Mama wanted no part in it, he showed me." Her lips lifted. "I got pretty good too. Though not near as good as Luke. He can shoot an apple off a tree by its stem."

While such an ability was impressive, Addie couldn't get past the thought of Luke putting a rifle in the hands of his young sister. "I'm surprised your mother allowed it."

The girl's flushed cheeks relayed the truth.

Addie's eyes widened. "She doesn't know?"

Lydia lowered her voice. "Please don't tell her. Mama would faint if she knew I handled a rifle."

Pursing her lips, Addie held back a smile. "If your mother is ever to know, it won't come from me."

"Thanks." Lydia grinned up at her. "Wanna know another idea of Luke's I really like?"

"What's that?"

"Sending you here."

Warmth flowed through Addie as her newfound friend returned to milking. While her mind cautioned her to hold this family at arm's length, her heart longed to embrace the sense of belonging. With a deep breath, she chided herself for her moment of weakness. This family and this way of life were not her own.

Nor could they ever be.

The rhythm of Lydia's milking tapered off, until it stopped altogether. Her pail nearly full, she dished out a small bowl for Basil and covered the remainder with a cloth. Standing, she gave Penny a pat on the rump. "That does it."

A woman's humming drifted through the open barn door, bringing a smile to Lydia. "And just in time. There's Mrs. Perkins now. Come on. I'll introduce you."

Following her outside, Addie scanned the path leading to the house. She slowed her pace at sight of the dark-skinned woman walking toward them, a sizable basket in the nook of her arm. She waved to them, and Lydia lifted an arm in greeting. "Mornin' Mrs. Perkins."

Addie balked. Mrs. Perkins was a woman of color? She'd never even considered the possibility. Martha and Lydia had spoken so highly of her and Mr. Perkins ... as equals—a thought so foreign to her Southern upbringing it roiled in her chest.

Lydia paused beside her. "Is anything wrong?"

She held back her words a moment before letting them trickle out like molasses. "No. It's just. I never thought she'd be ..." The word stalled on Addie's tongue, unwilling to sully the girl's opinion of the woman.

Or her.

Lydia's blank stare confirmed she had no inkling what the trouble could be. "What is it?"

Collecting herself, Addie shook off her misperception. "Nothing. I'm fine."

They started on, reaching Mrs. Perkins a few yards shy of the house. Dressed in a well-fitted, tan-and-white day dress, with her ebony hair in a loose chignon, the woman in no way resembled the shabbily dressed, tattered look of a slave. Instead, she appeared almost refined.

She bowed her head in greeting, a wide smile spreading over

her face. Her gaze fluctuated between them, finally settling on Addie. "Good mornin', ladies. Who's your friend, Lydia?"

Lydia set the pail of milk on the ground, then straightened. "This is Adelaide Hanover. All the way from Richmond."

The woman's eyes flared, the fervor seeming to bleed from her face. "*Richmond?* You don't say?"

With a brisk nod, Addie pursed her lips, uncertain which of them was less comfortable.

"What brings ya all this way? You two related?"

When Addie offered no reply, Lydia intervened. "No. She was injured in the fire there. Since she had no family, Luke sent her here to stay while she mends."

"Well now, I'm sorry t' hear you're ailin'. But you're in good hands with Miss Martha and Miss Lydia."

"They've been very kind." Addie met the woman's gaze only an instant before letting it fall away, her words coming out stiff, forced. Conversing with a colored person on the same social level felt unnatural. It just wasn't done. At least not in her experience.

A creak of the house door broke the moment of awkward silence. Martha stepped onto the porch. "Good morning, Celia. I see you're getting acquainted with our new houseguest."

"Yes. My, I don't think I've ever met someone from as far south as Richmond." The nervous tone in the woman's voice made Addie wonder if she would rather they hadn't met.

Martha descended the steps, a basket of bottled milk and tin of butter in tow. "It is quite a jaunt. Luke's on his way back there now."

The dark-skinned neighbor's head jerked backward. "Why, that dear boy's headed the wrong direction. With the war ended, I figured he'd be on his way home one of these days."

"He assures us it will be soon." Martha smiled as she and Mrs. Perkins swapped baskets.

The visitor shook her head and grinned. "My, how I miss that young man. He was always so good to check in on Hal and me."

The insight into Luke wasn't surprising. He seemed to have a heart as big as Dixie. Yet, the endearing look on the woman's face left Addie a bit disconcerted. To hear her speak of Luke with such familiarity, as if he were her own, was unnerving.

With a resolute smile, Mrs. Perkins clutched the basket of milk tighter. "Lord willin', he and Andrew will both be home b'fore summer sets in."

Martha returned a long sigh. "I certainly hope so. It seems they've been gone an eternity." She gestured to the surrounding acreage. "And look at these unsightly fields. They're more overrun with weeds every day."

"Do ya want Hal to work up a plot? He'd likely be able to manage a small section."

"Oh, no. Thank you. That won't be necessary. I'm certain they'll get to it eventually."

"Well then, I'll be getting on." With an affirming nod, Mrs. Perkins turned to Addie. "Nice to meet you, Miss Hanover. I hope your stay here is a pleasant one."

Addie returned the well wishes with a rigid dip of her head. Plainly there was much she didn't grasp about this Northern way of life.

Which was precisely the reason she intended her stay here to be a short one.

LUKE WAITED for Private Newberry to dismount, then peeled himself off the leather seat, more saddle-sore than he cared to admit. Two days of solid riding was more than he'd managed in quite a while.

Cass arched his back and stretched out his arms. "How long till you figure we reach Richmond?"

Though they'd avoided towns and taken shortcuts whenever possible, the burden of added weight had slowed progress. "Another day and a half, I'd say."

"That long?"

One glance at his whiny companion scratching his belly had Luke wishing their destination was just over the next ridge.

He wasn't sure who had it worse—him, with Newberry's foul breath on his neck and incessant jabbering, or the horse, shouldering the excess load. Even with one of them striding alongside from time to time, the mount's strength was worn thin.

Slipping his haversack from his back, Cass squinted at the grove of trees on their left. "I reckon I could shoot us some supper, if'n you trust me to tote a loaded rifle."

Trusting him was arguable in itself but keeping him quiet long enough not to scare off game was the truer challenge. The man yammered more in a single hour than Adelaide and Miss Van Lew had spoken the entire trip. Luke cleared his throat. "I might, if you allow me the same privilege."

The private's gray eyes shifted side to side. "On second thought, you seem a purty good shot. Why don't I stay and set up camp while you fetch us some game."

Luke arched a brow. "I'd sooner suffer through an empty stomach than leave you alone with my horse and provisions."

Shoulders drooping, Newberry thrust out his lower lip. "You don't trust me. I'm cut to the core."

With a shake of his head, Luke reached to retrieve his bag of cartridges. "Coming from a man who just this morning was willing to shoot me for no good reason, I'd say I've a right to doubt your motives."

"You're a Yank. That's reason enough t' shoot ya." He snorted and flashed a toothy grin. "But then, you're the likeable sort, so I promise not to."

Luke's stomach rumbled, reminding him of the task at hand. Clutching his Springfield, he headed toward the timber. "Let's *both* go get us some grub."

Hours later, he and Private Newberry reclined by a crackling fire, bellies only half-filled. With a groan, Cass leaned forward on his log seat. "Ain't there a town around we can get us somethin' decent to eat? That squirrel meat wasn't enough to snack on let alone satisfy."

Luke paused from spreading his blanket on the ground and sat back on his haunches. "I've some hardtack in my haversack I'll be happy to get rid of."

Even in the shadowy twilight Luke caught the look of disgust on his companion's face. "I said somethin' *decent*."

With a soft chuckle, Luke laid on his blanket and stared up at the darkening sky. "Unless I miss my guess, the nearest town's more than six or seven miles from here."

The private straightened with a jerk. "That's not so far. Let's go."

Not budging, Luke looped his hands behind his head. "The horse needs a rest and so does my backside. Besides, I'm short on cash."

"Yeah. Me too." Cass gave a loud huff and settled down on his blanket. "Hey, Gallagher. Whatcha gonna do once your stint is up?"

A spattering of stars twinkled overhead, taunting the ache inside Luke. If he had his way, he'd call it quits now. "Return home to the farm just as quick as I'm able."

"Where's home?"

"New York. Near Elmira."

Cass turned on his side, propping himself up on his elbow. "You got a gal? Ya look a bit young for a family."

The query stirred a vision of Adelaide, her delicate features and raven-black hair. Luke dismissed the beguiling image as quickly as it blossomed. No sense dwelling on what could never be. "No one special."

"That's too bad." Shifting onto his back, Newberry released a long breath. "Me? I cain't wait to get home to my Sally Mae." I don't suppose you'd let me borrow that horse of yours so as I can have a mount the rest of the way?"

"Horse isn't mine."

Newberry's head lifted. "You steal her? Didn't figure you for a horse thief."

Tiring of the conversation, Luke retrieved his Bible from his haversack. "I'm not. She belongs to an acquaintance of mine in Richmond."

With a curious grunt, Cass ended the exchange.

In the few blessed moments of silence, Luke tilted the page toward the firelight, starting where he'd left off reading the book of James.

"What's that you're reading?"

He pointed a finger at the spot where he'd been interrupted. "The Bible."

"Huh. That somethin' you do regular?"

"Most every morning."

"Mornin'? Then why are ya doin' it now?"

Luke was starting to wonder himself. "Because I had an unexpected visitor and didn't get to it this morning."

Long silence followed. "Oh."

One verse later, his companion spoke again. "Sorta dark for readin', ain't it?"

Luke swiped a hand through his hair and snapped his Bible shut. Honestly, the man would test the patience of Job. "You know, you're right. I think morning would be better."

Another low grunt sounded, followed by blessed stillness and the steady drone of nightlife.

Smothering a yawn, Luke glanced at the burly soldier stretched out on the ground at the far side of the campfire. Either he'd finally decided sleep was more enticing than chatter, or his thoughts were churning and up to no good. Luke turned on his side, facing his bulky companion. Though they seemed to have made their peace, he intended to keep one ear and eye open.

26

April 30, 1865
Sunday, 5:30 a.m.

A shuffling noise stirred Luke from restless sleep, the dim light of early dawn encompassing him. Last night's fire had dwindled to hot embers and a thin plume of smoke. A quick glance at the spot where he'd last seen Private Newberry had Luke springing to his feet. He scrubbed a hand over his face. Exactly what he'd feared. After hours of listening to the man's fitful snoring, Luke had finally succumbed to fatigue. Sometime in the wee hours of morning, the renegade soldier must have snuck off.

The creak of leather revived his hopes. He spied Cass at the edge of the timber seated atop the bay mare, securing his rifle and bedroll. Luke took a step toward him. "Don't do it, Newberry."

The private stared at him, a conflicted scowl washing over his face. "Sorry, Gallagher." He tapped his heels into the horse's flanks, propelling her into a gentle trot.

Luke strode toward them. "We had a deal."

"I promised not to shoot ya. Didn't say anything about not

stealin' your horse." He goaded the mare into a canter, calling over his shoulder. "Tell your friend thanks for the ride. The trip home'll go a lot quicker this way."

"Newberry, wait!" Luke ran after him, shouting, "I won't make it back in time. They'll think I've deserted." Cupping his hands to the sides of his mouth, he raised his voice louder. "Is this how you repay a kindness?"

With a backward glance and a callous shrug of his shoulders, the soldier galloped on.

Tossing his kepi to the ground, Luke kicked the toe of his brogan at the sod. He'd been a fool to trust a Reb. Even a little. Other than being a bit annoying, Newberry hadn't seemed that bad a fellow. But, no matter how cordial they'd become, the Rebel soldier had deceived him.

He lifted his eyes to the heavens. "I tried to do right by him, Lord. Where did I go wrong?"

As if in answer, the sun crested the horizon like a ball of fire, giving him the sense God was there and still in control. He'd given the man a chance. That's all he could do. Anything more was up to the Lord.

Snatching up his cap, he turned toward the campsite. At least he still had his rifle and provisions. But on foot, he'd never make his furlough deadline. His best bet would be to search out the nearest town and send a wire explaining his predicament. If they court-martialed him, he'd almost deserve it.

He reached in his pocket and surveyed the meager sum of money he needed to make last until his next pay. Maybe someone at the livery would take pity on him and loan him a horse for a lesser amount. If not, he had a long trek ahead.

His stomach rumbled. With his time constraints, hunting down breakfast wasn't an option. *Hardtack it is.* He grimaced, his tastebuds revolting at the thought. Reaching in his haversack, he pulled out the rigid, tasteless cracker and broke off a chunk. What he wouldn't give to be seated at his mother's table eating eggs and bacon, or pancakes.

Instead, here he sat, hungry, alone, and duped by a renegade soldier. He reached for his Bible. This being Sunday, he could at least afford a short time for Scripture before heading out. On foot, he'd have lots of time to pray. Namely that that no-account Reb would have a change of heart or run smack-dab into Union forces less charitable than Luke.

———

"WOULD you like me to help you get ready for church service?"

Lydia's request was one Addie had expected and prepared for. Yet, she hesitated, knowing her response would not be well received. She drew a steadying breath. "I ... won't be going."

Martha's eyes flared wide then leveled, indicating if Addie were her child, that would not be an option. "Why not, may I ask?"

The nagging ache in Addie's head tempted her to claim not to feel well. Instead, she squared her shoulders, refusing to cushion her response. "Because I don't believe in God."

The declaration produced an audible gasp from Lydia and a hasty clank of Martha's coffee cup against its saucer. She studied Addie, a blend of disbelief and sorrow swirling in her eyes. "I'm saddened to hear that."

Addie lowered her gaze. The confession wasn't completely true. Deep down she knew this world hadn't come about by happenstance. That the Lord created and sustained it. But like a child attempting to block out a bad dream, she chose to push away the One who had the power to prevent her hardships and hadn't.

"But I was so looking forward to introducing you to everyone." With a disheartened frown, Lydia stood and gathered her and Addie's breakfast dishes. "Couldn't you come this once? You might enjoy it."

When Addie failed to respond, Martha laced her fingers together on the table and peered up at her daughter. "No need to coerce, Lydia. Adelaide knows her mind. She must make her own decision what to believe."

A wave of relief washed over Addie. She would rather them think her a heathen than sit through church service with a hypocritical spirit.

Martha cleared her throat, a slight hesitancy in her voice. "Does ... Luke know of your views?"

The question both confused and astonished her. Why would Martha ask such a question? Did she think Luke would not have sent her had he known? Or was she worried Addie's lack of faith would tarnish her son if they became too attached?

Heat flamed in Addie's cheeks. She knew Luke well enough to realize he would never take up with someone who didn't share his deep convictions. His mother should know no less. Mustering her resolve, she met Martha's gaze, surprised to see compassion in her eyes instead of condemnation. "Luke is aware of how I feel. Though I'm not sure why that matters."

Martha opened her mouth as if to speak then pursed her lips as though thinking better of it. Instead, she offered a weak grin and rose from her chair. "Can you manage here on your own while we're away? A couple of hours at most."

"I'm certain I'll be fine."

Depositing the breakfast dishes in the washtub, Lydia pivoted toward them. "I'll stay with you if you wish some company."

Addie cast a quick glance at Martha and shook her head. "That's not necessary. Truly. I don't wish to interfere with your worship. I'll ... sit on the porch and enjoy the scenery while you're away."

With an affirming nod, Martha took up her cup and saucer. "Splendid. We'll get you situated before we leave."

"Thank you." A sense of satisfaction spilled over Addie. Her hosts had proven more gracious and understanding about the matter than she'd anticipated.

And yet, the gratifying feeling vanished when Martha paused, hopefulness streaming in her eyes. "But if you should change your mind, the church building is up the road about a mile."

Nodding, Addie suppressed a grin. She could certainly see where Luke inherited his tenacious faith. And though, at times, she wished she could share such a commitment, it could never be. Not as long as she clung to the memory of all she'd lost.

And that, she surmised, would be a lifetime.

27

April 30, 1865
Sunday, 11 a.m.

The late morning sun beat down on Luke, and he pushed his kepi higher on his forehead to wipe his sweaty brow. Surely a town couldn't be much farther. Though he tried not to harbor bad feelings toward Private Newberry, every step pounded the man's selfishness in deeper.

Luke's complaints to the Lord had been many over the past few hours. But holding a grudge only brought further grief, so he'd taken to praying for the private's soul instead. *Convince Cass of the wrong he's done me, Lord. May his heart be stricken with guilt, so he won't take advantage of anyone else. May he come to know you and live his life in a whole new manner.*

Opening his canteen, he took a long swig, the tepid water less than satisfying. The hours of walking had provided a lot of time to reflect and pray, not only for his thieving friend, but Adelaide as well. She truly was a troubled soul, blaming God for all the hurt she'd endured. If only he had the right words to convince her otherwise—that the Lord longed to comfort her, not cause her pain.

The clop of hooves coming at him from the far side of a grove of trees revived his senses. He slid into the underbrush, gripping his loaded rifle tighter. The farther south he traveled, the more likely he was to meet up with a hostile rather than a friend. His encounter with Newberry was evidence the end of the war hadn't signaled peace.

Squinting against the midday sun, Luke watched a man on horseback emerge from around the grove of trees to his left. His jaw dropped at the gray-clad soldier riding toward him. "I don't believe it," he whispered under his breath. He stepped into plain sight, rifle aimed at the intruder.

The bulky soldier raised his arms. "Don't shoot, man. I come friendly-like."

Luke kept his Springfield trained at the renegade soldier. The big oaf deserved to squirm a little. "Cass ... Newberry. What are you, lost? Riding in circles?"

He started to lower his arms, but at Luke's signal, raised them higher. "Not me. I've been lookin' high and low for you, Gallagher."

Half humored and half agitated, Luke glared at him from behind his rifle. "Why's that? You forget to steal the rest of my provisions?"

Cass gulped, a bit red in the face. "No. I came to return your horse."

Not quite convinced, Luke squinted up at him, gradually lowering his gun. "What changed your mind?"

The private shrugged and dropped his hands to his sides. "I don't know. After I rode a ways, I got t' feelin' guilty and doubled back. Just hadn't the heart t' see you in trouble on account a me. Not after what ya did t' help me."

With a shake of his head, Luke rocked back on his heels. "Well, I'll be. Then my prayers weren't wasted on you after all."

Cass rested his forearm on the saddle horn and sounded a nervous chuckle. "Now, I wouldn't blame you a bit if you left me behind. But, bein' the God-fearin' man you are, I was sort of hoping you'd see fit to let me ride along."

Looking him in the eyes, Luke weighed his options. Either he could take revenge on the man and leave him stranded the way he'd been, or he could take him at his word and show mercy a second time. Confident his prayers had been answered, there seemed but one choice.

He cleared his throat, shifting his haversack to a more comfortable position. "I figure if you came all this way to right your wrong, the least I can do is let you tag along."

All the air seemed to expel from Newberry's chest. He motioned to Luke, a wide grin replacing his worrisome glower. "Well then, hop on, Gallagher, and let's get moving. But *I* ride in front this time."

Luke laughed out loud as he sauntered over. Though he could argue the point—the horse being his, bickering over such a trivial matter didn't seem important. God had answered his prayers, and in no small way, softened the heart of the self-centered, head-strong Reb.

Hope surged through him as he accepted Cass's arm up. If the Lord could use a bit of kindness and prayer to alter the hate-filled heart of a Confederate soldier, He could do the same with Adelaide. Maybe all she needed was a little time and a few more words of persuasion.

ADDIE GAZED out over the landscape, the breeze brushing softly against her cheeks as Martha and Lydia disappeared down the worn path. Though there'd been nothing more said about her attending church, Addie had sensed sadness in Martha's eyes as they'd left for service without her. She'd hated to disappoint, but her heart just wouldn't have been in it.

She breathed in the sweet essence of lilac, the blooms on the plants at the corner of the yard just beginning to open. The serene setting helped ease some of the pain in her head. After a lifetime of dwelling in a city with a view hemmed in by buildings and crowds of people, the rolling hills and vast expanse of green fields and meadows was breathtaking.

If for no other reason, she was grateful for the opportunity to come to this place and witness its untold beauty. She could almost sense God's presence in a place like this. Unwilling to give into the yearning, she pushed the impulse away.

The sound of humming drifted on the breeze, pulling her attention to the worn path in the distance where a dark-skinned man and woman in Sunday dress strolled arm in arm. Though the woman's broad-brimmed hat concealed her face, her slender build and lively hum resembled that of Celia Perkins. The man's hobbled gait was consistent with what she'd heard of Mr. Perkins' frail health.

She slouched lower in the wicker chair in hopes they would pass without noticing her. But as they neared the house, the woman turned her face toward Addie and raised a hand in greeting. Unable to respond in kind, Addie merely offered a weak nod, assuming they would continue on. But with a few private words to her husband, Mrs. Perkins coaxed him into the yard.

Addie's stomach lurched, the thought of conversation with the couple unappealing. What could they possibly have to say to one another?

Celia Perkins tipped her head to the side as they neared, a questioning look in her eye. "Mornin' Miss Adelaide. It's unusual to find someone home this time of a Sunday mornin'. We figured you'd all have left for church service by now."

Straightening in her chair, Addie cleared her throat. "Martha and Lydia have gone. I chose not to."

The slight hesitation transformed into a terse grin. "Well, I imagine you need some time to settle in."

Addie nodded, her gaze drifting to Mrs. Perkins' companion.

Looping her arm tighter through his, the woman's voice took on a more cheerful tone. "Oh, this here's my husband, Hal."

Only a smidgen taller than his wife, the man's skin was a shade darker. Though creases lined his brow, his dark eyes oozed with vitality. He tipped his felt hat, flecks of gray spattered among his head of black curls. His full lips spread in a welcoming smile. "How do, Miss Adelaide?"

A twinge of pain shot through her forehead as she returned a polite, yet guarded nod. "Mr. Perkins."

His brow furrowed. "You feelin' poorly, Miss Adelaide? You looks a mite peaked."

"I'm fine. Just a bit fatigued from the trip." At least that was her hope.

His eyes trailed to her bandaged hands. "Celia tells me you've suffered some burns."

"Yes." Not wishing to prolong the visit, she kept her answers concise, her tone less than inviting. She hadn't asked for this visit and longed to reclaim her solitude.

He gestured toward her hands. "What're they treatin' your injuries with?"

"Lead paint mixed with linseed oil." Not that it was any of his business.

Mr. Perkins scratched at his chin, his face scrunched like he'd bitten a sour gooseberry. "That might soothe the burns a bit, but won't do much in way of healin' 'em. Might even do ya some harm."

Addie worked her tongue over her teeth. Who was he to criticize the methods of those who made medicine their practice? "And I suppose you have something better?"

With a firm nod, he shared a smile with his wife. "Sure do."

"And what might that be?" Addie's sarcastic tone seemed to have no effect on the man.

He smiled up at her, his straight, white teeth glowing with optimism. "Honey."

Addie sat forward in her chair, uncertain she'd heard him correctly. "Hon-ey?"

"Yep. You swathe your burns with honey, and they'll heal in no time. I'll send a tin with Celia next time she heads this way."

Addie willed herself not to laugh. The idea was absurd. Honey was something you spread on biscuits, not burns. Gathering her wits, she forced a smile. "I-I don't wish to trouble you."

With a shake of his head, he jutted his lower lip. "No trouble a 'tall. Glad t' do it."

Celia tugged at his arm. "We'd best be off t' prayer meeting."

He patted her hand. "Yes, love." He tipped his hat to Addie, his smile so genuine it melted some of her resolve.

"I'll stop by first thing in the mornin'," Celia called as they strolled away.

Addie slumped back in the wicker chair, a bit dazed. These Northerners were a strange lot. In one short exchange, the Perkins' had dismantled a lifetime worth of assumptions regarding people of color. She'd thought them uneducated, with no capacity to think or feel. And yet, other than their allusion to the healing power of honey, Hal and Celia Perkins seemed intelligent people with a deep sense of love for each other.

Thus far, her entire experience with Yanks had been not at all what she'd expected.

Either Luke, his family, and even his neighbors were an unusual sort—or not all Yankees were the devils she'd thought them to be.

28

Richmond
Monday, May 1, 1865

Private Newberry pulled back on the reins, staring out ahead of them. "There she be. A mere shadow of what she once was."

Luke leaned to see past the man's bulky frame to where the city of Richmond lay sprawled in the distance. Butted up against the wide James River, the Capital City looked almost as much a shambles as when he'd arrived nearly a month earlier.

Cass shifted his heels as if to tap the horse's flanks, then paused. "You sure about this, Gallagher?"

"You have my word."

Newberry turned his head to the side, talking over his shoulder. "It ain't *your* word I question. No offense, but you bein' just a corporal, it's your higher ups that worry me. How 'bout us partin' here, and I'll be on my way?"

He started to dismount, and Luke tugged him back into the saddle. "It'll be fine. I'll explain you've a long trip ahead and in need of a fresh mount. Simple."

"That's more than decent of ya, Luke, but me goin' in there

amongst that mob of Yanks is like unearthin' a worm in a chicken coop."

"The war's over, Cass. There's no cause to detain you. President Lincoln wanted lenience shown to the Confederacy."

As if unconvinced, the private made no effort to press forward.

Luke nudged him on the shoulder blade. "You don't really want to go the rest of the trip on foot if you don't have to, do you?"

"N-no."

"Then let's get going so you can head back to that family of yours."

Newberry's back straightened. "I hope you're right, Gallagher." With that, he tapped his heels against the horse's flanks. The mare eased into a slow walk, the long days of travel having snuffed the life from her gait. Newberry's little jaunt and added weight hadn't helped either. But the worn-out bay would soon be in for a well-deserved rest.

When they reached the outskirts of the city, their approach garnered wide-eyed stares from all sides. Likely there would never be a more improbable sight than a pair of soldiers from opposing sides riding in on the same horse.

With a humored nod, Luke surveyed the array of Federal soldiers who'd paused from their work to gawk. Numerous Richmond citizens emerged from their houses, mouths agape.

Luke could almost feel the tension frothing inside Private Newberry as they ventured deeper into the city. The Rebel soldier remained rigid, seldom hazarding a glance to the left or right, until he turned his head to speak. "Where to, Gallagher?"

"Head toward the Capitol building. My company should be around there somewhere."

An affirming nod his only response, Newberry angled the horse left. Luke marveled at the soldier's change in nature. That Cass had come to trust him enough to risk entering a den of

Federal soldiers spoke volumes of how far they'd come in a few short days. God alone could bring about such change.

"Hey! There's Corporal Gallagher!"

The familiar guttural voice of Private Cummings pulled Luke's attention to the cluster of soldiers up ahead. "Slow up, Cass. That's my company."

The bewildered group of soldiers dropped their picks and shovels and ambled toward them.

"Whatcha doin' riding on back of a Johnny Reb, Corporal?" Private Fenton's pointed question brandished both stunned curiosity and humor.

Luke looped his leg over the horse's back and slid to the ground. "He didn't like my driving,"

A wave of laughter erupted from the soldiers as Cass dismounted and stood beside Luke, a humored grin lining his lips. The group fell silent as Sergeant Delmar and Lieutenant Fowler pushed their way to the front. The lieutenant scowled at Luke and Cass beneath his thick beard. "Who's this Reb, Corporal, and why are you parading the streets of Richmond with him?"

Not wishing to jeopardize Cass's trust or risk losing his superior's confidence, Luke took a moment to weigh his response. "We crossed paths a day's journey outside of Washington, sir. He was on foot and headed in the same general direction, so I suggested we travel together."

Cass glanced Luke's way, brows pinched as though surprised he'd tempered the details of their first encounter.

Sergeant Delmar's gaze darted between the two. "You traveled all that way with a no-account Reb who more than likely was on the run for desertion?"

The lieutenant glared at Luke. "Sort of risky on your part wasn't it, Corporal? By the looks of him, he could have waylaid you and left you to the vultures."

Cass opened his mouth as if to speak, but clamped it shut

when Luke gripped the back of his arm. "We had an understanding, sir."

The lieutenant studied Luke through close-set eyes. "So, what do you propose we do with this Rebel traveling companion of yours?"

Mustering courage, Luke drew in a breath. "He's on his way home to reunite with his family in North Carolina and needs a fresh mount to get there."

A snicker sounded from the lieutenant. "Good horses are hard to come by even for our own soldiers, and you expect me to commission one to a Johnny Reb? I think you've been on leave too long, Corporal."

Undeterred, Luke tipped his chin higher. "Maybe so, sir, but it was President Lincoln's wish to reunite our nation. What better way to marshal in peace than by aiding a Confederate soldier in need?"

Lieutenant Fowler's upper lip twitched beneath his mustache as Luke and he locked eyes. At last, he broke off his gaze and tugged at his gloves. "Well, it's against my better judgement, but I suppose it wouldn't hurt to check with the livery. See to it and report back here when you're through."

Pulling himself to full height, Luke gave an open-palm salute. "Yes, sir."

With a hasty tug of the reins, Luke motioned for Cass to follow.

Falling into step beside him, the oversized private expelled a gust of pent-up air and whispered, "Gallagher, I believe you could talk a polecat down from a tree."

Luke tossed him a sideways grin, giving the mare a pat on the neck. "A little prayer doesn't hurt either."

With a shake of his head, Cass sank his hands in his pockets. "I have a feeling it was them prayers of yours that routed me back to you in the first place. Don't know why else I'd double back."

The confession couldn't have thrilled Luke more. "I did pound on Heaven's door quite a bit on your behalf."

They fell silent, ignoring the stares of onlookers as they meandered their way along the street. When they reached the livery, Cass cleared his throat and pivoted toward Luke. "Never thought I'd say this to a Yank, but I'm obliged to ya. I'd still be foraging berries and hidin' out if it weren't for you. Doin' you a bad turn just wouldn't have set right. I'd have lived with guilt in my gullet the rest of my days."

Luke gave the private a soft slug on the arm. "Remember that next time you cross paths with someone else you're inclined not to like."

Cass gave a hearty laugh. "I'll remember."

Luke returned a satisfied nod, still amazed how the Lord had taken him and Cass from sworn enemies to distrusting companions to unlikely friends.

Hope stirred in his chest. Now if only God would work a similar transformation within Adelaide.

ADDIE OPENED her eyes to a light-drenched room, the thin bedroom curtains stirring with the gentle breeze. The nagging ache in her head that had kept her up half the night had blossomed into a full-fledged throb. Surely the headaches weren't a result of her blow to the head? Nearly a month had passed and the injury had been quick to heal.

She eased onto her back and stretched her legs out until her heels touched the footboard, mind foggy. Why hadn't Lydia awakened her?

Or had she?

Addie vaguely recalled the youngster rapping on her door at first light and speaking her name, but she'd been too tired to answer. What had she done to cause this fatigue? Even with yesterday's restful day, she couldn't seem to rally.

Perhaps this Northern air didn't agree with her.

Easing into a sitting position, she swung her legs over the side of the bed. The room began to spin, and she blinked her eyes shut. Something most definitely wasn't right. Faint voices drifted from outside her window, assuring her the others were indeed up and about. She stood on wobbly legs and ambled toward the window. From this vantage point, she could merely hear and not see who was speaking. Though she couldn't distinguish the conversation, she recognized first Mrs. Perkins and then Lydia's voice.

Heaviness pulled at Addie's limbs. Lowering her head toward the open window, she drew a deep breath. "Lydia?"

The conversation lulled, followed by the approach of soft boot steps. A moment later, her young hostess stepped into view. "You're finally awake. I couldn't rouse you earlier so let you sleep. I'll be up shortly." She lifted her arm, a silver tin clasped in her fist. "Look what Mr. Perkins sent you. Honey. He says it'll be good for your burns."

Addie managed a slow nod, light-headedness forcing her to her knees. "I ... I'm not feeling well. Could you help me back to bed?"

The smile vanished from her young friend's face. "I'll be right there."

Closing her eyes, Addie bowed her head and leaned into the windowsill. Whatever this was had her firmly in its grip. As helpless as she'd been before, she was more so now.

Was she dying?

For a brief moment the thought was almost a comfort. Death would reunite her with her father and brothers. A weak smile touched her lips. As well as the mother she'd never known. But just as quickly, a terrifying thought snatched the comfort from her.

"Whoever shall deny me before men,
him will I also deny before my Father which is in Heaven."

The Scripture pounded in her head like a gavel pronouncing sentence. She'd denied the faith she'd once clung to. Such an offense would surely separate her from, not only her family, but God and Jesus for all eternity.

Her heart leapt to her throat. Luke had been right in saying her soul wasn't ready for death.

She struggled to breathe, her mouth as dry as cotton.

Lord, help me, I must live.

I must.

29

"Was ails her, Doctor Royce?"

Martha's pointed query pierced Addie's muddled senses. She stared up at the pasty-complected doctor at her bedside, awaiting his response.

Removing his stethoscope from his ears, he sat back with a sigh. "I'm not certain. She has no fever and no sign of infection. Other than a bit of a low heart rate, I find nothing physically wrong."

He lifted Addie's eyelids one at a time. "How long have you been experiencing headaches?"

"About a week, but they've worsened over the past couple of days."

"And you've no other symptoms?"

Addie shrugged. "Just a bit of fatigue and light-headedness. I did incur a head injury in the fire. Could that be the cause?"

He examined the scar on her head. "I don't think so. Head trauma would have presented itself sooner after the incident, and the wound seems to have healed nicely."

Gently lifting one arm and then the other, he took a closer look at her burns. "This residue of white on your arms. Have you by chance been treating your burns with white lead paint?

"Yes, mixed with linseed oil."

"How long?"

His furrowed brow troubled her. "Nearly a month. Why, is that a problem?"

"Possibly."

"What is it, Doctor?" A hint of alarm told in Martha's voice.

Doctor Royce returned his stethoscope to his black bag, his mouth growing taut. "Though we're not sure why, some patients develop symptoms with long use of lead paint. Symptoms very similar to yours."

Swallowing her angst, Addie ventured the question plaguing her. "Are the symptoms ... life threatening?"

To her relief, the doctor shook his head. "Not particularly. The effects build up over time. That's why you're experiencing these symptoms weeks after treatment began."

"What should be done?" Martha's obvious concern warmed Addie.

"The paint must be stopped at once. Without its use, her symptoms should gradually subside. But we need to find an alternative method to treat the burns."

Lydia stepped toward them and held out the tin of honey. "What about this? Mr. Perkins claims honey heals burns."

To Addie's amazement, rather than scoff at the idea, the doctor's brows lifted. "Hmm. Not a bad thought. Honey does boast some healing qualities. In fact, some people swear by it."

Addie balked. "Surely there must be something better to use."

With a shrug, Doctor Royce gestured toward the tin. "Honey is available and certainly more healthful than what you've been treating with. The idea holds merit."

"Please try it, Adelaide." Lydia's eyes were pleading as she eased down onto the mattress. She truly had every confidence in her neighbor's odd remedy.

Still hesitant, Addie merely gnawed at her lip.

Doctor Royce gave her arms another glance. "Your wounds

seem to be healing rather slowly for a month's time. Let's apply the honey a couple of weeks and see what happens. Agreed?"

With a reluctant nod, Addie's mouth twisted. "I suppose it's worth a try."

The silvery-haired physician rapped his fingers on his black bag. "Good. I'll check back in a couple of weeks." He peered at her through wire-rimmed spectacles. "That is, unless you're getting no better, and I need to return sooner. But let's assume that won't be the case."

Martha smiled down at Addie. "We'll see she gets the best of care."

A strange sort of sensation coursed through Addie as she met the woman's tender gaze. She'd expected Martha and Lydia to view her as a burden, an intruder within their tranquil household —especially after discovering her lack of faith. Instead, they had accepted her and her plight with open arms, doing all they could to make her stay comfortable.

Such kindness could only stem from a sincere heart.

Martha pivoted toward Doctor Royce. "Thank you, Doctor. I'll see you out." She paused beside the bed and placed a hand under Addie's chin. "We'll have you on your feet again in no time."

Addie mustered a weak grin, embracing the comforting words. Unlike Lydia, who seemed to resent her mother's nurturing, something within Addie craved the motherly attention. Her entire life, she'd wondered what it would be to have a mother to confide in and care for her. In his own way, Papa had tried to express fondness, but had lacked the comforting aura a mother could supply. Even her short time with Aunt Polly had been characterized by aloofness rather than tenderness.

A tumult of emotions ambushed Addie's heart as she watched Martha accompany Doctor Royce to the door. She'd resolved not to like Northerners. But, like the city of Richmond, the walls around her heart were beginning to crumble.

"NEVER THOUGHT I'd see the day you'd go traipsin' around with a Johnny Reb. What got into you, Gallagher?"

Luke tugged off his boot, Sergeant Delmar's barbed comments stinging a bit. He met his superior's questioning stare, determined to be as forthright as his lesser position allowed. "I just did what I'd want a fella to do for me if I was on foot and hundreds of miles from home."

The sergeant's expression softened, a hint of a grin edging onto his lips. "I suppose I'd expect no less from you." He leaned forward, elbows on his knees, his demeanor turning somber. "You're a good man, Luke. One of the few individuals I know who really lives what he professes. Almost makes a believer out of me."

Luke stilled in mid-tug, leaving his second boot dangling half on and half off. He peered over at his companion, the evening shadows inside the tent making it difficult to discern if his words were genuine. Though honored by the sergeant's praise, it was the long-awaited confession that thrilled Luke. For nearly a year, he'd prayed for wisdom how to reach his stubborn sergeant's heart. Now, it seemed, the Lord was using a simple act of kindness to penetrate the man's hardened shell. "Almost?"

Delmar locked his fingers together in front of him and let out a sigh. "Let's just say, you've got me wondering if there's somethin' to this faith of yours."

Luke's lips lifted. He'd waited a long time for this. Stifling the urge to give a loud shout, he reached in his haversack and pulled out his Bible. "It's all in here. Everything you need to know."

The sergeant shook his head. "I can't take that. Your nose is in it every morning."

"We'll share it. I'll read mornings and you evenings." Flipping to Matthew, Luke shoved it toward his friend. "Start here in the Gospel of Matthew. Just skip all those names and start at verse eighteen with the account of Jesus' birth."

Delmar hesitated then took it from him, holding it as if it were a newborn baby he didn't know what to do with. "What if somethin' don't make sense?"

"Then just ask." Luke finished pulling off his boot and laid back on his cot. "I don't claim to have all the answers, but I'll help where I can."

The sergeant slid the lantern closer and thumbed through the stack of thin pages. "There's no way I'll get all this read by the end of the week."

Chuckling, Luke looped his hands behind his head. "What's your hurry?"

"Haven't you heard? They found Lincoln's killer a few days ago at a farm outside Port Royal, Virginia."

Luke nodded. "I read that in a Washington newspaper. Hopefully that'll squelch any thoughts of rebellion against the Union."

"Yeah well, there's more." A telling grin spilled onto Delmar's lips. "We're being deployed to Washington by week's end."

Luke jerked his head toward him. "You're not serious?"

"No foolin'. There's to be a huge parade of the armies to celebrate the end of the war. We'll likely be mustered out soon afterward." The sergeant let out a laugh. "Seems you came all this way just to turn around and head back."

A bit stunned, Luke could only gape at him. He lay back, his thoughts turning to the lush, green hillsides of his rural home, the fields awaiting planting, and the joyous faces of Ma and Lydia. No matter how much traveling he had to do, he'd not complain. So long as it meant he'd be returning home.

Another image sifted through his mind—that of a raven-haired beauty whose violet eyes and soothing voice had chiseled their way into his heart. He'd not expected to see her again, but this soon, their paths would most certainly cross. He would simply have to guard his heart and pray that, like Sergeant Delmar and Cass, the Lord would find fertile ground in which to sow His truths.

30

Friday, May 5, 1865

Martha set the tin of honey and clean strips of cloth on the dresser and pulled the chair up beside Addie's bed. "How are you feeling this morning?"

Sitting up, Addie smiled over at her. "Better. My headache is much more tolerable."

"I'm pleased to hear it." Martha began peeling back the thin layer of honey-soaked cloth around Addie's arm. "Hal and Celia will be thrilled as well. They've asked about you more than once."

Recalling her harsh attitude toward the couple, Addie hung her head. "I suppose I owe them a thank you. Their remedy seems to be working."

"It does at that." Martha pulled away the bandage and examined the burns. "Your arms look better every day."

Addie glanced at the white and pink blotches of skin. Though still unsightly, her arms looked less angry than they had days earlier. She bent them at the elbow. "I can tell a definite improvement in movement. They aren't nearly as stiff."

With a grin, Martha reached for the tin of honey. "I'll be sure to tell Hal and Celia. I'm certain they'll be by again to check on you."

Addie swiveled her legs over the side of the bed, letting her arms drop to her sides, "I don't see why they should care about me." Especially after the standoffish way she'd treated them.

Martha paused and touched a hand to Addie's cheek. "We all care, Adelaide. The Lord, included."

Pricked by the comment, Addie bit the inside of her cheek. She thought she had Northern folks figured out. Now, she wasn't so sure. They were all so confusing. Why should any of them concern themselves with her?

Why should God?

And yet, she could sense the genuineness in Martha's eyes. She truly did care, as did Lydia and Luke. Why else would they sacrifice so much on her account?

Papa had often said God had a plan for her, that He loved and watched over her no matter where she was or what she went through. Was it possible God hadn't willed her father and brothers to die? That she'd placed blame on Him that rightly belonged to the war and fallen world? Did He truly love her even though she'd spurned Him?

It certainly seemed He'd been blessing her since coming to this compassionate home.

Her chin quivered. Since Luke had pulled her from the ruins.

Mrs. Perkins' familiar hum sounded outside the window, breaking through Addie's ponderings.

Martha reached for the strips of cloth. "That sounds like Celia now. Let me get you bandaged and dressed, then I'll go give her your message."

Blinking moisture from her eyes, Addie caught her companion by the arm. "If I may, I'd like to thank her in person."

Martha smiled. "She'd like that."

In that instant, something broke free within Addie. And though she wasn't certain what to make of it, for the first time since her father and brothers had died, she sensed her heart begin to open.

———

Richmond
May 5, 1865

LUKE SECURED his haversack and took one last sweeping glance around Richmond. Mere days after his return, he was leaving the ruined city.

For good.

This time on foot.

Excitement vibrated through the group of soldiers like children on Christmas morning. Ninety-five miles lay between them and their nation's capital, which made Luke a bit envious of Cass's good fortune to have been supplied a horse for the remainder of his trip.

By now, his friend was likely back at home in the loving arms of his wife. Would he remember their venture and someday tell his children the story of how he'd shared meals around a campfire and ridden into Richmond astride the same horse with a Union soldier? He snickered at the thought, fully intending to share the tale with his offspring—should he be blessed to have any.

Sergeant Delmar stepped up beside him, staring at the mass of gutted buildings. "Well, Gallagher, sounds like this is it. Can't say I'm sorry to leave."

With a shake of his head, Luke cast him a sideways glance. "Me either. Just wish we could've left Richmond in better shape."

The sergeant widened his stance, crossing his arms over his chest. "She's better off than when we found her, but you're right. These poor folks still have a heap of work t' do before the place is back on her feet."

The downtrodden expressions of the Richmond onlookers robbed Luke's moment of joy. "What'll become of these people?"

"Likely the government will step in and help 'em out. They may not go along with some of the changes, but they'll manage."

The words were little comfort when Luke considered the thought of Adelaide someday returning and making Richmond her home. This was no place for a young woman alone. If he could only convince her of that. But the girl had a mind of her own.

And plans that didn't include him.

31

Gallagher Home
Wednesday, May 10, 1865

A ddie strolled alongside Lydia, breathing in the morning air. Days of being cooped up inside from lack of energy made a walk through the countryside exceptionally inviting. Though the surrounding fields had grown more weed-infested since her arrival, the vastness of the lavish, hilly landscape captivated her.

Lydia shook her head. "Papa would be mortified to see the fields in such a state. I only hope Drew and Luke return in time to put in a crop."

Addie had to admit, even at this stage, that would take some doing.

The rumble of a buggy drew their attention further down the worn path. A trail of dust announced its speedy approach. "My but someone's in a hurry," Lydia exclaimed. Her eyes widened as the buggy came into full view. "Why that's Mr. Perkins' rig, and Mama's with him. Something must be wrong."

Addie struggled to keep pace as Lydia sprinted down the path toward the buggy. With labored breaths, Addie trotted along behind, her mind filled with troubled thoughts. Had something happened to Luke? She spurred herself faster, arms hugging her chest.

But as they neared, Martha's expression was one of joy, not sadness. She waved her arm in the air, a letter clasped in her gloved hand. "A letter from Luke!"

An elated Lydia pressed her hands together, bobbing up and down as Mr. Perkins tugged the horse to a stop beside them. "Is he coming home?"

"Not yet." Martha took Mr. Perkins' offered hand down and slid her basket of goods from the floor of the buggy. "Thank you for the ride, Hal."

"My pleasure. And I can't think of a better piece o' news t' give Celia." With a tip of his hat, he slapped the reins down, spurring his horse into a steady trot.

Moisture pooled in Martha's eyes as she turned toward Addie and Lydia. "Luke's heading to Washington. There's to be a Grand Review of the Armies on the twenty-third. He wants us to meet him there a few days prior and attend the festivities." She swallowed as if struggling to catch her breath. "Soon afterward, he'll come home to stay."

A nervous twinge worked through Addie. She'd not expected him so soon. Part of her rejoiced at the thought. The rest of her quivered as she recalled the tender way he'd looked at her when they parted.

The way she'd looked at *him*.

Lydia's jaw slackened. "That's less than two weeks away. Oh, I can hardly wait."

Pressing the letter to her chest, Martha's gaze settled on Addie. "He wants all of us to attend."

The words coiled their way around Addie's throat, threatening to choke off her air. Attend a parade celebrating Union victory? Never. To endorse such an event would be like turning her back on her family. Her very existence. She clenched her jaw, averting her gaze to the hem of her dress. "I'm sorry. I don't wish to offend, but I could never attend such a celebration."

The slight hesitation and exhaled breath hinted the words were not ones Martha had hoped to hear. "We'll speak of it later. For now, I wish to relish the news at least one son will soon be home."

"What about Drew?" Lydia's query pierced Addie's fogged mind, and her eyes lifted.

Martha shook her head. "Nothing just yet, but Luke did say he might be detained."

A giggle sounded from Lydia. "Oh, yes. A *girl*. She must be quite something to catch Drew's eye. I wonder if we'll meet her."

"Never mind all that." Her voice still tinged with excitement, Martha's reprimand held little sternness. She returned her gaze to Addie, her expression sobering. "Luke included a note for you, Adelaide."

A burst of heat flamed in Addie's cheeks. Luke had written *her*? Though she longed to know what message the note contained, reading it in private sounded more appealing. "Could you take it to my room?"

"Certainly." Martha gave a brisk nod, then paused. "Oh, by the way, Adelaide, I ran into Doctor Royce in town. He inquired about you, and I told him you were faring much better. He intends to be out early next week to check on you."

Early next week. That allowed a few more days to strengthen her limbs. If she could prove herself capable to Doctor Royce, Martha would almost certainly allow her to stay.

But right now, reading Luke's note was foremost on her mind.

LUKE TOOK a swig from his canteen, the noontime sun beating down on him. Lifting his kepi, he swiped a hand over his dampened brow and stared out ahead of him to the company of exhausted, yet eager, soldiers. More than halfway to Washington, with still dozens of miles to go. Somehow knowing this was their final march made the long journey a bit less taxing.

A wave of nervousness coursed through him. Nearly two weeks had passed since he'd posted his letter. By now it must have reached home. How had Adelaide responded to his note? He gritted his teeth. He should never have disclosed his feelings so openly. Would she resent him? Worse yet was the thought Ma might read the note.

Would she?

He'd know soon enough. Even if she hadn't, she had a way of seeing right through to his core.

"Won't be long now, huh, Gallagher?"

Luke glanced to see Sergeant Delmar peering out over the sea of soldiers, his mop of blond hair protruding from beneath his kepi. "Sounds that way."

Delmar crossed his arms, his sleeves tight against firm muscles. "I can't count the number of times I almost didn't survive this war. First thing I'm gonna do when I get home is drop down and kiss the ground. Seein' as I've no one better t' kiss."

Luke smothered a grin. "I know what you mean." He popped the cap back on his canteen, gazing over the war-torn men. "When you consider all who lost their lives, those of us who remain need to count ourselves blessed."

Seeming not to hear, the sergeant's eyes glazed over. "Fellows fell left and right all around me, while I just kept a goin'. Yes sir, I figure God must have some purpose in lettin' me live."

Stunned such a comment would originate from his sergeant, Luke gaped at him. "He must at that."

The hue in the sergeant's face deepened as he shot a glance at Luke and lowered his voice. "I've, uh, been readin' that Bible you loaned me. Some of it's sort of hard to grasp, but I think I'm gettin' the gist of it."

Luke stood taller, overjoyed by the confession. "That's good to hear."

The sergeant raked a hand over his jaw. "Never thought I'd see the day I'd read the Good Book of my own accord. Never been one for religion. But then, I've not been around someone so bent on gettin' me saved as you neither."

A smile edged across Luke's lips as he gave a mock salute. "Glad to oblige, Sergeant. But I think the Lord's nudging had more to do with it than I did."

The command to press forward rippled through the regiment of soldiers, bringing the conversation to an abrupt end. Luke's step was a bit lighter as he took his place beside the men. They had more ground to cover.

As did Sergeant Delmar.

32

Addie stared at the note laying unfolded, face down on the quilt. She tried to convince herself Martha had opened it out of convenience, knowing Addie's rigid fingers could not manage the delicate paper. Still, she wondered if her hostess read its message. She wouldn't blame Martha if she had. Addie was no match for Luke. They were from two different worlds.

She reached for the letter, noting the handsome writing. Fine penmanship for a man. *Miss Adelaide,* it read in bold letters. Awkwardly, she flipped it over and spun it toward her. With unsteady breaths, she read the opening lines, imagining Luke's masculine voice saying the words.

Dear Adelaide,

> *I hope you are finding rest and healing in Ma and Lydia's care. Hopefully Lydia hasn't pestered you too badly. She can talk the ears off a stalk of corn if given half a chance.*

Addie smothered a grin. He knew his sister well.

> *Only days after my return to Richmond, I was astounded to*

learn we were to travel to Washington before the month's end and soon be mustered out of the army. I know you will likely balk at the idea of attending the parade.

She arched a brow. He knew her as well.

But regardless, I hope you will come. I don't wish you to feel uncomfortable, but more so, I want you to be looked after and cared for. And I wish to see you.

Warmth radiated through her as she read the endearing words again and again. She curled her feet up under her on the bed, the thought of Luke unraveling her. Yet, to be honest, she was just as eager to see him.

But not even *he* could persuade her to make the trip to Washington.

A nervous tingle rippled through her. If she were able, she would leave this place and be on her way to find Clarissa. And yet, something about Luke and his family drew her like a magnet. The terrors of Richmond and the war seemed far away here, like a nightmarish dream that had vanished with the light of morn.

Her feelings for Luke baffled her. One moment, she wished never to see him again; the next, she longed never to be apart from him. His soothing presence conflicted with the life she'd envisioned. This temporary haven—however pleasant—could not undo the person she was. Her roots were in the South, and that is where she belonged.

Her *and* Clarissa.

No matter the girl's uncertain origin, they were family, bound together by blood. No one could negate that fact.

The letter's final lines tugged at her concentration, pulling her back to the page.

I realize you blame God for your hardships, but look at all the good He's done. He allowed you to be found amid a heap of rubble when others did not survive. He ensured you received medical care and that you were supplied a safe place to heal.

I can't undo the pains of your past, but if you'll allow Him, the Lord can heal your wounded heart. Despite our differences, I miss you, Adelaide.

Respectfully, Luke

The words left Addie fidgety and unsettled, like a child forced to sit when she wanted to play. In truth, she missed him as well. It was typical of Luke to see God at work in the midst of trouble, while she gleaned only pain and sorrow. They were on different planes where the Lord was concerned.

She lay back on the bed with a sigh. Which was exactly why they could never be together.

A tap on the bedroom door brought her back to a sitting position. "Come in."

The door widened and Martha peered in. "I'm not intruding, am I?"

"No, not at all." She made an awkward attempt to flip the letter over. Only managing to crinkle it.

Venturing closer, Martha smiled. "Have I given you time to read Luke's letter?"

Addie glanced down at the note then back to Martha. Did she already know what it said ... or would she seek to find out? "Yes. I finished just now."

To Addie's relief, her hostess made no attempt to glance at the letter. "May I sit?"

With a nod, Addie slid the page behind her to make room, confident this was more than a mere social visit.

Easing onto the bed, Martha locked her fingers together in her lap. "Have you been comfortable staying with us, Adelaide?"

"Yes. You've both been very kind."

With a prolonged breath, Martha glanced around the small bedroom, eyes filled with remembrances as they paused on various items of Luke's—the daguerreotype of him and his brother and Lydia as youths, the pair of worn boots resting against the wall, and the oak trunk at the foot of the bed.

Her smile deepened. "What a joy to think of Luke returning home soon. It seems but a short time ago I was tucking him into bed and reading him stories. Now, he's a grown man. How I wish time didn't pass so quickly."

The tension in Addie's shoulders eased as she witnessed Martha's love for her son. Would her mother have loved her as much? She swallowed. "I suppose he'll be needing his room back."

Martha gave a gentle sigh. "I'm sorry for the inconvenience. I didn't expect him to return so soon." She leaned toward Addie with a grin. "Though, I'm not complaining, mind you. Andrew's room will do just as nicely. And when he returns, we'll simply move you in with Lydia."

A sense of relief trickled through Addie. Martha's hospitality seemed to know no bounds. Though still intent on finding Clarissa, it comforted Addie to know she was welcome to stay as long as necessary.

"Now." Martha's pat on the leg reclaimed Addie's focus. "Let's discuss this trip to Washington."

The relaxed conversation gave Addie courage to speak her mind. "Please don't ask me to go. I don't wish to disappoint Luke or cause anyone grief, but I can't bring myself to do it. Truly."

"I understand, dear, but consider at least traveling there with us. If you don't wish to attend the festivities, we'll all understand. But with you unable to function on your own, I don't see any way around you going."

Addie sat straighter, determined. "I'm gaining more use of my arms every day. Perhaps given time, my hands will follow."

A shroud of doubt overshadowed Martha's features. "Even so,

we'd be gone several days. You could never manage so long on your own."

"I will. Somehow." She leaned forward, voice pleading. "It's nearly two weeks until you leave. Please. Allow me that time to mend and prove myself capable."

The creases at the corners of Martha's mouth deepened. "All right, Adelaide. If you feel that strongly, we'll wait and see how you're faring when the time nears. But I suspect Luke will be disappointed if we leave you behind. He seems to have grown quite fond of you."

Heat singed Addie's cheeks. Had Luke conveyed that knowledge in the letter to his mother, or had she indeed read the note intended for Addie? She moistened her lips, pushing aside her reservations. "Then he'll understand why I can't come."

Martha studied her with a focused gaze and then flashed a lopsided grin that so resembled Luke's it nearly melted Addie's heart. "I suppose he'll have to ... *if* you're able when the time comes."

With a resolute smile, Addie eased back. Though it felt odd to have a woman she'd known only a short time guiding her decisions, Martha plainly wanted what was best for her.

Like a mother would.

The thought warmed Addie. Rather than resent the boundaries being imposed upon her, they seemed almost a comfort. A hedge of protection leaving her feeling safe, valued. Papa had been rather lenient in her growing up years. Probably too lenient. Allowing her to wade through her own choices— good and bad. As had Aunt Polly.

But regardless of Martha's good intentions, Addie could never concede to going.

33

Washington D.C.
Friday, May 12, 1865

"You ever see such a hoard of soldiers, Corporal?" Private Cummings gawked at the slew of Union soldiers and pup tents peppering the outskirts of Washington. "There must be nigh onto fifty or sixty thousand."

Stepping up beside him, Luke shook his head then nodded toward the company approaching on their left. "And more on the way, it appears."

"Is this all of us, the entire Federal army?"

Luke shook his head. "Only a fragment of the Army of the Potomac. Sherman's troops are setting up camp across the Potomac at Fort Runyon."

Sergeant Delmar moved to the front of the men and barked out instructions, his tone and expression firm. "Secure your tents, then the remainder of the day ... you're free to spend at your own choosing." A moment of stunned silence followed, then excited shouts burst from the soldiers. Bone-weary after long months of skirmishes and being on the go, the privates seemed to find renewed strength in the afternoon of liberty.

Private Fenton tipped his kepi higher on his head. "You mean we can go into town? Do whatever we want?"

Delmar's rigid expression softened. "I'd say we're all due for a bit of free time after what we've been through. We'll tackle preparations for the parade startin' tomorrow." He crossed his arms, his bushy brows drawn together. "But watch yourselves. Remember, you're not mustered out of the army yet."

"Yes, sir." With that, the husky private let out a holler and scurried after the others already unpacking their tents.

Luke shared a wide grin with the sergeant. "Never seen him move so fast."

"Funny what the right motivation will do."

Leaning on his musket barrel, Luke surveyed the vast swarm of soldiers darkening the landscape. Was his big brother among them? If so, he'd likely never find him in such a multitude. At least their chance meeting in Richmond assured him Drew had survived the war.

Their father's death still stung deep. His absence left a huge hole in their family. Especially for Ma. It would be tough to fill his shoes in a number of ways, not least of all keeping up the farm. This late in the season, Drew and he would have a lot of catching up to do in the fields.

He squelched a grin. Hopefully, Drew's lady friend wouldn't delay him too long.

Luke's gaze shifted to the city beyond, to the newly completed Capitol dome and the partially constructed Washington Monument. Here, for the first time, the army of the Potomac would converge with Sherman's Western armies for a Grand Review, parading through the streets before scads of onlookers. Including the newly appointed President Johnson and other top officials.

And yet, it was his family Luke ached to see. His family ... and Adelaide. Try as he might, he couldn't stop hoping she would come. But, deep down, he knew she wouldn't.

Her embittered heart wouldn't let her.

Which, to be honest, was probably for the best. The less time spent with her, the less temptation he'd have to let his fondness deepen.

Gallagher Home
May 12, 1865

"Remarkable." Dr. Royce gently twisted Addie's arm side to side. "You've made great strides these past couple of weeks." He sat back in the bedside chair, his eyes expressing deep satisfaction. "And how are you feeling now?"

Addie cut a glance at Martha and Lydia standing just inside the doorway. "Much better, thank you." Even if she weren't, she would have feigned improvement. Anything to convince Martha to let her stay.

"Good. Apparently, Hal's honey did the trick." Removing his wire-rimmed spectacles, the doctor smiled at her. "Your arms have improved to the point I think you can safely go without your trappings."

A flurry of mixed emotions bombarded Addie. While eager to rid herself of the bothersome dressings, the thought of baring the hideous scars left her queasy. Though sleeves would hide the ugliness of her arms, her rigid, stippled hands were certain to draw unwanted attention.

She stretched out leathery palms. "What about my hands? They're too misshapen to fit into gloves, and I can barely manage the simplest of tasks."

With furrowed brow, the doctor reached to examine her fingers. At last, he held out his palms, slender and smooth for a man's. "Try gripping my hands."

Hesitant, Addie stared at him.

"Go on," he coaxed. "Give them a squeeze."

She slid her hands under his, her marred flesh experiencing

little sensation of warmth or softness of touch. Concentrating, she willed her fingers to curl around his. Her hands quivered as she worked to tighten her hold, barely able to apply any pressure before dropping her hands to the mattress. "I can't."

He placed a comforting hand on her shoulder. "Have patience. Your nerves and muscles were badly damaged. Keep exercising your fingers. In time, they'll regain some of their agility."

"Some?" Addie's stomach lurched. "But not all?"

Doctor Royce scratched at his pallid cheek with a sigh. "I'm afraid the damage might be too extensive to regain full use. But one never knows. Time does have a way of healing wounds."

Addie's lower lip trembled. Time would not heal *her* wounds. She was scarred in body and spirit with no one dear to share her sorrows. Nor would there be. What man would want to look upon such unsightly blemishes?

No. Her disfigurements had destined her to a lifetime of loneliness. Unwanted and unloved.

Luke's handsome features invaded her thoughts. Though he seemed to think something of her, he deserved someone attractive. Not an undesirable woman laden with scars.

Doctor Royce patted her arm. "Keep your spirits up, young lady. You should be quite pleased with the improvements you've made."

True. Her progress had heightened since she'd arrived— thanks to Martha and Lydia and, she supposed, Mr. Perkins. But not enough to suit her. She mustered a shallow grin. "Thank you, Doctor. I will."

He stood and pivoted toward Martha and Lydia, his diminutive frame barely eye level with theirs. "You're taking excellent care of her, ladies. Keep challenging her. Let her grip your hands as I've done or squeeze something pliant to gain muscle strength."

"Like a cow udder?" Lydia spurted, taking a step closer.

With a chuckle, Doctor Royce lifted his doctor's bag. "Why

yes. Milking is an excellent suggestion. It may prove difficult at first, but the steady rhythm would be helpful, and it wouldn't require meticulous use of her fingers."

Addie nearly groaned out loud. Her young friend seemed determined to engage her in the distasteful activity. But then, Penny would need milked each day Martha and Lydia were away. Her mind reeled. If she practiced, perhaps she could use that as a reason to stay behind.

Sitting taller, Addie peered over at Lydia. "When can we start?"

ADDIE FLOPPED down at the supper table with a dispirited sigh. The aroma of baked ham and mashed potatoes wafted up, stirring her appetite, but doing little to squelch her disappointment.

Sliding onto the chair across from her, Lydia peered at her with meek eyes. "Don't be discouraged, Adelaide. Dr. Royce said it would take time."

"Time is what I don't have." The disgruntled words slipped out before Addie could prevent them.

Eyeing her, Martha draped a napkin over her lap. "I take it the evening milk session didn't go well?"

With a frustrated huff, Addie slumped back in her chair, the spindles creaking under the added pressure. "I can't even wrap my hands around tight enough to grip."

In characteristic calmness, Martha folded her hands on the table and released a long breath. "If your heart is so set on not going to Washington, why don't I ask Mrs. Perkins if she would come stay with you while we're away?"

Addie shot forward in her chair, the thought disconcerting. "Oh no. That's not necessary."

Martha's brow creased. "But you just said ..."

"Well, perhaps a bit of help with the milking wouldn't hurt, but there'd be no need for her to stay with me. I'd manage somehow." Addie interjected.

"But there is so much you're unable to do. How will you cook or tend to your personal needs? I wouldn't feel right leaving without someone to watch over you."

Addie gnawed at her lower lip. Plainly Martha was as unswerving on the matter as her. They would simply have to compromise. "We still have a few days. I'll work at doing more on my own. Perhaps Mrs. Perkins could simply stop by morning and evening to milk and check on me."

Martha's pale blue eyes sparked of approval. Her chin dipped. "Fair enough. We'll see how these next few days go and take it from there."

With an affirming nod, Addie eased back in her chair. She'd won the battle.

The question was, would she be able to accomplish what she professed?

———

SERGEANT DELMAR NUDGED Luke on the arm. "What say we head into town and have a look around?"

Luke tested the tension in the tent string one last time then turned to his superior. He'd had no time for sightseeing on his last visit. It would be nice to take in a few of the city's sights this time around. "I'm all in. Let's go."

The entire city was astir as they made their way onto the bustling streets of Washington. Reminders of the still grieving citizens were everywhere—in the flags flying at half-staff, the black crepe ribbons adorning the windows and pillars of buildings, and myriad woman dressed in black with no one at their side.

"You see much of this place when you were here before?"

"Only the Willard Hotel and the train depot." Luke dodged

the onslaught of soldiers and pedestrians crowding the walkways. "It wasn't nearly this busy then."

"We'll never get anywhere this way." The sergeant paused and took a glance around. Raising his voice a notch, he gestured down a side street. "Let's head this way."

With a nod, Luke started after him, eager to leave the frenzied thoroughfare behind. "I hate to think how overcrowded this place will be in another week."

A jeweler's storefront caught his eye, and he slowed to a stop before the array of gold pocket watches, rings, and sparkly necklaces in the window. He'd never taken notice of such finery before, had never even stepped foot inside a jewelry store. And yet, he perused the display of shiny gold and silver pieces. Searching.

At last, his eyes latched on what he unwittingly sought and an uneasy twinge surged through him.

He sensed someone at his shoulder, harried breaths sounding in his ear. "What's of interest?"

Luke shifted his feet, unwilling to venture a glance at his superior. "I need to stop in here a minute. You go on. I'll catch up."

Delmar let out a grunt. "You can't be serious. We'd never meet up again in this mass of people."

"Then hold up a minute. I'll be right back."

"Why? You've got a pocket watch and you say you have no girl, so what are you after?"

Luke gripped the door latch. If he shared his reason, the sergeant would never let him live it down. "Just wait here."

Ignoring the sergeant's agitated huff, Luke pushed the door open, causing the bell above to jingle. Short on cash, he wasn't sure he could even afford the item. Even if he could, it would leave him with little to nothing until his next pay.

But in his mind, it would be money well spent.

34

Gallagher Home
Thursday, May 18, 1865

"You did it!"

"Nicely done, Adelaide."

A wide grin etched across Addie's lips, Lydia and Martha's words of encouragement a sweet melody in her ears. She'd labored long and hard to gain enough control of her hand to hold a utensil and actually bring food to her mouth. Perhaps her daily attempts at milking had done some good after all.

While her fingers still lacked the dexterity to feed herself without making a mess of the table or her dress, every improvement was a step toward freedom.

Freedom to tend to her own needs.

Freedom to live life again.

Hope welled within her as she chewed the small forkful of potatoes. In time, she was determined to not only master feeding herself, but buttoning and unbuttoning her dress, and pinning her own hair. But for now, she would be content to convince Martha she was capable of managing on her own. At least for a few days. Surely, she could survive that long without constantly being watched after.

Setting her fork down, she swallowed the bite of food. "So have I convinced you I won't starve while you're away?"

"Perhaps." Martha's azure eyes twinkled. "Though you're liable to lose a pound or two of your already slender frame by the time we return."

With a teasing grin, Addie leaned in closer. "Well, if I do, I promise to make up for it once you return."

Chuckling, Martha touched a hand to Addie's shoulder. "I'll hold you to that, dear."

Unaccustomed to such tenderness, Addie tensed. For weeks, she'd endured the pokes and prods of nurses and doctors as a patient. But, as she met Martha's gaze and viewed the warmth in her eyes, something within her melted.

She blinked, the full gist of Martha's words sinking in. "Then you're agreeable to me staying?"

Nodding, Martha let her hand fall away. "I spoke with Celia yesterday. She and Hal have agreed to check in with you mornings and evenings when they come to milk Penny. Basil and the horses can tend to themselves. I'll leave you an assortment of food, and I wouldn't be a bit surprised if Celia doesn't shower you with some of her own."

The welcome news bubbled inside Addie like fresh spring water. Resisting the urge to hug Martha, she merely smiled. "Thank you. When do you leave?"

"First thing Saturday morning. Luke said in his telegram Washington is quite overrun with visitors and thought it best we arrive a few days ahead of time. We'll return late in the day on Thursday."

Mention of Luke stirred unwanted feelings within Addie. She gave a slow nod, tamping down the ache to see him. "Will ... Luke be with you?"

Martha sat back, moistening her lips. "Unfortunately, no. He's not certain when he'll be home. But soon."

They held each other's gaze as if attempting to decipher one another's thoughts. Addie had a feeling Martha understood her heart better than Addie knew it herself. She glanced at her half-filled plate. Both knew she wasn't deserving of Luke.

They were North and South. Faith-filled and faith-less.

What the Bible called "unequally yoked."

Though, thanks to Luke and his family, Addie had come to the realization not all Northerners were bad, she couldn't entirely let go of her deep-seated bitterness toward the North ... or God.

The time alone would be good for her, if for no other reason than to clear her head. She needed to prepare herself for Luke's return, lest she go weak in the knees the moment she set eyes on him.

That would never do.

They were friends. Nothing more.

To hope otherwise would only break one—or both—of their hearts.

"WHEN WILL YOUR KINFOLK ARRIVE?"

"Day after tomorrow." Luke rubbed the cloth along his rifle barrel outside the tent, trying to look and sound indifferent, while inwardly teeming with eagerness. In less than forty-eight hours Ma, Lydia, and hopefully Adelaide would arrive by train, making him all the more eager to return home.

"You better hope you can find 'em in that mob of people. The city's so cluttered with civilians, I don't see how there'll be room for us soldiers."

"Oh, I'll find them all right." Nothing could keep him from it. He stopped polishing and stared at the sergeant. "How about you? Do you have family coming?"

Delmar leaned back on the stump he was seated on and stretched out his legs, crossing them at the ankles. "Nah. I've no one but my folks, and they're too feeble to battle this crowd. Didn't even ask. I'll surprise 'em when I get home."

With a nod, Luke returned to polishing his gun stock.

"Say, ain't you got that gun spiffed up yet? You're gonna rub the shine right off."

Luke flashed a mischievous grin. "Gotta do General Meade proud in front of the President and General Grant. Not to mention the host of onlookers."

Sergeant Delmar shook his head, his gaze flicking to the bulge in Luke's pocket. "Say, you never did tell me what you bought at the jewelers."

The question was one Luke had hoped to escape. He eyeballed his Springfield, doing his best to cloak his response. "Didn't know I needed to."

The sergeant looped his hands behind his head. "Aah ha! I knew it. You're holding out on me. You've a girl and aren't sayin'."

Heat rose in Luke's cheeks, and he rubbed harder at the polished metal. If he relayed the truth, Sergeant Delmar was sure to twist the facts and make more of the situation than necessary. Better to keep the man guessing than bare all. He shot the sergeant a furtive glance. "My mother and sister are coming. What makes you think it isn't for one of them?"

The moment of hesitation assured him he'd given Delmar something to consider, but the sergeant soon broke the quiet with a soft snicker. "I might believe that if your face wasn't so red."

Luke's hands stilled, the sergeant's perceptive grin piercing his defenses. He should have known he'd give himself away. Might as well fess up ... at least to a point. "All right. It's a gift for the girl injured in the fire."

Sergeant Delmar's eyebrows shot up. "That pretty little filly? That's right. She went to stay with your family while she recouped. No wonder you're eager to get home."

"She's no sweetheart. Only a friend."

Delmar's smile deepened. "Uh-huh. And I'm next in line for the presidency." He chuckled. "Ha! You couldn't fool a three-year-old child with that honest face of yours."

With a heavy sigh, Luke leaned his rifle against the corner of the tent. If the sergeant didn't hold rank over him, he'd give him something to think about besides pestering. But as that wasn't an option, Luke snatched up his uniform jacket and plopped his kepi atop his head. "Think I'll go for a walk."

"Ah now, don't go off sore. I was only teasin'."

Donning his jacket, Luke weaved his way through the myriad soldiers, more angry with himself than the sergeant. He could take being teased about a lot of things, but his heart wasn't one of them.

Especially when his faith and his emotions were at odds.

The sounds of laughter and music faded as he reached the outskirts of camp, his dew-soaked brogans swishing in the tall grass. He paused, the vibrant evening sky morphing to deep blue. Raising his eyes heavenward, he glimpsed the first glittering stars of evening.

With a cleansing breath, he pushed aside his agitation and soaked in the chatter of nightlife. Nothing quieted his spirit as much as being surrounded by nature. The thousands of flickering campfires dotting the landscape didn't hold a candle to the splendor of God's creation.

Luke could think more clearly out here. Alone with God.

He fingered the small box in his pocket, Adelaide's delicate features invading his thoughts. His intentions were pure. The gift, one of friendship not romance. Hopefully she'd see it that way. And yet, he'd be fooling himself not to admit he wished for something deeper. Would being around her again only make things worse? The thought left him ill-at-ease.

Keeping his distance would be his best bet.

Though, Lord help him, it wouldn't be easy.

35

Gallagher Home
Saturday, May 20, 1865, Dawn

"I wish you were coming with us. I worry about you here alone."

Lydia's sweet admission tore at Addie's resolve. "I'll be fine. Really."

They shared a brief hug then parted with a smile. The morning sun barely crested the horizon as the driver helped Lydia onto the buggy seat. "I'll tell Luke *hello* for you."

Addie nodded, that all too familiar flutter churning inside her. She had better get a handle on that before his arrival.

Slipping on her gloves, Martha cast a quick glance toward Addie. "Celia will be by this evening to milk Penny and check on you. There are corncakes, syrup, milk, and berries in the kitchen for breakfast and fresh bread and smoked ham for dinner." She paused, shoulders sloping downward as her gaze settled more fully on Addie. "Are you certain you're up to this?"

Touched by her concern, Addie grinned. "Don't worry. I'll manage."

The tension in Martha's face eased, and she brushed a loose strand of hair from Addie's brow. "Of course you will. And if you need anything at all, Mr. and Mrs. Perkins are just down the road."

Addie nodded and leaned into Martha's unexpected embrace. The older woman held her close, giving her torso a gentle squeeze. Not since Addie was a young child had she been embraced so tenderly. When she'd fallen from her pony and her father whisked her up in his arms and quieted her sobs by gently wiping tears and dampened hair from her cheeks. Over and over, he'd kissed her forehead, his masculine voice soothing her with soft words. *"You're safe now, sweet Adelaide. Papa has you. Don't cry, child."*

A long-forgotten feeling of love and security enveloped her as Martha whispered in her ear, "God be with you, Adelaide."

Addie closed her eyes, drinking in the indescribable sense of belonging. Her throat thickened. Somehow, she didn't even mind the reference to God. Martha's faith was as genuine as Luke's, and her words were heartfelt ones.

With a soft pat, Martha loosened her hold and stepped back. "We'll send a telegram to let you know we arrived safely. I've arranged for Hal to retrieve it for you."

The woman's thoughtfulness knew no bounds. Addie blinked back moisture. "Thank you. Have a nice time."

She touched a hand to Addie's cheek, her own eyes damp. "Goodbye, dear."

"Goodbye." Addie could hardly squeeze out the word, emotion robbing her of speech.

The driver offered Martha a hand up, then turned the hired buggy in the direction from which he'd come.

Addie responded to their waves with an awkward one of her own. A surge of loneliness spilled over her as the buggy faded into the distance. She inhaled a determined breath. If she could manage this place a few days, independence was not far off. Weeks earlier, the thought would have invigorated her. Now, the closer the time for leaving became, the more it frightened her. Where would she go? She still had no notion of how to locate Clarissa. How would she fund her travels or have money to live on?

She stared at her damaged fingers. Who would hire her with such distorted hands? What sort of job could she even do?

But one question plagued more than any other—how could she bear to leave this family who'd taken her in as one of their own?

B & O Railroad Depot
Washington D.C.
May 20, 1865, 4 p.m.

THE LOCOMOTIVE'S BRASH whistle announced its approach, stirring Luke from the granite pillar he leaned against inside the elaborate railroad station. The passenger train braked to a stop, the screech of metal on metal cutting through the flurry of activity. Shouldering his way closer, Luke craned his neck to see past the hoard of people gathering to load and greet travelers.

His eyes darted from one stream of exiting passengers to another, with no sign of either his mother or sister.

Had they missed the train?

He wiped moist palms on his trousers. Or maybe Adelaide *had* come and they were waiting for the crowd to clear to avoid the risk of someone jarring her injured arms. By now, he hoped she had at least regained some use of her limbs.

Minutes passed and the crowd began to thin. Surely, he hadn't misread Ma's telegram. He slid his hand in his pocket to retrieve the message, and his fingers snagged against the jewelry box. He swallowed. Would Adelaide take the gift for more than what it was intended? Worse yet, would she be offended?

He couldn't worry about that now. He had his family to locate.

As he slipped the telegram from his pocket, a familiar voice called his name. Glancing up, he spied Lydia at the train's top step, face aglow, hand lifted in greeting. She motioned to someone behind her, and his mother emerged, her blue eyes sparking when she glanced his way. Shoving the missive back in his pocket, he waved and started toward them.

With careful steps, the pair descended, arms laden with baggage. Luke's gaze shifted to the person behind them, and his shoulders drooped.

No Adelaide.

Pushing aside his disappointment, Luke rushed to meet them. With a giddy laugh, Lydia dropped her satchel and flung her arms around his neck. He braced himself against the unbridled lunge and twirled her around in his arms. Setting her on the pavement, he drank in her thinning face and long, golden hair framed by a navy-blue bonnet. "You're prettier and more grown up every time I see you."

A shy smile hovered on her lips as she rested her hands on the front of his uniform jacket. "It's only been a few weeks. Surely, I haven't changed that much."

"Seems longer."

Ma dropped her things and leaned for a warm embrace. Luke kissed her on the cheek. "So good to see you again, Ma. I was beginning to wonder if you'd missed your train."

"Just some difficulty retrieving our baggage. How are you, son?"

"Better now that home isn't far away." Luke took a casual glance around, unable to flout the sting of disappointment. "Adelaide didn't come, huh?"

His mother arched a brow. "Are you surprised?"

"Not really." All at once, the box grew weightier in his pocket. He'd hoped to give the trinket to her in person. Now he had little choice but to send it home with Ma and Lydia. "Who's looking after her?"

The two shared a look before Ma answered. "Hal and Celia are checking on her and helping out where needed, but, for the most part, she's looking after herself."

Luke nearly choked on his tongue. "But she can't handle ..."

Ma raised a hand to silence him. "She's come a long way in a short while. You'd be amazed how well she's doing."

Lydia grinned up at him. "She's even trying to milk Penny. Though, I admit, she hasn't quite got the knack of it."

Unconvinced, Luke shifted his feet. "But, to stay by herself so long. Do you think she can manage?"

Ma reached to give his hand a squeeze. "I had the same concern, but she's strongminded, as I'm sure you know. With her determination and our prayers, she'll be fine."

Forcing a weak grin, Luke shoved aside his uncertainties. What could he do but pray and trust the Lord to look after her? To be truthful, he wasn't sure what bothered him worse—the thought of her being left alone ...

Or the fact she was edging closer to leaving.

THE WICKER PORCH chair creaked as Addie stretched her legs out in front of her with a sigh. What a long day. Time seemed to creep by with no one to visit with. And it was not yet supper time. She perused the worn path, glimpsing only a rabbit nibbling clover along its edge. Her shoulders sagged. Never would she have imagined looking forward to Mrs. Perkins' visit. And yet, she found herself listening for the neighbor's familiar hum.

Penny bawled from inside the barn, eager to be relieved of her tight udder. The usually annoying sound was a welcome one today. Even a cow provided a bit of living, breathing company. Though Addie had yet to squeeze out one drop of milk, her grip had improved with each attempt. Enough so, she was willing to give it another try. Wouldn't Mrs. Perkins be surprised to find the milking done ... or at least started?

Standing, she took another glance at the road. The neighbor nowhere in sight, Addie headed toward the barn, intent on proving herself capable not only to Mrs. Perkins but to herself.

The scent of straw and hay filled her nostrils as she entered the barn. Penny lifted her head, chewing her cud and sounding a soft "moo." Addie flexed her fingers in attempt to limber them for milking. Scooping up the milk pail, she forced out a breath. "All right, Penny. We both know I'm no good at this, so help me out and let your milk down, will you please?"

Penny continued to chew, but turned her head when Addie moved the three-legged stool beside her. Giving the cow a tentative pat on the rump, Addie placed the pail under her and eased down onto the oak stool.

She could do this.

Her hands trembled as she slowly gripped the warm udder. She squeezed and tugged downward, working to give enough pressure to produce milk.

Nothing.

Over and over, she tried, yet the bucket remained dry. With a discouraged huff, she increased her pace. Penny's leg lifted, and with a loud bawl, she kicked the empty pail aside. With a soft squeal, Addie lost her balance and toppled from the stool. "You fool cow."

Muffled laughter sounded from the open barn door. Mrs. Perkins strolled toward her, a basket in her hands. "Mmm. Mmm. That technique of yours needs some work, Miss Adelaide. This here cow ain't gonna give milk lest you ease her into it."

Picking herself up off the straw-filled floor, Addie brushed the back of her dress. "No amount of *easing* can bring milk from this cow. She hates me."

Mrs. Perkins gave a loud cackle and set her basket aside. "She don't hate you, child. You jus' need t' learn to work with her, not again' her." Righting the stool, she stroked a hand along Penny's side. "Ain't you ever heard the phrase 'you catch more flies with honey than vinegar?' An animal likes a gentle touch and a soothing voice."

Addie reached out her arms. "With these hands, there's no such thing as gentle."

Casting her a sideways glance, Mrs. Perkins retrieved the milk pail. "That jus' means you have to work all the harder to win her over. Pat her side and rest your forehead against her flank, like this." The dark-skinned woman leaned into the cow rubbing her hand down toward the udder.

Addie feigned no interest but watched out of the corner of her eye. When steady pings sounded at the bottom of the pail, she whipped her head for a better look. "But how ...?"

Mrs. Perkins stopped milking and sat back with a smile. "You see? All it takes is a bit of patience and lettin' the animal know you can be trusted."

Addie shrugged. "You make it sound so simple."

"It is, once you get the hang of it." Mrs. Perkins stood and brushed her hands together. "Now you try."

With a shake of her head, Addie took a step back. "Oh, no. I've been trying for weeks without success."

"Yes. But now you know what you was doin' wrong."

Addie hesitated. A fortnight ago, she wouldn't have paid any mind to what the woman said, but after her husband's honey remedy worked in her favor, and now Celia's success with milking, it was difficult not to accept her words at value.

Mrs. Perkins tapped the stool. "Come on, child. Don't give up so easy."

Some of the fire of determination rekindled inside Addie. With a timid step forward, she made an internal list of the instructions the woman had given. Soothing voice. Gentle touch. Forehead against flank.

Renewed hope stirred within her as she eased down onto the hard stool. She gave Penny a soft pat and leaned into her side.

"That's right." Mrs. Perkins bent close to Addie's ear. "Now, take hold of her udder and give a gentle squeeze, like you're massagin' someone's foot."

Addie clasped uncooperative fingers around the front two teats and began the steady motion, mimicking the same speed and rhythm Mrs. Perkins had implemented. After several fruitless attempts, she slowed her pace, shoulders drooping. "It's no use."

"Keep going, young'un."

With a discontented huff Addie resumed her rhythm and almost startled when, after a few more tugs, a stream of white sprayed into the bucket. She grinned, the tension in her shoulders relaxing a bit.

"Now you're getting it."

By the time the pail held a couple inches of milk, her hands tired and began to cramp. She sat back on the stool and stretched them out in front of her.

"You want me to finish, Miss Adelaide?"

"Yes, please." Addie stood and moved aside for Mrs. Perkins to take her place. In a matter of minutes, the bucket was filled. "My but you're quick."

Mrs. Perkins chuckled. "Years of experience, child." Covering the milk with a cloth, she gave Penny a final pat on the rump and stood, bucket in hand. "Now then, what else can I help you with? You had supper? I thought you might enjoy some comp'ny, so I packed us some fresh corn muffins and a tin of beans."

Addie stiffened. Though indebted to both Mr. and Mrs. Perkins for their help, the thought of socializing with them still brought her discomfort. "No need to bother."

"Nonsense. That's what I come for." Mrs. Perkins gestured to the basket in the corner. "Bring along the basket of eggs and honey."

"Won't your husband be expecting you?"

"I left him plenty. He'll not miss me a smidge."

Reluctantly, Addie retrieved the basket, then turned to her companion. After the woman's help, it seemed rude to send her away, but Addie's upbringing demanded it. "I-I thank you for your offer, but there's no need to stay. I'm really not very hungry."

Mrs. Perkins' eyes studied Addie as if looking past the surface to her very soul. At last, she nodded, the luster in her eyes dulling. "I see. Well, you keep that food anyway. You're apt to get hungry later on."

Ashamed, Addie mustered a faint grin. "Thank you. And I appreciate you teaching me to milk Penny."

Mrs. Perkins' mouth twitched but fell short of a smile. "Hal and I will stop by on our way to church in the mornin'. I'll jus' see to this milk and be on my way."

She paused, gesturing toward the basket Addie carried. "Funny thing about eggs. Some's brown and some's white. But they all taste the same. Seems the Good Lord made no distinction between the color of the shell and what's inside."

Addie glanced at the cluster of brown and white eggs then at Mrs. Perkins, her dark eyes searching Addie's. It didn't take much to catch the deeper meaning in her words. Was it true skin color didn't matter to God? That He didn't value one race over another?

If so, Addie stood condemned. From the start, she'd been standoffish with the couple, as though they were of lesser worth than herself. Perhaps a part of her even blamed colored folks for the war. Evidently Mrs. Perkins had detected the slight.

Addie fell into step behind Celia as they headed toward the house. She and Mr. Perkins were so different from the colored folks Addie had encountered. It had her wondering if the slaves were as simpleminded and lacking as she thought they were.

Or had they merely been so beaten down they'd had no spirit left to display?

Her stomach gripped. Had the North been right all along?

She trembled at the thought.

Another glance at the eggs turned all she'd ever known upside down.

THE HOUSE SEEMED EXCEPTIONALLY QUIET, now that Addie was alone again. She emptied the egg basket and set it on the counter, still pondering Mrs. Perkins' poignant words. Distracted, she nearly overlooked the slip of paper tucked inside. With clumsy fingers, she unfolded it and saw *Galatians 3:28* scribbled across it. Was the note meant for her?

Addie started to toss it away and then stopped, curiosity tugging at her. She laid the note aside, but her eyes kept pulling back to it. What did the verse say? She'd be unable to rest until she knew.

Recalling the Bible on the dresser in Luke's room, she went to retrieve it. She sat on the bed and laid the Bible open atop the quilt. Though she'd once relished reading Scripture, it had been years since she'd opened a Bible. A few awkward flips brought her to the New Testament and several more to Galatians three. Running her fingers along the page, she paused on verse 28.

> *"There is neither Jew nor Greek,*
> *there is neither bond nor free,*
> *there is neither male nor female:*
> *for ye are all one in Christ Jesus."*

Addie's brow pinched. She recalled reading the verse when she was younger, but never fully understood it. Why had Celia felt the need to point it out? As she read over the verse again, its meaning became clearer, chipping away at the biases she'd fostered since childhood.

Neither bond nor free. Her heart beat faster. Did God condemn the buying and selling of slaves? How many times had she witnessed masters demeaning or beating their slaves and turned a blind eye? And yet, the thought of Mr. or Mrs. Perkins being whipped or chastised left her nauseous.

Ye are all one in Christ Jesus. The verse left no doubt God places equal value on everyone, and that one's faith in Jesus was the true measure of worth.

She swallowed. If all were equal in God's eyes, slavery was wrong, and the very core of her upbringing was in question.

She placed the Bible in her lap, for the first time in a very long while drawn to Scripture. After reading further in Galatians, she turned to the Gospels. She'd forgotten how cruelly Jesus had been treated by the Jewish leaders. He'd been whipped and beaten, even killed for no fault of His own. How had God stood by and watched without intervening?

As with her family.

Her mind churned back to another time when her heart was full of questions. One night at bedtime, she'd asked Papa, "Why did Mama die?"

He'd pulled her close and kissed her head. "Everyone dies, Adelaide. Some sooner than others."

"Even Jesus?"

"Yes, even Jesus."

"But Jesus was God's son. Why did He have to die?"

"So, we could be with Him and God someday. God loved us so much that He sent Jesus to die in our place."

She pulled away. "Then why do we die?"

He stroked her pigtails. "If we accept Jesus, only our bodies die. Our souls go to be with Him. Remember, Jesus didn't stay dead. God has power over death and brought Him back to life."

She leaned her head against him. "So, is that where Mama is? With Jesus?"

"Yes, honey. With Jesus."

That following Sunday she'd gone forward to be baptized, and her life had changed. She'd felt a deeper kinship with not only Jesus, but her mother. At least for a while. When the war came, that joy had been stripped away. Her prayers for Papa and her brothers unanswered.

If God has power over death, why didn't He save them?

Her stomach clamped tighter. And yet, hadn't Jesus's prayer to be spared gone unanswered as well? But, despite His pleas to be spared the agony of the cross, He'd prayed God's will be done.

Addie closed the Bible, more confused than ever. She needed answers. And she knew where she needed to find them.

36

Stafford Hotel, Washington D.C.
Sunday, May 21, 1865

Luke stood and pushed in his mother's chair as she joined him at the table. "Where's Lydia?"

"Still trying to piece herself together," she answered, her voice barely audible over the noise of the hotel restaurant. "She'll be down shortly."

Luke slid onto the chair beside her. "How did you sleep?"

"Tolerably." One eyebrow lifted. "I suppose I'm too accustomed to the quietness of the country. Do people never sleep in this town? I heard merriment most of the night."

"The city was booming when we arrived, but with the huge influx of people it grows more chaotic every day. It was a challenge to even find an available hotel room."

"I can believe that." The man at the table behind jostled Ma's hat as he stood. Reaching to readjust it, she took another glance around the crowded room. "I don't believe I've ever seen so many people crammed into one place."

Luke brushed crumbs from the stained, white tablecloth. "Not quite the Willard, is it?"

CYNTHIA ROEMER

She smiled at him. "I'll not complain, so long as we're together."

Luke reached for her hand, drinking in the sight of her. Though the creases around her pale blue eyes had deepened and the flecks of gray in her hair were more visible than when he'd left home, she was a beautiful sight to behold. Yet, it didn't seem right his father wasn't beside her. "Any word from Drew?"

She shook her head, her smile fading. "No. Nothing."

He squeezed her hand. "I wouldn't be concerned. Not every company was sent here, and he did say he'd be delayed. I'm sure you'll hear from him soon."

"I'm certain you're right." She glanced at the wall clock. "Do you suppose we'll make church service?"

Withdrawing his hand, Luke sat back in his chair, still struggling to hear above the commotion. "The church isn't far. If we take a horse-drawn streetcar we should be fine."

His mother's eyes turned thoughtful. "I wonder how Adelaide's faring?"

Mention of her stirred his own restless thoughts. "I still find it hard to believe she's improved enough to stay on her own."

"She struggled for a time. The paint she was using as treatment had ill-effects on the poor dear. Hal suggested honey be applied to her burns instead, and that seemed to make all the difference."

"I'm surprised she was willing to try it."

Ma grinned. "Oh, it took a bit of coaxing, but she didn't put up too much of a fuss."

"I'm relieved to hear it." Luke knew first-hand how stubborn she could be ... and how captivating. He cleared his throat. "I don't suppose she's had a change of heart where God's concerned? I'd hoped being around you and Lydia might have an influence on her."

Even in the crowded room, Ma's hesitance rang heavy. She drew a long breath. "Not much, I'm afraid. She still refuses to

254

attend church service, but I've tried to leave the persuading to the Lord."

Leaning forward, Luke locked his fingers together on the table. "I believe she once had faith. But her wounded heart left her embittered toward God." He stared at the vacant chair across from him, speaking as much to himself as his mother. "If I could only find the right words to convince her He isn't to blame for her sufferings."

Ma placed a hand on his arm, pulling him from his reverie. "It's God's job to change someone's heart, Luke. Not ours. Sometimes prodding only makes matters worse."

"Sometimes not saying anything doesn't work out so well either," Luke murmured, bittersweet memories of his lost friend flashing across his mind.

Ma's heavy sigh assured him she caught his meaning. "You can't go on blaming yourself over Jacob, son."

Four long years had passed since his friend had drowned in the swollen river. Luke could still see him being sucked under by the raging current. In an instant, he was gone, along with any hope of his soul being saved. "He was my best friend, and I never once shared my faith with him."

"You're placing too much blame on yourself. You weren't the sole influence in his life. We all make mistakes, Luke. None of us is perfect."

He set his jaw. "Maybe not, but I figure I need to do all I can to ensure others don't suffer the same fate."

Including Adelaide.

"As do we all, but you can't *earn* God's grace, son. No matter how hard we try, only Jesus can make us right with God."

Luke's shoulders drooped, the truth of her words hitting him like gale-force winds. Is that what he was doing? Trying to work his way back into God's good graces?

Impossible. To even attempt such was cheapening Christ's sacrifice. His motive for sharing his faith should be love, not guilt.

Forgive me, Lord.

Ma leaned closer, her voice mellowing. "On the other hand, prayer can soften the hardest of hearts. If the Lord wills, Adelaide will come around."

The comforting words seeped into the recesses of Luke's soul, reviving his spirit. "I never stop praying for her."

She gave his arm a brisk pat. "Neither do I. Because, if I'm not mistaken, my son is quite fond of her."

His eyes lifted, and he met her telling gaze with an unsettled grin. "Is it that obvious?"

A perceptive smile wedged across his mother's face. "Let's just say, I sensed your caring went beyond her physical well-being the moment I saw you together."

The noise around them seemed to still as his inward thoughts churned. He raked a hand through his hair. "I do care for her, but it would never work. Not when she doesn't share my beliefs."

Ma calmly wet her lips and nodded. "You're right, son. Until her calloused heart softens, your strong faith would always stand as a barrier between you."

The words only reinforced what he already knew. Better men than him had fallen at the hands of an ungodly woman. He couldn't let that happen. He wanted no part in a relationship that was doomed from the start. Edging back in his chair, he folded his arms across his chest. "Anyway, from the sounds of it, she'll be leaving soon. So, it doesn't much matter how I feel."

"I don't know. She doesn't seem quite as eager to leave as she did at first. I believe she's come to like staying with us."

The news sparked a nervous tremor within Luke. The girl was as unpredictable as a summer storm. He'd hoped she would settle in, but never expected it of her. Now he wondered if it would almost be easier if she were gone. Though the thought left him empty. "If she's still there when I get home, I'll just keep my distance."

Ma touched a hand to his cheek. "You're a godly man, Luke,

and I know you'll choose wisely who to spend your life with. But I want you to know, I've sensed Adelaide's attitude softening, and I believe there's hope."

Luke's gut clenched. Hope was good. But hope alone wasn't enough.

Mr. Perkins brushed his hands together. "Well, young lady, things is all taken care of."

"Thank you." Addie followed him from the barn out into the yard, his prominent limp forcing her to slow her pace.

Dressed in her Sunday best, Mrs. Perkins rose from the porch chair to meet them. Not her usual chipper self, her humming had stilled, and her smile had been exchanged by taut lips.

Addie's stomach knotted, certain the neighbor's depleted spirit was a result of yesterday's rebuff. Had she inadvertently hurt the kind-hearted woman? Mr. Perkins had excused his wife's aloofness by saying she didn't wish to soil her Sunday clothing. But her stoic expression spoke of something deeper.

Attempting a smile, Addie offered a kind word. "You look very nice."

Mrs. Perkins gave a curt nod and tugged at her husband's sleeve. "We'd best be on our way, Hal, or we'll be late t' church service."

With a tip of his felt hat, Mr. Perkins turned to Addie. "Good to see you up and about, Miss Adelaide."

"Thank you." Sweaty palmed, Addie trailed along behind. Since last night, her mind couldn't seem to rest. She'd lain awake for hours toying with the idea of seeking answers to her questions at church. So, she'd risen early to wipe the smudges from her black taffeta and did her best to pin her hair and tie on a bonnet in case she found the courage to actually go.

If she disliked the service, Martha and Lydia would never

know she'd attempted it—unless Mr. and Mrs. Perkins divulged her secret. But now that the moment was here, courage failed her. Was Mrs. Perkins so miffed she would refuse a request to accompany them?

The couple turned onto the path, arms linked. Addie's pulse quickened as she sensed the opportunity slipping from her. Torn from within, she at last found her voice and blurted through shallow breaths. "M-May I go with you?"

The pair froze in place and shared a puzzled look before pivoting toward her. Eyes wide, Mr. Perkins, scratched his cheek. "You wanna go t' church service? With us?"

Addie hesitated, finding their rounded eyes and slackened jaws almost humorous. "Yes. If I may."

Mr. Perkins motioned to her, his stocky frame jiggling with delight. "Glory be. Well come on then. You've a ways farther t' tread than us."

Venturing a few steps closer, Addie knit her brows. "You don't attend the same church as Martha and Lydia?"

A chuckle sounded from Mrs. Perkins. "Why no, young'un. There is white churches and black churches. You see, even the North has its prejudices."

The very thought seemed to contradict all the North fought for. Addie wavered, mind reeling. Walking into a church alone after all these years was intimidating enough, but doing so in a Northern church was nearly inconceivable. Perhaps she should rethink this. She looked at Hal and Celia, their faces vibrant. To back out now would be awkward, if not impolite.

Leaden feet carried her forward. Though her mind and body ached to turn and seek refuge inside the house, something in her soul begged her to press on.

THE SOUND of muffled singing vibrated from within the white, frame building, a cross atop its small steeple. More than once,

Addie considered turning on her heels, but held steady. Though her hand shook as if shivering from the cold, she put it to the door latch. She hesitated, contemplating how she would draw the least attention.

With the service already started, she could hopefully slip in unnoticed to a back pew and conceal her blotched hands beneath her skirt. When the service ended, she would leave during the final hymn. If all went as planned, no one would even know who she was or where she'd come from.

Drawing a deep breath, she inched the door open. The singing blared louder as the door hinged wider. The congregation stood shoulder to shoulder, facing the tall, lank song leader at the front, allowing Addie to slip in with only a few curious turns of the head. She skimmed the fuller-than-anticipated church building, and her heart plunged. Every seat appeared filled.

A cluster of people stood near the empty coat racks along the back wall. Ill-at-ease, Addie faltered. What had possessed her to come to a church filled with Northerners? If she left now, none would be the wiser. An older woman in black caught her eye. Scooting to make room, she motioned Addie over. Not wishing to be rude, Addie pushed aside her fears and went to stand beside her. She returned the stooped woman's warm smile, experiencing a sort of kinship with another who was grieving someone dear.

Grateful for the inconspicuous place to stand, Addie locked her hands together behind her. The harmony of voices lifted in song helped calm her restless spirit. Though unfamiliar, the hymn's beautiful words and melody called to her like a forgotten friend.

My Jesus, I love thee. I know thou art mine.

She'd always loved to sing. Even now, her voice longed to hum the catchy tune. Instead, she listened in silence, doing her best to fade into the backdrop.

When the song ended, the congregation took their seats, leaving Addie and the rest of those standing more exposed. A hush fell over the group as the preacher strode to the pulpit, his straight, sandy hair slicked back against his scalp, giving him a hawk-like appearance. He gripped the outer edges of the pulpit, deep-set eyes perusing the crowd of onlookers. *"Where were you when I formed the foundations of the earth? Who can number the clouds? Who provideth food for the ravens?"*

The preacher's booming voice echoed through the packed building, a baby's soft coo and the shuffle of feet the only sounds to break the stillness. Holding up his worn, leather Bible, he stepped to the side of the pulpit, his brunet eyes darting from one face to the next. "These were questions asked of Job when he was suffering loss and hardship. Job was a righteous man who followed the Lord wholeheartedly, and yet he was stripped of his wealth and possessions, even his sons and daughters. Soon after, he was stricken with painful boils and in such misery he wished he'd never been born."

Riveted on his every word, Addie's heart thumped in her ears. She'd forgotten the story of Job, how he'd lost everything —family, possessions, even his health, all in a short span of time. She flexed her hands, memories of the agony she'd suffered from her burns flooding back. Could boils have felt much different? But while her injuries had been confined to her hands and arms, Job's painful sores had covered his entire body.

The pastor paced along the front of the church, clutching his Bible to his chest. "In the midst of his hardships, his wife and friends advised him to curse God and die. But despite their urgings, he held fast to his faith and refused to blame God."

He seemed to look straight at her then, and the blood drained from her cheeks. Wasn't that what she'd done? Blamed God for her sorrows? She stared at the oak floorboards, lest the insightful pastor glimpse the shortcomings in her soul.

"Oh, he questioned God, asking why all this had happened to him, even cursed the day he was born. But he refused to give in to the temptation to turn his back on the Lord." A volley of "amens" sounded from the congregation, the pastor's words slicing through Addie's very core.

"How many of us question God in face of hardships? How many times have we blamed God when it's Satan's wiles that buffet us? This war has stolen much from many, and yet God has not forsaken us any more than He forsook his servant, Job."

The pastor opened his Bible to its center. "Scripture says Job repented in dust and ashes for his doubts and misconceptions. Perhaps hard times have caused you to question the Lord's goodness or to doubt his sovereignty. Do you need to repent as well?"

Tears pricked Addie's eyes as she pondered the pastor's words. While Job had merely questioned God, she'd turned her back on Him. Blamed Him for her losses. Her throat tightened, and she stifled a sob.

The older woman next to her held out a handkerchief. Addie tensed, hesitant to expose her ugly hands. When the dear woman waved the kerchief closer, Addie resigned her insecurities and lifted her hand to take it. Rather than a look of repulsion or pity, the woman's wrinkled hands fastened around hers, producing a sniffle and added tears from Addie.

The minister's voice struck up again, his tone lighter. "Those of you who've suffered loss, take heart. God did not leave Job in despair. The final chapter tells of how the Lord blessed Job beyond what he'd ever experienced. My friends, God longs to restore your lives as well. You need only to repent and put your faith in Him. And if you've never given your heart to Jesus, come now, confess your sins and be baptized."

As the congregation rose to their feet for the final hymn, Addie edged toward the door, heart drumming in her chest. She'd come seeking answers to her prejudices and instead found her gravest failing was resentment toward God. How wrong she'd been to blame Him for her hardships.

She bowed her head. *Forgive me, Lord.*

As the church filled with song, several made their way down

the aisle. Addie paused, an irrepressible pull bidding her to stay. She clutched tighter to the handkerchief dampened with her tears, the walls around her heart beginning to topple. Could God truly restore her life as he had Job's?

Such a hope seemed too incredible to fathom. And yet, in this room filled with strangers, she sensed God's power and presence.

And, for the first time in a long while ... peace.

Sweet release spilled over her, and her spirit lifted. Whatever the future held, she would no longer face it alone. With a deep breath, instead of bolting for the door, she stepped toward the center aisle, her frailties forgotten.

37

Washington D.C.
Tuesday, May 23, 1865

A cannon blast split the morning air—the signal to advance. Major General Meade, astride his horse, Blackie, led the way. Eighty-thousand strong, Grant's Army of the Potomac descended along Pennsylvania Avenue like a river of blue, every step and movement precise. Never had there been such cause to hold heads high as now, in this Grand Review of the Armies.

A gentle breeze cooled Luke's sweat-dampened brow as he craned his neck for a better view. For the first time since he'd arrived in Washington, flags had been raised to full-staff. Likely for the first time since President Lincoln had passed.

Though the air teemed with vitality, no one spoke. All eyes were riveted on the soldiers fanned out ahead of them, and all ears were tuned to their superiors as they awaited the command to begin their trek from the Capitol to the White House lawn.

Long minutes passed. At last, the signal came, and Sergeant Delmar moved to the front. "This is it, men. Look sharp."

Standing taller, Luke shouldered his rifle, spacing himself evenly between the sergeant and the soldier to his left. His heart hammered, a rush of pride coursing through him as the company fell into step, bayonets gleaming in the sunlight.

Scores of spectators lined the mile and a half stretch, waving flags and shouting cheers to the celebrated soldiers. Welcome banners and red, white, and blue bunting now decorated the buildings where, days earlier, black crepe had signaled a nation in mourning.

Cavalry patrolled the street, keeping the jubilant crowd at bay. Voices raised in song added a spring to Luke's stride. Though he kept his head straight, his gaze flicked from side to side. Ma and Lydia were out there somewhere amid the throng of people, though there was no way of knowing where. Knowing they'd come was enough.

As they neared the White House lawn, the president's pavilion came into view. Out of the corner of his eye, he caught a glimpse of General Grant alongside the newly appointed President Johnson. He pulled his eyes to the soldiers ahead of him as he passed the highly decorated reviewing stand, the hair on his arms standing on end beneath his uniform. If ever there were a day to celebrate, this was it—a day marking freedom and an end to war and bloodshed.

With each step, the box in his pocket thudded against his thigh, reminding him not everyone had cause to celebrate. Thoughts of Adelaide toyed with his concentration, drowning out the sounds of celebration. Her lack of desire to share in this day was understandable. While the Union gloried in their victory, thousands of Confederate soldiers and civilians were returning to desolate homes and tragic loss.

His heart grieved for them and for this broken nation. Given time, would it heal?

Would Adelaide?

When Ma and Lydia returned home, the trinket in his pocket would travel with them. Perhaps, sending it would shed a bit of joy to Adelaide ... and spare him the awkwardness of facing her with it in person.

ADDIE STOPPED MILKING and flung her cramped hands back and forth to stimulate the blood flow. In the dim light of the barn, she peered in the milk pail, excited to see nearly twice the amount she'd milked that morning. "Well anyway, I'm improving."

Mrs. Perkins peeked in the bucket and grinned. "You sure are, child. B'fore ya know it, you'll not need help a 'tall."

Addie stood, allowing Mrs. Perkins to take her place on the three-legged stool. "Won't Martha and Lydia be surprised?"

"Mmm. Mmm. They will indeed. When do you expect 'em back?"

Addie raised her voice to compensate for the steady spray of milk. "On the Thursday afternoon train."

"Well then, you won't be needin' Hal or my help much longer. Don't hardly *now*, 'cept milkin' Penny here." Celia leaned back and patted the cow's rump. "I've sorta missed milkin' since we sold our Dolly. Gonna miss *our* time together too, now that we're on friendlier terms." She tossed Addie a wink.

Addie forced a grin. Over the past couple of days, she'd come to look forward to the Perkins' visits. Rather than shoo them off, she'd begun to engage them in conversation. Since Sunday, she'd tried to work up courage to apologize for her rudeness, but so far hadn't found the words. Obviously, her attempt to treat the Perkins with more respect had spoken for her. "I appreciate all you've done to help. I realize I haven't been the easiest to get along with."

With a dismissing wave of her hand, Celia returned to milking. "That's all past now. It's plain the Good Lord's got ahold of your heart, and it's made all the difference."

Addie's spirit lightened. Her renewed faith had rid her of the resentment and bitterness pent up inside her—toward God, toward blacks, even toward Yankees. For years, she'd been held captive by her own misconceptions, believing Satan's lies that

God was to blame for the hardships she faced. She knew better now. And though she didn't know what the future held, for the first time in a long while, she had hope.

"There we are. All finished." Easing off the stool, Celia turned toward Addie, hands on hips. "Anything else you need before I go?"

She started to shake her head, then caught herself, cutting a glance at her black taffeta gown. Leaning against the barn timber, she grinned over at Celia. "Actually, there is one thing."

38

Gallagher Home
Thursday, May 25, 1865

A ddie turned side to side in front of the bedroom mirror. She didn't wish to be vain, but she'd forgotten how she looked in a color besides black. The time for mourning had ended. Shedding the taffeta dress seemed a fitting outward response to her inner heart change.

Celia had embarrassed her with endless praise, insisting on doing the chores yesterday and today to keep Addie from soiling her new dress. Miss Van Lew's taste for clothing suited her. The long-sleeved, white blouse, offset by a navy-blue bodice and full blue-and-white checkered skirt, was as fine as any Addie had ever worn.

A chuckle bubbled in her throat. How would Martha and Lydia react when they saw her? Of course, they'd instantly note the change in appearance, but wouldn't they be stunned when Sunday arrived, and she willingly accompanied them to church service?

Her stomach roiled. What would Luke think of the change?

She eased onto the bed. Poor Luke. He'd tried so hard to

convince her of God's goodness only to have her spurn his attempts. Now, weeks later, she'd come to the realization on her own, with a bit of nudging from Celia and the pastor. Not to mention Scripture.

So much had changed since she and Luke had parted. When she first arrived, she'd been sated with bitterness. All she'd wanted was for her arms and hands to mend so she could be on her way. She'd given little thought to her soul needing healed as well. And though finding Clarissa was still foremost in her thoughts, leaving this place, this family, would be harder than she'd anticipated.

Especially once Luke arrived.

The sound of a carriage rumbled outside the window. Going for a look, she gave a soft titter. "They're back."

As quick as her plentiful dress allowed, she downed the stairs and made her way onto the porch. Even at a distance, she could see Lydia's outstretched arm and head protruding from the opening of the hired coach. With great satisfaction, Addie lifted her hand in greeting. She'd missed the two of them more than she cared to admit.

Strolling out onto the lawn to meet them, she subconsciously watched for signs of Luke. Though they'd said he wouldn't be coming, still, she hoped. When she saw he indeed wasn't with them, her spirit plummeted.

She shook off the disappointment as the coach rolled to a halt before her. Lydia squealed with delight and bounded from the hack without waiting for the driver's help. Her rounded eyes perused Addie. "Just look at you. You're beautiful."

Addie deflected the compliment with a shy grin and an accolade of her own. "And how refined you are in your big city attire. Why, you look every bit of sixteen."

Lydia giggled and reached to give her a hug.

Relaxing into the sisterly embrace, Addie couldn't suppress a smile.

Martha paused beside them. "Why, Adelaide. You're

stunning. And to think we feared we'd find you half-starved and desperate for our return."

Heat flooded Addie's cheeks as she released her hold on Lydia. "Mr. and Mrs. Perkins were very generous to help. Though I am so pleased you're back."

Moisture brimmed in Martha's eyes, and she stretched out her arms. Addie leaned into her, touched by the tender way the older woman's cheek pressed against hers. She breathed in the scent of lilac, an inexpressible longing to stay wrapped in Martha's arms steeling over her.

As they relinquished their hold, the driver deposited their satchels on the porch. With a tip of his hat, he collected his pay and returned to his hack, leaving the three of them to converse.

Taking up their things, they strolled to the house.

Addie held open the door. "How was your trip?"

Lydia's eyes sparked. "Grand. But my, Washington was swarming with people. More soldiers and spectators than you could ever imagine. We even got a glimpse of President Johnson and General Grant as they were leaving the reviewing stand."

Not as impressed as Lydia might have liked, Addie merely nodded and followed them to the parlor. There was only one soldier she cared about seeing, and she nearly regretted the missed opportunity. She eased down onto the settee alongside Martha, attempting unsuccessfully to squelch the question burning her lips. Smoothing her dress out under her, she cleared her throat. "And how is Luke? Did you find him well?"

With a soft grin, Martha laced her fingers together in her lap. "Quite well. Though eager to be done with the army and on his way home."

Addie dropped her gaze, brushing a pretend speck from her skirt. "And ... will that be soon?"

She could almost sense Martha's smile deepen. "He believes so, though he can't be certain."

The thought of further delay made her heart sink. Though the added time would allow her more opportunity to heal.

"He sent you a gift."

Lydia's elated tone broke through Addie's reflections, and her head lifted. "A gift?"

"May I give it to her, Mama?"

Motioning with her hand, Martha chuckled. "Go ahead."

Addie waited in eager anticipation while Lydia rummaged through the inseam pocket of her dress. At last, she produced a small box and held it out to Addie, a bit of pout in her lower lip. "He was cruel and made us promise not to peek."

Martha leaned closer to Addie, a hint of humor in her voice. "And it took every ounce of constraint for Lydia to *keep* that promise."

With a shrug, Lydia flashed a sheepish grin.

Addie stifled a laugh. She could understand the young girl's curiosity. The tiny box held intrigue for her as well. What could he have sent? She resisted the urge to retreat into the solitude of her room to open it in private. Such an action would be making more of the incident than necessary. With awkward fingers, she worked to pry open the lid. After several failed attempts, it finally pulled free, and Addie drew in a breath.

"A new locket." Lydia bent for a closer look. "How pretty."

Addie fought back tears, the thoughtful gesture so typical of Luke, but one she hadn't anticipated. She gently rubbed her finger over the rose etched at the front of the shiny necklace. "It's lovely."

"Would you like help putting it on?"

She blinked away the moisture pooling in her eyes as she met Martha's gaze. "Yes, please."

Trying to curtail the surge of welling emotions, Addie took another glimpse at the necklace then handed it to Martha. As she pivoted away, gentle hands brushed her hair to one side. Warm fingers touched the nape of her neck, working to unclasp Aunt Polly's charred locket.

As Martha slid the necklace from around Addie's neck, she

leaned close to Addie's ear. "I'll put this in the box for safe keeping."

"Thank you." Tarnished though it was, the keepsake was the only tangible reminder of her family, outside of the few photos her aunt had stowed. She glanced down as Martha slipped the new locket in the charred one's place. This would be *her* locket to fill—if ever she were blessed with a family of her own.

Martha gripped Addie's shoulders. "There now, let's have a look."

Turning toward her, Addie couldn't hold back a grin.

Martha clasped her hands together. "Splendid. The perfect offset for your new dress."

Lydia leaned for a better look. "Just wait'll Luke sees how pretty you look."

A bit unearthed by the comment, Addie reached for the box with her aunt's locket and stood. "I ... think I'll take this up to the room and put it with my things."

"A fine idea." Martha braced her hand on the arm of the settee and rose to her feet. "Lydia and I have some unpacking to do. And I, for one, am eager for a quiet evening and a good night's rest after all the hubbub we've endured."

Excusing herself, Addie started from the room, the jewelry box tucked in her palm. A puddle of nerves at the thought of Luke's return, she fingered the locket around her neck. Luke must have sacrificed a great deal to purchase such a lovely piece. Did he care for her more than she realized?

As she upped the stairs, her stomach knotted. Was there any real hope of a future for them? How could there be, with her determined to find Clarissa and return south?

Luke's home was here. Though some of the barriers between them had toppled, her newfound faith was no match for his seasoned convictions. He likely would never consider her worthy of his affections.

Perhaps he had no interest in her at all but had merely given the locket out of kindness.

A sigh escaped her as she started down the hall to her room. She wasn't even certain of her own feelings—other than the thought of seeing him again made her a bit addle-headed.

A thud sounded at her feet. She paused and glanced down, cringing at sight of the open box and charred locket lying in pieces. "Oh no," she groaned. In her distraction, the box must have slipped from her inept fingers.

Stooping to pick up the broken keepsake, she chastened herself for being so careless. A tiny slip of yellowed paper beside one of the dislodged photos caught her eye. What was it? Something to help hold the photo in place?

Addie struggled unsuccessfully to clasp it between her fingertips and finally flipped it over with her thumb. Faded words stared up at her from the aged scrap of paper. Unable to read what it said in the dimness of the hallway, she shoved everything in the box and hurried to her room. Plopping down on the quilted mattress, she reached to brighten the bedstand lantern.

Her curiosity piqued, she emptied the contents of the box onto the bed and sought out the slip of paper. Heart drumming, she moved nearer the light and read the faint words:

Stuart and Emma Banks
1334 Bayberry Road
Copperville, Pennsylvania

Addie cupped a hand over her mouth, not knowing whether to laugh or cry. *Thank you, Lord.* Who would have guessed Clarissa's whereabouts had been around her neck the entire time?

She clutched the tiny slip of paper to her chest. Now that she had an address, all she needed was the means to get there.

And the fortitude to leave Luke and his family behind.

SERGEANT DELMAR FLOPPED on his bed of blankets and scrubbed a hand down his face. "I don't know about you, Gallagher, but I'm glad that's over. Two full days of parades and fightin' crowds is about more than I can stomach."

Luke tossed his kepi aside and rested his elbows on his knees. "But you have to admit, it was quite a sight. Something to carry with us the rest of our days."

Nodding his agreement, the sergeant jutted his lower lip. "It was at that."

Luke laid back on his makeshift cot, listening to the chortle of insects outside the dimly lit tent. He smothered a yawn, still trying to absorb all that had transpired. Washington had quieted considerably since the throng of people left the city. Ma and Lydia's short visit had come and gone in a blink, leaving him more eager than ever to return home. He turned to the sergeant. "So, what happens now?"

Delmar finished unlacing his brogans and slid them off his feet, revealing several haphazardly stitched holes in his socks. And one he'd missed. "We travel to our state field rendezvous points where we'll receive our final pay and eventually get mustered out."

Luke cocked himself up on his elbow. "Do you know when?"

Delmar sniffed and wiggled his toes. "From what I hear, could be as soon as Monday."

"Where's New York's rendezvous point?"

The sergeant glanced at Luke out of the corner of his eye, his lips curving upward. "Somewhere you may have heard of. A town called Elmira."

"Wahoo!" Luke flopped back down on his bed of blankets with a grin. In a few days, he'd be back at his hometown for the first time in more than a year. That final paycheck couldn't come soon enough after spending all he had on Adelaide.

By now she'd have the locket in hand. Or, better yet, around her neck. What he wouldn't give to have seen her reaction. But it was better this way. Keeping his distance was easy from hundreds of miles away.

He raked a hand through his hair. The question was, how would he manage it when they were living in the same household?

39

Monday, May 29, 1865

Addie leaned her head against the barn beam and brushed a hand down Basil's back, her fingers barely able to sense the fur's softness. The short-haired, orange cat purred in her lap, easing some of the restlessness pent up inside her. Since finding Mr. and Mrs. Banks' address, she'd thought of little else. Though her heart ached at the thought of leaving this place—and Luke—she had to at least try to locate Clarissa and see about making a home with her.

She glanced at her hands, their blotchy color and rough texture something she would never grow accustomed to. Surely there was some means of employment she could manage. A job where her unsightly hands wouldn't draw attention. She would need travel money as well as some for herself and Clarissa to live on.

If the girl was willing.

But first Addie had to find a way to reach her.

"Here you are. I've been looking everywhere for you."

Startled by Lydia's unexpected approach, Addie scrambled to

her feet, sending Basil scampering away with an unhappy "meow."

Lydia eased back. "I'm sorry. I didn't mean to startle you."

Addie brushed straw and cat hair from her skirt. "I suppose my mind was elsewhere."

A wispy grin slipped across Lydia's lips. "And would that *elsewhere* include a certain brother of mine?"

With a sorrowful shake of her head, Addie gripped the gold locket. "Just the opposite."

"What do you mean?" Lydia's face lost its smile. She studied Addie a moment, then her eyes widened. "You're not thinking of *leaving?*

Addie hesitated. "Not immediately. Soon though."

"But why? Just when Luke is about to return. He'll be heartbroken. And Mama. Did you see how happy she was when you attended church yesterday?"

"I know." Addie pressed down the lump in her throat. "You've all been wonderful."

Moisture pooled in her young friend's eyes. "Then why go?"

Addie swallowed, attempting to purge the tremor from her voice. She'd not expected the thought of leaving to be so heart-wrenching—for either of them. "There's something I need to do. A place I need to go."

"But where? Surely not Richmond?"

"No. Not Richmond." With a steadying breath, Addie eased back down on the strawed barn floor. "Remember the young cousin in the photo you asked me about on the train?"

Lydia dropped down beside her. "Yes. I remember you didn't want to talk about her."

"Well, her name's Clarissa. My aunt apparently gave her up when she was a baby. I've never met her, but she's living somewhere in Pennsylvania with a Mr. and Mrs. Stuart Banks."

"And you want to find her?"

Addie nodded, the quiver in Lydia's voice making answering difficult. "She's all the family I have left."

The reply seemed to drain the vitality from her friend. Lowering her gaze, Lydia toyed with the straw bedding. "So, if you find her, will she return south with you?"

A twinge of uncertainty coursed through Addie, and she released a long breath. "That's what I need to find out."

———

B & O Railroad Depot
Washington D.C.
May 29, 1865

LUKE GLANCED at the lofty clock tower at the front of the train depot for what he hoped was the last time in a long while. Washington was nice for a visit, but right now, all he could think of was home.

A whistle sounded in the distance, announcing their train's approach. Sergeant Delmar thumbed over his shoulder to the group of soldiers. "There's our ride, men. Let's go meet it."

Shouts poured from the excited privates as they broke formation and herded toward the depot entrance.

The sergeant held up his arms to regain control. "Hold up there, fellas, you're not mustered out of this army yet, so let's act like soldiers."

The group quieted and mumbled, "Yes, Sergeant."

Stepping inside the crowded depot, Luke and Sergeant Delmar struggled to keep the line of privates intact as they wove their way through the host of other soldiers eager to get where they were going. Luke's steps grew lighter as he caught a glimpse of the train at the far side of the hundred-foot carhouse. In a few short hours, he'd be back in Elmira.

So close to home he could taste it.

As the engine groaned to a stop in front of them, a cloud of warm steam rolled from beneath. Looking a bit like cattle being prodded to market, the soldiers tightened their ranks to make room for unloading passengers. Luke ran a hand along the smooth rifle barrel, eagerly awaiting his turn to board. He watched the faces of the men, each expression sated with renewed hope and longing.

Private Cummings leaned toward him, raising his voice above the racket. "How long till we head home once we reach Elmira?"

"Hard to say. Hopefully just long enough to receive our final pay and muster out." Though, with so many soldiers being mobilized, Luke had a feeling it would take longer than any of them realized.

And right now, four miles from home seemed nearly as far as two hundred.

"ADELAIDE? WHERE ARE YOU, DEAR?"

Martha's faint call from the direction of the house stirred Addie and Lydia to their feet. Apparently, Lydia wasn't the only one looking for her. She stepped from the barn into plain sight. "Over here."

In a rather eager fashion, Martha motioned for her to come, cupping a hand to the side of her mouth. "A friend of yours is here to see you."

Addie knit her brow. "A friend? To see me? Who ..." She sucked in a breath, sharing a hopeful glance with Lydia. "It must be Luke!"

The pair hiked their skirts and took off at a rapid pace, slowing as they reached the porch steps. She'd not expected him so soon. Was she ready for this?

Martha met them at the top, her countenance more stoic than Addie would have imagined for her son's homecoming. "He's in the parlor."

Addie eyed her. She was teasing. She must be. To retain the element of surprise.

Her stomach clenched. Or had something happened? Why

hadn't Luke come looking for them himself? Had he been injured?

Addie paused to check herself over, wishing she'd had opportunity to glance in a mirror and make herself more presentable. She clasped a hand to her locket, assuring it was in place. With bated breath, she pushed open the door, Lydia at her heels. The hall clock ticked loud against the stillness, and she slowed her step to match its cadence.

With a soft giggle, Lydia nudged her from behind. "Go on."

Legs atremble, Addie rounded the parlor doorway, eagerly awaiting Luke's ready smile and wheat-blond curls.

Instead, she stopped short, clutching a steadying hand to the doorframe, the blood draining from her cheeks.

Simon.

40

"Hello, Addie."

Addie's insides recoiled at the sound of Simon's gruff voice speaking her nickname. After weeks of hearing only Northern talk, his Southern twang sounded almost foreign. "How did you ..."

Taking a step forward, he raised a hand to silence her. "Aah! Save your questions. I'm sure these fine ladies don't want troubled with all our doings."

Addie snapped her mouth shut and glowered at him, her heart pounding in her ears. This man was unpredictable, dangerous ... and evidently resourceful. No telling what he would do if she exposed his true identity.

Simon's gaze swept past her to Martha and Lydia. "Might I have a word in private with Miss Hanover?"

Addie peered over her shoulder at Martha and Lydia, distraught to see the worry in their eyes. Seeking to reassure them, she forced a slight smile. "It's all right."

Like a pair of reluctant children being sent to bed early, they eased from the parlor and slid the door shut behind them. Secretly, Addie hoped they would listen in on the conversation, but knew well enough they would not stoop to something so intrusive. As soon as their boot steps faded down the hall, Simon flopped onto the settee and looped his arms behind his head. "This is a pretty good setup. You found the perfect place to hide." He perused the furnishings, then settled his gaze on Addie, his lips spreading in a smirk. "Almost."

"How did you find me?"

His smile deepened, exposing a row of yellowed teeth. "Nurses talk, given the right incentive. Jus' took me a while to pinpoint exactly where your Yankee beau lived."

Addie's heart leapt to her throat. "If you've hurt Captain Sally or Miss Jane, I'll ..."

"You'll what?" He snickered. "Don't fret your pretty head. All I done is put enough scare into 'em so they'd talk." He stretched out his legs, crossing them at the ankles. "Where is that runt of a beau of yours anyway? From the looks of the fields, he's sluffing his duties."

Ignoring the comment, Addie blew out a breath. "What do you want, Simon?"

He folded his arms over his chest. "I think you know the answer to that."

Addie slid her tongue over the back of her teeth, nose flaring. "If it's money you want, you'll have to wait. I'm just now regaining use of my hands and arms. If you'll give me an address to send you the funds, I'll mail them to you as soon as able."

The settee creaked under his weight as he jerked forward. "If you think I'm gonna give you another chance to run off, you're daft. Nuh-uh. I'm staying right here until you take me to Clarissa." He leaned forward, elbows on his knees. "You *do* know where she is. Don't you?"

It was an accusation rather than a question. *Forgive me, Lord.* She shook her head. "No. I don't."

He glared at her. "I think you do."

Fearful her expression had already relayed too much, she let her gaze fall away.

She heard more than saw Simon hop to his feet. Sidling over, he stood mere inches from her. His voice softened. "Now that I think of it, Polly may have had the smarts to hide her somewhere up north here. Am I right?"

Taking a step back, Addie pursed her lips, refusing to answer.

He inched closer. "I see you have a new locket. I'd be interested in seeing Polly's old one. Do you have it?"

"That's none of your concern." She edged back, and her foot knocked against the baseboard, jolting her to a stop.

He pressed closer, shooting her heartrate to a rapid pace. "Look. All you need do is tell me where she is, and I'll be on my way."

Find Clarissa. Don't let him have her. Her aunt's haunting words echoed back, sending a chill down her spine. Her chin lifted. "And if I don't?"

"Then I guess you're stuck with me." He pinned her in with his arms, his coarse breath assaulting her. "And if you breathe one ill word about me to your friends, I'll make certain they never speak to anyone again."

She turned her head, but not before glimpsing the sizable knife bulging beneath his shirt. Her breaths shallowed, the threat coiling its way to her heart. "Why are you doing this? What right have you to Clarissa or to extort money from my aunt, and now me, for that matter?"

Lowering his arms, he took a step back, a smug grin lining his lips. "I have every right."

Addie stood taller, mustering her resolve. "And why's that?"

"'Cause, I'm the girl's father."

NUMBNESS TORE at Addie as she led Simon from the parlor to the porch, still trying to absorb his confession. It couldn't be. It just couldn't. Why would Aunt Polly take up with the likes of Simon?

A sickened feeling washed through her. Unless he'd forced her against her will.

The admission explained why he'd wielded such a hold over her aunt. And perhaps even some of why he wished to locate Clarissa. But if he cared for the girl, why had he willingly taken money in exchange for not seeing her all these years? It didn't make sense.

Was the man even capable of caring for someone?

As Addie and Simon emerged onto the porch, Martha and Lydia stared up from their wicker chairs as though eager for explanation.

But Addie had none to offer.

If she exposed Simon, her dear friends would pay the penalty. But to break her promise to Aunt Polly and share the whereabouts of her daughter with such a man was inconceivable. *Lord, what am I to do?*

Martha clasped her elbow, brow furrowed. "Are you all right, dear? You look a bit shaken."

Addie forced a grin. "I'm fine."

As though unconvinced, Martha held her gaze a moment longer before she spoke again. "Mr. Banner tells me he's also from Richmond. How are you two acquainted?"

Mr. Banner?

Addie jerked her head toward Simon. How had Martha come by the surname so easily when he'd kept it hidden from her? Was it even his true name? She eyed him, trying to come up with an adequate response. "Mr. ... *Banner* was an acquaintance of my aunt. He and I have only recently come into contact."

Simon flashed what looked to be a warning glare before brandishing a smile at Martha. "But I soon came to think of her as I would my own daughter."

The very thought made Addie nauseous, his emphasis on the word *daughter* not escaping her.

"I've grown quite fond of her myself." Martha smiled at Addie then shifted her gaze to Simon. "Richmond is quite a distance. What, besides a visit with Adelaide, brings you all this way?"

"Work." The word slipped from Simon far too easily, as though rehearsed. "Employment's a mite hard to come by in the South right now."

Martha gave a slow nod as though detecting the sarcasm in his voice. "And what sort of work do you do?"

Addie held back a grimace, her palms growing clammy. She prayed he would not divulge his appalling profession and tarnish Martha and Lydia's opinion of her in the process.

Simon crossed his arms over his chest. "You name it, I can do it." He strolled to the edge of the porch, staring at the weed-infested fields. "This is a fine place, Mrs. Gallagher, but it appears you've no one to work your ground."

"My sons will be home soon. I'm certain they'll make up the slack when they come."

The tension in Addie's shoulders eased at Martha's declaration. The last thing she wanted was for Simon to be about the place.

With a slow nod, he jutted his lower lip and returned his gaze to the surrounding landscape. "Even so, by then these weeds will be that much harder to knock out and the plantin' further behind. I'd be happy to work the fields so they're ready t' plant once your sons get here. Assuming you have horses to pull the plow."

Addie bristled, wishing she were out of Simon's line of view, so she could give Martha some sort of warning. Instead, she prayed Martha would see through him on her own.

"We have horses, but I'm afraid no means to pay you."

"Food and board suits me for wages."

Addie bit her lip to keep from speaking out. No matter how good-natured the offer seemed, Simon was a menace to not only her, but the Gallaghers as well. The sooner he was sent on his way the better.

Martha tapped her cheek, seeming to weigh the offer. At last, she nodded. "All right, Mr. Banner. You can start tomorrow. But with no menfolk about the place, you'll take your meals and bed down in the barn."

"Fair enough." The triumphant smirk Simon flashed Addie sent a chill down her spine.

Clearly, her safe haven was safe no more.

41

Camp Rathbun, Elmira, New York
Monday, June 5, 1865

"How much longer are they gonna keep us holed up here, Sergeant? All they gotta do is give us our pay and send us on our way. How hard is that?"

Luke paused from polishing his brogans. Private Cummings posed a good question. A full week had passed since arriving in Elmira, and Luke was as eager as anyone to make the final trek home.

Sergeant Delmar glowered at the private. "Us and a half-a-million other soldiers. B'sides, what've you got to complain about? Poor Corporal Gallagher's within walkin' distance of his home and stuck here with the likes of you."

The reminder was one Luke could have done without. He gave a soft sigh. "You can bet our wages are held up in some bureaucratic entanglement. Our turn will come."

Cummings raked a hand over his face. "Yeah, but all this waiting's enough t' drive a fella mad."

Delmar cleared his throat. "If you're bored, we can always run more drills."

"Noooo ..." A wave of moans echoed through the group of soldiers. One tossed a boot at Cummings. "Quit your bellyachin' b'fore we all pay."

Stifling a grin, Luke stared through the cracks of the tall fence surrounding the former military training facility. The town had grown considerably since he'd last seen it. The coming of the railroad and military outpost seemed to have brought in a slew of people and businesses.

His gaze drifted in the direction of his home, and his heart reeled. Just four miles separated him from his family. Being so close and yet unable to go there was like winter without a spring.

He felt a nudge on his arm and looked to see Sergeant Delmar motioning to him.

Standing, Luke looked past him to the row upon row of white frame buildings that had, until the war's end, housed Confederate prisoners. Though a few prisoners remained, most had been allowed to return home.

A privilege he and many others were still waiting to enjoy.

He followed the sergeant into their quarters. Delmar took a thorough glance around as if ensuring they were alone and then leaned closer, voice low. "Word has it we'll likely be mustered out later this week."

Luke's spirit lifted. "That's great news. I take it you don't want the men to know?"

"Not till it's certain. No sense getting their hopes up."

"Understood."

A sense of satisfaction as well as loss settled over Luke as he returned to the group of soldiers who'd served under him and with him. The past year and a half had been spent battling alongside these men. They'd become like brothers, fighting for a common cause. Soon, they'd return to their normal lives. Some to farms or trades. Others to jobs as surveyors, bankers, or proprietors. All seeking to forget the horrors of war and be reunited with their families and loved ones.

Which was exactly what he planned to do.

"I DON'T LIKE THAT MAN." Lydia whispered to Addie as they rounded the corner of the house, baskets of fresh garden goods in tow.

Addie's gaze flicked to Simon out in the east field, taking another swig from his canteen and watching their every move. Though he'd made some headway with the fieldwork over the past week, his efforts were mediocre at best. She looked away and leaned toward Lydia. "He seems to spend as much time gawking and taking breaks as working."

Lydia nodded in agreement. "I don't see how the two of you are acquaintances."

Addie fought the urge to divulge the truth about Simon, but instead pursed her lips. The man was dangerous. If he thought, for an instant, she had disclosed his true intentions, no telling what he might do. "I know very little about the man and had no inkling he would come here."

Studying her, Lydia softened her voice even more. "You don't like him either, do you?"

Her young friend was more perceptive than Addie gave her credit. She would need to be careful how she responded. "There are those I like better."

Lydia snugged her basket tighter, her eyes again fixed on Simon. "Have you noticed how intently he watches us? It's unseemly."

An icy chill worked its way through Addie. She knew all too well Simon's disreputable behavior and couldn't hold back a warning. "Keep away from him. He ... can't be trusted."

Lydia's eyes widened. "What do you mean?"

Before Addie could respond, Martha stepped onto the porch, water jar and lunch tin in hand. "Lydia, would you take Mr. Banner his lunch? Then come have your own."

"I'll take it," Addie offered, setting her basket of produce on the porch.

"Thank you, dear."

Taking the tin and jar from Martha, Addie tried to stem her frayed nerves. Each day Simon seemed to grow bolder and more impatient. The less contact he had with Martha and Lydia the better. She cast Lydia a quick glance then averted her gaze, hopeful her young friend wouldn't pass on what little Addie had confided.

With poised steps, she crossed the yard to the field where Simon was working. Since the moment he set foot on the property, she'd not felt safe. Nor would she, until he was gone.

Removing his gloves, he swiped an arm over his brow and waited for her to approach. Rather than gratitude, a scowl lined his lips. He snatched the water jar and lunch tin from her with blistered hands. "If you think I'm gonna put up with this much longer, you've got another thing comin'."

Addie glanced over the poorly-worked field with a shrug. "Coming here was your idea, not mine. As was plowing the fields. Though I'm sure the Gallaghers are grateful for your ... help."

Simon's sneer deepened. "My patience is wearing thin where you're concerned. Either you tell me where I can find Clarissa, or that pretty little friend of yours and I are gonna get acquainted real quick like."

Heat surged in Addie's cheeks, and her muscles tensed. "You lay one finger on her and I'll ..."

"You'll what?"

She floundered, struggling to control the shakiness in her voice. "Just stay away from her. She has nothing to do with this."

"She does now. Purty young thing like that would make a fine substitute for Clarissa. And she looks to be a couple years older. More suitable for grooming."

"Grooming?" Addie's gaze flicked from one of his eyes to the other. "For what?"

One corner of Simon's mouth lifted in an appalling smirk. "To work for me, of course. Someone so young and fine will bring in more money than you or Polly could pay in a lifetime. I put up with Polly's meager payments until the girl was old enough. She's still a mite young, but she'll soon come into the trade."

Addie pressed a hand to her mouth, nearly retching at his words. "*That's* your intentions? To throw Clarissa to a pack of ravenous wolves to be molested and used?"

He jutted his lower lip. "Ah, now. Don't make it sound so vile. I prefer to think of it as providing a ... service."

She worked to quiet her voice. "But she's your daughter!"

His bushy eyebrows lifted. "And what better way to get acquainted than to make her a part of the family business?"

Holding back a groan, Addie cast a glance over her shoulder to ensure Martha and Lydia weren't within hearing range. Relieved they were nowhere in sight, she turned back to Simon, hands on hips. "You're more despicable than I imagined."

"What can I say? If you're not savvy with turnin' Clarissa over to me, there's always your blonde friend. She's a lot handier than trying to track down Clarissa. And a Northern girl like that would be a real delicacy for our boys down South."

"You beast." Addie reached to slap him, and he caught her by the arm. Pain surged through her, and with a moan, she clenched her teeth.

He shoved her arm away with a grin. "But a wealthy one."

She rubbed her wrist, her mind racing. Money seemed all this loathsome man valued. "W-What if I can somehow come up with the money? All of it. At once." Though she hadn't a clue how.

He shook his head. "Uh-uh. The time for paying me off is past. Like I say, one of these girls would be a goldmine. Just name which one, and I'll let you be."

"How could you even suggest such a disgusting thing? I'd never agree to surrender one of these girls to you."

Simon glared at her, his slate-gray eyes narrowing to slits.

"You've got till the week's end. After that, I'll make your mind up for you."

"Then take me." Addie's mouth quivered, the very thought leaving her nauseous.

"Huh. I might've considered that early on, but you're damaged goods with those ugly burn scars. Nah, it's either Clarissa or the girl."

Addie rocked back on her heels, all the blood draining from her face. The insult poured from Simon's lips as easily as if he'd told her he liked the color of her hair. Was she so worthless and pitiful that not even someone so vulgar as Simon valued her?

He took another swig from his water jar, then eyed her once more. "And remember, breathe one hostile word about me to anyone and sweet Mrs. Gallagher won't live to see the next sunrise."

Unable to find her voice, Addie pivoted away from him, praying she could compose herself before reaching the house.

What am I to do, Lord?

Lydia had become like a sister to her. And Clarissa *was* family. How could she sacrifice either of them to the likes of Simon?

With a heavy heart, she tromped through the yard, too numb for tears. Running away would do no good. He'd merely nab Lydia and force her into a life so contemptible Addie shuddered to think of it.

She wrapped an arm around her unsettled stomach. There had to be a way.

42

Camp Rathbun, Elmira, New York
Friday, June 9, 1865

"Here you go, Gallagher. Thanks for the loan."

Glancing down at the leather-bound Bible Sergeant Delmar held in his hand, Luke shoved it toward him. "Keep it."

"You sure?"

Luke looped his haversack over his shoulder. "I'm sure. I've another one at home and you've a lot more reading to do."

"Thanks." Delmar flipped through the thin pages. "You read all this?"

"Every word." With a lopsided grin, Luke scratched his cheek. "Well, maybe not *every* word. Books like Leviticus and Numbers I sort of skim."

"Ha! I'll remember that."

The sergeant's expression sobered, and he stuck out his palm. "You're a good corporal, Gallagher. A good man." He wagged his head side to side. "A bit young and impulsive maybe, but a good man nonetheless. I've enjoyed serving with you."

Luke gave his hand a firm shake, a flurry of emotions swirling inside him. "Same here. Hope we meet again someday."

Clutching his Springfield in one hand, Luke offered a final salute with his other. The bittersweet moment would stick with him a lifetime. As he walked through the gate toward the outskirts of town, an uncontrollable urge to shout spilled over him. Other soldiers followed suit, tossing their kepis in the air and turning the street into a raucous din. The spontaneous merriment soon dissipated as each man routed himself toward home. They were different men than when they'd joined up. Most, like him, not much more than boys when they'd pledged to fight.

As the street quieted, Luke retrieved his kepi and dusted it off, staring down the road ahead. It was time to get on with his life, begin anew. Shouldering his rifle, he started off, a spring in his step. The four-mile jaunt would seem as nothing compared to all the marching he'd done the past year and a half.

He grinned. Plus, he had a lot better incentive to get where he was going.

THE RUMBLE of a buggy stirred Addie from her prayers—something she'd been spending a lot of time at, of late. Since renewing her relationship with the Lord, it seemed her situation had gone from bad to worse. Simon could have given her until the end of the decade to make her choice, and it wouldn't have helped.

She would never allow him to have either girl.

As the sound of the approaching buggy intensified, she peered out the window of her upstairs room and immediately recognized Mr. Perkins' rig traveling at a hasty clip. Her breath caught when she recognized the soldier seated next to him.

"Luke." The whispered name was spoken with both endearment and apprehension.

How would Simon react to his being here?

She had to warn Luke.

With a hurried glance in the mirror, she scurried from the room and down the stairs. As she eased open the door, Martha and Lydia trotted down the porch steps to greet the buggy. Mr. Perkins tugged the horses to a stop, flashing a wide grin, his white teeth contrasting with the darkness of his skin. He gave Luke's shoulders a hardy squeeze. "Looka who I found wandering the road on my way from Elmira."

A beaming Luke hopped from the buggy, and immediately was smothered with hugs and kisses. For one brief moment, his eyes locked on Addie's, and all her burdens seemed to lift. She cast a tentative glance to the field, giving a relieved sigh at sight of the deserted horses and plow. Had Simon been scared off by Luke's arrival?

Or was he merely biding his time until he could gain the upper hand?

When he broke free of his mother and sister's embrace, Luke turned to Mr. Perkins. "Thanks for the ride, Hal."

"My pleasure. Wait'll I tell Celia you're home. She'll be cheerier than a lark."

With a wave goodbye, Luke turned to face Addie, his smile deepening. "Good to see you, Adelaide. You're looking well."

He was looking well also. So well, Addie curled her toes to keep from rushing into his arms. "Good to see you too."

A moment of awkward silence passed between them before Luke turned away. An ache welled in Addie's chest. He'd hardly seemed to notice her new dress or her fashioned hair. She scolded herself for caring. Had she expected him to fall at her feet?

Addie hid her hands behind her. Like every other man, he would view her as marred, blemished.

And yet, she'd thought him different. Someone who could see past her flawed appearance to her inner self.

Luke panned the fields, his gaze stalling on the abandoned horses and plow. "I can see Drew and I have our work cut out for us, though it looks as if someone has made an attempt to start."

Martha took his arm. "That's Mr. Banner's doing. He's an acquaintance of Adelaide's from down south." She lowered her voice. "But the poor fellow doesn't seem to have much knack for hard work."

"A friend of Adelaide's?" Luke turned questioning eyes on her.

Determined not to disclose Simon's identity in front of Martha and Lydia, Addie fumbled for words. Perhaps she could hint to Luke without the others realizing. "He's … more acquainted with my aunt than me."

Luke's eyes searched hers, but it was difficult to determine if he'd understood.

With a glance around, Martha knit her brow. "I wonder where he's off to? Well, you can meet him later. Come inside and get settled."

He pulled something from his pocket and waved it in the air. "You might want to have a look at this first. While in town, I stopped by the post office."

Martha's face lit as she snatched it from him and read the handwriting. "It's from Drew."

Lydia squealed and pressed closer. "Is he coming home too?"

With swift movements, Martha unfolded the letter and gave it a quick scan. "Yes! He'll be home in a few days." She glanced up, eyes sparkling. "And he's bringing a surprise."

A curious grin spilled over Luke's lips. "One guess what that is."

Martha's eyes moistened. "Both sons home within a fortnight. What more could a mother ask?"

Wrapping an arm around her shoulders, Luke leaned his head against hers. Lydia wedged her way in, and he looped his other arm around her, unspoken love passing between them. Addie turned her head to stem the flow of tears. Weeks earlier, the happy reunion would have brought her sorrow and envy. But, knowing this family as she did, she rejoiced with them and even yearned to be a part of it.

CYNTHIA ROEMER

As she gazed into the distance, her stomach knotted. Simon was lurking out there somewhere. Watching. Waiting. While Luke's presence brought some semblance of security, she knew all too well what Simon was capable of.

The sooner she could alert Luke of his presence here, the better.

LUKE UNHITCHED the horses from the plow, a bit agitated this *Mr. Banner* would go off and leave them unattended in the hot sun. Who was he, anyway? And what was he doing following Adelaide all over the countryside?

Adelaide.

He'd barely been able to tear his eyes from her. She was more beautiful than he'd remembered. Having shed her mourning garb, she'd be an even greater temptation. He couldn't allow himself to become more attached.

Looping the ends of the reins over his shoulders, he gripped them farther down with his gloved hands. At least he had farm work to occupy him. That would give him ample time to pray she'd see God for who He truly was.

"You've made your mother and sister extremely happy."

Luke jolted at Adelaide's gentle voice.

"I'm sorry. I didn't mean to startle you."

Relaxing his hold on the reins, he turned toward her. Unable to restrain a grin, he drank in every contour of her face. "I guess I'm more used to my sergeant's voice than a woman's."

She returned a soft smile, fingering the chain around her neck. "I wanted to thank you for the locket. It was very thoughtful of you."

He shrugged, heat flaming in his cheeks. "I figured you couldn't go around wearing that singed one of your aunt's."

Her expression sobered, and he regretted dredging up the

memory. "I also want to thank you for sending me here. Living with your family has ... changed me."

A little surprised, he nodded, his gaze flicking to the farmhouse in the distance. "Ma and Lydia are pretty special."

"Yes, they are." With a hasty glance around, she inched closer, seeming as uneasy as her close proximity was making him. Her voice softened to a whisper. "That's why you need to know they're in danger."

"Danger? What sort of danger?"

Moisture pooled in her violet eyes, and her chin trembled. "Simon's here."

"*He's* Mr. Banner? How did he find you?"

The concern in Luke's voice was both gratifying and unsettling. "He coaxed the information from one of the nurses at the Richmond hospital."

Luke's cheeks flinched. "Has he threatened you?"

With another cautious look around, Addie leaned closer until she could almost feel the warmth of his cheek against hers. "It isn't safe here. If he thinks I'm warning you, there's no telling what he'll do."

Nodding, Luke feigned checking the harness straps. "Do Ma and Lydia know who he is?"

Addie shook her head. "I've kept it from them. But I'm worried he might harm Lydia. His intentions are ... too deplorable to speak of."

"Maybe my coming was enough to spook him."

"He wouldn't give up so easily. I'm certain he's out there somewhere." She scanned the tree line to the north, the very thought making her squeamish.

"You may be right." Taking hold of one of the horse's bridles, Luke clicked his cheek and tugged the team forward.

Addie walked alongside, enjoying the sense of security and

strength Luke's presence brought. Holding her dress out of the freshly plowed soil, she took careful steps, glancing at him out of the corner of her eye. He seemed different, more distant. As if he didn't want her here.

And yet, she couldn't deny the concern on his face when he'd learned about Simon.

A piercing scream sounded from the direction of the house. They locked eyes, knowing instantly whose voice it was.

Lydia.

Leaving the horses, Luke barreled across the yard toward the back of the house. Addie ran after him, shoving frantic thoughts aside to pray. *Please, Lord. Help Luke reach her in time.*

When she rounded the corner of the house, Martha, Luke and Lydia were standing together at the edge of the garden, Lydia sobbing in her mother's arms. Breathless, Addie clutched a hand to her chest. "Is she all right?"

Luke nodded. "Lydia said he took off into the timber when he heard me coming. The coward." He balled his fists, edging toward the house. "I'll get my rifle and go after him."

"You'll do no such thing. He could be lurking anywhere, and we need you here."

At his mother's request, Luke reneged, though his eyes scanned the woods like a hunter in search of game.

Martha loosened her hold on Lydia, brushing a hand down her mussed hair. "Are you sure he didn't hurt you?"

"I'm fine." Lydia pushed back, lower lip puckered, her torn dress and tattered look suggesting otherwise.

She shifted her gaze to Addie. "It was Mr. Banner. He had a knife and tried to force me to go with him. Why would he do that?"

Addie struggled for a response. "I ..."

"He's obviously deranged," surmised Martha.

Lydia squared her shoulders. "I bit him and stomped his foot with my boot heel. That's when he heard Luke and Mama coming."

Good girl. That should make Simon think twice about carting Lydia hundreds of miles against her will. Addie could almost envision the man's irritation.

Lydia fingered the large tear in her sleeve. "Look. He tore my dress."

"Your dress can be mended. What matters is that you're safe." The tremor in Martha's voice belied her calm exterior.

Addie dropped her gaze to the ground beneath. "This is my fault. I never should have come."

"My dear, you can't possibly blame yourself for this man's dishonorable actions."

Though Martha's words were a comfort, there was no denying the truth. "But it's on my account he's here."

"Then blame me." Luke's masculine voice broke in. He stepped toward her, and her eyes lifted. "I sent you here."

"What's this all about, son? I have a feeling there's more to this than we've been told."

Addie searched Luke's azure eyes, gaining courage from their resolve. It was time they knew the full story. About Simon. About Aunt Polly. About Clarissa.

Every ugly detail.

Saturday, June 10, 1865

Addie peered out the window to the field where Luke was plowing. She leaned her forehead against the windowpane, watching him skillfully guide the team to turn the earth in deep furrows. How different he looked in civilian clothes. Though equally as handsome.

Despite his qualms about not staying nearer the house, he'd given into their assurances and gone to the field. Though his head often veered in their direction. Under instruction not to go outside alone and only when necessary, she and Lydia had taken to their room like a couple of caged birds.

"Shall I tell Luke you've been admiring him from afar?"

The sound of Lydia's giggles brought a rush of warmth to Addie's cheeks as she moved away from the window. "I'm not ... admiring him. I've just not observed someone plow before."

"You never watched Mr. Banner that way."

Despite the tease, Addie bristled. "I'd not wish to watch that awful man do *anything*."

Lying crossways on the mattress, Lydia drooped her legs over the side of the bed and stared at the plastered ceiling. "This is certainly no way to live. How long do you suppose we'll have to stay cooped up like this?"

"Until Luke flushes Simon out I suppose."

"Ugh. That could be weeks, or even months."

Addie sighed. If she thought leaving would end the matter, she would have Luke whisk her away in a heartbeat. But Lydia was as much in danger now as her.

If anything happened to the dear girl, Addie would never forgive herself.

Penny's familiar bawl sounded from inside the barn. Lydia popped off the bed like a bee had stung her, a smile replacing her glower. "Sounds like Penny's eager for her evening milking. At least we have that to occupy us. Come on."

Addie grinned at her friend's eagerness. "I wasn't aware milking was such a treat."

"It is when it's your only entertainment. Let's go."

Addie could hardly keep pace as Lydia frolicked down the stairway. "We're going to milk Penny, Mama," she announced as they passed the kitchen.

"All right, dear. Be quick about it and keep a close watch."

Stepping out onto the porch they took a cautious glance around. As they downed the steps, Lydia leaned close to Addie's ear. "More than a day has passed without sign of him. Maybe he's gone."

"Maybe." Addie knew Simon better than to think he'd give up so easily. But not wishing to frighten Lydia, she held her tongue. The poor girl had been through enough.

They strolled side-by-side toward the barn, casting leery glances in either direction. The evening sun still held warmth as it shone an amber glow over the landscape. The scent of earth carried on the gentle breeze, and Addie again glanced to the field where Luke was plowing. He'd worked all day with only a short break for lunch. With all this going on, would she ever have opportunity to spend time with him?

Tomorrow being Sunday, perhaps they'd have more time

together. She smiled to herself. Wouldn't he be stunned to learn her heart had softened toward God? Could that even be what fueled the distance between them?

Suddenly, tomorrow couldn't come soon enough.

As they reached the barn doorway, Penny's large, brown eyes stared back at them, and she sounded an impatient bawl. Hands on hips, Lydia tilted her head to one side. "No need to grumble. We're coming."

With a soft chuckle, Addie turned to retrieve the milk pail from the side of the door. Her breath caught when a hairy hand grasped her arm, and Simon emerged from the shadows. She gave a soft scream, his firm grip bruising her still tender flesh. She pivoted, seeing sheer panic in Lydia's eyes. "Run!"

Lydia hesitated but an instant before sprinting from the barn with a frantic cry.

Addie kicked at Simon with the toe of her boot, and he groaned, his hold loosening long enough for her to slip from his grasp. He lunged, pulling her down by the legs. Addie hit the barn floor with a loud "*umph*," the air expelling from her lungs.

Still half dazed, she spit out bits of straw and dirt. She cringed as Simon's brutish arm wrapped around her waist, lifting her to her feet. "Looks like you'll be going with me after all, Addie Hanover," he spewed.

The very sound of her name on his lips made her flesh crawl. She fought against him, until the cold steel blade of a knife lodged against her throat. She stilled, her heart pounding against the wall of her chest.

Simon's heavy, foul breath nearly choked her as he placed his mouth to her ear. "Not a sound." He tightened his grip until she could hardly breathe. "You'll not get away so easy as your young friend. Now, let's go before she alerts the whole countryside."

He shoved her from the barn, his belt buckle pressing into her spine. Unable to turn her head without the knife blade pricking her skin, Addie's eyes searched for signs someone might be approaching.

Her heart sank when her limited view revealed no one. Too far out to hear the commotion, Luke would have to glance this way to know anything was afoot. *Oh, please Lord, help Lydia reach him in time.*

Addie trembled beneath Simon's harsh grip. As frantic as she was to regain her freedom, all she could think of was how thankful she was Lydia had escaped.

And hopefully sought help.

Simon dragged her to the back side of the barn where a saddled chestnut mare stood tethered. One that strongly resembled Mr. Perkins' horse. A sense of dread pierced her heart. Had Simon harmed the couple?

The pressure of the blade beneath her chin slackened, and in its stead, a rank-smelling bandana covered her mouth. Simon snugged it around her head, pulling hair out by the roots as he tied it in place. Addie's insides roiled. If he expected her to put up with this treatment all the way to Richmond, he had another thing coming.

She'd not give him a moment's rest.

Now that she'd made her peace with God, death seemed less frightening than being subjected to the life Simon had in mind.

She tried to wriggle free, and he spun her toward him, his thick fingers pressing into her shoulders. He gave her a firm shake. "Make this easier on the both of us and stop squirmin'."

As she raised her hand to slap him, he clasped her wrist, squeezing it until her legs buckled. "You're a spirited one, all right. That'll work to your favor where you're headed."

Unable to speak, she pinned him with her glare. For the first time in her life, she understood what it must feel like to be enslaved, and it appalled her.

With a smirk, he pulled a rope from his pocket and looped it around both wrists. As he tied it into place, her unfeeling hands grew even number.

She ventured a glance around. Why hadn't anyone come?

Had Lydia indeed panicked and hidden in her room instead of alerting Luke?

Surely not. She was much too brave and resourceful.

Her breath caught as Simon hoisted her onto the horse. She fumbled for the saddle horn, struggling to sit upright. As Simon gripped the pommel and lifted his boot to the stirrup, she saw her chance. Drawing her leg back, she planted a mighty kick to his chest.

He fell backwards with a groan. "Why you ..."

Heart thumping, Addie clicked her tongue against her cheek and sounded a loud "Yah!" The horse surged forward, throwing her off balance. Within three strides, she dropped to the ground. Ignoring the pain in her backside, she scrambled to her feet and poised to run.

The click of a pistol held her in place. "Move one inch farther, and I'll shoot."

Addie turned to face him, the gag keeping her from rendering a reply.

Hurried footsteps sounded from the front of the barn, stirring hope within her.

As the sounds grew closer, Simon cast a frenzied glance toward the timber. His eyes narrowed as he turned them on Addie. "You're more trouble than you're worth."

A tremor coursed through her as he pointed the Derringer at her and steadied his aim. Backing away, Addie shook her head.

Smoke puffed as he pulled the trigger. A lifetime seemed to pass in that split second, Closing her eyes, Addie curled her arms over her head and squatted on the ground. Hoping, praying his aim wouldn't be true.

Something brushed against her, knocking her from her feet.

A second shot fired from behind, and Simon gave a mighty roar.

Harried boot steps and frantic women's voices grew closer. Addie fought for air, her breaths coming short and fast. Opening her eyes, she stared down at her dress, expecting to see a blood stain or feel the searing pain of a bullet.

But there was nothing.

How had he missed her?

She ventured a look, and saw Simon flailing on the ground, obviously badly injured.

Sounds of weeping from behind startled her. She turned, eager to assure everyone she was okay.

But a moment's glance conveyed the true reason for their grief.

Not three feet from her, Luke's lifeless form lay stretched on the ground, Martha and Lydia crouched on either side.

The blood drained from Addie's face. *Oh Lord, no!*

Scrambling toward him, her mind played over what had happened, trying to make sense of it. Something had swiped against her just after the gun went off.

Tears brimmed in her eyes. Simon hadn't missed. Luke had shielded her.

Her whole body went limp as she held back a sob. He'd taken the bullet intended for her.

44

Sunday, June 11, 1865
1:30 a.m.

"Your son's a lucky man, Mrs. Gallagher. The bullet lodged very close to his heart. An inch lower and you wouldn't have needed my services."

Addie's blood ran cold at Dr. Royce's sobering statement. She glanced at Luke, his ashen face and still form so foreign to his usual hearty appearance. He'd nearly died saving her.

Foolish man.

Warmth surged through her. *Foolish, yet wonderful.*

"Wasn't luck that spared him." Martha continued to stroke Luke's damp forehead, her eyes never straying from his face. "The Lord was watching over him."

"I'll not argue that." Dr. Royce finished drying his hands, then rubbed bloodshot eyes, the difficult surgery and late night taking their toll.

Thankfully Lydia had had the wherewithal to ride to retrieve both him and the sheriff while Martha and Addie helped get Luke to his bed. He'd rallied just long enough to walk upstairs before fatigue and blood loss rendered him too weak to continue.

Worry lines creased Martha's brow. "How ironic that he should survive the war only to be gunned down at his own home."

Addie's shoulders weighted with guilt. Did Martha blame her for this?

Lydia strode over and placed a hand on her mother's arm. "Luke's young and strong, Mama. Just you wait. He'll be back on his feet in no time."

Chin quivering, Martha cupped a hand over Lydia's. "That's right, dear."

Dr. Royce finished putting away his supplies. "The effects of the chloroform won't wear off for a while yet. He'll likely sleep the remainder of the night, so I suggest you get some rest."

She drew a deep breath and released it slowly. "I'll sit with him a while."

"If you like, I'll stay the night."

With a shake of her head, Martha gazed up at the weary doctor. "That won't be necessary, Doctor. We've inconvenienced you enough. Thank you for all you've done."

Nodding, he closed his black bag. "I'll be back to check on him in the morning." His gaze flicked from Lydia to Addie. "You young ladies see Mrs. Gallagher gets some rest."

Lydia patted her mother's arm. "He's right, Mama. You look tired. I'll stay with Luke."

The ache to do something chiseled its way through Addie. She edged closer, choking down the boulder-sized lump in her throat. "Please, may I stay with him?"

Three pairs of eyes swung in her direction. In the awkward moment, Addie wrapped her arms around her middle to still them from trembling. Her gaze locked with Martha's, expecting bitterness and blame. Instead, her pale, blue eyes seemed to brim with understanding. Without a word, she leaned to kiss Luke's forehead, then rose to her feet. "I'll see you out, Doctor."

As Martha passed, she stretched out her arm, and Addie latched onto it as though it were a lifeline. "Let me know when he awakens."

Grateful for the woman's trust, Addie gave her arm a gentle squeeze, a hint of a smile touching her lips. "I will."

Doctor Royce paused beside her and held out a small, glass bottle filled with reddish-brown powder. "He's liable to be in quite a bit of pain when he wakes. Mix a pinch of this with a glass of water and give it to him."

"Yes, Doctor." Taking the bottle, Addie turned and saw Lydia standing beside her still as a statue but for her quivering chin. Addie searched her young friend's moist eyes, not knowing how or what to comfort.

Lydia's lips moved as if to speak, but instead she thrust her arms around Addie, sobbing.

Melting into her embrace, Addie struggled to keep a hold on the bottle, as well as her emotions.

A sniffle sounded in her ear. "I was so scared."

"Me too." Addie let her tears roll unhindered, squeezing her friend tighter. Even in the midst of uncertainty, a deep sense of kinship seemed to bind them.

As Lydia's hold slackened, she whispered in Addie's ear. "God watched over us."

Addie's lips lifted in a weak grin. "Yes. He did."

Drying her eyes on her sleeve, Lydia cast a glance back at Luke. "Come get me if he wakes up."

"I will."

As Lydia exited, Luke's steady breaths seemed to grow louder. Striding over, Addie set the medicine bottle on the stand table and watched his chest rise and fall. He looked so helpless, so fragile. This whole incident seemed a nightmare.

Fear coiled its way around her heart. What if he didn't pull through? What if he died like everyone else she'd ever cared for?

She brushed the back of her fingers over his cheek, letting her tears flow freely once more. He'd sacrificed himself for her.

Been willing to die for her. No one had ever done anything so loving.

Except Jesus.

The thought surfaced from deep within.

She swiped the tears from her cheeks. It was true. Jesus had willingly died in her place. Forgiven her when she'd rejected and blamed Him for all the hurt. She needed to trust Him now. With Luke.

No matter what.

Bending over, she kissed Luke's forehead, the warmth of his skin breathing renewed hope into her heart. She placed her hand on his arm and bowed her head.

"Lord, I don't claim to understand your ways. Like Job, I question why You do the things You do. I'll never understand why I didn't have the chance to know my mother, or why Papa, Thomas, and Eli had to die. I used to see only the bad, all the wrong. But now I know You can bring good out of hardship. Your ways are indeed higher than ours."

Her throat hitched. "Luke taught me that."

"Thank you for bringing him into my life. Thank you for protecting him, not allowing the bullet to pierce his heart when it easily could have. He's such a man of faith. I can see why You might want him with You, but I ... I need him. Please don't take him from me. But, if You choose to, I won't hold it against You. Thy will be done, Lord. In Jesus' name."

Addie's eyes blinked open, plunging more tears to the already dampened bedsheet. Luke lay unmoved, his breaths steady and unchanged. And yet, through the blur of moisture and fatigue, she thought she noted a slight upturn to his lips. Was it her imagination?

"Can you hear me, Luke?"

Though the words fell void, her hope remained.

THE SOUND of a moan in Addie's ear stirred her from light sleep. Though the room itself remained dim, the first hint of daylight filtered through the curtained window. With a sudden recollection of what had happened, she popped her head up from the corner of the mattress and sat back in the chair. "Luke?"

No response.

She was certain he'd made a sound. With a sigh, she rubbed the crick from her neck. When had she fallen asleep?

Prying her eyes wider, she relit the lantern wick that had burnt to a nub.

Another moan returned her eyes to Luke. Twin lines now creased the bridge of his nose—a sign the effects of the chloroform were wearing off.

Leaning over him, she brushed a stray lock of hair from his temple. A trace of blood stained the bandage covering much of his bare chest. "I'm here, Luke."

His eyes flickered open. He cringed, squinting up at her. "Guess I ... caught the bullet ... after all. Didn't know if ... I'd make it ... in time."

"Shh." She rubbed a hand along his brow. "Save your strength."

With a slight nod, he took a hard swallow. "Is everyone ... okay?"

Her heart melted at his undying concern for his family. "Everyone is fine."

The muscles in Luke's face relaxed as if those three words made everything right with the world.

A glance at the open door reminded Addie of her promise to wake Martha and Lydia, but she couldn't bring herself to. Not yet. For a few glorious minutes, she wanted Luke to herself. "Are you in a great deal of pain?"

He gritted his teeth. "Like I've been kicked by a mule."

She reached for the bottle of powder. "Well, Doctor Royce

left some pain medicine that should help." She stirred some into a glass of water.

Propping his head up with her hand, she put the glass to his mouth, her fingers struggling to hold it in place. A few sips were enough to make his face pucker. When he turned his head, she set the glass aside. "Shall I tell Dr. Royce you're a disagreeable patient?"

"I've seen what too much does ... to people. I'd rather have my ... wits about me."

"Well, there must be something I can do to ease your pain." She wrung out a dampened cloth and dabbed his sweaty brow. "I suppose I should let your mother and Lydia know you're awake."

"I'm sort of enjoying ... the nurse I have."

A rush of warmth cloaked her cheeks, and her lips lifted. Apparently, he was equally content with just the two of them. "It seems we've switched roles. The patient has become the caregiver."

"That's not all that's changed." His blue eyes searched hers. "I heard you praying."

"You did?" She drew her hand back, the blush in her cheeks deepening as she tried to recall her exact words. "Everything?"

"Enough." A twinge of pain trounced his attempt at a grin. "And to think how much time I've ... wasted trying to think of a way to ... persuade you God isn't the enemy."

She resumed dabbing his forehead, her lips pulling taut. "Then you know you didn't have to do this, that my soul was ready."

"But I did." He moved his hand to hers, and the warmth in her cheeks filtered through every inch of her. "You've given me more reason than ever to want you to live."

Moisture pooled in her eyes as she leaned closer. "But you could have died, and where would that have left me?"

"But I didn't die."

The gleam in his eyes stole her defenses, and she became more keenly aware of the feel of his hand caressing hers.

"You're awake!"

Lydia's excited voice stirred Addie to her feet, and she flashed a nervous grin. "Yes. I-I was just coming to get you."

She locked eyes with Luke and shared a telling grin, their moment of intimacy ending far too abruptly.

Yet it was enough to make her long for more.

Dr. Royce folded his stethoscope and took a step back. "Well, young man, you've cheated death and won, but it will be several weeks before you'll be doing any field work or other strenuous activity."

Luke raked a hand over his stubbled jaw. Laying off a few weeks of work was a small price to pay for having a bullet in his chest. But it wouldn't do his family any good with no crops in the field. He gave a soft sigh. "Sounds like Drew's got his work cut out for him when he gets here." He turned to his mother. "Sorry, Ma. I never figured on being laid up."

She leaned to kiss his forehead. "You just concentrate on getting well. The crops will wait. And Hal has offered his help, if need be."

"Are he and Celia all right? When I recognized their horse, I feared Simon might have harmed them."

Ma smiled. "Lydia returned their horse and spoke to them this morning. They're fine, and plan to visit you soon."

The doctor returned the instrument to his black bag. "I'd stay and chat, but I have another house call to make ahead of church service." He cast a sweeping glance around the room before returning his gaze to Luke. "And you seem to be thriving under the care of these three lovely ladies. Which is more than I can say for the man you shot. When and if he recovers, he'll go straight from the infirmary to jail."

"Man I shot?" Luke hadn't thought to ask what had become

of Simon. But he was sure of one thing—he hadn't shot anybody. "It wasn't me. I didn't have a gun."

Adelaide's jaw dropped, her confusion seeming to exceed only the doctor's. "Then who shot him?"

A straight-faced Lydia toyed with the tip of the thick braid draped over her shoulder. "I did."

Luke watched his mother's face, expecting to view utter shock. Instead, her expression revealed little change. Either she'd witnessed the act or guessed their secret.

"You, Lydia?" Doctor Royce's tone harbored disbelief.

With a diminutive nod, Lydia's eyes lifted. "Luke was too far away, so I went to the house to get his hunting rifle." Her eyes moistened. "I only meant to scare Mr. Banner off, but when I saw him shoot Luke, I just ..."

Luke reached a hand out to her, and she rushed forward, burying her face against his shoulder. Her warm tears dampened his skin as he placed his good arm around her. "You did right, Lydia. If you hadn't acted, no telling what he would have done."

Ma's gaze fluctuated between him and Lydia. "He's right, dear. You did what was necessary. Though I'm hard-pressed to know how you acquired such a skill?"

Lydia's head lifted, and Luke tossed her a wink. "Luke thought it best someone know in case we needed to protect ourselves, so he taught me before he left."

Ma's gaze landed solidly on Luke. "I thought as much."

He flashed a reluctant grin. "You gotta admit, the lesson wasn't wasted."

"Well, if this isn't one for the newspapers." The doctor raised his hand and moved it through the air as he spoke. "Soldier saves girl. Sister shoots intruder."

Witnessing the distress in his mother's eyes, Luke cleared his throat. "Uh, Doc. I think we'd rather keep this incident to ourselves. It's not one we're too fond to recall."

The doctor shrugged. "Suit yourselves. A doctor's confidentiality means I'll not breathe a word. But news like this has a way of spreading." Clutching his bag, he nodded at first Luke, then his mother. "I'll check back in a couple of days."

"Thank you, Doctor."

As Ma and Lydia followed Dr. Royce from the room, Adelaide lingered. She edged closer, her violet eyes fastened on his. "You and your sister are both quite remarkable. You deserve a hero's fanfare."

His lips spread in a grin. "I'll settle for the peace and comfort of home."

"I don't blame you." Dropping her gaze, she tucked her lip behind her teeth.

"What is it?"

She hesitated, then looked him in the eyes. "I know where Clarissa is, my aunt's daughter. Now that Simon's no longer a threat. I need to go to her."

Though Luke's heart sank, he tried not to convey it in his voice. "Where is she?"

"Copperville, Pennsylvania. Have you heard of it?"

His brow pinched. "Copperville. Why that's down in Sullivan County. Not more than a day's ride from here." He forced a grin. "Tell you what. Soon as I'm travel-worthy, I'll drive you there myself. Lydia can ride along as chaperone."

She released a long breath, her expression brightening. "I'd like that."

Though he shared her warm smile, deep down he wondered if he was losing her before he even had her.

45

June 19, 1865
(Eight days later)

The "clunk" of wood splitting drew Addie to the back of the house. At sight of Luke wielding an ax, she shook her head and sighed. "I don't think chopping wood is what Dr. Royce had in mind when he said to take it easy."

Luke gave her one of his endearing, lopsided grins as he placed another chunk of wood on the stump. "It's not hard. All I do is lift the ax and let gravity do the rest. Watch." With a twist of his wrist, he lifted the ax over his head with one arm and let it fall. As it splintered down the center, the hunk of wood flew in two directions. He wriggled his eyebrows at her. "See?"

Her mouth twisted. "Well, it's hardly restful."

"I can't sit idle all the time. It goes against my nature." His winsome smile made arguing impossible.

"They're coming!" Lydia's excited voice reverberated from the front porch.

"Must be Drew." Luke wedged the ax in the tree stump. "Let's go."

Addie fell into step beside him, a bit nervous how Drew

would respond to her. What would he think of a Southerner living under their roof? *Her* brothers would have taken offense if she'd allowed a Northerner into their home.

She hung back in Luke's shadow as they rounded the corner of the house. Meeting new people had never been her strong suit, especially those who might find her presence intrusive. She caught a glimpse of Martha and Lydia greeting a dark-haired man and woman on the front porch, peals of laughter mingling with joyful chatter.

"Hey, hey, big brother. 'Bout time you got here," Luke called as they approached.

All eyes spun toward them, and Drew's face lit up when he saw his brother. "Luke!" Leading the woman by the hand, Drew strolled to greet him. Though the brothers shared few like features, Addie noted similarities in their square jaws and sideways smiles.

Drew's attempt at a hug met with Luke's outstretched palm. "Better settle for a handshake."

Drew's dark brows turned downward as he cut a glance at the bulge of bandages beneath Luke's shirt. He gave his brother's hand a gentle shake. "What happened to you?"

"Ah, I'll fill you in later. I'd rather talk of pleasant things." His gaze drifted to Drew's companion, her eyes the color of honey and a kind smile lining her lips. "Like who this is with you."

"This is Caroline." Sliding an arm around the woman's slender waist, Drew and she shared a loving glance. "My wife."

Luke thumbed his hat higher on his head. "Your *wife*? Well, I'll be. How'd you manage that with a war on?"

"I'm not sure, but with your injury, you oughta be glad I did. She's a nurse."

Caroline's shy grin shifted from her husband to Luke. "More like a nurse in training."

Addie rocked back on her heels. Though not as thick as her own, she detected a definite Southern twang to Caroline's voice, her style of dress and loose chignon quite similar to her own. Had Drew married a Southerner?

"Don't let her fool you. She stitched me up in the middle of nowhere with nothing but a needle and horsehair." Drew lifted her hand to his lips, obvious love and pride telling in his eyes.

Caroline's delicate fingers, decorated with a wedding band, swayed Addie to slide her blemished hands behind her back. Everything about Caroline appeared flawless.

The sort of woman Luke deserved.

Luke eyed the couple. "Is that how you two met?"

Raising his voice a notch, Drew glanced at his mother looking on from the porch. "Now, that's a story to tell over some of Ma's good home cooking."

She motioned to them. "Come on in. Lydia and I'll have victuals on the table in no time."

"We'll be right behind you. But first, Luke, aren't you going to introduce us to your friend?"

Though tempted to slink back into Luke's shadow, the touch of his hand at the small of her back held Addie in place. "This is Miss Adelaide Hanover of Richmond."

"*Richmond?*" Drew's tone escalated. "You're a long way from home. Much farther even than Caroline."

Addie's head dipped. She wasn't certain where home was anymore.

"I've always wanted to visit Richmond," Caroline's gentle tone cut through Addie's fog.

With a nod, she returned a warm smile. "Where are you from?"

"Near Frederick, Maryland. Along the Monocacy River."

"Sounds pretty."

"Oh, it is." Caroline took a sweeping glance around. "Though I must admit, New York is every bit as lovely."

Addie met Caroline's gaze, her friendly nature putting her more at ease. Caroline looked to be only a couple years older than her and someone she might enjoy getting to know. But as the four of them strolled toward the house, easy chatter rolled from her three companions. Caroline seemed to fit in like she belonged here.

Where did Addie fit?

She strolled along in silence. As kind and accepting as this family had been, it wasn't her own. She had but one blood relative—Clarissa. And Addie's heart would not be settled until they were together.

46

Stuart Banks Residence
Copperville, Pennsylvania
June 24, 1865

Addie glanced over her shoulder at Luke and Lydia seated atop the buggy. Luke flashed a reassuring smile. A half-mile outside of town, the impressive estate only heightened Addie's already rattled nerves. With a deep breath, she tapped the knocker down twice. Taking a step back, she waited for what seemed an eternity. Light footsteps approached the door from within, and she shifted feet to keep her legs from trembling. She'd waited months for this. Would they even let her meet Clarissa?

The door swung open, and a slender, red-haired maid peered out at her. "May I help you, miss?"

"A-Are Mr. and Mrs. Banks at home?"

"Yes, miss. May I tell them who's calling?"

"Adelaide Hanover. Polly Hanover's niece."

The maid's thin brows knit. "Come in, please."

With a tentative glance back at her friends, Addie stepped onto the plush, red carpet lining the hallway. A full-length mirror at the end made the hall seem to go on forever. She followed the maid to the spacious parlor, a huge stone fireplace decorating the far center wall. A piano graced the bay window to her right, while on her left, an ornate table displayed an abundance of photos.

The couple obviously wasn't hurting for money.

"Please, have a seat. I'll let them know you're here."

Ill-at-ease, Addie inched onto the lavish settee. Her eyes veered toward the array of daguerreotype photos and portraitures behind it, most of which included various stages of Clarissa's life from infancy to present. What a different life she'd had with this couple than she would have had with Aunt Polly.

But affluence alone did not bring happiness. The Clarissa in the photos looked happy, but was she truly?

The swish of a dress and muffled voices sounded from the hall. Addie sat straighter, doing her best to conceal her scarred hands. The couple, trim and refined in their stance, strolled toward her, their expressions quizzical. Mr. Banks nodded to her. "Miss Hanover?"

"Yes." Standing, Addie worked to school her voice. "I'm Polly's niece. Adelaide."

"Also from Richmond, I presume?"

"Yes." Her thick drawl obviously conveying her Southern roots.

Mrs. Banks' olive eyes harbored misgiving. "What can we do for you, Miss Hanover?"

"I'm afraid I have some rather grim news to relay." Addie moistened her lips, trying to piece together her words. "My aunt was ... killed in a fire during the Richmond takeover."

Mrs. Banks drew in a breath. "Oh, no!"

A soft sigh escaped her husband. "We wondered why we hadn't heard from her. We're truly sorry."

Choosing her expressions carefully, Addie forged on. "I recently learned of my aunt's relationship with ... your daughter,

Clarissa. I have no other family. I wonder if you might allow me to become acquainted with her?"

The couple exchanged an anxious look. Clearly disturbed by the request, Mr. Banks slid an arm around his wife's waist. "I'm not certain that's a good idea. Clarissa knew Polly only as a distant relative." He softened his voice. "She has no inkling she's ... adopted."

"I understand that. And I don't wish to disrupt your lives, but she's my only living relative, and I'd like very much to have the opportunity to meet and get to know her." Something within Addie balked. That wasn't entirely true. Until this moment, she'd had every intention of making Clarissa aware of their kinship. Perhaps not immediately, but soon. In hopes she would want to come away with her. But seeing how attached Mr. and Mrs. Banks seemed to the girl had her doubting she could follow through with her plans.

Before they could respond, the front door opened and shut and footsteps trailed down the hall. "Mama. Papa. Who's that in the buggy out ..." The loud query came to an abrupt end as a chestnut-haired girl rounded the corner to the parlor. Her eyes fastened on Addie. "Oh. Hello."

Addie's heart leapt, her eyes glued to the girl's face. The twelve-year-old had Aunt Polly's sloped eyes and held her mouth just the same. Likenesses Addie hadn't detected from the photos. "Hello, Clarissa."

Clarissa cocked her head to the side. "Do I know you?"

"No, but you knew my ..." Addie paused, taking heed to Mr. and Mrs. Banks' pleading expressions. "*friend* Polly."

The girl's face brightened. "That's what it is. Your Southern accent sounds much like hers. She's nice. It's been a while since she's come for a visit. Is she all right?"

Rather than answer, Addie turned to Mr. and Mrs. Banks. "Could Clarissa and I have a few moments? Please?"

The couple wavered before finally making their way to the

door. Mrs. Banks slid a hand down Clarissa's sleeve. "We'll be just down the hall."

Mouthing a "thank you," Addie waited for them to take their leave, then patted the settee. "Sit down, Clarissa."

The girl ambled over, her face pinching when she noticed Addie's scars. "What happened to your hands?"

Tamping down her insecurities, Addie kept her blemished fingers in plain sight. "They were burned in a fire."

"Oh, I'm sorry."

"Thank you." Addie drank in the girl's features, choking down the emotions this moment entailed. How much should she divulge? If Aunt Polly had remained silent about her identity all these years, perhaps she should too. And yet, Clarissa was all she had left. Someone Addie had longed to know from the moment she'd learned about her. She drew a deep breath. "I've come to tell you Polly won't be able to visit you anymore."

The girl's face scrunched. "Did something happen to her?"

"Yes. She ... died in the fire that burned my hands."

"Oh, how sad. Thank you for telling me. I would have wondered what happened to her."

Addie swallowed. *Nothing but death could have kept her away.* "Coming here to see you made her very happy."

Clarissa shrugged. "That's what Mama and Papa said, so they let her keep coming. The poor dear. I'll miss her visits."

Though the girl seemed genuinely sad, there was no real depth to her sorrow. No true attachment like Polly might have wished.

Clarissa tilted her head to the side. "Say, maybe you'd like to come in her place?"

Addie bit her cheek, a torrent of emotions coursing through her. Though less contact than she'd hoped for, the invitation was one to which Aunt Polly would have heartily approved. She grinned. "I'd like that, with your parents' approval, of course."

"Oh, they won't mind. They're the best."

The comment was all Addie needed to tip the scales of

silence. Obviously, Clarissa was content here with the only family she'd ever known.

And though it broke her heart, Addie couldn't bring herself to take that away.

BEFORE ADELAIDE EVEN NEARED, Luke saw the anguish in her eyes. Apparently, the visit hadn't gone as planned. He was glad Lydia had tired of waiting and walked to the mercantile. It would give him time alone with Adelaide to feel her out.

Offering her a hand up, he slid to make room for her on the buggy seat. "Everything all right?"

She shook her head but gave no explanation.

Deciding not to press her, he released the break and tapped the reins across the horse's rump. "Lydia walked to the mercantile. I told her we'd pick her up on our way through town."

Adelaide's only response was a slow nod, and he was beginning to think it would be a long trip home. But, before they'd traveled ten paces, she let out a huff. "I couldn't do it."

He peered over at her. "Couldn't do what?"

"Tell Clarissa who I am or who Aunt Polly was. The old me could have, but not the person I am now."

At a loss for words, Luke struggled how to respond. "Is there a chance you can visit?"

"Yes. I at least have that. But if I return to the South, those visits will be few." She pulled in a jagged breath. "She has a good life here with Mr. and Mrs. Banks. To disrupt that would only confuse her. She might even come to resent me." Her voice grew weepy. "She's all the family I have left, and she'll never even know it."

Resisting the urge to pull her into an embrace, he kept his gaze glued to the path ahead, the turn of the carriage wheels filling the void. He cleared his throat. "You know, Adelaide, family doesn't have to be blood related."

She gave a soft sigh. "I suppose not."

"Ma and Lydia adore you, and Drew and Caroline have already taken a shine to you."

"I've grown fond of them as well."

Luke glanced at her out of the corner of his eye. "And then ... there's me."

She sniffled, meeting his gaze with an inquisitive stare. "You?"

His heart raced in his still-sore chest, hands growing clammy. On impulse, he swerved off the road and guided the horse to a secluded grove of trees, slowing their pace over the rougher terrain. Now was as good of time as any to express how he felt about her.

If he could manage it.

"WHY ARE WE STOPPING?"

The flush in Luke's cheeks deepened as he set the break. "'Cause I have something to say, and I want you to hear it." He wiped his hands on his trousers, looking tenser than Addie had ever seen him.

He was beginning to make her nervous. "What is it?"

Edging closer to her on the seat, he reached to clasp her hand. "I know you have your heart set on returning south, but I ... want you to stay, Adelaide. I'm asking you to stay. You have a home with us if only you'll accept it. We all care about you."

"I know." She dropped her gaze. "I'm fond of all you, too, it's just ... so different from what I thought my life would be."

"Sometimes God has a way of changing our plans and creating better ones."

She nodded. The Lord had definitely altered her life in ways she'd never anticipated.

Luke's fingers cupped her chin, and her eyes lifted. "When we get home, if you're willing, I'd like the chance to court you proper."

Addie's heart thrilled and then plummeted just as quickly.

You're damaged goods with those ugly burn scars. Like a demon from the past, Simon's chilling affront came echoing back. Addie tried to pull her hand away, but Luke held it fast, the creases above his nose deepening.

He didn't understand.

Her mouth quivered. "You don't want me, Luke. I'm scarred and ugly. You deserve better."

Exhaling a breath, he whispered her name. "Adelaide."

A tremor ran through her as he drew her into his embrace. She melted into him until she could hear his heartbeat. Secure in his arms, she nuzzled her cheek against his warm shoulder.

His face dipped lower, and he pressed his forehead against hers. "Don't ever view yourself as scarred. You're beautiful just as you are."

Addie gazed into his eyes, seeing not rejection or pity, but deep-seated affection and acceptance.

Finding her lips, Luke claimed them as his.

She slid her arms around his neck and returned his kiss with all the fervor the depths of her core could muster. A bit breathless as they parted, she knew at once her heart was knit with his.

Lifting her marred hand to his lips, Luke kissed it tenderly, his voice so soft she had to pause to hear. "Jesus had scars, and there was never anything so beautiful."

Tears welled in her eyes as she choked back a sob. It was true. Jesus' hands *were* scarred. Out of love, He'd willingly suffered in her place. She tipped her head higher, warmth surging within her. No longer would she allow herself to be held captive by Simon's lies.

Or her own.

God loved and accepted her as she was, and apparently Luke did too.

He brushed the backs of his fingers against her cheek, gazing at her with an intensity that she'd never seen. "Please say *yes*."

In that moment, all her misgivings melted away. Her yearning to return to her beloved South no longer held interest. Her heart was here now. With Luke and his family.

Her family.

With a nod, she smiled at him, grateful for his love. "Yes."

Unbridled joy told on Luke's face as he sounded a loud "Woohoo!" He gave her another tender kiss, then took up the reins. "Let's go home."

With a chuckle, she looped her arm through his. She was no longer Addie, the bitter, sorrowful, lonely girl of Richmond. She was Adelaide—loved and treasured daughter of the King. The Lord had indeed blessed and restored her life as He had Job's, giving her a mother, siblings, and a godly man to love. Clarissa would always be a part of her life, but Adelaide had found her place of belonging.

A place only God could have designed.

She fingered the gold locket around her neck and smiled, certain there was indeed hope beyond wounded hearts

AUTHOR'S NOTE

This second book in my Wounded Heart Series, though not quite as profoundly steeped in historical detail as Book One (*Beyond These War-Torn Lands*), also contains an array of history and historical figures woven into its storyline. As I delved into the historical details of Richmond at the time of its capture, I found several fascinating particulars. One was the colorful character of Miss Elizabeth Van Lew.

In case you're unfamiliar with Miss Van Lew, she was indeed a spy for the Union living and orchestrating her undercover ring right in the crux of Richmond. This daughter of Richmond was educated in Philadelphia and held strong convictions against slavery. As in my story, it was her true aim to bring an abrupt end to the war and with it, slavery. To ward off suspicion, she would often chatter on to herself while walking the streets of Richmond and do other oddities that earned her the nickname "Crazy Bet."

While from a well-to-do family, Miss Van Lew spent her family fortune in her efforts to aid slaves. By the war's end, her funds were all but depleted. While my fictionalized Miss Van Lew is not affluent, she is able to aid Luke and Adelaide with some of their needs.

Besides Miss Van Lew, I enjoyed throwing in glimpses of General and Mrs. Lee, and President Lincoln. Captain Sally of the Robertson Hospital in Richmond was also a real, historical person I enjoyed meeting in my research efforts. I also discovered the Capitol dome had newly been completed at this time and the Washington Monument was underway.

Much of my research revolved around the fall of Richmond. What a complex moment in history that was, when Jefferson Davis and his army fled, setting the city ablaze to keep anything of value from falling into Northern hands. I found it fascinating that President Lincoln and his son, Tad, paid the ruined city a visit not much more than 24 hours after the Southern army and leader's departure. Most amazing, was the fact that Lincoln strode through the streets of Richmond nearly unsupervised, surrounded by those he'd struggled so hard to free. It was a day he'd long awaited. Sadly, we know from history, his joy was cut short by assassin, John Wilkes Booth, mere days later after the war ended.

Following Lincoln's death, the Nation was in mourning. In attempt to relieve the oppressive sorrow, a Grand Review of the Armies was assembled in Washington on May 23rd, 1865. I enjoyed learning about this piece of history that is often overlooked. Thousands upon thousands of soldiers from both the Army of the Potomac and Sherman's Western army converged and paraded down the mile and a half stretch of Pennsylvania Avenue between the Capitol and the White House before top officials such as General Grant and the newly inducted President Johnson. Placing Luke in the midst of the action was so much fun.

I hope you enjoyed Luke and Adelaide's story, and that you learned something about the time period along the way. I dearly love blending Spiritual truths and growth of character into the pages of history. For a deeper understanding of the insights into this novel, be sure to check out the Discussion Questions I've included with readers and Book Clubs in mind.

If you enjoyed *Beyond Wounded Hearts*, I welcome you to delve into my Prairie Sky Series and Book One in my Wounded Heart Series. I love interacting with readers and am available for virtual Book Club Q & A discussions.

For more information, check out these resources I used in researching and writing *Beyond Wounded Hearts*:

Book Sources:

April 1865: The Month That Saved America, by Jay Winik, Perennial, New York, 2002

The Fall of Richmond, by Patrick Rembert, Louisiana State University Press, 1960

In the Wake of Battle: The Civil War Images of Mathew Brady, by George Sullivan, Prestel, New York, 2004

Web Sources:

https://www.youtube.com/watch?v=cLHUPdvLlJQ

https://www.styleweekly.com/richmond/lee-house/Content?oid=1477657

https://richmondmagazine.com/news/features/fall-of-richmond/

DISCUSSION QUESTIONS FOR BOOK CLUB & GROUPS

1) As the novel opens, we see Adelaide extremely bitter toward Yankees. With her family and home taken from her, we can easily understand her reasoning. But as she comes to know Luke, her opinion of Yankees softens a tad. What caused her change of mindset? Why is it wrong to judge an entire people group based on one's own limited experiences?

2) Luke blames himself for not sharing his faith with his friend, Jacob, before he died. How did feelings of guilt play out in his relationship with Adelaide? Sergeant Delmar? Cass Newberry? Initially, his drive to share his faith stems from guilt. Are guilty feelings productive or destructive to our lives? Read Ephesians 2:8 and I Peter 2:24. How can these verses ease the guilt of sin that weighs us down?

3) Adelaide has to work through not only her preconceived notions about Northerners, but also Richmond citizen, Elizabeth Van Lew, who she deems a traitor. What convinces Addie to not hold Miss Van Lew's actions against her? Is there someone you've held a grudge against that in getting to know them you've come to accept? Is there someone you need to love

regardless of your differences of opinion? What is one small step you can take to bring about reconciliation or peace?

4) As Luke becomes more attached to Adelaide, he struggles to keep his feelings for her in check. Knowing she doesn't share his faith, he determines there can be no future for them. Why is it dangerous to become emotionally/romantically entangled with someone who doesn't share our Christian convictions? What does Scripture say about being "unequally yoked"?

5) Aunt Polly's charred locket holds a secret from her past that shocks Adelaide, but instead of placing judgement on her aunt, Addie dwells on how to find Clarissa. Why is finding her cousin so important to her? What can we learn from Adelaide's forgiving attitude toward her aunt's imprudence? When we become savvy to a piece of gossip, do we pass it on or do our best to snuff it out?

6) Luke never ceases to pray for Adelaide to regain her love for the Lord. What do James 5:16 and I Peter 3:12 say about prayer? Why is it important to pray for those who are unbelievers or those who have fallen away from God?

7) When Adelaide travels north to stay with Martha and Lydia, she has no intention of developing an attachment to either of them. And yet, she finds herself drawn to Martha's motherly ways and comes to think of Lydia as a sister. What causes this transformation? How does Addie's lack of knowing her own mother play a role? Have you ever had someone fill a need in your life as a surrogate parent or sibling? Have you expressed to that person how special they are to you?

8) When Luke meets up with Cass Newberry he tries to offer him the same kindness he would anyone else. How does he respond when his attempts seem to backfire? How do Luke's

prayers work to change Cass? Have you ever given up on someone only to find that your efforts made a difference in their life after all? Why should we never give up on God changing a person's heart?

9) More than once Adelaide falls prey to the lie that she is "damaged goods" due to her disfiguring burns. Has your self-esteem ever suffered due to someone's thoughtless words or your own misconceptions about yourself? Read the following Scriptures: Matthew 10:37, John 3:16, Psalm 36:7, Psalm 103:11, Psalm 117:2. What do they say about your worth to God?

10) The theme verse for *Beyond Wounded Hearts* is Proverbs 16:8: "*When a man's ways are pleasing to the Lord, he makes even his enemies to live at peace with him.*" How does Luke exemplify this verse? Are there difficult people in your life who you might influence for the better by living for Christ? When is it most challenging to live out a Christ-like attitude in daily life?

11) Adelaide is determined to not only find Clarissa but to whisk her away from the life she'd been living. But, after seeing how much her adoptive parents love her and how content she is, Addie sacrifices her dream of them being together. How might Luke's example and her renewed faith have played a part in her decision? Do you feel she made the right choice in not telling Clarissa who she was?

ABOUT CYNTHIA ROEMER

Cynthia Roemer is an inspirational, award-winning author who enjoys planting seeds of hope into the hearts of readers. Raised in the cornfields of rural Illinois, Cynthia enjoys spinning tales set in the backdrop of the mid-1800's prairie and Civil War era. .

Cynthia feels blessed the Lord has fulfilled her life-long dream of being a published novelist. It's her prayer that her stories will both entertain and encourage readers in their faith. Her Prairie Sky Series consists of Amazon bestseller, *Under This Same Sky, Under Prairie Skies*, and 2020 Selah Award winner, *Under Moonlit Skies.* Her fourth novel, *Beyond These War-Torn Lands*, is set during the final year of the Civil War and is Book One in her Wounded Heart Series. *Beyond Wounded Hearts* is the second book in the series.

She writes from her family farm in central Illinois where she resides with her husband of twenty-eight years. She is a member of American Christian Fiction Writers. Visit Cynthia online at: www.cynthiaroemer.com

ALSO BY CYNTHIA ROEMER

Beyond These War-torn Lands

Wounded Hearts—Book One

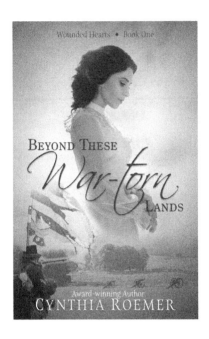

While en route to aid Confederate soldiers injured in battle near her home, Southerner Caroline Dunbar stumbles across a wounded Union sergeant. Unable to ignore his plea for help, she tends his injuries and hides him away, only to find her attachment to him deepen with each passing day. But when her secret is discovered, Caroline incurs her father's wrath and, in turn, unlocks a dark secret from the past which she is determined to unravel.

After being forced to flee his place of refuge, Sergeant Andrew Gallagher fears he's seen the last of Caroline. Resolved not to let that happen, when the war ends, he seeks her out, only to discover she's been sent away. When word reaches him that President Lincoln has been shot, Drew is assigned the task of tracking down the assassin. A chance encounter with Caroline revives his hopes, until he learns she may be involved in a plot to aid the assassin.

Get your copy here:

https://scrivenings.link/beyondthesewartornlands

Under This Same Sky

Prairie Skies—Book One

Becky Hollister wants nothing more than to live out her days on the prairie, building a life for herself alongside her future husband. But when a tornado rips through her parents' farm, killing her mother and sister, she must leave the only home she's ever known and the man she's begun to love to accompany her injured father to St. Louis.

Catapulted into a world of unknowns, Becky finds solace in corresponding with Matthew Brody, the handsome pastor back home. But when word comes that he is all but engaged to someone else, she must call upon her faith to decipher her future.

Get your copy here:

https://scrivenings.link/underthissamesky

Under Prairie Skies

Prairie Skies—Book Two

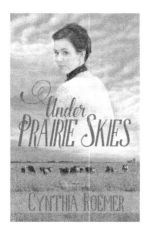

Unsettled by the news that her estranged cousin and uncle are returning home after a year away, Charlotte Stanton goes to ready their cabin and finds a handsome stranger has taken up residence. Convinced he's a squatter, she throws him off the property before learning his full identity. Little does she know, their paths were destined to cross again.

Quiet and ruggedly handsome, Chad Avery's uncanny ability to see through Charlotte's feisty exterior and expose her inner weaknesses both infuriates and intrigues her. When a tragic accident incites her family to move east, Charlotte stays behind in hopes of becoming better acquainted with the elusive cattleman. Yet Chad's unwillingness to divulge his hidden past, along with his vow not to love again, threatens to keep them apart forever.

Get your copy here:

https://scrivenings.link/underprairieskies

Under Moonlit Skies

Prairie Skies—Book Three

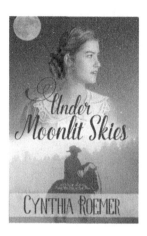

She had her life planned out - until he rode in

Illinois prairie - 1859

After four long years away, Esther Stanton returns to the prairie to care for her sister Charlotte's family following the birth of her second child. The month-long stay seems much too short as Esther becomes acquainted with her brother-in-law's new ranch hand, Stewart Brant. When obligations compel her to return to Cincinnati and to the man her overbearing mother intends her to wed, she loses hope of ever knowing true happiness.

Still reeling from a hurtful relationship, Stew is reluctant to open his heart to Esther. But when he faces a life-threatening injury with Esther tending him, their bond deepens. Heartbroken when she leaves, he sets out after her and inadvertently stumbles across an illegal slave-trade operation, the knowledge of which puts him, as well as Esther and her family, in jeopardy.

Under Moonlit Skies won first-place in the Western Fiction category of the 2020 Selah Awards.

Get your copy here:

https://scrivenings.link/undermoonlitskies

MORE HISTORICAL ROMANCE FROM SCRIVENINGS PRESS

Strong Currents by Delores Topliff

Columbia River Undercurrents—Book Two

When German Christian, Erika Hofer, opposes Hitler, church leader Dietrich Bonhoeffer helps her flee to her uncle John Hofer along the Columbia River in America's Pacific Northwest. Erika finds acceptance and support but also suspicion, hatred, and an attempt on her life.

American pastor's son, Josh Vengeance, joins the US Navy to serve his country, but is injured at Midway Island and invalided home. While healing in body and spirit, he joins a network of colorful individuals, including John Hofer and his niece, Erika, who defend their homeland as volunteers.

Can two wounded young people move past betrayal and disillusionment to find love and freedom during a world at war?

Get your copy here:

https://scrivenings.link/strongcurrents

***Window of Opportunity* by Heather Greer**

The Stained-glass Legacy Series—Book One

Faith and duty drive Evangeline Moore to protect her father's pristine image as a judge in Harrisburg, Illinois. Her resolve's biggest test? Dot, her childhood friend. With Evangeline beside her, Dot's desire for the Roaring Twenties' glitz and glamor leads the pair into questionable situations.

Born into a Chicago mob family, Brendan Dunne understands duty, but faith puts him at odds with his father's demands. Even when his brother James's propensity for trouble lands them in Harrisburg, the truth is undeniable. To their father, the lines he won't cross mean Brendan will never measure up.

When circumstances push Brendan and Evangeline together, unexpected events create opportunity to break free of family expectations. Will they be brave enough to forge their own path before the window closes on their chance to change?

Get your copy here:

https://scrivenings.link/windowofopportunity

Redemption's Trail by Betty Woods

Trails of the Heart—Book Two

Newly widowed with her second child due in a few months, Lily
Johnson has nowhere to go until Toby Grimes, her late husband's boss,
asks her to stay on as housekeeper at his ranch. Remaining in the house
Mr. Grimes built for her and her husband is an answered prayer. But
malicious gossips see her godsend job as a ruse for a sinful dalliance
since her employer is a nice-looking, single man.

God and a lot of others turned their backs on Toby during the war, so
he returns the favor by keeping to himself. Yet the need to care for and
protect Lily overwhelms him. The way she tugs at his heart scares him
more than going into a losing battle.

Unwilling to allow anyone to destroy a fine woman's reputation, he
proposes a marriage of convenience. After much prayer, Lily accepts.
Her first marriage was a love match made in heaven. The second leads
down a trail only God knows. The peace she has concerning a marriage

to a troubled man she doesn't love begins a walk of faith to a destination neither she, nor Toby, can guess.

Get your copy here:

https://scrivenings.link/redemptionstrail

Quench your thirst for story.
www.ScriveningsPress.com

Stay up-to-date on your favorite books and authors with our free e-newsletters.

ScriveningsPress.com

Made in the USA
Las Vegas, NV
05 May 2023